City of Desire

Upper Broadway Street looking south with the spire of Trinity Church in the background (ca. 1835)

City of
Desire

SIDNEY MORRISON

RIVERWOOD BOOKS
ASHLAND, OREGON

Riverwood Books may be purchased for educational, business, or sales promotional use. For information, please write:

Special Market Department
Riverwood Books
PO Box 3400, Ashland, OR 97520
Website: www.whitecloudpress.com

Cover and interior design by Christy Collins, Constellation Book Services
Cover photo by Debra Thornton Photography, www.debrathornton.com

First edition: 2017

17 18 19 20 21 10 9 8 7 6 5 4 3 2 1
Printed in the United States of America

Library of Congress Cataloging-in-Publication Data

Names: Morrison, Sidney, author.
Title: City of desire / by Sidney Morrison,
Description: Ashland, Or. : White Cloud Press, 2017.
Identifiers: LCCN 2017005709 | ISBN 9781940468495 (hardcover)
Subjects: LCSH: Jewett, Helen, 1813-1836--Fiction. | Prostitutes--New York
  (State)--New York--Fiction. | Robinson, Richard P. , 1817---Fiction. |
  Trials (Murder)--Fiction. | Corruption--Fiction. | New York
  (N.Y.)--Fiction. | GSAFD: Legal stories. | Mystery fiction.
Classification: LCC PS3613.O77775 C58 2017 | DDC 813/.6--dc23
LC record available at https://lccn.loc.gov/2017005709

To my wife, Karan, who always believed in me, and to Lieutenant John W. Foreman, who by saving my life made it possible for me to write this book.

Acknowledgments

I can't say enough to express my gratitude to those who read drafts of this novel and provided invaluable feedback and offered suggestions. Of course, I am ultimately responsible for the book's quality, but I know that it is better because of their contributions. My thanks to Clarissa Garlington, her son, Todd Garlington, Dr. Anthony Lee, Constance Lue, Dr. Kikanza Nuri-Robbins, Tadia Rice, David Langness, Janice Lineberger, and finally, Kimberley Cameron, a literary agent who years ago encouraged a young novelist to persevere.

My cheek was still warm from her kiss, my body ached beneath the weight of hers. If, as would sometimes happen, she had the features of some woman whom I had known in waking hours, I would abandon myself altogether to this end: to find her again, like people who set out on a journey to see with their eyes some city of their desire.

–Marcel Proust, *Swann's Way: In Search of Lost Time, Volume 1*

PART 1

Chapter One

Death always leaves a mess.

When Judge Nathan Weston heard of Helen Jewett's murder, he thought first about unwanted publicity. As soon as he saw the news item on page three of Saturday's *Eastern Argus*, Portland's main newspaper, with its reference to the "Horrid murder and arson" of Helen Jewett from Hallowell, Maine, he knew he had to plan carefully a response to the expected inquiries.

His wife, Paulina, who usually did not travel with him on the court circuit, was with him in Portland and was more sanguine about the possible danger.

"Hallowell is only two miles from Augusta," she said, with cheerful indifference, "but it might as well be on the other side of the moon. How can *anyone* in the press think that, just because she was from Maine, we knew her? Maine is a big state, after all, and there is no mention of our name."

At first fascinated and appalled, they read carefully the graphic descriptions of the New York sex trade and the mortifying details of Helen's fall into seduction and prostitution, somehow punctuated by her aliases: Maria Stanley in Portland, Helen Mar in Boston, and Helen Jewett in New York. They agreed, Manhattan was a den of iniquity.

But they could not fathom the vulgarity, indeed, the depravity, of James Gordon Bennett's decision to print a description of Helen's murdered body.

"This is unspeakable," said Paulina, tossing the *New York Herald* aside.

Weston made no comment. The offending passage had triggered memories and stirred the slightest hint of desire. Even in death, her beauty could not be denied.

"Slowly I began to discover the lineaments of the corpse, as one would the beauties of a slate of marble," he read. "It was the most remarkable sight I ever beheld—I never have, and never expect to see such another. 'My God,' exclaimed I, 'how like a statue! I can scarcely conceive that form to be a corpse.' Not a vein was to be seen. The body looked as white, as full, as polished as pure Parian marble. The perfect figure, the exquisite limbs, the fine face, the full arms, the beautiful bust—all surpassing in every respect Venus de Medici. For a few moments I was lost in admiration at this extraordinary sight, a beautiful female corpse that surpassed the finest statue of antiquity."

But when the couple returned home, the Thursday edition of the *Eastern Argus* shattered Paulina's complacent theories and any of Weston's lingering reveries when it reprinted long *New York Herald* extracts citing names, places, and associations.

Bennett reported, "In Augusta, Maine, lived a highly respectable gentleman, Judge Western, by name. Some of the female members of his family, pitying the bereaved conditions of young Dorcas Dorrance, invited her to live at the Judge's house. At that time Dorcas was young, beautiful, innocent, modest, and ingenuous. Her good qualities and sprightly temper won the good feelings of the Judge's family. She became a *chère amie* of his daughters—a companion and a playmate."

"Oh my God," moaned Paulina, fanning herself with the newspaper as she paced the library. "This will *ruin* us."

Weston urged calm, but Paulina could not be appeased, reading the offending passages again and again, emphasizing key parts for inaccuracies, distortions, and absolute lies to assuage her fears, fanning the newspaper even more vigorously, and shaking her head to accent her denials.

Matters worsened whey they received a lawyer's letter, forwarded from one of their sons in Portland, asking for an interview. Now sickened with dread and made dizzy by panic, Paulina asked again and again: How did Jamie Bennett find their oldest son? Who else was now caught in his sticky web? What would the neighbors think? When would this storm pass?

Determined to remain poised and focused, Weston calmly reviewed the major points of their projected response. Five days had passed since he first saw the *Eastern Argus* news item, and he knew exactly what had to be said . . . and what had to be ignored.

"We will send a letter to the *Herald* and the *Argus*," he said, "but the *Argus* will get it first."

"Good," declared Paulina, with a deep intake of air. "We can trust Winthrop Smith. He will support us, unlike that disgusting and most disagreeable James Gordon Bennett, who makes a cheap paper even cheaper. He *cannot* be trusted, and he has no respect for the facts. He didn't even have the correct name."

"We will provide the correct name, of course: Dorcas Doyen, not Dorrance. No matter: She changed her name often enough."

They then began to list the facts and, as the evidence accumulated, their voices lightened as grim satisfaction became almost giddy exoneration:

"We will admit that she resided with us," Paulina said.

"She was received into our family as a servant girl," Weston noted.

"Her father asked us to take her in. He was an unfortunate drunk."

"A man of intemperate habits."

"That's better," said Paulina, now smiling. "You always have the right words for the occasion. Your being chief justice is no accident, my dear."

"Thank you, my dear. And I must carefully describe the nature of Dorcas' service, because we must not, in *any* way, imply that we were derelict in our supervision of her and thus contributed to her ruin."

"We were good to her. We sent her to the common schools on several occasions."

"Yes, and she showed a remarkable quickness of apprehension and cultivated a taste for reading."

"Not only there," corrected Paulina. "We indulged her *here*. She could freely use our library."

"But we never had any intimations of improper conduct. *Never*."

Paulina frowned at this point. Delicately correcting her husband, she pointed out, "Rumors *did* come to my attention just before she left us. Remember, my dear? I heard rumors to her disadvantage, and when I asked Dorcas about them, she protested, and I believed her."

"Unfortunately, the reports to her prejudice became so general that we could not believe them unfounded," explained Weston.

"Her subsequent character confirmed all the stories we heard," Paulina replied, casting aside any suggestion of wistful regret. "But we cannot, for it would be unseemly, offer details of those stories."

"She was seduced," added Weston. "We don't know by whom."

"No young man ever came to our house," said Paulina.

"And then she was gone," said Weston.

"Be sure to be correct with the chronological facts, my dear," Paulina replied. "Lawyers love to find errors with judges of the court."

"She came to us in the spring of 1826, having turned thirteen in the previous fall, and she left us at eighteen. Those are the indisputable facts. And she was, I believe, very faithful in the performance of what was required of her."

"But, and this is a significant *but*, my dear," Paulina said, lowering her voice, "She *misrepresented* the condition in which she resided in our family. It seems that she left the impression with friends, who spoke to those vile reporters, that she was almost a member of the family, like a ward, an orphaned ward. She was *not* an orphan or a member of this family. She was always a servant. A good servant, but still a *servant*."

"And she abandoned herself to a profligate life after she left us," concluded Weston.

"True," declared Paulina, "and yet we can't end the letter on that note; it is too harsh, too judgmental. We cannot appear unfeeling or cruel."

"Certainly not," Weston added. "A tragic end followed her profligate life. Both are to be deeply deplored."

Satisfied that all of the major points had been covered, Paulina straightened the folds of her dress, a gown of light blue with white lace at the neck and wrists. As she rose to leave the library, where they could discuss serious matters without their six children interrupting, she concluded, "Be sure to end the letter with some kind of declaration of the moral lessons to be learned from this unfortunate business."

"I mustn't end with certainties, my dear," said Weston, with a solemnity worthy of his time on the bench. "The tone throughout will be discreet, even circumspect, but to end the letter with a moral to the story might suggest that we have told a tale and not the truth. I will say only that I sincerely hope the catastrophe, cruel as it was, may not be without its moral uses."

"Splendid," said Paulina, "and of course you will end with a reference to your obedient servitude."

Weston smiled at the reference to the formal closure still in use but losing popularity in a more democratic time, the age of Andrew Jackson, Martin Van Buren, and the mob.

"Of course," he said. "Some traditions are worth keeping."

"Then can we keep to our promise to not talk about Dorcas? We promised to never mention her again."

"But recent events require adjustments," said Weston wearily.

Paulina frowned and conceded, "Very well, then. Let's review everything that happened. so there are no disagreements when people ask, for once they see our letter, people will ask."

"Our friends will *not* ask, " asserted Weston, secure in the solidarity of their circle in Augusta. "And our enemies will make up want they want, as did Dorcas, who had quite a gift for lying."

"I rue the day that Hannah Dillingham recommended her when I said I needed extra help, " Paulina replied. "Thank goodness, we're still friends. But Dorcas Doyen certainly managed to put a strain on our friendship when things started to deteriorate. Poor Hannah, she felt guilty about it all."

"We forgave her long ago," Weston clarified.

"So we did," Paulina replied. The reticence in her voice forced a raised eyebrow on the judge's high forehead.

"So we did," he repeated, emphasizing his own moral high road.

Unfortunately, more bad news came from Boston a week later, and Paulina collapsed onto the drawing room sofa as Weston read the assertion in the *Daily Advocate* that Helen Jewett was "brought up in the family of an eminent Judge of the Maine Supreme Court" and was "seduced by a son of the Judge."

"This can't be," she moaned. "Oh my God, how could this happen? How?"

"If you are talking about reprints from the gutter press, this should not surprise you," Weston answered coldly, more upset by Pauline's hysteria than by the accusation. "If you are referring to seduction, then it was not possible. Nathan Junior was away at college, and the other boys were too young. Please, Paulina, take control of yourself. I will make sure the editor receives the facts and issues a retraction. Remember the facts, Paulina, the facts."

He sat absolutely still, determined to remain calm and not to excuse *more* excess. He didn't worry for a moment about Pauline's health, even though her eyes were closed and she had one hand at her neck. He could only wait. Yes, the circumstances were extraordinary, but this scene of female weakness was all too familiar.

Finally she asked, "When will that girl forever *stay* out of our lives? Please, Lord, *when?*"

He did not answer.

———•———

Dorcas was nine when John Doyen sent his youngest daughter away. It was not uncommon for fathers to send daughters away as servants; the small wages helped growing families. And John had enough children in his house, with his older daughter, Nancy, and three young boys. John also saw service to the Dillinghams as an opportunity for his bright, precocious daughter. At six she could read the Bible, and at seven she wrote letters with a penmanship a judge's clerk would envy.

When Dorcas returned from the Dillinghams' after four years, her father's hopes for her were fulfilled. She had proven herself a hard worker, cleaning and washing in a household of eight children, and she never complained in her letters home about the endless hours, the dirty diapers, the heat of summer and the bitter winters. These were the mere facts of her experience.

The educational benefits of living with the Dillinghams were also obvious. Hannah Dillingham was a teacher at the Cony Academy for Girls, and she and her husband had a large private library, one of the largest in town. Dorcas was free to use the library when her work was done. Dorcas never reported that Mrs. Dillingham also provided private tutoring, but clearly Dorcas had absorbed a wealth of knowledge from listening to Hannah and Pitt Dillingham and their guests as she served them at the dinner table. Dorcas had an incredible memory; she could repeat lines of conversation and accumulated small volumes of interesting facts and pieces of information, especially about history and literature. John Doyen was not surprised. When Dorcas was small, she could recite pages of scripture after reading them once or twice.

John' new wife, Lydia Dutton, was not impressed. At twenty-three, she was a constant critic of her stepdaughter. Despite her obvious skills, Dorcas could never meet Lydia's high standards. The linens were not white enough. Dust could still be found on the backs of chairs. Plates were removed from the table too slowly. And her attitude was even worse. "She puts on airs," Lydia complained. "Just because she lived with the Dillinghams doesn't make her better than us."

Dorcas was unhappy. Her mother had died while she was at the Dillinghams', and her father, a widow for only a few months, married a woman twenty years younger than himself. It was bad enough that Lydia seemed like an older sister; she was also beautiful, vain, mean, ignorant, and stupid.

Dorcas silently endured the criticism for months; the other children were spared. Then she went to her father, seeking relief.

"Please, father," she begged, finding him alone in the parlor for the first time in weeks. "Tell her to stop. Tell her to leave me alone when I want to be alone, when I want to read. I can't even walk across the room without her finding fault. She tells me not to slam a door before I have even approached it!"

"You must do as she says. She is your mother now."

"She is *not* my mother," Dorcas replied, her contempt deepened by his callous disregard for her grief and loyalty to a woman who was the complete opposite of Lydia Dutton.

John Doyen's voice deepened, its chill cutting and hard like ice. "You will do as I say," he said. "You will *not* come to me with your complaints and excuses. You know your place, and until you leave this house, you will abide by my decisions . . . and hers."

"Then send me away," Dorcas declared. "You did it once; you could do it again."

John started to rise from his chair. Dorcas stepped back, immediately recognizing she had gone too far. His green eyes, the mirror image of hers, widened. She had never seen him this angry.

"You dare to speak to me as if you are my equal? I am your father, damn you, and my wishes are to be respected *always*. Do you understand me?"

He was yelling now, and Lydia rushed into the room and closed the sliding doors behind her. "John, we can all hear you. The boys are frightened, and I cannot deal with their tears and questions."

Suddenly, as if released from a trance, Dorcas turned from the rage in her father's eyes to Lydia's whining supplication, and sneered, "Everything isn't about *you*. You somehow can even turn my brothers' tears into *your* tale of woe."

As if encountering a madwoman, Lydia asked incredulously, "John . . . what?"

Before Dorcas saw the rise of his hand, it slapped her face with sharp, twisting force. "You shut your vile mouth now!" John exclaimed.

"I told you, John, she had to go," Lydia said, vindicated at last. She registered no surprise at John's sudden violence.

"I will find a place," John said, returning to his chair. He resumed reading the newspaper, his anger disappearing as suddenly as it had erupted. "Dorcas, you may leave us."

Humbled, Dorcas replied softly, "Yes, Father."

But her humiliation did not prevent her from hiding her undiminished contempt for Lydia. And as Dorcas, tall for thirteen and equal in height, passed Lydia, she stared at her stepmother with wide, open eyes.

Lydia stepped back, and implored softly, "John?"

But Dorcas was out of the room, closing the door behind her, and she remained just outside to hear the aftermath. Eavesdropping was an essential part of the servant's trade.

"This is too much, too much!" Lydia declared.

"I told you. I will take care of it."

"How?"

"I am making inquiries. She will be put out to service, of course, and hopefully she will remain there until she reaches her maturity."

"Will she be ruined by another family like the Dillinghams?"

"Ruined?" asked John. "She did well by them. And if I am fortunate, I will find a family even better for her."

"You defend her pride, her contempt for me, for all of us?"

"I do no such thing, but she is a special child deserving special circumstances."

"Then when she returns, she will be worse, far worse."

"She will have better prospects; perhaps she will meet someone . . ."

"Then you *do* want her to be better than us!"

"Most parents want better for their children. It's natural."

"I cannot, I *will not* endure her judging me, making me feel as if I am worthless."

"How can a child do such a thing?"

"I cannot endure it," Lydia insisted. "I will not. You must choose. We cannot both be in the same house."

"I *have* chosen," John said. "She goes, you stay; and if she comes back, she cannot stay for long. She will work somewhere else, not here. She is my daughter, but you are my wife, and I love you."

"Good," Lydia replied, smug triumph in a single word.

It was a miscalculation. John offered an immediate correction: "But don't *ever* ask me to *not* love my daughter, or to choose my love for you over her. I will love you both in my own way, even if it means that she and I are apart. Is that clear?"

Dorcas did not hear Lydia's answer because she had walked away from the door, but she had heard enough to know that she was loved. Still, she could not deny the aching sense of loss. Her mother was gone, and now her father was sending her away from his house and her sister and brothers, perhaps for good. She took some comfort in his acknowledgment of her place in his heart.

"You are named after a very special woman in the Bible," John once said after she had asked why she wasn't named Emily or Elizabeth, Emma or Mary, the most popular names of the day. "You can read about her in the New Testament, the Acts of the Apostles."

Dorcas found her name in Acts 9:37. "Now there was in Joppa a certain disciple named Tabitha, which by interpretation is called Dorcas," the Bible declared. "This woman was full of good works and alms-deeds which she did."

But then she died.

The account of her death was short and brutally direct:

And it came to pass that she was sick, and died: whom when they had washed, they laid her in the upper chamber.

The disciples sent unto Peter two men, desiring him that he would not delay to come to them. Then Peter arose and went with them. When he was come, they brought him into the upper chamber: and all the widows stood by him weeping, and sewing the coats and garments that Dorcas made, while she was with them. But Peter put them all forth, and kneeled down, and prayed: and turning him to the body, said, Tabitha arise. And she opened her eyes, and when she saw Peter, she sat up. And he gave her his hand, and lifted her up, and when he called the saints and widows, presented her alive. And it was known throughout all Joppa; and many believed in the lord.

Dorcas took no comfort in the knowledge that she was named after a good woman who died and was resurrected by the hand of the Apostle Peter. She hated the very sound of her name. Even Tabitha was better.

At ten she vowed that when she had the chance, she would change her name. At thirteen, as she was about to leave home again, she still hated it. But now she appreciated its association with resurrection, with renewal, with the chance to start over.

In the spring of 1826 there would be no apostle, no proofs of the miraculous ways of the Lord. She would be on her own, making her own way in the world under the banner of her own *new* name: Mary, Maria, or Helen. She didn't know where she was going, but she was not afraid. Future arrangements were in her father's hands, but her character would be of her own making. Lydia Dutton would have no hand in this. None.

The Westons of Augusta, Maine, had other plans.

Chapter Two

The Westons were not the richest family in Augusta; that distinction belonged to Paulina Weston's sister Martha and her husband, Ruell Williams, who lived in a fourteen-room mansion on Cony Street. Nevertheless, the Weston house impressed most visitors to Augusta, and it certainly impressed Dorcas, who marveled at the good fortune that had come her way when she entered the spacious white house in the center of town near the Kennebec County Court House.

While she waited outside the parlor, John Doyen spoke briefly with the Westons; then he was gone. There were no tears, no protracted farewells. He had made a business arrangement, and he expected his daughter to fulfill her obligation without complaint. "Be good, and do a good job," was all he said before giving Dorcas a perfunctory hug.

She stood absolutely still, her arms at her sides, refusing to cry.

On that first day Paulina Weston also made her intentions clear, as Dorcas stood silently before her and Judge Weston in the parlor: "Of course, you will have all the duties that come with maintaining a household with six children, and I expect you especially to clean the house thoroughly, since we entertain frequently and must maintain appearances commensurate with our position in society. And you will help with the young children, who need constant supervision. You will serve at the table, and wash our clothes, and tend to my needs, whenever they arise."

This was as expected; domestic service was grueling work from dawn to dark, with little rest during the day. But then Paulina, beaming with self-satisfaction, said, "And we have decided to bestow on you the benefits of our supervision and moral commitment. You will remain with us until you reach maturity, at eighteen, and as such you will go where we go—to church, on family visits, even on walks to Mr. Spalding's bookstore. We understand that you are an intelligent girl, and so we will send you to school when time permits. And you may read books in our library, again when time permits. Our town will surely know of the wonders that beneficence can bring to an orphan such as you."

Dorcas silently objected. Her mother was dead, but her father was still very much alive. She was definitely not an orphan. But she focused instead on the particulars of Paulina's list of benefits, and smiled broadly before saying, "Thank you, Mrs. Weston. I will prove myself worthy of your esteem."

"Now listen to her, Mr. Weston," said Paulina, delighted. "She will be quite an asset to us, and to the children, with such a command of language. How did you learn to speak so well? Oh, of course, you watched the Dillinghams for years, but I don't think even Mrs. Dillingham has your command, your poise, your spirit."

Still grateful to the Dillinghams, Dorcas looked down at her scuffed shoes to avoid detection. Her eyes were clear, open windows to her soul; their deep green seemed to intensify the clarity of her inner response.

Dorcas duly noted that Paulina was enthusiastic but disloyal, and perhaps someone not to be trusted.

Paulina continued brightly, "Mr. Weston, you should take this opportune moment to show Dorcas our library, the largest in Augusta."

He immediately corrected her: "The largest in the entire state."

"Yes, the largest in the entire state, with many novels. We certainly don't subscribe to the view that novels are dangerous for young girls, corrupting their morals and other nonsense—wasting time, creating dissatisfaction with ordinary life. On the contrary, novels show the power of imagination over the facts, isn't that so, Mr. Weston? The facts are boring, all too boring."

Judge Weston interjected grimly, "Even so, I *must* deal with the facts."

"Oh, I know that," conceded Paulina, with a wave of her hand. "But who needs to read the facts during our private moments, when we need respite from the realities of the day? I prefer not to read about war, slavery, and Whig party when I have some spare time, which comes not often when you have as many responsibilities as I have. Six children is a grave responsibility."

Judge Weston stood. "I will take Dorcas to the library now. Come, young lady."

"She is not a young lady yet," said Paulina, annoyed. "Only our ward."

But Weston did not bother to reply. He left the room, Dorcas following behind him at a respectful distance. He looked back and smiled, saying, "If you like books, this will be paradise."

The library's walls were filled with books from floor to ceiling. There were piles of books on the floor in all corners of the room, on the desk, and on the two tables near the fireplace. Immediately, Dorcas was tempted to count the volumes to reinforce Judge Weston's' obvious pride. By comparison, the library at the Dillinghams' was paltry indeed.

Weston sighed. "It should be more organized, " he said, "but when you come you will be able to explore, pick, and choose. I only ask that you return what you borrow to where you found it. That is the only way I remember what's here."

"I can put them in order, sir, from A to the end of the alphabet, starting there on the right," Dorcas offered.

"Oh, you won't have time for that, young lady, not with four boys running around, and a little girl besides. You will be a great help to my daughter Catherine; we call her Cassy, and you will meet her shortly."

"Yes, sir."

He looked around the room, and said, "Where can you possibly start, with so much before you?"

Dorcas did not know what to say, and hesitated. Weston answered his own question, declaring with a slight lift of his chin, "I know, when the time comes, you can start with novels by Sir Walter Scott, or Edward Bulwer-Lytton, or that five-volume story by Miss Jane Porter, *The Scottish Chiefs*. Have you heard of them?"

"No, sir."

"Good," he exclaimed brightly. "You will have the great pleasure of new discoveries. That is why I keep on buying: to relive those moments of first discovery, of opening that page and reading those *new* words for the first time, and meeting a new voice. Do you understand what I mean?"

Dorcas was astonished that Judge Weston was talking to her at all; and his open honesty and curiosity simply stunned her. She didn't know how to answer his question, even though she knew the only one possible. Yes, of course, yes.

Still looking down, Dorcas managed to mumble, "I only have my Bible."

"Ah, yes, the Bible with its old words that should be forever new and yet become stale with blind, rote use. I have a few around here somewhere." He took a quick, distracted glance around the room. "Your father said you know the Bible."

Although surprised that her father had reported this information, she only said, "Yes, I remember some things in it."

"Can you recite a psalm?" he asked.

Finally, Dorcas looked up, proud to demonstrate her incredible memory. "Which one?" she asked.

"Which one?" Weston asked, amused and still skeptical. "How many do you know?"

"All of them," she replied softly.

"All of them!" exclaimed Weston. "We all know the twenty-third. How about number twenty-five?"

Dorcas began reciting: " Unto thee, O lord, do I lift up my soul. O my god, I trust in thee, let me not be ashamed, let . . ."

"Number one hundred and fifteen," interrupted Weston.

She obliged with the opening lines: "Not unto us, O Lord, not unto us, but unto thy name give glory, for thy mercy, and for thy truth's sake."

"Psalm seventy-eight," said Weston, shock in his voice.

"Give ear, o my people, to my law; incline your ears to the words of my mouth. I will open my mouth in a parable. I will utter dark sayings of old."

"Where is one of those Bibles?" Weston walked to his desk. "One of them is around here somewhere."

After a few seconds, he found the volume. "At least it was on my desk," he said somewhat sheepishly. "I am at least respectably religious."

He opened the thick book, his index finger randomly finding the Book of Proverbs. He started reading the first words that caught his eyes, "The preparations---"

Dorcas recited the opening lines of Proverbs Sixteen, "The preparations of the heart in man, and the answer of the tongue, is from the Lord."

"Oh my God!" exclaimed Weston. "You know everything in here. You know it all!"

Dorcas shook her head. "No, sir, I don't, just the things I like, the sounds, the words, the stories."

"So you don't like the rules in Exodus or Leviticus? The laws, the boring facts?"

"I know some of them," she replied meekly.

"And the New Testament?"

"Most of it, and *all* of the Gospels."

"How is this possible?" cried Weston. "How can you remember all of this? I read all the time, and I cannot remember so much. How do you do it?"

"I can't explain it, sir. After I read something, and I copy it, or I write under the lines, or put a circle around what I have read, I see it like a drawing before my eyes, and I describe the drawing."

He protested, "But the eyes see so much, and still they cannot see everything, or remember everything. In my courthouse I hear eye witnesses who cannot remember the most important details, and they were there when a crime happened!"

Dorcas became uncomfortable; it seemed that her display had rattled the judge's perception of what was possible. He might blame her for inspiring his confusion and doubt. She looked down, preparing herself for a verbal attack.

But instead, he said warmly, "We want you to go to Sunday school, but what will be there for you to learn?"

"I need to understand what I remember, sir," Dorcas replied.

"Good answer," he intoned. " A very good answer, but the teacher at the First Congregational Church will not know what to do with you."

"Please don't tell them what I know, sir. Please," she pleaded, suddenly recalling the anger of Lydia Dutton.

"Why?" he asked, frowning with concern.

"I get into trouble, sir, with some people. They think I am showing off, or trying to be superior."

"There *are* superior people," noted Weston, "and all people aren't created equal."

"Please, sir, please."

Weston chuckled and leaned slightly forward to say, his eyes bright with mischief, "This will be our secret, then. I will tell Mrs. Weston and Cassy that you have read the Bible, but I won't mention to them how much you really know, or to the Reverend Tappan or Mr. Dolittle, the Sunday school teacher. You will be a prodigious student, and they will believe themselves to be your inspiration."

"Yes, sir," said Dorcas, looking down again. She sensed danger.

"It would indeed be awkward if you demonstrated the true extent of your knowledge. Prodigies are rarely appreciated."

"I am only a servant girl," she replied.

"A very smart, very pretty servant girl," he observed, "and the Westons will all soon realize our good fortune in having you come to us. Now let us return to Mrs. Weston so that you can meet Cassy and the other children."

———·———

It was another five months before Dorcas earned the opportunity to return to the library. Paulina insisted that Dorcas prove herself worthy of this benefit, and Judge Weston saw no harm in a short probation. In the meantime, Dorcas worked diligently with the washing, dusting, and cleaning, and became a friend to sixteen-year-old Cassy, who had her hands full supervising and entertaining Nathan Junior, thirteen; Daniel, eleven; George, ten; Charles, four; and Louisa, three. Although she was three years older than Dorcas, Cassy seemed younger. She was short, thin, and pale; she spoke softly and moved slowly, her shoulders hunched as if always prepared for some crisis or disaster. She was certainly overwhelmed by the noisy physicality of her brothers and the constant demands for attention, intervention, and approval from everyone.

Experienced with the Dillingham brood, Dorcas insisted on the consistent enforcement of rules and advocated a daily nap for the youngest children.

"You need a break," she told Cassy. "No more of this running around until they drop at different times of the day. At least for a couple of hours we can get things done without constant interruption."

"Mother will have to agree," Cassy noted.

"Of course," said Dorcas, nodding. "But we will make our case on *her* behalf. She deserves time away from them, too. Everyone will win, and the children will not be so disagreeable in the late afternoon and evening. It will be difficult, at first—this change in their schedule—but we will all see the benefits soon enough."

Paulina agreed, and Dorcas was proven right. Relieved and grateful, Cassy turned more and more to Dorcas for advice and began to speak openly with her when they took walks through town after church on Sunday.

"Father told us that you really know the Bible," Cassy observed one afternoon. The sky was clear, and a gentle breeze stirred the air, making the dogwood trees tremble.

Dorcas stopped, feeling the shock of betrayal. Judge Weston promised. Why couldn't he keep a promise?

But Cassy said nothing that revealed any knowledge of her servant's gifts. She continued, "And yet you don't seem pious, like those dour women who wear piety openly like a corset on the outside of a dress."

Dorcas giggled, enjoying both the image and Cassy's surprising evocation of it. "I only read it," said Dorcas, "and remember some lines for Sunday school and my own enjoyment."

"Enjoyment? Surely, your reading has inspired a deeper faith in the Lord."

Tired of dissembling, Dorcas stopped and turned to face Cassy directly, now two friends, not young mistress and servant.

"No, my reading has not inspired piety or a deeper faith in the Lord. I am only more confused, and yes disturbed by His ruthless revenges against entire nations, wiping out thousands of men, women, and children for the failures of a king, or the snubbing of a prophet. The Lord is bloodthirsty and He is cruel, insisting on rules that we no longer follow, sacrificing children and stoning women. I can't pray to a being that will comfort one moment and strike you down with a bolt of thunder the next. And He has *never* answered my prayers, anyway."

And He took my mother while your silly mother is still here, she almost shrieked but did not, maintaining her self-control by the thinnest shred of decency.

Horrified by this stream of blasphemy, Cassy could only stare, her eyes and mouth wide in utter disbelief.

Dorcas fell silent, stunned by the force of this revelation of one of her deepest secrets. She began to shake, sure that finally she had gone too far, even with Cassy, who clearly had reached the limits of intimacy and patience.

But then Cassy softened her face and voice as she replied, "Oh, Dorcas, *what* has happened to you to make you say this? What terrible thing has brought you to see everything, even the Lord's work, so darkly?"

Dorcas could not answer, still shaking at the prospect of ruining her chances for a better life with the Westons.

Cassy stepped closer and took Dorcas into her arms. "Please don't tell anybody else you think this way. Please, don't. I certainly will not."

"I know they use to burn people for saying things like this," Dorcas said. "Will you pray for my immortal soul?" She hated asking this question because she no longer believed in heaven or hell, eternal salvation or damnation, but she was desperate and needed to make amends, quickly.

Cassy's concerns, however, were more immediate, as she explained, "This is a small town, and everybody knows everybody's business, or certainly more than they should. Reputations are all we have to protect, and I don't want people to believe that you are some dangerous *free thinker*. What you said will shock even Father, who is more tolerant than most. I don't want mother and father to have cause to send you away. I want you to stay. Please don't jeopardize things by talking like this. If you really need to talk like that, just talk to me, and I will listen. But you must promise me that you won't say anything like this to anyone else in Augusta."

"Yes," Dorcas promised without hesitation. She didn't want to lose a friend who was now like a sister; and clearly, Cassy needed a sister older than little Louisa.

"Good," concluded Cassy, placing her arm under Dorcas' arm so that they could resume their walk. "It's such a beautiful day today."

Dorcas kept her promise, but it did not prevent future disagreements, and few things exasperated Dorcas more than Cassy's attitude about their next-door neighbors, the Foyes.

"We can't talk with *them*," said Cassy, a slight twist of her small mouth indicating her disdain. "As you can see, they are *colored*."

Cassy and Dorcas were on another stroll, enjoying an unseasonable summer breeze; the humidity and the mosquitoes had thankfully retreated for another day.

"But they are your, *our* neighbors," replied Dorcas, surprised that Cassy, usually a gentle soul, was so vehement about this.

"They are *beneath* us," explained Cassy, matter-of-factly.

"How?" Dorcas asked, trying to hide her growing annoyance.

Cassy turned to her, saying sharply, "Dorcas, for someone as smart as you, I can't believe you are so *blind* to the obvious. Because Mr. Foye owns property and has a successful business and lives near us does not make him our equal. He is a *negro*."

"Is he a nice man?" asked Dorcas. "What about his daughter? I see her working in the garden sometimes."

"What difference does that make?" Cassy asked, her responses getting more heated with each challenging question from Dorcas. "They are beneath us, as some people *must* be."

"Your family is better off than most, Miss Cassy, and there will always be some who have and some who have not. But how does color put him there, beneath us?"

"It just is, Dorcas, and you cannot associate with Annabelle Foye, or with any other of the black people in this town ... and thank God, there are not that many."

The mention of God provoked Dorcas: "But King Solomon didn't refuse to receive Bathsheba because she was black, and he gave her many gifts."

Cassy suddenly stopped and pushed Dorcas in the shoulder with her right hand. "Don't you dare show off to me," she snapped, her face twisted with rage. "You are just the help, and your job is to do what you are told and listen to your betters and believe as *we* believe."

Dorcas stood completely still, staring at the shy, reserved girl who, when provoked by a threat to her closed mind, lashed out to insult her only friend. But the uncomfortable truth could not be denied, even if it reared its ugly head only today. In the order of things, Dorcas would always remain a servant beneath her teenaged mistress. Their friendship was a charade, a show of affection that one slight question or comment could instantly obliterate.

"Or at least keep your silence about it," Cassy added, softening when she saw the shock on Dorcas' face.

"Yes, Miss Cassy," Dorcas replied softly, her disappointment in her own folly now deeper than sadness. *I should have known better*, she thought. *Did I really think things could be different between a mistress and the help?*

"Now, let's not be too serious," said Cassy, returning a smile to her face. "We can't let the color of someone's skin get between us, and we can at least be thankful that we are *not* black."

Dorcas did not dare a reply and waited for Cassy to introduce a safer subject for conversation . Finally, Cassy obliged, saying with excessive sweetness, "Oh, Dorcas, the steamboat ride up the Kennebec will be perfect for such a day as this."

"Yes, Miss Cassy," Dorcas agreed, grateful that Cassy was at least trying to make amends. She could no longer trust Cassy with absolute certainty, but she needed her friendship, such as it was. Although she enjoyed her moments of bookish isolation, Dorcas recognized her own essential nature. She preferred the company of others, delighting in gossip and conversation, and she thoroughly enjoyed watching the parties, picnics, and cotillions, the sewing sessions and chess matches, the constant round of visitors, and the piano lessons and recitals that consumed the time of the elite in Augusta, Maine. She worked before, during, and after these occasions, cleaning the house, helping to prepare the huge amounts of food expected at formal dinners, and serving at the table. Dorcas watched everything with meticulous care. She was going to rise in the world and be a lady. Her school was in session every day of the week, including Sunday. And eventually Augusta, and perhaps Boston and New York, would recognize its prize student, a woman of independent means, excellent taste, and refined manners—a true heiress of the age.

—◦—

The last highlight of that first year with the Westons was the lavish Thanksgiving dinner held at the home of Ruell Williams. His mansion on the east side of the river overlooking the town was the perfect setting for a multifamily gathering, and Dorcas was one of five servants needed to help with the preparations and serving guests at the bountiful table.

Dorcas had never seen so much food. Big meals were customary at even humble tables in Maine, but the Williams' dining table, with three extensions, seemed to groan under the weight of the food on top. Under the table was the rug made of thick green baize, strategically placed to receive the crumbs and grease droppings that inevitably fell to the floor during the enthusiastic consumption of meats and vegetables, mounds of ham with apple sauce, beefsteak with stewed peaches, salt fish and onions, eggs and oysters. After this first course, the first of two table clothes were removed to make way for the under cloth and the service of sweet pastries, pies, preserves, apples, walnuts, and chestnuts.

Preparing so much food was difficult enough, but at least she could see and hear the enjoyment of every thick slab of meat and morsel of breads. But no one could see or truly appreciate the amount of work required for rubbing the mahogany dinner table with brush and beeswax, or the intense ironing of the damask tablecloth that could not be folded. No crease was allowed to dim its smoothness, and it had to hang in a spare room the day before.

With the women sitting at one end of the table and the men at the other, and having to constantly negotiable movement between the table and a sideboard for the storage of beverages and the display of silverware, Dorcas had difficulty keeping track of any conversations. She was especially annoyed when she could not follow the heated exchanges between Mr. Williams and Mr. Rufus Breck about the ineffectiveness of the American Colonization Society. Mr. Breck saw colonization as the only solution to America's race problem, and Mr. Williams saw colonization as a wasteful and useless solution. "We can't send all of the negroes there," he asserted. "There are too many."

Then Paulina called Dorcas to the other end of the table, and Dorcas had to hear, as she removed plates and cups, Paulina's delight with the newly installed Venetian blinds. "After all," observed Paulina, "views should be shut out to prevent distraction during the afternoon."

Dorcas groaned, still disappointed by the ceaseless flow of insipidity out of the mouth of the woman, but she was grateful that Mrs. Weston granted her permission to join the family after dinner for the piano recital in the octagon parlor room.

"For all your hard work today, my dear, you've earned the privilege," said Paulina.

After the men had withdrawn for coffee and expensive Madeira wine, everyone gathered in the octagon parlor at the south end of the house, where Cassy played the piano for the assembled guests. She played Mozart and Haydn sonatas, using sheet music recently imported from London, with great precision and moving eloquence in the slow sections of each piece. For someone so shy and awkward in direct conversation, especially with men and older boys, Cassy displayed absolute confidence at the keyboard, and with the applause that came at the end of each piece, Cassy stood and smiled with a slight nod, silently acknowledging that this recognition of her talent was rightly deserved.

As much as Dorcas enjoyed the music, she could not keep her eyes away from the extraordinary French wallpaper covering the eight walls of the parlor. The paper depicted a lush tropical scene, where South Sea natives prepared to greet the famous Captain Cook, whose ships waited on the horizon. Before bare-chested seated men, groups of bare-breasted women, scores of them with feather headdresses and scarves, danced in celebration, pointing their arms to the sea as their thick legs, exposed at mid-thigh in shimmering togas, responded to drums and long reed instruments. Their shameless joy stirred an intense longing within Dorcas for the absolute thrill of pure freedom, a state where nothing but sheer pleasure mattered, where reputation was irrelevant, where fear of recrimination and reprisal had no place, where the body could speak silently on its own terms, woman to man, man to woman, woman to woman, even man to man.

She flushed at such thoughts and suddenly looked around to see if anyone noticed her reddened hand, burning cheeks, and the moisture on her forehead. No one, thank goodness, seemed to notice or care, but Dorcas took only small comfort in their indifference as she felt a flow of moisture within her private parts. She shifted in her chair and lowered her head, as if this could stop what was happening. But her mind could now only see entangled arms and legs, the raw humping of buttocks, and she could hear only the groans of sexual delight. Dorcas suddenly recalled the words of Solomon in his song, and this inconvenient blasphemy only intensified the lust within her:

My beloved is white and ruddy, the chiefest among ten thousand/His head is the most fine gold, his locks are bushy, and black as a raven/His eyes are as the eyes of doves by the rivers of waters, washed with milk, and fitly set/ His cheeks are as a bed of spices: his lips like lilies, dropping sweet smelling myrrh/His hands are as gold rings set with the beryl: his belly is as bright ivory overlaid with sapphires/His legs are pillars of marble, set upon sockets of fine gold/ His mouth is most sweet: yea, he is altogether lovely. This is my beloved, and this is my friend/Awake, o north wind; and come thou south;

blow upon my garden, that spices thereof may flow out. Let my beloved come into his garden, and eat his pleasant fruits.

She was so rattled that she conflated the text of the fourth and fifth chapters of the Song of Solomon, but this unusual error did not register or matter; she only knew that she could never return to the octagon room if she had any hopes of becoming a lady.

Unfortunately, matters only worsened when she returned to the Weston library that night.

Chapter Three

"**D**orcas, please come to the library after you help put the children to bed."
Judge Weston's voice was casual, warm, and undemanding. Because it was so late, almost ten o'clock, Dorcas thought the request unusual, but she hurried to complete the children's preparations for bed, believing that finally the judge was going to grant her access to the library without restrictions.

"Come in, and sit down here next to me," he said, his voice now strange and almost hoarse. "And close the door."

This was an unnecessary order. The door of the library was always closed, occupied or not. And no one, absolutely no one, could enter without the judge's permission.

He sat at his desk with his back to the door, and didn't turn around until Dorcas stood beside him. The fire in the fireplace had burned out hours before, but the oil lamps on the desk and the table near the door illumined the dark room with a golden glow. The curtains were drawn.

"Sit down," he said more softly. Her chair had been moved from the corner of the room so that it faced his chair.

When she sat down, he stood; sitting there she was overwhelmed by his physical presence for the first time. He was a short man, only three inches taller than Dorcas. But his thin frame and broad shoulders, and his youthful appearance in a dark, finely cut jacket befitting his station, made him seem big and frightening somehow. He was forty but looked twenty-five, and men and women openly commented, even in his presence, that for a judge he seemed young. Now sitting so close to him, with her eyes on his midsection, Dorcas suddenly wished that his belly pushed out the buttons of his waistcoat, that the skin of his hands was wrinkled, that he was old and less attractive.

He sat down, facing her, and said, "Give me your hand."

Dorcas hesitated, and he instantly asked in a cold, contemptuous voice, "You *dare* to oppose me?"

She didn't answer and looked to the door. With the same tone of disdain, he added, "You know no one will come in; even if they knock, they know that if I don't answer, they *can't* enter and disturb me, not even Mrs. Weston."

Dorcas felt faint as her heart raced. She knew something terrible was going to happen, and the mention of Mrs. Weston's name made the moment even more repugnant.

Weston took her hand and placed it in his lap, never taking his eyes from Dorcas' wide-eyed look of panic, commanding her silence without uttering a word. Then he pressed her hand deeper, until she could feel a bulge rising under the soft, dark wool. He groaned and his head fell back into the chair, as if a powerful inner force had overwhelmed him.

Had he fainted? Dorcas wondered. Confusion, anger, bewilderment, and self-condemnation overwhelmed her. *Why is this happening to me? Did he see me look at that wallpaper in the parlor? How could he do this, a judge with a wife and six children?*

"Harder," he said hoarsely.

Not knowing what he meant exactly, Dorcas pressed the open palm of her right hand into his crotch.

"No," he said softly, then gently pushed her hand away, without letting go of it. Dorcas thought her ordeal had come to a quick end and closed her eyes to concentrate on hearing his curt dismissal. But she was wrong. He released her hand and began to unbutton his trousers.

No, no, no, she wanted to scream when she realized what he was doing. *Please don't show me that!*

She was horrified, but also curious. She had seen the private parts of babies and young boys, of course, and there were the occasional paintings and prints of almost naked men. Once she had stumbled upon a group of loud and naked teenage boys playing in a pond, and she was surprised that some of them had long, swollen poles of flesh extending from hair and two sagging sacks of skin below their bellies.

Enthralled, she had watched in absolute silence, and only turned away when one boy, dropping to his knees, pulled at another boy's penis and put it into his mouth.

But nothing had prepared her for *this*—seeing and touching a grown man's most private parts.

Weston reached within his trousers and underwear and pulled out his penis, now fully erect, with thick veins under the reddened skin pulled back to reveal a large cap at the top. As she feared and hoped, it was ugly, repulsive. She could not fathom any pleasure associated with touching it, kissing it, or having it in her body.

Weston took Dorcas' hand again and placed it around the shaft at the middle. He kept his own hand over hers as he said, directing her as he looked into her eyes, "Hold it tight, and pump the skin up and down like this."

He demonstrated with his own hand before releasing it so that Dorcas could perform the movement independently. She complied, moving slowly, afraid to make a mistake and anger him, and at the same time startled by the soft, supple feel of his flesh.

"Quicker," he said, objecting even has he groaned, "Much faster."

She did as she was told, and he moaned, "Yes, yes, yes, that's it. Yes."

He started rolling from side to side as if he had lost control of his body's movements. Dorcas began to lighten her grip to stop the convulsions. He immediately cried out, "No, don't stop. No!"

Dorcas obeyed and continued on, keeping her eyes closed. The embarrassing abandonment of self-control was too painful to watch. How was it possible for this man, a pillar of the community, to become, in a matter of minutes, a mass of twitching legs, spasms, and groans? And now, fully aware of the pungent smell of Weston's compromised, sweating body, Dorcas felt light-headed, as if she was about to faint.

Finally, he said, "Ah," and Dorcas immediately opened her eyes to witness a white, viscous liquid flow over her fingers.

Surprised and instantly repulsed, she pulled away her hand; this time, he didn't try to stop her. He gathered the folds of his shirt and covered himself before saying simply, "This happens. It will wash off."

Dorcas didn't know where to turn or what to say. He noticed her confusion and added, "Don't wipe it on your dress. I have a cloth for you to use."

Taking the white cloth from the desk, he handed it to Dorcas, who quickly wiped the semen from the fingers of her right hand.

Weston was standing again. He buttoned his trousers and vest, and put on his frock coat. As if giving final directions to a clerk in his office, he said, "You will say nothing about this to anyone. If you do, no one will believe you, and I will toss you into the streets for telling so damnable a lie. Your father will not take you back because of the disgrace. So, you will take the best course and continue to do as I tell you. When I call for you to come to me, you will come, and you will do again what you did tonight. And you will do it better and better, like any good student. Goodnight, Dorcas. You may go now. I don't expect any questions, and I have nothing more to say to you. Again, good night."

She left the room, never looking at him as she passed, her steps soft but firm. As soon as she had closed the door behind her, she leaned against it and began to tremble as a deep sob welled up from her heaving chest. But immediately her instinct for self-preservation forced her to step away from the door. Even a slight rattle could anger Judge Weston, awaken the entire family, and arouse suspicion. Dorcas scanned the rise of the staircase, looking for her escape to the sanctuary of a darkened room and the gentle snoring of innocent children. She hurried up the staircase, stepping lightly, and only when she had reached the top of the stairs did she allow herself to cry. Even then she cried soundlessly, not wanting to awaken the children and face their questions.

She covered her mouth, sure that if she did not she would scream.

Tomorrow demanded a casual, unassailable brilliance. She needed time to prepare reasonable lies to counter the natural curiosity of the young ones, and the natural suspicions of their older sister. She assumed that by morning her prepared explanations would come, but her mind raced with questions now. *What should I do? What should I say if asked?*

By the time she was undressed and had slipped into bed, without bothering to wash her hands in the water bowl, Cassy entered the unlocked room and asked, holding a candle to Dorcas' face, "What did Father *want?*"

"He wanted to talk to me about using the library." Dorcas immediately replied, not looking away.

"Couldn't that wait for the morning?" Cassy asked.

"I can't explain your father's timing or schedule, or question when he wishes to see me, you, or anyone else," Dorcas said, carefully controlling her voice to hide her annoyance and rising fear. After living with Dorcas for months, Cassy Weston had becoming increasingly adept at reading the implied messages behind even slight modulations of tone in Dorcas' voice. Dorcas could only hope that the dark room hindered Cassy's interpretative skills.

"Did he grant you unfettered access to the library then?"

Dorcas hesitated. She was a good liar, but she couldn't take the risk of contradicting Judge Weston.

"No, he didn't," she replied, deciding that her answers needed to be as brief as possible; extended answers only made matters worse.

"Then what took so long?"

Dorcas almost snapped, "Were you counting the minutes?" but she refrained, saying only, "He talked about his latest acquisitions."

"At ten at night, and with *you?*"

Even a simple "yes" was dangerous, but Dorcas answered anyway. "Yes."

She waited, now refusing to look away from Cassy's belligerent eyes. In this test of wills, Dorcas knew she had the upper hand. There was nothing incriminating Cassy could possibly get out of her. Only the judge could betray her, and he was committed to a shared secret. Dorcas looked around the room to see if Cassy had awakened the children, but they did not stir. There was no mistaking the power of Cassy's jealousy.

"We shall see about this!" Cassy hissed. Then she turned away, leaving Dorcas to wonder what, if anything, Judge Weston would say about the time spent in the library.

Weston took the initiative the next morning by declaring at breakfast, before any questions or probing commentary, "Last night I discussed with Dorcas my satisfaction with her service here. And, believing that she has fulfilled and even surpassed our highest expectations, I offered her access to the library, as I originally promised. I expect that she will make the greatest use of it as she pursues her self-education."

Offered liked a final verdict, no cross-examinations were expected or permitted. Mrs. Weston and Cassy exchanged furtive glances but avoided direct eye contact with Weston, who only smiled. His smug benevolence seemed to expand his chest under his cravat and waistcoat.

Serving dishes when Weston announced his decision, Dorcas discreetly watched for signs of disapproval, but the faces of Paulina and Cassy had hardened into white marble masks of indifference.

"Well," Weston continued, clearing his throat, "there will be obvious rules for Dorcas' use of the library. During the afternoon, when the children are taking their naps, Dorcas may use the library when I am not at home. And in the evening, she may come to the library to peruse and select books for her private study. On occasion, I will summon her to the library so that I can discuss with her readings and the lessons she has learned. On these occasions we are not to be disturbed, as I take my tutelage most seriously."

"How generous of your time," Paulina said, the thinnest of smiles on her lips.

"Indeed," said Weston, "for she has *earned* my solicitude."

Dorcas could not resist a glance toward Cassy as she moved around the room; but a mere glance was enough. The mask had cracked at the eyes, and Cassy revealed black spheres like eclipsed suns burning with aureoles of rage.

Dorcas turned to the judge and said what was only appropriate under the circumstances: "Thank you, sir."

She had received her reward at a price she was willing to pay. Her memory of the titles in the library lifted her spirits, and she eagerly anticipated the first time she could enter the room alone and feel the bindings in her hands, the firm but soft paper, the delicate printed letters on hundreds of pages. There were stories to savor, information to acquire, and dreams to nurture, and in exchange she would have to submit to Judge Weston's requests. For hours of reading, she only had to give minutes to his carnal pleasure. Would his demands increase, she wondered? Would he expect her to kiss his private parts, or spread her legs so he could enter her? She shuddered at the mere thought of painful intercourse, and the embarrassing indignity of a man on top of her, but she brushed aside these concerns, noting that she would have more valuable time with Judge Weston than anyone else in his family. There were fates worse than being the favorite of Judge Nathan Weston of Augusta, Maine.

The year passed with comforting familiarity, the round of picnics, cotillions, dinner parties, sewing circles, walks, games, boat rides, and church services filling the Westons' calendar and creating the exhausting and expected work for the servants. Dorcas performed her duties with due diligence, even though she never received a compliment or any expression of appreciation for her domestic skill and dedication after Judge Weston's announcement about the library. But she didn't need them, having earned the undivided attention of Weston two or three times a week.

He took his tutelage quite seriously, offering Dorcas his own lifetime reading list, with specific recommendations for a fruitful beginning of her education. The list's length overwhelmed her, its sheer magnitude underscoring the limited time available to her. But Weston understood, saying gently, "Now don't worry. We'll begin with plays and poems, the shorter works, Shakespeare, the lyrics of Keats and Byron. The great histories and novels will come later—Gibbon, Richardson, Sir Walter Scott, and more. I prefer the English writers. Unfortunately, we do not have the years yet as a national culture to produce works of comparable quality. James Fenimore Cooper doesn't belong in such esteemed company. You will begin with "Romeo and Juliet" and "Julius Caesar," a fitting contrast for our exploration of the complexities of human nature."

Dorcas could only stare at the man who spoke to her as if her feelings and opinions mattered, and she was pleasantly surprised whenever her sessions did not end with touching him. He actually seemed to enjoy talking to her and answering her questions, once she became comfortable asking them. After three sessions, when she listened to his monologue and performed her sexual duties in absolute silence, she found the courage to ask a question. His reaction was immediate—an expansive smile, bright eyes, and an eagerness to instruct that touched her in a strange way. He pursued his sexual agenda with grim determination, giving orders in ugly, clipped tones, never smiling even when his hunger was satisfied, and refusing to look at her when she was done. But there was joy in his literary instruction, and true communication between them. Each had a need to know and understand the other's taste and interests.

Eventually, Weston escalated his sexual demands.

One day he told her to lick the shaft of his penis and then take it into her mouth. She frowned, failing to hide her revulsion, then flinched when she saw the anger in his eyes. Suddenly, he grabbed her by the back of her head and pushed it forward.

"Open it," he demanded, and Dorcas resisted, wimpering, "Please. I can't. Please."

"Open it," he insisted, his voice so cruel and remorseless it frightened her. She now tried to relax her mouth and resist the urge to gag as tears filled her eyes.

Weston gently pushed and pulled her head, moaning until he released her and fell into the back of his chair. Dorcas needed to empty her mouth, and turned away looking for a cup, a napkin, anything that could relieve her revulsion and contempt. This was, indeed, a dreadful and undignified business.

Although he never apologized for his sudden cruelty, Weston never behaved like that again, even as he wanted and needed more. Once he had shattered the plot of his carefully crafted play, he was gentle, almost furtive, when he began touching her breasts, lifting her skirts, and probing the flesh between her legs. Sexual intercourse now seemed inevitable, and although she feared the pain and possible pregnancy, she calmly accepted it when it came, relaxing her body and breathing evenly when Weston took her hand, led her to the carpet in the middle of the floor, and asked her to lie down. After he knelt before her, lifted her skirts, and covered her body with his heavy chest, Dorcas could see them both from above, as if she hovered near the ceiling on softly undulating wings, looking down to the couple below.

But she could not hear. Weston moved his uncovered hips without groaning. She received his thrusts without flinching, sighing, or gasping. The wood in the fireplace did not crackle, and the rain rattled the windows no longer.

This separation of body and spirit surprised Dorcas for only a moment. Then relief overwhelmed her. She could maintain her distance and not feel remorse or shame. Somehow, all this was happening to someone else.

There were a few other surprises that year. Cassy could not maintain her enmity, and after a month resumed her somewhat fractious friendship with Dorcas, preferring her company to righteous indignation. Cassy even took an active interest in her father's tutorials with Dorcas. If she could not have direct access to her father's mind and heart, then she could discover them through a talkative, opinionated intermediary.

Already a wealthy man, her father became even wealthier that year when the state legislature decided to move the capitol to Augusta and purchased land belonging to the judge for the new capitol building. Overlooking the city on a bluff near the Kennebec River, the spot seemed perfect, and the citizens of Augusta celebrated Judge Weston's and the city's good fortune with a parade, parties, and a constant flow of whiskey, brandy, and Madeira. The civic pride of a small town in the interior of Maine was now boundless, and its citizens were relieved of the sense of inferiority common to second cities. Portland had more people, but Augusta would be a capitol, like Boston and Albany.

Unfortunately, the reinvigorated civic pride of Augusta was not strong enough to withstand the sting of criticism from the town's most famous visitor in 1827; and when she published her account in another one of her travel books, she had only one good thing to say about Augusta—it had one worthy family, the Westons, and that family had the good fortune of employing an extraordinary servant girl.

Anne Royall was notorious, earning her reputation by traveling alone throughout the country, taking copious notes on every occasion, including conversations with prominent citizens, and then publishing her usually unflattering accounts in a trilogy series called *The Black Book*. By coach and train, she roamed the country, exposing the morons, jackasses, boors, and contemptible puppies who failed to impress her. The local newspapers always announced her impending arrival, as if acknowledging her self-importance. She was an irascible busybody, but the hunger for approval was so great, and a gnawing sense of inferiority so pervasive, that Americans from New Orleans to Augusta invited ridicule for the slightest chance of printed flattery.

At first, Dorcas did not think much of her brief encounter.

Opening the door, she said softly, "Good afternoon, and welcome to the home of Judge Weston and his family. Please come in."

With a wave of her hand, Dorcas directed Mrs. Royall to the parlor, where Mrs. Weston waited to receiver her.

Stepping into the parlor first, Dorcas announced, "Madam, Mrs. Royall."

"Thank you," Mrs. Royal replied with a slight bow of her head. "You are a delightful young lady, and thank you, Mrs. Weston, for receiving me."

Mrs. Weston nodded slightly, but before she could even sit down, Mrs. Royal had a question.

"Who is that girl, and where did she come from?"

Paulina frowned, taken aback by this sudden interest in a servant, but she answered quickly to bring the subject to a merciful close: "She is an orphan girl, whom we took in and have raised."

"A dove so mild," Mrs. Royall observed.

"You may leave us now," Paulina said to Dorcas, who was only waiting for the signal to depart.

Except for a passing annoyance with Paulina's inaccurate reference to her as an orphan, Dorcas dismissed the appearance of Mrs. Royal as just another in the constant parade of visitors. And whatever were their impressions of the famous visitor, the Westons did not share them with her until *The Black Book* was published months later. It was only then that Dorcas regretted meeting the woman.

Harlow Spaulding's bookstore on Water Street, so close to the Westons' that Dorcas could reach it with a five-minute walk, advertised the sale of Mrs. Royall's three-volume work, and scores of eager citizens, including Paulina Weston, purchased copies to read what the acerbic Mrs. Royall had to say about them.

Dorcas could not afford the cost of the book, but the young and friendly bookstore owner pointed out the key passages for her to see. She openly groaned, feeling the wounded pride of her adopted town, when she read Mrs. Royall's opening assault. "The citizens of Augusta," she asserted, "are a long ways behind the citizens of Hallowell, in urbanity and good breeding—no comparison."

But Mrs. Royall had only praise for Judge Weston, and Dorcas smiled as she read about the man whose name Mrs. Royall could not manage to spell correctly. "Judge Western and his family alone would secure the reputation of any place which might have the honor of his residence," she wrote. "The Judge is of low stature, but very dignified; he said he was forty years of age; I would suppose him at once, not more than twenty-five—he is the youngest looking man of his age in America. In his manner he is frank, polite, and easy as the evening gale, and at the same time the most commanding and dignified man in the United States, and I would suppose among the most learned judges; there is something in the tone of his voice originally pleasing; and take him on any ground, he is altogether one of our first men; he is a long way ahead of any Judge I have met north of Washington City."

Dorcas was amused that Mrs. Royall could be so right and so wrong about Nathan Weston. Of course there was no way for her to know his secret desires or detect his hypocrisy, but Ann Royall seemed to be only a boorish snob incapable of writing a graceful sentence.

But Dorcas gasped when she came to the next paragraph. In fact, she almost dropped the book when reading it.

"But of all the families I saw," wrote Mrs. Royall, "I was most astonished at a little girl in the capacity of a servant. I generally (and doubtless others do, too) form my opinion of the master and the mistress of a house by the servant who opens the door. If I find the servant civil and polite, the master is certain to be so. But if I find the servant insolent, I never fail to find a thorough, proud vixen in the house. When I knocked at the door of Judge Western, it was opened by a little girl of about eleven years old, who saluted with inimitable sweetness, and with a graceful wave of her hand, invited me to take a seat on the sofa. What an easy matter it must be, I thought, to be polite when this child has become so perfect in the art. After exchanging salutations with the family, I could not forebear a remark upon the little girl—expressing my astonishment at her graceful manners . . ."

Shaking her head, Dorcas said to Mr. Spaulding, "Oh no, oh no, oh no."

"What could be wrong?" he asked, his brown eyes widening.

Unable to speak for a moment, she pointed to the offending passage, and he said brightly, "Isn't that a most pleasant surprise? She managed to say something nice after all, and she wrote about *you*. Can you believe it? Too bad she doesn't mention your name."

Grimly, Dorcas noted, "Mrs. Weston is mentioned only *once*."

"But it is nevertheless a compliment."

"As a reference to her taking care of *me*," Dorcas explained. "No, this is *not* good, not good at all. Oh why did Mrs. Royall have to come to the house and then write a book with us in it?"

"I'm sorry you feel this way, Dorcas," Spaulding said, closing the offending volume, "but the book is selling quite well, and I need the money."

"I'm sorry, but I need to go," replied Dorcas. She hurried out of the bookstore, preparing herself for a chilly reception on her return.

Paulina was in the parlor waiting with her copy of the book in her lap.

"Dorcas, I need to speak with you," she announced solemnly. "And we shall be *alone*, you and me."

Feeling helpless and completely isolated, Dorcas blurted out, "It's *not* my fault. I *didn't* write those words, and I *didn't* say more than a few words to Mrs. Royall when she called on us."

"On *us*?" asked Paulina, arching her eyebrows to accentuate the sarcasm in her voice.

"I meant . . ."

Paulina raised her hand.

"Stop now, Dorcas! You have far too much to say as it is, and you said enough that day to warrant Mrs. Royall's eternal approbation. Even I have benefited from knowing *you*."

She opened the book to the clearly marked page and read the offending passage, sneering at virtually every word: "She was a poor orphan child whom she took and raised. This is saying enough for Mrs. Western. This deed had more goodness in it than all the Bible and tract societies ever performed in their lives."

She paused, and then added, "Enough for Mrs. Western *indeed*."

"I am sorry, Mrs. Weston, "Dorcas mumbled, her eyes downcast.

"Let me make myself indubitably clear, Dorcas Doyen," declared Paulina Weston with a delicate, wry smile. "You will *never*, and I mean *never*, be a member of this family. And if any one dares to draw such a conclusion from this terrible book, I will make it my mission to set matters right and affirm your *low* status in this household. You represent *no one*, not me, not Mr. Weston, not my children. Mrs. Royall is a fool to think that she can draw conclusions about the most prominent family in Maine by the likes of you! Now get out of my sight."

Chapter Four

Once Cassy returned to Mr. Emerson's Academy for Young Ladies in Saugus just north of Boston, it was easier for Dorcas to develop a friendship with Annabelle Foye, the black girl next door. Paulina unintentionally opened that door when she praised Annabelle's gardening skills during a casual lunch with the judge, who was home for the afternoon before returning to the courthouse.

Dorcas had just offered the tray of tea and biscuits when Paulina said, as if Dorcas had disappeared, "You know, Mr. Weston, Annabelle Foye has quite an eye for beauty in the garden. Perhaps Dorcas can learn some things from her and improve our own garden, since ladies can't spend time in the sun and lead others to conclude—incorrectly, of course—that we are laborers, unlike negroes who are so used to working in the fields. Their skin absorbs the sun, and from everything I have heard and read, they are by nature disposed to such work."

"Our own Mr. Jefferson agrees with you, my dear. His *Notes on Virginia*, a curious volume written after the Declaration of Independence, says that blacks can only feel, not think, having no capacity for logic, or mathematics, or philosophy."

"Then you both agree that the labor of gardening becomes them," said Paulina with a satisfied smile.

But that satisfaction was immediately dashed when Weston observed, "*Notes* only proves that even great men can be blinded by prejudice and the need to self-justify. Those pages on blacks are utter nonsense. A negro designed Washington City, and black artisans and craftsmen did most of the work at Monticello. Besides, his views did not keep him from maintaining a longstanding relationship with one of his slaves, Sally Hemings."

Paulina raised her hand in protest. "Mr. Weston, remember that Dorcas is present," she cried. Dorcas froze in place. "Dorcas, please leave us now, child."

Weston turned to Dorcas as she prepared to leave, and said, "Annabelle Foye has put considerable *thought* into that garden. You can learn a few things from her."

Before Dorcas could reply even with a simple, "Yes, sir" Paulina interjected, "And the two of you might even become friends, which would make preeminent sense as you both function at society's lowest rung. Color, indeed, should not matter when you are looking up from the gutter to the heights forever barred to both of you."

"Paulina, that is *enough*," said Weston.

Paulina's eyes widened as if he had spit into her tea. She sputtered, "To rebuke me in front of . . ."

Dorcas was stunned, immobilized by embarrassment and fascination. She had never seen the Westons openly disagree before.

"You may go," Weston said without turning to Dorcas. "I know you have more to bring us, but we'll summon you with the bell when we are ready."

Dorcas hastened from the room, but she was unable to resist the urge to eavesdrop once she closed the door. She made a point of loudly walking away and returned softly, without her shoes, to the closed door, where she leaned her ear as closely as possible without pressing against the wood.

Weston continued his gentle rebuke: "Paulina, you need not remind Dorcas or anyone else at every opportunity that she is a servant. She is a smart girl and quite aware of her station. And I must remind you that we took her in so as to raise the possibilities for her elevation. True, she will never be our equal, but that doesn't mean that she is undeserving of opportunity."

Paulina's tone was cordial but unrepentant; she seemed to be speaking through clenched teeth.

"You are the head of this household, Nathan, and I too must recognize my place in it. But as your wife, I am due a measure of respect that is not in keeping with your obvious, and I mean *far too obvious*, regard for a servant girl."

"What are you saying?" he charged, the anger rising in his voice.

Weston always spoke evenly, never increasing his volume. But his rich baritone deepened sharply now.

"Even our Cassy has noticed," Paulina said. "Her tears have moved me and . . ."

"You dare to bring Cassy into this?" he roared. "Her opinion is irrelevant, and nothing will change the fact that she is my daughter and Dorcas is *not*. For all of your prattling about social standing and superiority, both of you seem far too threatened by a pretty, intelligent girl who has nothing else but us. We stand between her and the streets. We are all she has. She knows this, and so do you. So why are you so determined to remind her, and me, on every possible occasion of the obvious? We are not *stupid*."

Chastised like a felon before his judicial bench, Paulina said softly, "I am sorry, Mr. Weston, for offending you."

"Oh, Paulina, only *you* know how to make even an apology offensive," said Weston with a sigh, and then rang the bell summoning Dorcas, who stepped away from the door as softly as possible, put her shoes on in the pantry, and walked back to the parlor with a definite click to her heels.

———•———

Annabelle Foye proved to be a gracious and generous instructor. Older than Dorcas by three years, she patiently explained the steps needed for the successful cultivation of roses, daylilies, and hydrangeas, and all the annuals she mixed with them to create a seamless, luxuriant display. She grew vegetables in abundance, but took no pleasure in growing them.

"Just food," she declared.

And she showed no reticence when Dorcas finally asked her questions about racial matters.

"Why do you live here, when there are so few negroes in Maine? Don't you want to be around other people like yourselves? Wouldn't that be easier for you and your parents?"

"The more there are of us, the more we upset folks," Annabelle replied. "There have been ugly scenes, even riots, in Boston and New York."

"But why?" Dorcas asked. "Your skin is dark, but you're no different than people around here. You dress like us. You talk like us. You live in the same neighborhood."

"But I can't go to your church, and my parents will never sit in the Westons' parlor."

"That is ridiculous," exclaimed Dorcas, frustrated by the absurdity of one feature determining so much. What if her own green eyes made her a pariah?

"Most of my people are slaves, and because of that, people think we are all unworthy of respect," Annabelle explained.

"Then slavery should end," Dorcas declared.

"It should end, but I don't think that abolition will settle the matter. Slavery is not here. Maine came into the Union as a free state. Still, people look down on us."

Annabelle's father, born in Boston, was a master carpenter. His mastery earned him commissions from the wealthiest families on Boston's Beacon Hill, but the slurs, threats, and violence in a large city so angered and depressed him, he'd fled with his family to Portland, a smaller town. There he received similar treatment, and he considered moving on to Canada, the last stop on the Underground Railroad, where many free negroes had found a better life. But he was an American. The United States was his country, and he could not leave it. So he settled in Augusta, a town of almost four-thousand with about forty negroes. Augusta was not perfect, just better, with fewer ignorant, stupid fools.

"Some people look down on me," said Dorcas.

Annabelle smiled and touched Dorcas' hand. "But you can hide who you are, and where you came from. I can't."

"It's not fair!" Dorcas replied.

"No, it isn't fair, and I have cried about it many times. My mother and father have tried to make it easier by having money, a nice house, and some kind of recognition in the community. But no matter how well my father is dressed, no matter how much money he has, no matter how well he speaks, a total stranger on the streets will call him a *nigger*."

"That shows only a lack of class," Dorcas observed.

"But even the lowest of the low feel superior to my father, because he is black and they are not."

"You didn't choose to be black, just like I didn't chose to have green eyes and black hair."

"Skin is everything."

"Surely, you don't believe that?" asked Dorcas, saddened by Annabelle's fatalistic acceptance of the ways of the world.

"I have to," Annabelle said. "I am reminded every day, every minute—by looks, by comments, by questions, by the silences at the dinner table, by the newspapers, by a mere glance. You said that we are the same, you and me. We are *not*. You are free not to think about yourself every minute of the day, because everyone does not hold up a mirror from morning to night. You are *free*."

For the first time, Dorcas felt the force of open and honest communication, the sharing of heart and mind, and a trust born of vulnerability and mutual dependence between two people who were essentially equals, two young girls, almost women, struggling to define themselves in an insane world.

"May I be your friend?"

Annabelle smiled and, reaching out to take her hand, replied, "You already are."

Dorcas developed another friendship that season, responding to the attentions of Harlow Spaulding, who found in his teenaged customer the most enthusiastic reader of literature in town. Because she didn't have money, she couldn't buy the books in his store. And besides, she had Mr. Weston's library at her disposal. But Harlow didn't care. Dorcas was his best customer because she loved books, respected authors, and actually read whatever he recommended.

He wasn't handsome, having no features to turn a lady's fancy, except for his height. He was over six feet, the tallest man in town. He wore spectacles on a prominent nose, and his brown hair, combed to the back of his head, seemed too thin for a man of twenty-four. But his ready smile, his patient courtesy with all customers no matter how trying they could be, a deep voice that seemed to stir the air, and an expansive interest in everything from literature and the decorative arts to politics, news, and even gossip made him an attractive bachelor.

Harlow stocked his store with hundreds of books, maintained a lending library of recently published works, and also sold bugles, violins, flutes, calling cards, cologne water, backgammon boards, pens, embossed paper, and dice. All of these items and more he advertised in the *Maine Patriot and State Gazette*, a newspaper he also owned. It was one of Augusta's two newspapers and carried Democratic Party news, literary essays, and short items about love, courtship, marriage, and the nature of men and women. For Dorcas, he made several recommendations, the first being *The Scottish Chiefs* by Jane Porter.

She loved the five-volume work, a heart-stopping tale about William Wallace and other clan leaders who defended Scotland against English invaders. Dorcas identified with the novel's heroine, Helen Mar, a brave and beautiful girl who commanded troops and trembled before the man she loved. She admired everything about Helen, especially her remarkable ability to adapt to all circumstances, always finding the best ways to behave at the right time. Dorcas also developed a grudging fondness for the wicked stepmother, Johanna Mar, who had an adulterous passion for William Wallace, a passion he never noticed. This unrequited love touched Dorcas, for it reflected her growing feelings for Harlow, a cultivated man who was, most assuredly, forever beyond her reach. She was a penniless servant; he was the successful son of a prominent family in Hallowell.

As an eligible bachelor, he attracted attention, but he was not smitten, he confessed to Dorcas, who smiled surreptitiously with him at the flagrant display of female desire from Olivia Newbanke—the dropped fan, the slight lean into his chest, the blinking eyelashes, the deep sighs, the entire gamut of empty, hopeless strategies.

"I am waiting for the perfect girl," he observed. "Perhaps Miss Newbanke should read that Philadelphia article I reprinted in the *Patriot*. Respectability of character and purity of morals are essential qualities in close relationships, especially marriage."

Dorcas inwardly groaned. She could never claim purity of morals. Her activities in the Weston library, even under duress, made sure of that. But how would Harlow ever know? She would not be so stupid as to confess her deeds to him. Telling the truth was highly overrated.

"So what do you think about *The Scottish Chiefs*?" he asked at last.

She needed to share her opinions with someone who would understand.

Before she could answer, he continued, "It makes great sense to me that profitable lessons can be learned from characters in historical fiction, the good and the bad. For example, we have the chivalry of Richard II, and then we have the profligacy of Charles II, the range of human nature from which to draw an understanding of ourselves."

"But what if we draw the wrong conclusion? Is it our fault, or the author's?" Dorcas asked.

"Well, there are some authors who will inevitably lead us to the wrong conclusions, which is why we should, perhaps, never read Fielding, Rochester, or Smollett."

"Have you read them?"

"No."

"Then how do you know if . . ."

She stopped herself, annoyed that she could not sustain the deceptions integral to polite conversation for just a little longer. *I must work on this*, she thought. She shifted her position, saying instead, "And then what are the other good books?"

"There are books that are both educational and simply good to read. Try Richardson, Sir Walter Scott, Washington Irving."

"Are there other female writers like Jane Porter?"

"Well there is the other Jane—the Jane Austen of *Pride and Prejudice*, *Emma*, and *Mansfield Park*. She is amusing, with a biting wit, but nothing happens in her books except for courtship and marriage. Napoleon and Waterloo are not mentioned even once, even though she lived in England during the wars."

"She wrote about what she *knew*," Dorcas observed. As soon as she said it, she knew she had committed an error.

Harlow raised his eyebrow, and then he laughed aloud, throwing his head back.

"Oh, Dorcas, I just love knowing you. You can't seem to help yourself. You just say what you know, just like a man."

She didn't feel better for his saying this. Despite his avowals, she wanted him to acknowledge her identity as a young girl worthy of his respect and admiration. If so, she had a chance, however remote, of winning his affection. She tried again to ingratiate herself, saying with blatant coyness, "So what do you recommend from Mr. Richardson or Mr. Smollet?"

"Oh you should read Richardson. He's quite clever writing epistolary novels, stories told by characters in letters to each other. Most entertaining, reading people's inner thoughts. His letters are so good, not like ours."

"I don't write letters anymore. I used to, when I was younger and away from home. But my father is not interested in my feelings and opinions. He made that quite clear after I first arrived here. He said, 'Too many words for someone just cleaning house and emptying bed pans.'"

Another mistake! Self-pity and *a reference to excrement. When will I finally learn to shut up?* thought Dorcas.

"Oh, then write to me," Harlow said, smiling. "I love receiving letters. Most people do."

"I don't know much, but even *I* know that letters from a single girl to a single man in a small town like Augusta wouldn't be acceptable. There would be talk about it, and the Westons would not appreciate even the slightest suggestion of scandal."

"You're right, of course, and wise for one so young."

"I'm not *that* young."

Can't you just agree with the man, and leave it at that?

"No, you are not. In fact, you're an amazing girl."

"Thank you." She enjoyed the simple and obviously heartfelt compliment.

"You are smarter than most people around here, men and women."

That's not too hard. This is Augusta, not Boston, she almost said. But she chose discretion, knowing that to say this would insult him, a native. She repeated her thanks instead.

"Now let me get you that Richardson," he said, turning to a nearby shelf.

———·———

Her literary education continued with Judge Weston presenting her a key.

"This is to my cabinet, which I always keep locked," he explained. "You are not to take the key from this room, but once I show you where I keep it hidden, you can always find my treasures when you need them."

He turned to his desk and said, "Here I have a secret hiding place, and it's just for the cabinet I am about to show you."

Need? What need? she wondered, irritated by his habit of talking about his feelings as if they were hers. Instead, she asked, unable to suppress her surprise, "Treasures?"

"Now don't jump to conclusions, Dorcas. I'm not talking about gold, jewels, or anything like that. I'm talking about books, hard to obtain books."

"Oh," she replied, unable to hide her disappointment.

Weston chuckled.

"I'm *not* that rich, Dorcas. And besides, if I had jewels, I wouldn't keep them in the house for some thief to get at."

"My mistake, sir."

"No apologies needed," he said, going to his cabinet. "Now let me see."

He opened it wide and reached for a pile of volumes, some small, some large. He returned to his desk with them, and said as he put them down, "I could give you my list of the cabinet's contents, but that would be meaningless. You can go through them when you want to, but I brought these out so that you can get an idea of what is in store for you."

Dorcas noticed then that he had an erection and waited for him to open his trousers and begin the customary explorations. But he continued on as if she was unaware of his physical excitement.

"These are books and illustrations that I get from Europe. They are hard to find, and thus very expensive. They will show you the ways of the world beyond Augusta, and you will learn about the possibilities before you, as they remind me."

His voice was hoarse now, and he turned away as he placed the right flap of his jacket over his crotch.

Dorcas didn't know what to do or say, so she waited, staring at the books and knowing, given what he had just said, that no good could come from them.

Finally, he turned around, and his voice had a restored calm that was oddly reassuring. "This is the first time I have ever showed these to anyone. I am sorry for acting in haste. Perhaps another time."

What could be so terrible? she thought impatiently. *What could a book do to me that he has not done already?*

Sometimes she had to satisfy him twice a day, the hurried rush to unbutton trousers, the stifled moaning, the twists and turns of a man in the grip of climatic release now only inspiring her irritation and impatience. After the initial shock and self-loathing, Dorcas enjoyed her power, however fleeting, over him. Here was the most important man in Augusta, Maine, writhing under her hand, his fancy clothes and all the other symbols of his prestige made silly by their irrelevance. Lust was more than the great equalizer, it debased with casual ease.

She almost snapped at him, her curiosity now frustrated. But she controlled her voice, saying as evenly as she could, "Sir, I'm most interested in what you are disposed to share, right now."

She didn't have much time. There were some chores still to do, even though Paulina had retired for the night.

"Oh yes," he said, as if startled out of a sleep walk. "You should make sure to read John Cleland's *Fanny Hill* and Doctor Huntington's *Voyages to Darkest Africa and Other Forbidden Lands*. And take a close look at the prints from some of the best graphic artists from England and France. They have remarkable wit, as well as the power to enthrall."

He handed over part of the pile to her, and then hurried from the room, leaving her speechless.

She sat down, despite her need to complete the work of the day. She turned to the first page of the Cleland work and determined it was a tale of adventure written by a prostitute who had to explain the reasons for her fall into vice. She casually flipped a few pages and came upon the most detailed descriptions of sex she had ever encountered.

After reading one passage, she turned to another, then another. They all followed the same pattern: Fanny meets a customer, she provides sexual satisfaction, and she moves on, collecting money and appreciation because she never fails to extol the size of a man's member and his self-regard. Clearly, Fanny is in charge, and she controls with a sense of humor.

Dorcas tried not to laugh. Young ladies, she knew, were not supposed to see humor in such things. But she giggled anyway.

The illustrations in the other books were more disturbing. The numerous scenes of fornication, with graphically detailed depictions of an amazing variety of sexual intercourse, did not shock Dorcas. But the details of body parts bothered her more—the enormous breasts, buttocks, and penises made crude and brutal by exaggerated proximity. And when she scanned the pages of the Mr. Huntington's trips to Africa, she almost dropped the book, so violent were the scenes of rape, torture, hanging, and mutilation perpetrated by white men against Africans so sexualized by the illustrators that little of their humanity remained. They were only holes to fill, breasts to suck, buttocks and hips to fondle, and huge penises to despise and then cut off. The slave traffic was unbelievably cruel, and monsters on ships came to Africa only to make money.

Why would Judge Weston show her all of this? Desperate, Dorcas looked vainly around the room, as if the walls and bookshelves could somehow reveal the answer to her silent questions. What message did he mean to leave with her? Were these books some kind of prediction, his way of telling her that her future fate was clear and irrevocable, despite the guardianship of the Westons . . . that the best she could hope for was becoming a well-read whore?

"No, this can't be true," she finally said aloud, as if by declaring her truth it became the truth for herself, for Judge Weston, and for all time.

She took the horrible books, placed them back in the closet, and locked them with the special key, swearing that she would never look at them again. Her silent oath seemed insufficient, and so she rushed to the other side of the library to find Judge Weston's copy of *Romeo and Juliet*. Touching its soft binding recalled memories of their mutual reading of scenes from the play, scenes that brought tears to the judge's eyes as he gently read the ardent lines of Romeo's incandescent devotion. Hearing them then, and recalling them now, Dorcas could not believe that a man so moved by such tender words could be so vicious a tormentor.

But she could not ignore his anger. At times it passed through him like convulsions after he made her do his sexual bidding. He seemed to blame her for bringing him to a depth he deplored and desired as well, his blue eyes narrowing to such thin slits she could barely see them. At such times she wanted to scream, as if her cries could awaken her from a bad dream.

But this was no dream. There was nothing she could do about it, at least for now. Her helplessness occasionally depressed her, but Dorcas did find some satisfaction, if not comfort, in the judge's bumbling, inarticulate guilt. In the mornings Weston always seemed relaxed from a sleep unbothered by a guilty conscience or regret. But Dorcas knew better; the facts inevitably emerged—the calculated coldness of his invitations to come to the library, the labored breathing when she entered the room, the sweat on his forehead, the curt dismissals after he withered in her hand. He hated her for knowing that she truly *knew* him.

And yet . . . and yet, she could not despise him, although she tried. She could not disregard or forget his defense of her, especially to Paulina. She could not dismiss his eager clarification of elaborate sentences and the explanation of obscure words. And she could never forget the gentle sounds of his evocation of Romeo's adoration of Juliet. Those words still echoed in her ears, their eloquence sweetening the air so deeply that nothing but the purest elements of earth and heaven mattered. Tears flowed from her eyes, as she mumbled the remembered words, *his* words recited to her on a night that seemed enchanted because he became that teenaged Italian boy declaring an endless love:

"O speak again bright angel/for thou as glorious to this night, being o'er my head/as is a winged messenger of heaven/unto the white turned wondering eyes/ of the mortals that shall fall back to gaze on him/when he bestrides the lazy puffy clouds/and sails upon the bosom of the air."

Chapter Five

Dorcas had become quite a beauty by 1830. Mirrors confirmed the obvious—lustrous black hair, a thin waist, unblemished skin whose whiteness matched the luminous cotton sheets she washed, high but delicate cheekbones that accentuated liquid green eyes, and small, almost red lips that didn't need added color. At seventeen, her breasts, round and firm, were too small, and her feet were too big. But she didn't fret about these limitations, counting on the requirements of current fashion—a tight, high-necked bodice and long, full shirts—to hide her flaws.

A casual promenade through the streets brought desired attention. Both men and women turned when she walked by. Men nodded their heads, tipped their hats, or winked their eyes before scanning her figure from head to toe. Some were so bold as to offer a compliment, and a few day laborers with grimy hands and dirty faces leered and gestured their futile hopes for sex behind a barn or in some ditch. Resentful ladies huddled to reaffirm their disapproval.

As she walked, Dorcas smiled and swayed her hips, never breaking her stride even when she noticed an attractive young man assessing her. But the time had come when she wanted more than furtive glances or crude street overtures. She wanted to experience what she'd read about in *Fanny Hill* and other works. Her body ached for the couplings described in the salacious prints Judge Weston secretly collected. Within a week, she had broken her vow to avoid them, her curiosity always stronger than outrage or dismay.

The pious critics in the *Maine Patriot* and literary journals were correct. Their worst fears were realized in the hopes and dreams of Dorcas Doyen. Novels and dirty pictures had corrupted her, revealing the vast possibilities for sexual pleasure if she were only willing to break the bonds of convention. Certainly her body was ready. The ache of her nipples, the sudden flashes of heat under her skin, and the liquid flow between her legs sometimes converged so powerfully within her that she would gasp and search for a chair or a wall to lean against. Dorcas now knew with absolute conviction that the advice in Frances Byerly Park's *Domestic Duties, or Instructions to Young Married Ladies*, and the other manuals and primers published for the ignorant and naïve, were wrong. Women were not sexless creatures who had to wait until men, gripped by passions uniquely their own, revealed the true nature of sexual feeling, awakening confused and ignorant virgins like princesses in fairytales. Dorcas knew better, and although only seventeen, she fully accepted the power of her allure and bided her time until the right opportunity came her way.

Harlow Spaulding remained out of reach. He recognized Dorcas' charms, but referenced them like an older brother wanting to protect his sister. He observed one afternoon, as they perused some of the latest arrivals in his store, "You know, Dorcas, I cannot help but see how the men look at you. You give them good reason since you have matured, but you must not be taken in by such attentions. If you succumb to them, and I have no reason to doubt your resolve to resist, the consequences will all fall to you. It's the way of an unjust world. Besides, men want angels to marry and adore; and you by right have every reason to be one of those angels."

These words stung like a neat and sharp cut made by the finest thin paper. Although well meaning, they only widened the deep chasm between her hopes and his expectations. She wanted to shout, "Look at *me*. Can't you see I love you? Can't you see I *adore* you?"

Instead, she said nothing about his advice that day, suspecting that he knew, somehow, the truth about her. But as much as she tried to accept his words as helpful admonitions, they angered her deeply. They perpetuated lie upon lie. There were no angels anywhere, and marriage, as far as she could tell, was based on deceit and gross self-interest. What angered her most, however, was the smug acceptance of the world as he defined it. His words left no room for change, for the possibility of an ideal making things right or better.

She looked at Harlow and felt, for the first time, like a plumed bird trapped in sparkling cage. Dorcas saw the future, and she shuddered. Always insisting on perfection, Harlow as a husband would keep her encased under glass on a pedestal in the corner of their bedroom. Every once in a while, he would lift the case and take her to their bed for his pleasure, and certainly not for hers. When done, he would return her to his prison with a smile, knowing that she was safe and secure.

Dorcas prided herself in being realistic, but at heart she knew she was a romantic idealist. She wanted more and deserved better. Surely there was someone out there who could see her true self and love her anyway?

Nevertheless, Dorcas could not relinquish her fantasies about Harlow, and she found some comfort in writing letters to him that she never posted. Modeled after some of the letters in Richardson's *Clarissa*, they were brief expressions of pure emotional release. No news or gossip, little social context to clarify the moment, only need and desire. Thus began a lifelong habit, and sometimes she wrote five or six letters a day. After Harlow Spaulding, she would post most of them.

In the meantime, she seized opportunities to demonstrate her attractiveness more aggressively, and if Harlow's blindness did nothing more, it finalized her resolve to find passion and attraction in one exquisite moment.

She no longer feared pregnancy, as she knew what to do to avoid it: Immediately after the act, one should squat over a bowl filled with tepid water, sulfate of zinc, and alum, and insert a plunger made from a wood spoon and cotton bandages to remove the man's seed.

Her opportunity for practice came from a surprising source.

———·———

The wedding of Catherine Weston to Frederick A. Fuller was the highlight of the spring season that year, marking the union of two distinguished families in the Maine countryside. An ancestor of the Fullers had signed the Mayflower Compact in 1620, and succeeding generations basked in the reflected glory of this momentous event. Frederick was not impressed. Nevertheless, the marriage of Frederick to Cassy provided Paulina relief from her greatest fear—the failure of her daughter to find a husband.

Frederick's proposal surprised Paulina even so. Cassy had grown an inch or two, and her dark blond hair now had a sheen that seemed to brightened her plain face. But she was still awkward in the presence of guests, looking down at the polished floors most of the time, adding little to conversations even in small groups of three or four and standing mute when surrounded by larger groups of girls.

Her piano playing was as breathtaking as ever. But she still couldn't sew a precise stitch and her cooking never satisfied. In fact, raised eyebrows and frowns were the usual responses to her culinary efforts. The Fuller house would have a hired cook, of course, as did all prominent families in New England, but Cassy's inability to acquire the full range of domestic skills deeply disturbed Paulina, who interpreted Cassy's failure as her own. Motherhood was serious business, and the proof of success for any mother was simple indeed: an attractive, well-mannered young lady appealing to a rich man.

Paulina had her own limits, however. As a teacher, she drew the line when it came to matters of the body and the bedroom. As a mother of six, she of course knew *what* happened, but as a teacher she had no models for useful instruction. Her mother had never said a word to her about it, and she would do the same. However, she saw an opportunity for Cassy when she noticed an advertisement in *The Patriot* for a traveling lecture show, "Dr. William's Anatomical Preparations in Wax." At the Masonic Hall between eight in the morning and four in the afternoon, Dr. Williams would explain the fundamentals of sex and human reproduction to men only, and *Mrs.* Williams would explain them to the ladies between four and seven in the evening. Admission was twenty-five cents.

Without warning, Paulina brandished the newspaper, pointing at the advertisement, and announced to a startled Cassy, "You *need* to see this exhibit; it is absolutely essential before the wedding day."

Cassy turned red when she read the ad.

"Mother, I can't!" she exclaimed. "Someone will see me!"

"Don't be ridiculous. We will go after all the men have left, so that no man will see you, for heaven's sake."

"You're going with me?" she asked.

"Well, of course. I have to make sure that everything is appropriate."

"But I can't talk to you about such matters!"

Paulina had a ready answer to this objection: "We'll bring Dorcas with us, and you can talk to her after we get home."

"Will you be there too?" Cassy asked, unable to refrain from challenging her mother, given the unsettling circumstances.

"My, my, we do have a lot to say, don't we, Cassy, on the eve of your wedded bliss?" Paulina asked, her blunt sarcasm hitting the mark. Immediately, Cassy froze and looked to the floor.

"Mother, I'm sorry," Cassy mumbled.

"Very well," Paulina declared, lifting her chin to accentuate her victory. "You and Dorcas can speak privately, like *step*sisters. Perhaps your education at school will have even in this most private of conversations some positive effect on Dorcas, who is attracting far too much attention in town. She can certainly benefit from further *refinements.*"

"I need more too," Cassy admitted.

"Well, of course, my dear. Your years at school can only benefit you and those around you."

Paulina repeated the word "school" with her nose pinched, as if smelling a stench. She'd insisted that Cassy attend one of the best finishing schools in New England and be prepared for "her place in society," and yet references to school and the possibilities for Cassy's possible advancements released resentment in Paulina like bile in the stomach. Cassy just might surpass her, and this she could *not* abide.

"Cassy, you must not disappoint me now," Paulina declared, perhaps too forcefully.

"How could I do *that?*" asked Cassy, obviously shaken.

"You don't know?" asked Paulina. "You have made a habit of it, I'm afraid."

Tears came to Cassy's eyes. "I never meant . . ."

Paulina's voice warmed slightly, but she maintained the severity of her folded arms and her pointed chin. "Of course, you didn't *mean* to. You couldn't help yourself. You are who you are."

"Then I will always disappoint you, even on my wedding day."

"You won't be the most celebrated bride, but . . ."

"You have *never* loved me," Cassy whispered, finally lifting her eyes to face her mother.

Paulina rose.

"Cassy," she hissed, "how *dare* you say such a thing to your own mother?"

"I apologize, Mother," Cassy replied, capitulating again.

"Good," said Paulina. "Let's not continue with this unpleasant topic."

"Yes, Mother."

"And *you* will tell Dorcas about the exhibit," said Paulina, avoiding another unpleasant topic. "And please *try* to be discreet."

"Of course, Mother. May I be excused?"

"At least you have not forgotten the basic rules of domestic civility," Paulina observed. "Soon you will be under Mr. Fuller's control, and you will be excused at his direction. I have prepared you well, then, with at least the basics."

This season was supposed to be one of the happiest times of Paulina's life, but now disappointment assailed her. Cassy could never be the daughter she had hoped for. Dorcas was nothing but trouble, and since her arrival, Nathan was no longer the husband Paulina had married.

She now hated their library.

Paulina couldn't say why, and she refused to think about it.

But she knew . . . somehow she knew.

Chapter Six

The "Anatomical Preparations in Wax" held no surprises for Dorcas, but she hoped for entertainment. Unfortunately, Mrs. Williams managed to suck the life out of her subject, her voice and posture as rigid as the wax figures beside her. She spoke in an even monotone and never established eye contact with the audience, looking over the heads of the assembled ladies, a small group who dared to show interest in so scandalous a subject.

She never asked for questions, and no one asked any, fearing that inquiries would appear unseemly and raise speculation about motive and state of mind. Of course, Cassy Weston, on the eve of her nuptials, had every reason for attending the exhibit and seeking clarification, but she kept her eyes closed during most of the presentation, and Paulina did nothing to open them. Only for a moment did Dorcas consider asking a question, her inner eye amused by a vision of consternation, its highlight Paulina Weston fainting into a heap of muslin flounces. But she refrained, choosing not to become a distraction before Cassy's wedding.

Paulina, Cassy, and Dorcas walked home in silence, even though the late afternoon heat in August gave them a safe topic of discussion. Their fans were useless, blowing gusts of humid air against sweating skin; their petticoats seemed to cling to every inch of their legs.

Once home, Paulina announced, "Mission completed," and went upstairs to her room without further comment.

Cassy waited until she heard the door to her mother's bedroom close, and then declared, "*That* was disgusting!"

Surprised by Cassy's vehemence, Dorcas almost came to Paulina's defense. Then Cassy continued, "That exhibit was utterly dreadful, disgusting, utterly dreadful."

She shuddered, wrapping her arms around herself. "What was mother *thinking?* I never felt more embarrassed in my entire life. Did we really need to hear and *see* body parts? I know mine, and hopefully I will not see *his*. Thank goodness it will be a wedding *night*."

Dorcas did not expect such a disclosure, and looked down. Then Cassy startled her by taking her hand and leading her from the hall. "Come with me," she said.

They went upstairs to Cassy's room, now exclusively her own since the engagement announcement. Still holding Dorcas' hand, Cassy closed the door and lead Dorcas to the bed, where they sat down together. Tears filled Cassy's eyes.

"Oh, Dorcas," she said. "I am *so* afraid. What am I to do? What should I do? I want to get married. I need to leave this house. But I don't know if I can do what needs to be done."

Dorcas remained cautious; their relationship was fractious and unpredictable. She remembered the sudden turns all too vividly; the most innocent statement could inspire blistering recrimination. Apologies usually followed, but Dorcas could no longer forgive. There were too many apologies, and no true reconciliation. By word, a subtle gesture, a mere look, Cassy never failed to remind Dorcas that she was her superior.

Encouragement seemed a safe enough tactic, so Dorcas replied, "Yes, you can do what needs to be done."

"He will hurt me."

"No," said Dorcas. "He loves you."

Cassy drew back her hand, and laughed. "Loves me? He doesn't love me!"

Dorcas leaned away, preparing for what would surely come; the cold brown eyes said everything.

"What do you know about it?" Cassy's voice was thick with contempt. "How could you possibly *know* what a man of his stature might think? You don't know him, and neither do I. I've heard he's a cad, a man about town. He knows women, *too many* women. And then he asks me to be his wife. *Me?* Why?"

Dorcas had no answer and dared not offer any conjecture, even though everyone in town assumed the marriage to be just another alliance between two prominent families. All she could think of saying was a softly spoken and sincere "I'm sorry."

A mistake.

"I don't need your *sympathy*," Cassy snapped, her face reddening. "Now get out of my room. I thought you would understand, but of course, I was wrong. I am always wrong about *you!*"

Dorcas rushed out, never turning to look at Cassy, who wailed like a child with a broken toy; the sound obliterated the last shreds of sympathy Dorcas had. Cassy deserved her misery.

Hurrying down the stairs, Dorcas did not worry about serious consequences for today's rupture. There would be cold stares and sarcastic comments for a while, but Cassy could not keep Dorcas from attending the wedding. The judge had insisted; as a ward of the Westons', Dorcas should attend it as a "family member" and not a servant.

When Paulina told her about the decision, Dorcas restrained her reaction. She was overjoyed, but said only "Thank you, "and immediately looked to the floor, avoiding the clenched jaw and cold eyes that signalized Paulina's disapproval. Cassy and Paulina were more alike than either of them realized.

"Yes!" Dorcas exclaimed after Paulina left. She'd expected to attend the wedding, but only as another pair of hands scrubbing and serving throughout a long day. She'd thought there would be no time to enjoy the festooned garlands of roses and shimmering candles at the Fuller house on Pleasant Street. But the decision made sense. She was now more than a servant of the Westons. She attended family picnics, parties, and other social events, and she sat in the family pew Sunday after Sunday at Reverend Tappan's Congregational Church. After four years, she deserved a discreet place in the family circle at a wedding.

Nevertheless, she would be careful. Sitting quietly in the back of the Fuller parlor, she would watch everything closely, especially the dancing, enjoy the music, and eat only small portions from the massive food platters. Her list mounted—no loud laughter, no uninvited comments, no clapping, no slurping of fruit punch, no sipping the Madeira, no tapping her feet to the music.

That Monday afternoon Dorcas was ready, dressed in a simple but beautiful pale green gown, decorated with tulle and lace. She wore no jewelry, having none and receiving not a single loaned bauble from either Cassy or Paulina. Dorcas noted the slight, but she didn't allow it to dampen her enthusiasm. She didn't need adornments; her flawless skin, her curling black hair, and the delicate lines of her nose and lips all declared the obvious. Cassy Weston needed vows, a new dress, and a bridegroom to be the center of attention. Dorcas Doyen could stand or sit, proud, beautiful, and alone.

Everything went according to plan: Guests from as far away as Portland and Boston filled the parlor. Reverend Tappan spoke briefly, shocking those familiar with his interminable Sunday sermons. The food was plentiful and delicious. Cassy Weston and Frederick Fuller seemed happy, smiling broadly when they received generous applause after the first dance. More approbation followed when Frederick dutifully danced the second dance with his new mother-in-law.

He then refrained from dancing for a while, ignoring the popular cotillion, instead moving about the room talking to guests, shaking hands, nodding his handsome head, and grinning like a satisfied cat after an ample meal.

The opening strains of a popular waltz emanated from the small orchestra in the outer hallway. Frederick stopped his comments in midsentence, without excusing himself, and crossed the room to ask Dorcas to dance.

As he approached, Dorcas could see all the eyes in the room widen with curiosity, surprise, and then dismay. But as if possessed, she could not turn her own away. She stared at Frederick, whose impish smile beamed satisfaction with the consternation he was causing. He was tall and broad shouldered, the tight cut of his brown coat emphasizing the size and apparent strength of his upper body. He was a lawyer, but he looked like an immaculate teamster or wheelwright. His small moustache and sideburns, unusual in 1830, added to his distinction.

"May I have this dance?" he asked, extending his right hand as he bowed.

"Oh, no, sir," whispered Dorcas, returning a coy nod. "I couldn't. It wouldn't be . . ."

Before she could continue, he took her by the hand and led her to the center of the dance floor, now suddenly open to accommodate the offending couple.

When he put his arm around her waist, necessary for the waltz, a collective intake of breath punctuated the opening beat of three-quarter time; another gasp followed when Frederick drew her close to him.

"You are stunning, absolutely stunning," he whispered.

"Thank you, sir," Dorcas replied, keeping her eyes now on him so as to avoid the scorn all around them. "But we are upsetting your guests."

"What can they say, that I can't dance with a member of my new family?"

"I'm *not* a member . . ."

He interrupted her. "By every measure save birth you are."

"That is not for me to say."

"But it is for me to say, and no one can object when I come to take you for a ride in the countryside without a chaperone. After all, I am a *married* man."

Dorcas did not like his tone; it seemed to mock the very ceremony that had taken place less than an hour before, and displayed a callous disregard for her current discomfort.

Then the music stopped in mid-bar.

"What is going on?" Frederick shouted. His angry tone gained him no supporters. All of the remaining dancers stepped away, widening the circle around Frederick and Dorcas. He hurried to the door, abandoning Dorcas in the middle of the dance floor. She was too embarrassed to move. Her embarrassment intensified when she heard shouting in the hall.

"Why did you stop playing?" Frederick demanded. "Who told you to stop?"

Dorcas could not hear the bandleader's answer, but Frederick's reaction provided it for everyone to know.

"Mrs. Weston had no right to tell you to stop. This is *my* wedding in *my* father's house. I will tell you what to play, and when to play it. Now resume that waltz until the end, and I mean to the very end. I know this music, and I will *not* be fooled."

After a pause, the familiar music resumed on the downbeat.

Frederick appeared at the door and scanned the dance floor for Dorcas, who had retreated to the side behind a group of young girls, who totally ignored her.

Undeterred, Frederick found Dorcas, took her hand, and led her to the center of the room. She didn't know what to do but comply. Frederick Fuller had taken absolute command, and he didn't seem to care what anyone else thought. His mortified parents stood like marble statues near the doorway; his new wife wept in the arms of a friend, and his dance partner prayed for the waltz to end.

No one else moved to dance, and Frederick bated his guests, "Don't you want to join us?"

When there was no response, he shrugged his shoulders, and said to Dorcas, "Then we have the floor all to ourselves." He swirled her about with even greater force.

"Please, sir," she pleaded. "Please."

"Don't play me for a fool, Dorcas Doyen," he said, grinning. "You and I both know you are enjoying every minute of this attention. Every minute."

He was absolutely wrong, but Dorcas saw no point in disagreeing with him. She simply waited for the waltz to end. When the final extended chord had played out, Frederick did not immediately release her. He whispered, "I will see you on my return."

He returned her to her chair behind the rest of the guests near the window of the west wall. Then he nodded his head once, bowed slightly, and walked away, leaving Dorcas to fear reprisals from all of the Westons, and to wonder why she wanted to kiss Frederick Fuller after all he done that Monday afternoon.

Chapter Seven

Nathan Weston had stopped asking Dorcas for "the touch," as he called her deft use of hands and mouth to arouse him. At the beginning, their sessions had happened two or three times a week, but they tapered off to once a week for several months, then twice a month, then once a month; then they suddenly stopped, without comment or explanation. By then Dorcas saw her manipulations as another distasteful chore, like emptying chamber pots, and when it was obvious that Weston was done with "the touch," she did not miss it; she had other interests. Weston never revealed a desire for intercourse again, and Dorcas refused to test his resolve.

Fortunately, he did not reject her. He still supported her privileged access to the library, and he continued his talks with her about literature, history, politics, and even religion, depending on Dorcas' incredible memory of scripture to challenge orthodox interpretations.

He also did not blame Dorcas for the scandalous waltz at the wedding, insisting that Dorcas receive no punishment. By accepting Frederick's request, she had behaved like a lady.

Weston also continued to talk with Dorcas about his family. He had misgivings about his son-in-law. Frederick Fuller was known for being brash, insolent, and even arrogant. These qualities assisted him in the courtroom but raised serious questions. Would he berate Cassy like a lawyer before hostile witnesses? Would he bring tears to her eyes again? Weston could have opposed Cassy's marriage to such a man, but he was grateful that Cassy had a husband from such a prominent family.

No one mentioned the waltz incident at family gatherings, and when Cassy and Frederick returned from their honeymoon in Boston and New York, Frederick demonstrated all the social graces that came with good breeding. He smiled, he waited, he acknowledged with a slight nod of his head; he never interrupted, never laughed with uproarious gusto, never smoked, slurped, or spit. He did everything right, so when he arrived in a new carriage that July and asked the judge if he might take Dorcas for a ride in it, Weston raised no objections.

"That went well, didn't it?" Frederick asked, marveling at his own performance. He drove Dorcas into the forest at the edge of town, a thick wall of maples and firs that seemed to make Augusta and the small towns on the Kennebec River mere outposts on the frontier, vulnerable to attack by Indians. Some tribes lived to the north, and there were still rumors of retaliation for stolen land.

"What do you mean?" asked Dorcas.

"You very well know what I mean," he replied, looking straight ahead as he tightened his grasp of the reins. "You're an outsider, and that makes you an astute observer. I was the perfect gentleman, and *you* know there's no such thing."

She quickly considered a safe response; she knew she was in dangerous territory, and her guide a creature of the filtered shade: beautiful on the surface, slick, smooth, and rotten underneath, like a killing mushroom.

"What do you want?" she asked flatly.

His answer was immediate. "You know that, too," he said, smiling.

"Then you presume," Dorcas said, now irritated by his low opinion of her.

He turned and glanced at the blankets behind him. "I want what you want," he continued.

"How do you know that?"

"Your eyes," he replied.

"Eyes can deceive, as your performance as the perfect gentleman proves."

"The best liars know the truth. That's what makes a good liar."

"Not if you lie so much you forget that you're lying."

He suddenly pulled at the reins and stopped the carriage. Then he turned to Dorcas with a dimpled grin that made her flush. He was even more handsome than she'd first recognized; somehow those dimples, the filtered light, the tight lines of his smile, and the wide sky blue eyes that suggested curiosity rather than anger stirred a desire to surrender to the moment. Indeed, she wanted to kiss him, as she had wanted to kiss him at the wedding party. Now she wanted to go with him to where he wanted to go. She knew the place; it was in her dreams, in the eyes of men in town, in the pictures she saw in the library, in the words of lovers, saints, and sinners.

"You could be a lawyer," he said, without sarcasm. "And one day we can continue this epistemological inquiry into the nature of truth. But for now, I will leave that to David Hume and Mr. Kant. I want you to come with me."

He stepped down from the carriage and came around to help Dorcas get out. "Wait here while I tie up the horse," he said.

She watched him move with the skill of a man used to being around horses. He gathered up the blankets from the carriage and said, "Come."

He led her to a small opening nearby. The trees cast a protective shadow, making it difficult for anyone to see them clearly from the road. Dorcas looked around. There was no one; she heard only the chirping of birds and a slight rustling of leaves.

"From the moment I saw you at the party, I knew this must happen. It was inevitable," he said, still maintaining the light tone of his voice. He dropped a blanket to the ground and opened it to a partial square, leaving one flap unfurled.

"You overestimate destiny's powers," she replied, annoyed. Rationalization didn't become him. Lust was lust, needing no excuses, at least not today.

His eyes flared. "You tread on dangerous ground. I could slap you for your audacity." He raised his right hand to emphasize his point.

She didn't flinch. Staring at his hand, she said, "*My* audacity brought us here?"

Then with a deep groan, he took her into his arms and kissed her, his tongue probing the curves of her mouth.

"Oh Dorcas," he finally said. "I *must* have you."

Of course he was determined to possess her, but Dorcas heard a hint of courtesy, a hurried appeal for consent, and said simply, "Yes."

She started to unbutton her bodice, but he took her hands into his, saying gently, "No, let me help you. I want to see you . . . *slowly.*"

This gesture unexpectedly aroused her more than anything he had done, and the nipples of her breasts hardened as he removed her outer garments. With only her undergarments remaining, they simultaneously dropped to their knees. They kissed again, then he reached for his own buttons, unraveling the catches as fast as he could. With his pantaloons now at the knees he lifted her and raised her skirt to her hips.

She lay down, feeling the rocks at her back and choosing to relax; at any moment he would enter her, and she would know *at last* adult manhood, surrender, and desire.

But suddenly he was on his knees and lifting her buttocks, moving her hips toward his face. Startled, she almost exclaimed, "What are you *doing?*" But she knew what he was about to do; she had seen the act depicted in numerous illustrations and described in several potboilers. She was curious about the possible sensations, but she had never expected to experience them.

Dorcas could feel his tongue, and she groaned, saying "Oh" again and again.

Then suddenly his entire body lay upon her, and he commanded, "Hold it . . . pull it, back and forth . . . put it in."

She complied.

He pulled away her hand, now an impediment, and rammed his hips repeatedly against her, producing a curious blend of accented grunts and pounding that made her almost giggle. Pressing against her chest, his body was heavy, compounding the pain between her legs. But then she relaxed, allowing herself to focus on the meaning of the moment, the fulfillment of expectation, the incarnation of passion, Wordsworth's splendor in the grass.

She cried out, "Oh my God, oh my God."

Her climax came before his, suffusing her with incredible warmth and super-sensitivity throughout her body, even in the toes of her feet. She considered for a moment the utter blasphemy of her exclamation just as he came to his own dutifully announced climax.

"Here it comes," he said through gritted teeth, lifted his chest by his elbows, and withdrew his penis to ejaculate on her belly.

The spell was broken, lines from Wordsworth forgotten, exquisitely raw feelings obliterated instantly, as she now worried about wiping away his seed. What could she use? She couldn't use her pantaloons, or her dress . . . certainly not her dress.

Frederick rested his head against her chest, taking deep breaths, the pause of the exhausted but satisfied. Then he sat up to examine himself.

"There's no blood," he observed coolly. "I wanted to be your first. But I didn't expect it, not with *you*. At least you won't have any Fuller bastards."

He pulled at the edge of the blanket and said, "Clean yourself with this."

Dorcas shut her eyes. The light seemed to intensify the pounding in her head, and she could not bear to look at him, this killer of another dream. Farewell folly, farewell fancy. How could she think that the perfect lover could also be the perfect gentleman?

Frederick had excited her in ways that her reading had not anticipated. She had surrendered completely to his touch and became mere flesh—raw, mindless, and free, without conscience, without fear. For a few blinding moments, she'd been an animal, acting on instinct and the absolute abandonment to her pleasure . . . until he opened his damn mouth.

She was more angry than hurt. So he thought she was an experienced whore. That didn't matter so much. The way she walked about town and looked at men, she had raised the possibility for that conclusion. What angered her was his relentless contempt. He could hide it for a while, with intense effort, behind the dazzling white mask of comedy. But a single word could provoke him to rip off the mask and reveal his true face.

He was no different from all the rest, that family of molesters, adulterers, bigots, and snobs, hypocrites all. She was sick of them.

And then she made her decision. She would leave the Westons before reaching her maturity at eighteen and be free of them, once and for all.

"Take me home," she said, rising to button her dress. The mention of the word "home" immediately soured her stomach; it was never her home, could never be hers.

"I'm not ready to take you home," Frederick replied, still on his knees, looking up at her with predatory intent.

"Then are you ready to take me by force?" Dorcas stared down at him. His blue eyes darkened, his entire face froze into a chilling white mask.

Frederick stood, pulling at his trousers and top button. He stepped toward her and said, "I could, you know, get away with it, because no one would believe you."

Dorcas did not move, replying with a calm, even voice, "But *you* will have more to lose. I'll be blamed for unleashing your animal nature, but you will have to live with a scandal your family will never be allowed to forget."

He stepped back, his open mouth slackened by shock. "*Who* are you?" he asked.

"I'm the girl you will pay if you ever want to have me again."

"That will make you a prostitute."

"Yes, but the money will be *mine*, and mine alone."

"There is a black man who works at the Barker Mansion house on State Street. He's called the doctor and procures . . . customers."

"I don't need a *pimp*." Dorcas dismissed the suggestion with a wave of her hand.

"Where have you learned such language?" Frederick asked, again taken aback.

"It doesn't matter," Dorcas replied. "I will be leaving Augusta."

"When?"

"I don't know, but soon, after I have earned a little to get me to Portland."

"I will you give you money for your services," he said, smiling again.

"And what is the going rate?"

He threw back his head, laughing and shaking his head. "You are amazing, absolutely amazing. I had no idea that you were this bold, this mature. I 'm sorry you have to leave."

"Augusta is too small, if we continue from today."

"If?" he asked, extending his hands to her. "Oh, there will be no ifs."

Frederick pulled her into his arms and Dorcas whispered, "And payment starts now. So how much?"

"Whatever you want," he said, laughing as he kissed her closed eyes.

———•———

By October there were rumors that had to be confirmed or denied. Leaving in her room a note signed by the both of them, Nathan and Paulina Weston summoned Dorcas into the parlor. Paulina spoke first, asking directly, "Is it true, the rumors going about town that you actively pursue *infamy?*"

What did the Westons really know? "Infamy" covered a wide range of sins and indiscretions, but the suggestion of sexual impropriety was obvious, and a heated denial would only complicate and perhaps prolong the season of her departure. Here was her opportunity, unexpectedly delivered by the Westons themselves, for a clean and immediate break. Say "yes," remain vague, and be done with it. Four more encounters in the forest with Frederick hardly merited the appellation "pursuit of infamy," but technically, she was guilty as charged.

Dorcas closed her eyes and waited. Sightless, she heard the swing of the pendulum of the clock on the mantelpiece.

After a long pause, she opened her eyes and said softly but firmly, "Yes."

Paulina fell back onto the sofa and, with hands clenching her bosom, moaned, "Oh no, oh, no, no, no, no, no, no."

Weston's face revealed nothing, but he gently touched Paulina's tight-clasped fist and said, "My dear, you must leave now. I have legal matters to discuss with Dorcas, and hearing such a discussion is not appropriate for a lady."

Paulina immediately unclenched her fist and turned to him, saying, "I should remain. This is *family* business."

"This is a matter of law," he said. "You must leave now, and I will call you back when I have completed my inquiries."

Paulina was reluctant. Weston deepened his tone, saying "*Now, Paulina.*"

She stared for a moment, then looked at Dorcas before rising slowly from the sofa.

"I will be waiting for your summons," her cold sarcasm surprising Dorcas. In four years, Paulina Weston had never used sarcasm, her favorite weapon, against her husband.

If blood had been spilled, Nathan Weston revealed not a single drop. He watched Paulina leave and waited until the door was completely closed before he asked his most crucial question, "Were you seduced?"

"Yes."

"By whom?"

"I cannot say."

"This is a matter of law. You are underage, and a wronged young woman can collect significant sums of money. Is he married?"

"No," Dorcas replied, still marveling at the judge's composure.

"Good. A successful suit is virtually impossible if it's someone you could not possibly ever marry. Did he promise marriage in exchange for your favor?"

"No."

"Who is he?"

"I can't say."

"You mean you *won't* say."

"Yes."

Weston stood and declared his verdict. "Very well. You must leave this house within the week. Of course you cannot receive a letter of recommendation from us for future service, given your debased behavior. It would raise questions about our own judgment in selecting you, and cast doubts about our ability to influence your character."

"Yes, sir." She saw no point in countering his arguments, even now when she had nothing to lose.

"And be reminded that anything you might reveal about family matters is subject to charges of libelous slander and would reflect poorly on your already damaged reputation."

This threat, not heard since the beginning of their sexual relationship, disappointed Dorcas. Long ago she had decided she would never reveal it; she remained grateful for his kind words, the special privileges, the education, the hours of conversation, the matchless library. She had found a measure of peace with the ugly past, and could not even blame him for throwing her out into the streets. But this unnecessary threat unraveled her scaffold of accommodations, and tears came to her eyes for the first time in months.

"Yes, sir" was all she could say, her voice shaking.

"You may go." He sat down again and turned to peruse a document on the side table. He was done with Dorcas Doyen, his banishment final and irrevocable.

"Yes, sir," she whispered again, going to the door. She didn't look back, unwilling to show any more tears or reveal her growing fears. How will I live? Where will I go? Who can earn my trust? Who will help me?

She needed encouragement, and so, on that bleak Sunday afternoon, she left the house, walked a few steps to Annabelle's house, and knocked on the *front* door to tell her only true friend in Augusta that she was leaving town forever.

PART 2

Chapter Eight

New York seemed the very city of her dreams. Its spires, cupolas, and ship masts shimmered in the late afternoon sun, a cluster of jewels at the tip of a long finger pointing to the open sea.

After two years in Portland and then Boston, Dorcas needed to come here. With a new name, she could escape the cold formalities of New England and recreate herself as a sophisticated "girl of the town" in the largest city in the country.

But first she had to board several cramped stage coaches to Providence, Rhode Island, traveling nine hours on the most common route between Boston and New York. Then she took a steamboat down the Providence River into Long Island Sound, passing into the widening sea beyond sight of land, the endless sky suggesting the limitless possibilities before her.

Dorcas was a dreamer but not a fool. She had delayed her arrival until after receiving word that the cholera epidemic, rampant during the summer months and killing thousands, had subsided. Residents who were able to escape the city were now returning, and businesses, shut down for weeks, were open again. The house at 55 Leonard Street, under the supervision of Mrs. Ann Welden, was ready to receive customers, and its newest girl, now calling herself Helen Jewett, disembarked from the steamship at Fulton Street and immediately proceeded to her new home, where she would earn five dollars a day. A tour of the city would have to wait.

Despite her brazen words to Frederick Fuller, she did not take any more money from him for sexual favors; nor did she seek out the one known procurer in Augusta. Once in Portland, she first tried domestic service at a brothel. Brothels were easy to find, and they all needed girls to wash clothes, dust, and clean rooms. Most of the domestic help lived elsewhere, but Helen, for convenience and out of curiosity, asked for a room; board was subtracted from her wages, and she received a room no bigger than a closet. She slept on the floor.

As a servant in a whorehouse, she was often fondled and grabbed by customers. Most of them assumed her services were free. After paying the other girls, they wanted a bargain, and she fought them off as best she could. Once, a huge man smelling of onions and whiskey pushed her into a closet, covered her mouth with a hand the size of her face, and raped her. He threatened to kill her if she told the madam of the house, but she told anyway, expecting solace and protection.

She received neither. With a dismissive wave of her hand, the madam explained the economic realities. "It is the occasional price of working here," she said, "and we certainly would not want to restrain the return of our *paying* customers, now would we?"

"But he hurt me!" Helen's eyes filled with tears as she recalled the terror, the heavy weight of the man's body, the pain, the dank smell of the closet.

"You're still alive," the madam replied wearily, waving her hand again. She was done. "Count your blessings."

Dorcas didn't reply, but she decided at that moment to change her occupation.

There were two certainties: She would not return home to her father and his wife, and she would not walk the streets.

Even if the relationship with her stepmother had been better, her father would not receive her after the scandalous gossip from Augusta. Appearances matter to aging hypocrites and he had lost interest in his daughter years ago. He'd stopped answering her letters, and she had stopped writing them.

Helen was too proud to become a streetwalker. It was dangerous and desperate, a sure sign that a girl had reached the end of her resources. She'd seen a few in Portland, and even more in Boston; they all had sallow skin and empty eyes blurred by hunger and gin, the favored pain killer for girls forced to do business in alleys and doorways, their sense of shame buried so long ago they could look at passing pedestrians and dare them to intervene as men lifted skirts, often from behind, and completed the transaction.

In Portland and Boston she learned her trade, moving from house to house and assuming different names—Maria Stanley, Maria Benson, Helen Mar.

After moving into her first house, a clean but dreary abode in a row of shabby houses on a narrow side street in Portland, she immediately looked for finer accommodations, something befitting a young woman raised in the households of the Dillinghams and Westons, surrounded by books, fine linens, and imported china.

She also discovered the value of the skills she'd first discovered in the Weston library, and she successfully used them to avoid intercourse with many of her customers, who paid well after acknowledging their surprise and delight with what she could do with only her hands and mouth.

Of course, intercourse was unavoidable, but clean customers—clean and generous customers—mattered more. She tried patience, having endured a parade of men, the ugly and the fat, the tall and the short, men with penises the size of acorns and the size of cucumbers, frightened boys and arrogant hustlers, the sober and the drunk. But one night a man arrived with filthy, soiled underwear, a man who couldn't bother to sweeten his breath or remove the mud from his skin.

She could not hide her disgust, turning away her face, closing her eyes, tightening her lips to avoid an intake of breath. She even pinched her nose, but nothing discouraged him. He laughed, saying without the slightest hint of offense, "I have enough money. What the house offers, I pay for."

And that was the problem, Dorcas realized.

She was in the wrong house; it attracted the wrong customers.

In one mixed-race house in Boston, she serviced men of different colors, travelers from distant lands, men covered in tattoos and speaking little or no English. And she discovered that most men were the same, a curious blend of pride and self-loathing, the need for approval and the urge to dominate, bullies and supplicants . . . fools all. She wanted to ask them, "Why do you hate your mothers?"

But none of this mattered.

Only money mattered, and only men with large amounts of it would be able to afford her. It was no guarantee, but at the very least the rich had servants to clean their underwear.

Now the sights and sounds of the new city demanded her attention. Now Helen Jewett, she would leave her reflections to another day and time. Never had she seen so many people or heard such noise.

Aboard a hansom cab, Helen appreciated the thin cloth wall between her and the thousands of pedestrians who crossed the bustling streets, darting between gigs, phaetons, and carriages as if mocking imminent death. Brown, fat pigs were equally oblivious, waddling in gutters full of mud, dung, and garbage, snorting loudly at the occasional but satisfying find.

Everything was for sale, and hawkers shouted prices on every street corner and in the fronts of stores that filled the first floor of almost every building, all of them lined up shoulder to shoulder as solid rows of brick wall. Street after street under huge signs and placards proclaimed the triumph of shameless commerce.

Broadway was the widest cobblestoned street she'd ever seen. Ladies and gentlemen dressed in the finest fabrics—the men in crisp, black, dark blue and brown coats, the women in bright gowns with fluttering ribbons and cloaks with opulent hoods—seemed like human ornaments before the magnificent stores, theaters, and residences on both sides of the street. Unfortunately, Broadway also had a horrible stink, which Helen tried to ignore. After all, what else could you expect in a city of thousands using open backyard privies and available street corners? Garbage collection was a random affair, and the horses, pigs, and dogs deposited sizzling piles of dung that festered for days. Indeed, Boston was cleaner . . . much cleaner.

West of Broadway, 55 Leonard Street, on the north side between Church and Chapel, was a large row house among three- and four-story private residences built in the Federal style popular in the 1810s and 1820s. The simple, elegant symmetry of the door and windows on the facades, the pristine whitewashed steps leading to black doors ornamented with a brightly polished knocker, and the absolute absence of litter on the sidewalk directly in the front of the houses suggested a neighborhood of substance and high repute. Helen could still hear the noise of Broadway, but this part of Leonard Street was a retreat that made the city seem far away.

The grinning driver, who had turned around to take a look at Helen whenever his carriage paused or stopped, gladly offered to carry her small two pieces of luggage up to the front door.

"Thank you," said Helen, smiling.

"The pleasure is mine, miss, since I will *never* be able to enter here. Can't afford it."

A girl, ten or eleven years old, answered the knock at the door, and Helen entered, saying only, "Mrs. Welden," as the driver dropped the luggage in the foyer and departed. "Please let her know that Helen Jewett has arrived," Helen added.

After two years as a prostitute, she never wanted to forget what it was to be young and powerless, always reminded of inferiority. But she could hear in her own voice the officious tone of the victim punishing others with the tools of her tormentors. She almost apologized.

"Please wait in the first parlor," said the girl, pointing with a blank expression, the serene mask of the servile everywhere.

Helen scanned the room quickly and found a seat near the fireplace. The elegance of the furniture, the rich tapestries on the walls, and the delicate china on the side tables confirmed her good fortune. At last she had found a worthy home.

When Ann Welden entered the room, Helen immediately rose. The mistress of the house was tall, full-figured, indeed almost fat, and yet beautiful, a mature woman with thin, lusterless streaks of grey in her hair that didn't detract from the youthful bloom of her clear skin and bright brown, almost golden eyes. Surely, if she was so disposed, Mrs. Welden could still entertain customers and earn an excellent income. Helen saw her own distant future and inwardly smiled.

"Miss Jewett, what a pleasure it is for you to arrive," the older woman said, extending her hand. "You are as pretty as I have heard. No, the testaments don't do you justice."

"Thank you, Mrs. Welden, and I will do *everything* to earn your approbation."

"You are well spoken, Miss Jewett, but I am more interested in the earnings you will bring to the house," Mrs. Welden replied.

"Of course." Helen nodded. "And the size of your receipts will tell the story."

Mrs. Welden maintained her smile, but her eyes narrowed ever so slightly, a signal to Helen that perhaps, just perhaps, she had gone too far. "And to what will you attribute your success?" asked Mrs. Welden.

"My versatility," Helen answered at once.

She'd had a reputation in Boston for initiating the unspeakable. Clients were shocked but delighted, and returned again and again with the comfort of knowing that they didn't have to *ask* for what they secretly desired—oral sex, anal penetration, bondage, simulated rape.

Mrs. Welden laughed, her face animated. She leaned forward for the first time, and said, "Oh, Miss Jewett, you are a *find*, and I think we will do well together. Please call me Ann."

The two women, now comfortable with each other, finalized arrangements. In a house of fourteen women, there must be clearly defined rules and procedures, and every penny had to be accounted for.

"You will, of course, need to be inspected," Ann added, after a detailed listing of house rules. "My girls must be clean."

Her narrowed eyes declared that no objections were acceptable; she smiled all the while.

"Our customers expect only the healthiest girls, and our doctor—Dr. David Rogers, a prominent physician, and so handsome and gentle, too—works for several houses in the city. His visits will come regularly, but they will be unannounced, you understand. Surprise insures me that you will be careful and *always* supremely conscientious about the close relationship between health and profit."

"Yes." Helen accepted the mandate without further comment. "And where will I meet most of my customers?"

"Ah, Miss Jewett, do you like the theater?"

"Yes, indeed."

"Good. Then let me tell you about the Park on Broadway. It's the best. Now come. We'll go to the back parlor and meet some of the other girls. They've been waiting for your arrival."

———·———

The New York theaters were not universally appreciated; one newspaper editor wrote, "To the theaters of this city, above all other places, is the iniquity that abounds to be traced. They are sinks of vice and pollution, houses of assignation and incipient prostitution—in four words, the Vestibules of Hell!" He exaggerated, of course, but any casual visit to the third tier of the Park, Chatham, Bowery, and Olympic theaters proved his basic point.

It was there, high above the stage and the first and second rows of boxes, unaccompanied women, alone or in groups, watched the performances below, chatted with friends and clients, and made appointments for sex and, hopefully, for dinner. In a theater where the house lights always stayed up, everyone knew what was going on in the third tier, and except for outraged moral extremists, no one seemed to care. The respectable and chaste patrons in the first and second tiers of boxes only demanded segregation and token discretion. Some citizens wanted to eliminate the common lobby, so there could be no comingling between respectable wives and daughters and prostitutes before the performance; but this proposal was rejected as unnecessary and too expensive.

The prostitutes knew the unwritten rules: Enter the lobby and take the stairs to the third tier and remain there for most of the evening. Men wishing to roam could leave the lower levels to laugh, drink, and make appointments above, and then return. Silence was not expected at any time; in fact, everyone talked during the performance, and people often interacted with the actors, acrobats, dancers, and musicians onstage. Rowdy and disorderly behavior from the women in the third tier, however, would not be tolerated, and arrests could follow.

The Park Theater, with its imposing four grey columns at the front, faced City Hall Park in a neighborhood that included the American Museum, Peale's Museum of Art, St. Paul's Episcopal Church, the College of Physicians and Surgeons, and Columbia University, a block west of Broadway. The area attracted thousands of residents and tourists every day, and more than two thousand filled the Park Theater for four to five hours for performances that included double bills of plays and *entr'actes* of music, or acrobatics.

Like all of the other patrons, Helen delighted in the plush, upholstered seats, the gas-lit chandeliers, the painted woodwork, and the ladies' lounges, with attendants serving food and drink. The actors were usually loud and bombastic, mutilating their lines with obtuse abandon. But Helen, at least at first, did not press her objections. In the first full flush of excitement as a new arrival to a great city, she granted to every symbol of the city's culture a special dispensation.

On her first day at the Park Theater she didn't care what was on the playbill, and she didn't recognize the title of the melodrama, "The Assassin's Knife." No matter. Except for the filthy streets, everything was better because it was in New York. She didn't mind the discomforts of anticipation. The quick, erratic beat of her heart, the prickly heat of her skin, and the sweat under her cotton gloves could not diminish the pleasure of being there.

The theater opened its doors early, allowing the ladies of the third tier to have a place to go two or three hours before a performance. "It gets us out of the house," explained one of Helen's new associates, a four-year veteran with assets no observer could deny. She had a pretty face and huge breasts. Even so, Helen liked Lucy Preston. One year older than Helen, she was smart and self-deprecating. One day after meeting each other, Lucy lifted her bosom under the cloth of her bodice with both hands and observed dryly, "Men think I am so lucky with *these*, and although they pay the bills now, they won't be so attractive when they fall to my waist." She giggled, and Helen laughed with her.

"Getting old has its prices," Helen replied, and a friendship was sealed with the taking of hands and a gentle hug.

Now Lucy was her tour guide and mentor, explaining the ways of New York one afternoon as they sat at the Park Theater two hours before a performance. A tall gentlemen with white hair but soft skin that made him seem much younger stood in a corner near the entrance with papers under his arms, staring at them with kind intensity.

"Who is that?" whispered Helen, leaning toward Lucy.

"The Reverend John McDowell," Lucy replied.

"What is *he* doing here?" asked Helen, genuinely shocked.

"You're new, and he'll introduce himself."

"But why?"

"To save you, of course. He pays visits to theaters and houses to reform us, to show us the way out of the darkness of our depraved lives."

"But you are not critical," said Helen, noticing in Lucy's tone a quotation rather than personal conviction.

"Oh no. He is the kindest of gentlemen. He truly wants to save us, and he has spent the past two years handing out Bibles in the worst neighborhoods, like the Five Points, leading prayer sessions, and setting up Sunday schools in almshouses and even prisons. But he has paid a *dear* price for his enthusiasms."

"How?"

"As you can see, Mr. McDowell is an attractive man, and he managed to convince a group of well-connected women to form a society. They called it the Magdalen Society, and they hired him to be its chaplain, missionary, and agent. The society also opened a house of refuge for repentant prostitutes, and last year they published a report that he wrote. The town fathers were *not* happy."

"What happened? What did he say?"

"He said that there was no less than *ten-thousand* prostitutes in New York. We are *supposed* to be invisible. And his report suggested, without naming names, of course, that members of prominent families frequent brothels." She laughed lightly with a wave of her hand, and added, "Ha! They do more than frequent; they *own* most of them!"

"I know how this ends," Helen observed grimly. "He took on the wrong people."

"Yes. There were several public meetings at Tammany Hall. People blasted the report. Even a grand jury was called to investigate the truth of his claim. There just could not be *that* many of us. After months of letters and protests, the society disbanded, closed the refuge, and left Mr. McDowell to do his work alone. But he wasn't cowed. He openly accused his critics of dumping prostitutes into the streets."

"You actually admire the man," observed Helen, when she noticed that he started to cross the room, tracts still under his arm.

"How can you not? He *is* bold."

"And threatens our income!" cried Helen before the Reverend McDowell reached them with a warm smile and an extended right hand.

He nodded his head. "As a representative of the Lord, I am here to save evil's newest recruit," he said, looking directly at Helen. This was said so sweetly, without even a hint of condescension, that Helen could not resist a smile.

"I thank you for caring," said Helen. "But it's too late."

"It is never too late," McDowell replied, his smile broadening.

"What do you offer, besides the promise of heaven?"

"Respectability, a new life."

"Can you pay my bills, give me a roof over my head?"

"No, I can't. But surely you must realize that you are being *used?*"

Suddenly, Helen was no longer charmed. Now put on the defensive, she was ready to dismiss him with the turn of her back . . . *after* a withering rebuke.

"Sir, you have failed in your mission," she said coldly. "I am *not* moved."

"Only today," McDowell replied. "Only today. But now is high time to wake out of sleep, for now is our salvation nearer than we believed. The night . . ."

Helen interrupted him by continuing the verse: "is spent, the day is at hand: Let us therefore cast off the works of darkness, and let us put on the armor of light."

"You know scripture," McDowell observed.

"Romans 13:11," Helen replied, her game of surprise still a source of delight. Prostitutes were not supposed to know chapter and verse.

McDowell nodded his head, handed a pamphlet to Lucy, and turned away, the smile never leaving his face.

"Well, that didn't go well," observed Lucy, falling back into her chair.

"How could it?" cried Helen, her voice high and tremulous, her usual sign of agitation. "Men like him must always be right . . . *always*. He *needed* my humiliation." She recognized the mask of civility dropped or ripped away to reveal the man needing relief or proof of his power over her.

"Oh Helen, I think you are wrong about him," Lucy replied. "What has he gained? He's lost his job and standing, and yet he still tries to make some lives better."

"He doesn't need a prostitute," Helen sneered. "His self-righteousness keeps him warm at night."

"Oh Helen, I must apologize," said Lucy sadly. "I didn't mean to make this afternoon unpleasant."

Helen started, as if coming out of a light sleep.

"Lucy, you don't have to apologize," she said, moved by her friend's concern. "You meant no harm. I'll be better prepared next time, and not take him so seriously."

"Yes," said Lucy. "I only meant it to be a light, casual exchange."

"Just tap me when I start veering into my dark, more serious direction. It's a bad habit. Maybe you can help me break it."

"You won't mind an oh-so-gentle tap now and then?"

"Now and then," she emphasized as words of caution.

She wanted a friend, not a parent with a zeal for correction.

Chapter Nine

As required, Dr. David Rogers came to inspect her, and immediately Helen noted two distinctive features—his age and the sound of his voice. She expected an older man, a fussy, distracted doctor in spectacles unable to hide his impatience or condescension even as he accepted the good fees that came with providing a needed service for a well-established business of ill repute. But Dr. Rogers, a medium-built man, was thirty-four and handsome in the symmetry of his ordinary features, brown eyes, a thin nose, and a rounded but even chin.

His voice most impressed her; it was the deepest voice she had ever heard, a rich bass as smooth as polished brass with a depth and resonance that filled the room even as he spoke casually. His words possessed a lilting musicality that suddenly put her in the Park Theater's third tier, marveling at the waves of sound from the voice of a great singer. As he spoke, Helen took a deep breath to calm the rapid beating of her heart.

"Miss Jewett, I shall be brief, and this inspection should not take too much of your precious time," he said, conveying no discomfort with the fact of sitting across from her in an upstairs bedroom. "Have you seen a doctor before?"

"Yes."

"Then this will not be too uncomfortable. I will not have you stand holding your skirts while I explore you on my knees, as do most of my colleagues. A most uncomfortable stance, and not conducive to accuracy."

Helen gulped lightly, not knowing what to say.

"Any questions?"

Before she could answer, he explained, "You will remove your underwear and lay down on the bed with your skirts pulled above your waist. I will use my right hand to touch you between your legs, in your private parts, to make sure that you are clean and able to perform your duties. Any questions?"

"No," she whispered.

"Very well. Do you have any water in the pitcher and a bowl we can use?"

"We?"

"You will need to clean yourself, and I will clean my hands, too."

"But why?"

He expressed no surprise, as if he had encountered this reaction many times before. "Just as when we clean our rooms, there is clarity. Dirt and grime obscure."

"I'm *not* dirty!" Helen protested, starting to rise from the chair.

"Please, Miss Jewett, I didn't mean to suggest that condition. From what I can see in your room and with your person, you obviously care. But dust and dirt can be invisible to the eye, and water and cloth can only improve matters. Certainly you prefer your customers clean, without dirt on their intimate parts?"

"Of course," Helen said with haughty emphasis, surprised by her discomfort. Dr. Roger embarrassed her, his clipped, detached words making her skin moist and hot.

"Then let us begin."

After washing as required, Helen removed her pantaloons and placed them out of sight on the floor, so that he could not see them. Acutely observant, as if watching a performance on stage, she noted the inconsistent oddity of this gesture. With what he was about to *see*, hidden pantaloons seemed silly and pointless.

But when she lay down on the bed, pulled up her skirts, and he sat down beside her on her left, he did not look between her legs. He said softly, "Spread your legs wider, please," and inserted his fingers into her vagina. His fingers were cold, and she flinched. He said, "You will get used to them in a moment."

She did, and then he asked, "Miss Jewett, what is this? What happened?"

She immediately replied, "What do you mean?"

"Miss, Jewett, please don't lie. Doctors need the truth from their patients, if we are to help."

"Is something wrong?"

"What happened, Miss Jewett? Something happened to cause these scars in your womb. I think I know, but you need to tell me."

He withdrew his hand, and Helen turned away, pausing to wonder if she should lie or tell the truth, a truth she had never revealed to anyone before. That voice, that sublime voice stirred a desire to trust the doctor, and she whispered quickly, fearing that with delay she would lose her resolve.

"I was raped in Boston, in the Back Bay, by a gang of men." She hoped that once spoken, the admission would lessen the weight of her memories.

"They hurt you. Terribly," Dr. Rogers said softly.

"Yes," she said, tears flowing from her eyes as she continued to look away. She could not face him. "After they took turns, one of them became very angry, I don't know why, and started to slap me again and again, and then, and then . . ."

"He thrust some object, some crude object, into you," Rogers continued.

"Yes, and I screamed and screamed. I thought they were going to kill me. Then they ran off. There was so much blood. And no one came to help me. *Nobody* came to help me." Her bitter words felt hot on her tongue.

"But you survived," Dr. Rogers said. "You survived, but did you see a doctor?"

"There was so much blood, and all I could think of was to use my skirts to fill me up and stop the bleeding."

"Then you didn't see a doctor?"

"No."

"You could have died, from the excessive bleeding or from fever. You are a strong, fortunate young woman."

She turned to face him, emboldened by the absence of accusation or final judgment.

"But . . ." she added.

"But there are scars . . . scars that will prevent you from having children."

"Forever?"

"I'm afraid so."

"A convenient consequence," Helen observed, turning away again. "I don't have the fear that most of us here have."

"I'm sorry."

"Don't be. I'm too selfish to be a good mother."

"I wish some other women were as scrupulous; there would be far fewer children to mend."

"Do you have children?" Helen asked. Immediately, she regretted the question because Dr. Rogers moved slightly away from her and said wearily, "No, I do not."

"There's still a need for good fathers."

"And you still bleed, of course, because if the scarring had stopped that, you would be dead already. And I can tell that your Venus spot is still intact."

Helen wasn't surprised that he knew about the spot; he was a doctor, after all. But now his reference to it seemed to shift the conversation from medicine to sex, to the survival of the source of a woman's sexual pleasure. When she wanted to feel intense sexual pleasure, she touched herself there. Sometimes, she told select men about it and requested a gentle touch of the hand or a delicate stroking of the tongue. What was Dr. Roger's suggesting? Should she be grateful? Was he seeking assurances for his own sexual satisfaction at a later date?

She closed her legs, and asked, "Is there anything else?"

As if reading her mind, he replied, "Miss Jewett, you presume. I am a doctor, and I can make reference without any hint of solicitation. Without this kind of detachment, I would not be able to serve Mrs. Welden or the other establishments. Why is it that so many of you think that once we see you or touch you we must, out of necessity, be consumed? Good day, Miss Jewett."

"I didn't mean to insult . . ."

"Good day, Miss Jewett."

After this inauspicious beginning Helen was then surprised when he returned a week later, left his card, and asked for a specific time and date that she would receive him in the parlor.

When he returned, she could not resist asking, "Why did you come back?"

He smiled, and said, leaning slightly forward, "You interest me."

His brown eyes glowed with mischief.

"How?"

"I looked around your room and noted your piles of books. I couldn't help but be intrigued by your choices, Shakespeare, Byron, the Bible."

"You'll need to pay for my time if you wish to discuss my reading habits," Helen said evenly.

He laughed, his head tossed back as if he had to take in more air to enjoy this moment.

"Miss Jewett, you take yourself much too seriously. But you are *practical*."

"I have to eat, and books are *not* free."

"Certainly. I also came to apologize."

"Apologize? Why?"

"I don't think I was sufficiently sensitive to the events that befell you in Boston, to the emotional consequences . . ."

Helen's voice rose to emphasize her displeasure. "Dr. Rogers, *that* was a private matter, a matter not appropriate to a parlor conversation now."

He sighed, his exasperation light but pointed nevertheless. "Miss Jewett, for one so young, you seem prone to pronouncements and denunciations."

"Would you rather I cry endlessly, seek your pity, or hide in my room? I am not a coward, and I don't hate all men."

"Perhaps we should go upstairs?" he said, looking toward the door even as he remained seated.

"A convenient, if profitable, change of subject," Helen observed.

"You prefer privacy, you said, if we mention certain matters."

"Six dollars," said Helen, her voice all business.

"You interest me," said Dr. Rogers, his eyes widened with curiosity. "Say something even more interesting."

She stood, staring at him. "I'm an abolitionist," she declared, scanning his face for a shocked reaction as she cast aside discretion. He only smiled.

"Now *that's* interesting," he replied. "Please tell me more."

Helen suddenly lost her nerve, believing her confession had compromised her support of the Antislavery Society and threatened the already precarious standing of abolitionists in the city. Blacks and their white supporters were being openly attacked on the streets.

She needed to assert herself before this handsome, fascinating man, but her pride had made her reckless and improvident.

"You can't say anything about this," she pleaded, gripping the folds of her skirt in her right hand. "As my doctor, you can't talk about private . . ."

"You are no longer my patient."

"What do you mean? You referred to your last visit. You apologized for a comment made as a physician."

"I am here as a customer," he declared. "Did you not quote a price for your services?"

He seemed to enjoy her befuddlement, smiling as he made comments with mocking insouciance.

Helen paused, taking a breath and trying to find the exact pitch for what she had to say next. "I make the decisions about services to be rendered, and I can be selective . . . *very* selective."

"Not yet, Miss Jewett, not yet. And besides, you need me. I can be good for business. I can spread the word about town. I have influence."

"Yes," was all she could say. He had won. In her business, reputation mattered most. If she was ever going to have clients with money, and lots of it, she needed access to them. Dr. Rogers was her bridge.

"When may I see you in your rooms?" he asked at last.

"Come tonight at eight, and I will be ready for you," Helen replied. "Be prompt," she continued, almost adding "please" as a perfunctory courtesy. But she omitted the word as too conciliatory, and left the room without looking back.

He was prompt that evening, and when they stepped into her room, he sat down at her desk and quickly scanned her books. Helen unbuttoned her bodice to signal the beginning of the business of the evening.

"Tell me something else interesting," he said looking directly at her. "No, something more than interesting, something provocative, suggestive, even obscene."

A man of words, she surmised, a man needing words to stir him. The sight of her naked breasts would not do. Helen thought for a moment, and remembered the lines from 1795's *Displaying the Secrets of Nature in the Generation of Man*, the perfect passage for a man by a man—a celebration of his penis.

She began: "Now will I storm the mint of love and joy and rifle all that's in it. I will enjoy thee, now, my fairest; come and fly with me to love's Elysium. My rudder, with thy bold hand, like a try'd and skillful pilot, thy shall steer, and guide my bark in love's dark channel, where it shall dance, as the bounding waves do rise and fall, whilst . . ."

She stopped, unnerved by the mockery in his eyes.

Grinning as he leaned back in the chair, he said, "My, my, my . . . bad poetry can deflate even the most amorous rudder."

"The obscene rarely rises to the level of art," said Helen defensively.

"Oh, it will do," he said,

"Then present your sword," she replied, alluding to a line in *Romeo and Juliet*.

Reaching into his trousers and pulling out his swollen penis, he said, "My bark is now ready."

"Are you going to use it or not?"

Dr Rogers put his organ back into his trousers, the stiffened flesh still protruding under the cloth. "No," he said, sitting up in the chair and covering his lap with his coat. "Not now, some other time. Now take off your clothes so that I can get a better look. You are a beautiful girl, a very beautiful girl, and I want a confirmation of my suspicion that the rest of your body matches that lovely face."

His tone, now coldly clinical, angered Helen even more, but she obliged him, a paying customer, and slowly removed her remaining garments, piece by piece, until she was naked before him. "Now?" she asked.

"No, not tonight," he said. "Another time. There will be another time, I promise you. Now put your clothes back on."

Helen did not appreciate the reference to a promise; it suggested her need for him rather than his need for her.

"Why are you doing this?" she asked.

"I will be asking the questions," he replied.

He waited. When she put on her chemise and paused, as if she had covered herself sufficiently, he said, "Everything. Put on everything."

Dr. Rogers then turned to a nearby book, perusing it casually until Helen had dressed herself. Only her hairpins remained on the table.

"Now what shall we talk about?" he asked.

"You tell me," Helen replied. "You must have chosen your favorites already."

"Smart girl," he acknowledged. "I will say a word as my gambit, and we will begin to talk about politics, history, the arts, current events."

"May I ask a question then?"

"No. Take a position; state a reaction. But no questions until I say we have reached that point in our conversation. And you are never to ask me questions about my medical practice, except as they relate to the sex trade, and those can only be asked on the day of my inspections."

"Very well," Helen replied, not asking the question that most disturbed her. How could this handsome, intelligent man, an experienced physician with a gorgeous voice and captivating smile, be so manipulating and demanding?

She thought she understood men, but this man confused and disturbed her.

As time passed, Dr. Rogers kept his sexual distance. Helen wanted him. But he refrained from intercourse, treating her like a virgin bride before the wedding night. It was strange, and she wondered if he could not sustain an erection during intercourse. Perhaps he had a medical problem himself? He seemed, however, genuinely interested in her allegiance to the cause of abolition. At their fourth session he asked about the origin of her commitment.

"A friend I once had," Helen answered simply. "She was colored and decent, and she proved in every way the falsity of any claim to superiority. She was a far better person than I could ever be, and she certainly was not inferior to the people of the town."

"And where was that?"

"I would rather not say. I don't want anything I might say to get back there and make her life any more difficult. It's difficult as it is, she being colored."

"Any slice into the bodies of two men, one white and one colored, will prove that we are all the same, under the skin, with the same hearts, lungs, and guts. The worms will eat us *all* in the end. But knowing this doesn't make me an abolitionist."

"I was in Boston when I saw a mob chase Mr. Garrison down the streets," Helen continued. "Because Mr. Garrison started the *Liberator* there, and because he demanded the immediate end of slavery and the equality of the races, people attacked his office. He barely escaped."

"Others watched, but they didn't become abolitionists," Rogers insisted.

"You don't know what it's like to be an *outsider*, to always see hatred in the eyes of others when you are on the streets."

"Surely you are not suggesting that whores and negroes have things in common?"

"Why did you use *that* word? Just when I was about to believe you were different from the others, you say something that makes you no better."

"I make no claim to superiority."

"You don't have to claim it. A word suffices: nigger, whore . . . there is a long list to chose from."

His thin smile disappeared completely, and he said softly, "Again, I apologize. I make no claim to perfection either."

"There is no chance of *that*, given what I know about you."

"I want to understand you," he asserted, leaning forward.

"Why? I am one among many others."

"No, you are not the many; you are *different*."

"We're *all* different."

"And despite your assertions of equality, everyone is *not* equal," pressed Rogers. "You are not equal to the other women in this house, and you know it. What is the point of pretending otherwise? Even after the Declaration of Independence,

Mr. Jefferson couldn't maintain that lie. Leave *that* to Mr. Garrison, Arthur Tappan, and their friends."

Helen sighed. She did not trust him enough to reveal that she financially supported the abolitionists because, in large part, she saw that support as her chance at some kind of redemption, some reclaiming of the self-respect lost in her decision to be a prostitute and the sometimes terrible consequences of that decision that defined her life. Helen had cast the idea of salvation into the dustbin of lost illusions, but she maintained the hope that simple acts of decency and charity—and donations, however small, to a worthy cause—would reduce the pain of regret and diminished hopes. She no longer feared the eyes of God; she only feared her own.

"Very well," she conceded, leaning back in her chair. "Then if so, why don't you *touch* me?"

"I pay you anyway," he replied.

"That's no answer," she said.

"It will have to do, for now."

Chapter Ten

Helen had a daily routine. She rose early, making sure the last customer of the night left before daybreak; then she cleaned and powdered herself before going down to gather food for a light breakfast in her room. She dressed herself for the morning, wearing a light shift and a cotton shawl in her cold room; she hated the feel of excess cloth against her skin even when the wind chilled the air. Before her morning meeting with the mistress of the house, she read Keats, Shelley, Wordsworth, and Byron each morning. Their words—vivid creators of the world, its radiant light and green pastures, the song of birds in the wind, the embracing blue skies—deepened her capacity for wonder. The profanities, sweat, and other fluids of the night became distant memories and she enjoyed, for at least an hour or so, the possibilities of enchantment.

But her reading also reminded her what it was she wanted most. She had tried detachment, the most practical response to being a prostitute. Every night she gave her body to stupid, silly men, but her heart—her idealistic, sensitive, and hopeful heart—was her own. And yet she yearned to give this to a loving and understanding man, some man who could not disappoint her as her father, Judge Weston, Frederick Fuller, and Harlow Spaulding had disappointed her. She wondered how her life would be different if her father had not taken her to the Westons' house, if Judge Weston had not ordered her into his library, if she had not wanted Frederick Fuller to seduce her. Fearing the self-accusation of weakness and sentimentality, she resisted tears. But at times, she felt the agony of regret, and a mere word from a great poet could suddenly burn like a searing match to the skin.

Today she felt like a fool for wanting Dr. Rogers to love her, to say that she was more than just a prostitute, that she held a special place in his heart. The shame of her need suddenly brought tears to her eyes as she read Lord Byron: "She walks in beauty like the night." So she turned to his *Don Juan* for comic relief. She then heard a knock at her door.

"May I come in?" asked Lucy.

Helen rose to unlock the door, opened it, and immediately returned to a small desk so covered with books there was no room for writing paper, or combs and brushes.

"What are you reading *now?*" asked Lucy. "The Bible?"

"No," said Helen, not looking up for the page and only slightly annoyed by the interruption. "Byron."

"Who?" asked Lucy, stepping into the small room. She too wore a light shift, but it was tied tightly at the waist, so as to emphasize the size of her bosom. Customers had definite preferences, and large breasts were popular.

Helen smiled, amused by Lucy's need to emphasize the limited range of her assets; at the same time, she took delight in teaching Lucy about literature and history, the world of the mind she had never explored. But Helen immediately recognized her own need. It was easier to embrace than deny: even to a friend, she had to demonstrate her intellectual superiority.

"The scandalous Lord Byron," Helen explained. "He wrote great poems, slept with women *and* men, including his own sister, and had a clubfoot. By all accounts, he was quite handsome. No, absolutely beautiful."

"Did he live in a castle?" asked Lucy.

"Castles, villas, mansions, apartments in London, on the continent. And while living a life of parties, balls, banquets, and continuous affairs, he found time to write books like this, *Don Juan.*"

"Don who?"

"Don Juan, Don Giovanni of Seville, Spain, the greatest lover in the world," replied Helen in an effusive rush to explain, celebrate a hero, and boast. " A man who seduced thousands and, because he would not repent, was dragged down to hell by the statue of a man he killed in a duel."

"Sounds like a good story," observed Lucy coolly.

"And a great opera too. Mozart . . ."

"Who?"

"Oh, never mind. Let me read you some lines. They are amusing and sharp and cunning. Many people hate this book because he couldn't even spare even his friends. But to be a target of Byron . . . what a way to die by the pen!" She sighed, savoring the moment. Lucy rolled her eyes.

"I'll read from the first canto," Helen said.

"The first what?" Lucy asked.

"The opening chapter."

Helen quickly turned to the well-worn page and started reading, her voice light and mocking, the perfect voice for this text as far as she was concerned. Helen could have recited it as well, entire chapters of it. But she refrained from revealing too much. She knew all too well the conclusions of stories about women who asked too many questions, who faced the searing costs of absolute truth: Lot's wife, Semele, Cassandra, and Eurydice. No, she would not show and tell all. She wanted a friend, especially now, and good lies always had their uses.

Helen read slowly, savoring every inflection of the sardonic yet beautiful verses, beginning with the opening lines:

"I want a hero: an uncommon want.

When every year and month sends for a new one,

Till, after cloying the gazettes with cant,

The age discovers he is not the true one,

Of such as these I should not care to vaunt,

I'll therefore take our ancient friend Don Juan—

We all have seen him, in the pantomime,

Sent to the devil somewhat ere his time."

Helen read the next four stanzas, and at the end of the reading, Lucy had no comment, only a question. "*Where* did you get such a book?"

"From a man I loved back in Maine," Helen lied. "He owned a bookstore, and as a token of our love, he gave me this book. I am so glad that I have it because when my family discovered I was seeing him, I was forced to leave town and leave him. This is the only gift I have from him, this and a few love letters."

She'd begun lying as soon as she left Augusta, and the lies flowed easily now, with slight variations, depending on the audience of the moment. Helen took great pleasure in the nimbleness of her improvisations. And given the potential dangers, she certainly could not admit that she stole the book from Judge Weston's secret collection. She would have preferred stealing it from the bookstore, if Harlow had dared to buy it. But he had not; he was too conventional, too concerned about public opinion. In any case, she certainly didn't want Harlow to know that she knew its existence. His esteem was too important, even after she had departed.

When she first felt the temptation to become a book thief, Helen realized that Judge Weston could never openly claim ownership of any of his special books. The exposure of his secrets would be too damaging. She had found the perfect crime, and only had to wait for the perfect time to commit it.

"I'm so sorry," Lucy said, her voice now tinged with sadness. "But don't you think it strange for a man who loved you to give you a book about a man who loved nobody?"

Helen changed the subject. "And how was business last night?"

As if relieved by the sudden change, Lucy replied quickly, "I did well. How about you?"

"I did well, but the gentlemen were all the same—pale, skinny clerks on the town with money to spend and time to waste. This neighborhood has so many different kinds and colors of people, but you would never know by those who come to our door."

"We don't worship or sleep together," observed Lucy, her lips tight with disdain. "If you want *that* you'll have to go to the Hook or the Five Points."

Helen's heart sank. Her new friend was another bigot in a city obviously full of them. Just within a few days the press reported five racial assaults on the streets, and a colored church was burned to the ground. Boston thugs had almost killed William Lloyd Garrison last year. Helen had hoped New York, a much larger and diverse city, would be more tolerant. As a demonstration of her liberal tendencies, Helen wanted to hire a colored girl as her maid. But she decided to wait for a time when racial tensions were not so high. In the meantime, she hired colored messengers to take her anonymous donations to the Antislavery Society.

"I want to see the Five Points, "Helen said, sitting up to punctuate her dismissal of a contemptible opinion. "When can we go?"

"Ladies can't go there!" protested Lucy, horrified. "It's too dangerous. And it is absolutely filthy, and full of colored people living with the lowest white scum. Thousands died there from cholera. It lives in the fumes, the stench. You can't be serious."

Helen raised her voice just enough to suggest bemused intransigence: "I'm told there have been no reports of pestilence anywhere in the city for weeks. Besides, we aren't going at night. And two strong women can scream loud enough and kick hard enough to fend off an attack. In Boston a man accosted me, grabbing me from behind. But I surprised him by quickly pulling away and kicking him between the legs. And I continued my walk. Some men are dangerous and stupid, but that is not going to keep *me* off the streets."

She suppressed the impulse to laugh at herself; how easy it was to utter the arrogant nonsense that had brought her to that alley in Boston. Nevertheless, a ride, if not a walk, in the Five Points would be another test of her claim to the public streets. And New York would settle the issue once and for all.

"Absolutely *not*," insisted Lucy. "I prefer living over touring. If you must, you will go alone. Even friendship has its limits."

Helen continued to smile. "Very well," she conceded, now even more intrigued by the famous neighborhood. "Let's go to Battery Park then. I hear it's lovely."

Lucy replied briskly, "Battery Park *is* lovely, and walking there is the fashionable thing to do."

"But there can't be the slightest hint of rain in the air. No mud will mar one of my best green dresses."

"We shouldn't dress too well, or call attention to ourselves," said Lucy.

"Our best dresses will be our *protection*," Helen replied, her arrogance now in full flight. From its heights everything seemed small, petty, and contemptible. She liked to believe that public opinion, and matters of fashion and popular esteem, mattered not at all. But she intended to court public opinion to her advantage. Celebrity would be good for business, and good businesses had to advertise.

"Now let's go down and settle our accounts with Mrs. Welden. She is waiting, I am sure."

"Yes, indeed," answered Lucy, turning to leave.

This time Helen didn't enjoy the escalating match of wits and the scoring of points. She was doing again what she had always done: preventing the full development of the friendships that seemed so natural a consequence of countless hours spent together; claiming to be a friend while insisting on a position of superiority; remaining aloof even when surrounded by laughter, card games, song, and dance; and pretending that true intimacy mattered when, despite her avowals, it did not.

Her ambition mattered more.

She wanted a friend, but sentimentality was cheap and useless.

Helen could silently vow to *be* a friend and become a confidant and listener. She could continue to share her knowledge and love of books, and now offer them as gifts of the heart from a sister at the family table. Lucy, Ann Welden, and the other women at 55 Leonard could now be members of a new family, the only family she had.

But money and fame had higher claims to her heart.

She had to be honest with herself. True friendship would have to wait.

Chapter Eleven

Helen wasted no time with small talk and coy delay in the front parlor, usually filled with cigarette smoke, loud laughter, and the smell of whiskey, as customers selected their favorites. She instead selected her own favorites, attracted especially to tall men, or men with large, thick hands, or men with green eyes like her own. She couldn't explain these preferences, they seemed arbitrary and capricious, but she knowingly used them to choose quickly the men she wanted, understanding full well that her feigned desire for them made them desire her. Men were quick to arousal, and with a few strategic touches, delicate finger strokes, the touch of her tongue, accompanied by words unworthy of a lady, Helen could expedite the transaction upstairs with impressive speed and earn more money in one night than the other prostitutes could in two. Day after day Helen achieved this, and Ann Welden offered her gratitude and appreciation. Helen Jewett was good for business.

Their arrest together in January had forged their bond.

To Helen, it came as a complete surprise.

One Eliphalet Wheeler, a Bowery Street butcher, filed a complaint of "disorderly conduct" against the two, and they had to appear in police court to answer to the charge.

Helen had never been arrested and, frightened at the prospect of spending any time in Bridewell, the old, decrepit holding jail west of City Hall, she demanded an explanation from Ann Welden, who received the summons with surprising equanimity.

"What is this?" Helen asked. "What did we do? And who is this man?"

"My dear, Helen, this is the usual charge against us," Ann explained with a wry smile. "It covers a multitude of sins. But essentially a citizen can claim that our very presence on the streets, especially in their neighborhoods, disturbs the peace."

"Where?" Helen asked, so agitated that she stepped too close to Ann, whose arched eyebrows alone could indicate a severe breach of etiquette.

"I have no idea where this man lives or works," Ann replied, her tone cold enough to startle Helen, who immediately stepped away, as if slapped in the face. "I don't know the man, but it doesn't matter. The law, thanks to our legislature making a law for *only* this city, allows for complete strangers to file a complaint, and for the city to collect bail. It is a moneymaking enterprise."

Ann chuckled at her own observation, inflaming Helen's protest even more.

"This is an outrage!" Helen paced the parlor as she struggled to comprehend this turn of events.

"Surely, my dear, girls were arrested in Boston and Portland? This can't be unknown to you."

"Of course," snapped Helen. "Of course there were arrests for open procurement on the streets, for fighting, for making a scene at theaters or dance halls. But for *nothing*, for just *being* in a neighborhood?"

"We don't know all the details. I don't know where this man lives or works. We will find out more at Bridewell."

"Have you been there?" asked Helen.

"Yes, and it is decaying on the outside and the inside. Some people are afraid to walk by and get hit by a falling stone. The city keeps telling us that it will be condemned, torn down, and replaced by a new, better jail, but so far, nothing. We won't have to spend much time there. We'll pay the bail, and return to the house."

"How much will we have to pay? Do we have to pay the same? You have more money than I will ever have." Her voice was still strained by fear and ignorance; nothing said seemed to appease or comfort her.

"We will find out more when we get there. And once we find out the bail, we can send word for a bondsman to get the money."

"This is not right, not right at all. This is hard-earned money, and why should I have to give it to the city if I didn't do anything wrong?"

Ann sighed, now more patronizing than comforting.

"Helen, every now and then the city shudders with moral revulsion about our work and feels the need to extract money to relieve the guilt that comes with allowing us to continue. It may appear that New York wants to discourage our work, but not really. We pay, and we go on."

"New York gets property taxes from the people who own these houses," Helen replied, now so abrasive that Ann frowned severely for the first time. "Why should we have to pay extra? We are just trying to make a living!"

"We can use the police courts, too, and file a complaint," added Ann. "Some customers drink too much, or hit girls who don't cooperate in the ways they want, and we can go to the courts and demand satisfaction. Some men would rather pay fines than see their names in the paper. It all works out. Now let's get ready to meet the judges of the police court. Please dress simply, dear; no exposed flesh, no perfume, no jewelry, no distractions."

Unconvinced, Helen took a deep breath, left the parlor to select a simple but tasteful gray dress with white flounces at the neck and wrists, and packed a small bag with toiletries.

They arrived at Bridewell within the hour.

Before they went inside the sagging building, Ann turned to Helen to admonish her, her voice gentle but firm.

"Do not act as if you are ashamed or afraid. Men with any kind of power love for us to grovel. They hate us all because we know how *little* they really are. Think of *that* when they get all puffed up with their rules and their authority."

Ann seemed amused by the prospect of another encounter with the city's police. Helen remained anxious, but she was no longer afraid, thanks to Ann's experience and poise. Now she looked on Bridewell as something more to despise than to fear, just another bloated shell ready to collapse from the rot within it.

A single man sat at the docket table; he was thin, of medium build, with a narrow, reddened face. Wearing spectacles, he looked over them and said in a surprisingly warm voice after Ann presented the summons: "Ladies, you are charged with committing the offense of disorderly conduct at the Bowery Theater by Mr. Eliaphat Wheeler of Bowery Street, and you can be released on bail at five hundred dollars for Ann Welden, and three hundred for Helen Jewett."

Stunned by the amount of money, Helen started to protest, but Ann immediately gripped her arm to silence her.

"We will pay after making the needed arrangements," Ann replied. "We, of course, do not have that kind of money with us at this time."

"You will need to stay here until the money comes," the keep of the watch docket book announced. "I will send word to a bail bondsman of your choosing."

"Very well," said Ann calmly.

They were led to a cell on the second floor of the building; it was small but clean, with two small beds. The nearby cells sat empty.

Once the cell door was closed and locked, and the police officer had left, Helen became agitated again.

"How are we going to pay the bond? I don't have that kind of money."

Ann's eyes narrowed, their glint hard and piercing.

"*That* I don't believe for one moment," she said. "Not with the rising demands for your services, my dear."

"I have expenses."

"Don't we all, and you pay them, leaving you with extra funds to support your books and wardrobe. You have a few pieces of nice jewelry. Please spare me your claims to poverty."

Helen and Ann spent three boring days at Bridewell, waiting for the bondsman to finalize arrangements. Fortunately, Helen had brought two books to read; it was her habit to take at least one book everywhere. Otherwise, she spent the time talking with Ann, sharing stories and listening to Ann's. Helen lied, exaggerated, and elaborated without fear of detection; unlike most liars, she did not get lost in the details of her fantasies. She remembered them as vividly as words on a page. She discovered that Ann had a similar story of family abandonment, but Helen did not remember as many of details of Ann's narrative. She was only interested in her own reactions, thoughts, emotions, and experiences.

The case of disorderly conduct at the Bowery Theater never went to a court hearing. Ann and Helen forfeited their bond after making a promise of good behavior in lieu of conviction and returned to work at 55 Leonard Street without serious disruption to their schedule or activities.

However, Helen decided after two months to move on.

The costs of living at 55 Leonard were too high. Helen was essentially an independent operator in a boarding house, paying Ann Welden ten dollars a week for room and board, and receiving four dollars for sex. But she learned that other madams at other houses did not take a cut of each fee the girl collected, as Ann did. Helen chafed at this exception. It made it more difficult for her to save the money she needed for the walking dresses, evening gowns, jewelry, bonnets, and shoes she desired. She was compelled to have more clients and perform more often at greater speed to pay her expenses and increase her savings. Even with her prodigious stamina in the bedroom, she was exhausted.

"Mrs. Welden will not like this," Lucy observed when Helen shared her decision. "Will you tell her?"

"Of course, I will inform her," Helen replied, insulted by the implication that she might sneak off in the middle of the night, like a thief.

"I will miss you," Lucy said, looking away. "Can we still be friends?"

"We can all live in different places, and see each other at the theatre, in shops, at the park. We can do the same."

"It will be different; the girls in the houses are like sisters."

"Friends can be as close as sisters, or even closer," said Helen, taking Lucy by the hands even as she suspected the truth of Lucy's fears. "72 Chapel is not that far away."

When Helen told Ann about the intended move, Ann only arched her eyebrows and said, with a calm so intense it threatened to unleash a storm of invective, "Give my regards to your new mistress." Helen almost gasped; never had a perfunctory courtesy sounded so dangerous.

Ann left the front parlor with no further comment, and Helen stared at the closed door, still surprised at the ease of this annunciation—no questions, no recriminations, no regrets.

"That was easy," Helen said aloud. "Too easy."

Helen wasted no time with needless speculations, instead rushing upstairs to pack her things. She would take small, personal items in a bag, and have her packages of books and clothes transported by hired hands. Fortunately, she did not have to wait until May first, the traditional moving day in the city; she didn't have that many possessions, and she would lease her new room from month to month, not year to year.

The house at 72 Chapel Street was smaller and less grand than 55 Leonard, but its diminished character suited Helen's purposes perfectly. Eliza Lawrence, the brothel mistress, had fewer overhead expenses and did not take a cut from Helen's fee for services. Helen was able to save even more for the resplendent gowns she planned to buy or have made.

Then Ann paid a visit.

———————

Wary but pleased, Helen received Ann in the main parlor. She had heard nothing from Lucy or anyone else about lingering resentments or animosity about Helen's departure from 55 Leonard.

Helen sat down, waiting for Ann to join her at the nearby chair. Then Ann swiftly crossed the room and slapped Helen on the face with such force that her entire head turned. Helen could only garble a startled question, "What?" before Ann slapped her again, this time with the back of her hand against the other cheek.

Helen tried to lunge forward out of her chair in a desperate attempt to protect herself, but Ann grabbed her by the hair and began shaking her head with one hand and scratching her face with the other.

"You bitch, you little bitch," Ann shouted. "You've cost me. You owe me, you ungrateful bitch."

Helen screamed, terrified. Ann was surely going to maim her. She seemed like a dog unable to stop a rampage, its rage so all consuming that no appeal could touch it. The skin of Helen's face burned, and she tried to cover her cheeks with her hands, instinctively protecting one of her most important assets. Helen then started to kick at Ann, using thighs and feet to push her away.

Suddenly three other women and a large teenage boy were in the room yelling and pulling at Ann, who continued her rant: "You *owe* me. I did everything for you. I pulled you out of the gutter, and you left me to come to this hole. You bitch! You ungrateful bitch!"

Ann had been pulled to the center of the room, her body still heaving from the force of her anger. She was not done or satisfied, and her face twisted with pure hatred. Her eyes bulged, and thick strands of disheveled hair lay against her skin like blackened meat on a line in a butcher shop.

Speechless, Helen could only stare at this vision of appalling ugliness. She felt faint, but she would not give Ann Welden the satisfaction of seeing her fall to the floor in a swoon.

Someone said to Ann, "You'd better leave now, or we'll have you arrested," and suddenly Ann assumed the calm demeanor of a cultivated woman.

"Very well," she replied, relaxing under the grip of the hands holding her. "You can unhand me now. I am finished. You can trust me."

They all looked to Helen for a signal, and she nodded her head. Released, Ann Welden declared, "Ingratitude is unforgivable," and left the room, followed by three of the four. Eliza Lawrence remained.

"I can't believe that," said Eliza. "What happened to her? She doesn't *need* you. You are not *that* important."

If these words were meant to console Helen, they failed, and she cried bitter tears. She hadn't mean to hurt anyone; she had only wanted to improve her circumstances. So she'd made a calculated decision that any intelligent businesswoman could understand. Surely, Ann Welden could understand this simple fact, or so it had seemed with her apparently graceful acceptance of Helen's decision. What had changed? Was her current success now an affront to her first sponsor?

"Nonetheless," Helen said, wiping tears away, "I do know I have rights, and this will not be the last she hears from me."

Three days later Helen, accompanied by one of the eyewitnesses, brought an assault and battery complaint against Ann, and Ann spent three days in jail.

Helen took great satisfaction in applying the lesson learned from Ann herself: The courts existed to be used by *all* citizens. Even prostitutes had rights.

But then Helen had second thoughts; after another three days, the charge of ingratitude rankled. She was grateful to Ann for bringing her New York, and for giving her a chance to start over in one of New York's finest establishments. Of course she had the right to leave; she was not a slave. But didn't Ann at least deserve more than two days' advanced notice? Had she not earned a heartfelt note of appreciation, and a warm embrace when it was time to go?

It was too late for that now. Such an attack was unforgivable, and the damage to their relationship beyond recovery.

But Helen decided she could at least do something decent, to show in some way that she was not the ungrateful bitch Ann said she was.

She paid Ann's five hundred dollars' bail, making sure the payment was not anonymous so that news of her generosity would travel quickly through the narrow streets of the Fifth Ward.

Chapter Twelve

Helen looked around the room, taking exquisite pleasure in each and every item in the small parlor of Dr. David Rogers on Chambers Street. She was now his "kept woman," a role she would play for as long as he was interested in having her stay. She could return to Eliza Lawrence's establishment at the end of this temporary arrangement, her place secured by Dr. Roger's payment of her room and board while she was away. He also gave Helen money to spend on clothes, jewelry, food, and entertainment while he was out making the rounds at brothels, seeing patients in his office or at private residences, and teaching students at the medical school, where he was developing new techniques for cutting up corpses and examining their internal organs.

But she was bored, and her earnings, substantial for a kept woman, had failed to relieve the frustration week after week of sitting and reading, sitting and waiting, hoping for more than brief exchanges of conversation. The original excitement of his invitation had long passed.

"Why don't you have a wife?" she asked one evening.

He arched his eyebrows. Helen had carefully modulated her voice to suggest mere curiosity, but clearly he heard accusation and saw effrontery, and as usual, he laughed at her, throwing his head back to punctuate her folly.

"Why, Miss Jewett, you *dare* to ask such a question?" he said. "This matter is none of your business."

"Miss, Jewett, still?" she replied.

"What's in a name? Yours is, no doubt, a fabrication anyway."

She waited, counting on his need to explain himself.

He obliged, saying, "Why have a permanent, legal arrangement for what I can have from time to time, all without the complications of household expenses incurred by a wife and brats, and their tireless need for my attention?"

"I want you," she said, carefully modulating her voice; she didn't want to sound desperate.

His eyes softened, mockery suddenly gone. Leaning slightly forward in his chair, he said warmly, "I was waiting for you to ask."

"I was ready from the beginning," she protested.

"That was business, a mere transaction. Now *I'm* ready."

Revealing no surprise, she rose from her chair and went to his bedroom, undressed quickly, and waited for him in the bed, covering her chest with the thin, embroidered cotton bedcover from the newest and most lavish emporium on Broadway, A.T. Stewart's. Proud of his purchase, Rogers had pointed out the bedcover's origin when she stood naked before him as he masturbated earlier in the week.

As she had feared, Rogers was a disappointment in bed. The enchantment of great expectation was dashed. She wanted a poet of sex, and Rogers had proved himself to be, despite that luxurious voice and his professional manner, an educated bully with odd tastes who performed the essential act with brief, perfunctory strokes.

Of course, she pretended to enjoy the moment, crying out with feigned astonishment at knowing his eminent climax. She moaned, rolling her hips to meet his. He was paying for the illusion and deserved a decent performance.

She would leave the poetry of sex to Bryon, Shakespeare, and frequent visits to the Park Theater, where she hoped to hear well-recited verses and meet a customer with good taste and an appreciation of her intelligence and literary refinements.

Even as her arrangement with Dr. Rogers continued off and on in the early months of 1834, Helen, searching for an even better clientele, decided to move again, this time to 41 Thomas Street, where Rosina Townsend did a flourishing business in two row houses connected to make an imposing structure with two staircases linked by a shared landing before the second floor. At the roof two large skylights illumined the entire vertical space between the floors. The furnishings were resplendent.

"Ah, Miss Jewett," said Rosina, another older beauty with poise and quiet confidence, "Your reputation precedes you. Dr. Rogers has been most complimentary. He knows us all, and Eliza Lawrence could only praise you, even after you left her."

"Yes, Mrs. Lawrence was most gracious. She said I would find success here."

"Eliza said more," corrected Rosina, her eyes a delicate registration of disapproval. She continued to smile. "She rightly told you that this is the top of our business, and that you would find success, if not happiness, here."

"Happiness is never guaranteed," confirmed Helen.

"We will do our best," Rosina replied.

"And what did Dr. Rogers say?" pressed Helen.

"He said that you would not disappoint us. He said you were bright, beautiful, and very well read. Your charm and intelligence will delight our clients, who will pay handsomely."

"Did he say anything more?" Helen asked, worried that he might have revealed too much of her history and interests.

Rosina frowned.

"What more is there to say, Miss Jewett?" she asked. "We do not indulge in graphic or salacious details."

Helen protested, "Oh, I didn't mean to appeal to vulgarity, Mrs. Townsend. You and your establishment could not possibly encourage or countenance even the slightest suggestion of it."

Helen pointedly scanned the expensive furniture in the parlor to emphasize her point.

"And when and if you leave us, Miss Jewett, I assure you I will not behave in the unseemly manner of Ann Welden. That assault was *truly* vulgar, most inappropriate and vulgar."

"I was shocked," added Helen, "and I promise you . . ."

Rosina's raised her hand to stop her.

"Please, Miss Jewett, do not attempt to promise your undying devotion, or even promise to stay here for the rest of your career. We are *all* vagabonds. I know."

Chastened, Helen looked down. She was surprised that Rosina had such an effect on her. She was both candid and kind, a rare combination Helen did not expect in an older woman with money and position. Paulina Weston could learn a few things from Rosina Townsend.

"After I tell you my basic story, you will tell me yours," said Rosina warmly.

Her real name was Rosanna Brown, and she was born near Albany, where she was married in the early 1820s. She and her husband moved to Cleveland, where he deserted her for another woman. She returned to her parents, but after a month she came to New York and tried working as a seamstress and then as a domestic servant in the home of a wealthy merchant named Henry Beekman. Work at the Beekmans' of Greenwich Street lasted for only a few weeks, and Rosina turned to prostitution as a way to make a satisfactory living, working in her first brothel in 1826. By 1828, she ran a house at 28 Anthony Street, and then in 1829 at 41 Thomas Street.

"It's a typical story, Miss Jewett," concluded Rosina, "but not a common one, as you can surely see."

Rosina looked at specific pieces of furniture around the room and then stopped to stare, emphasizing her possession of the huge mirrors that reflected back the splendor of her paintings and tapestries, and her own mature beauty.

"I am very good with money and organization. The owner, who cannot be known to you, *ever*, is quite pleased. Now tell me your story briefly, and I mean *briefly*."

As required, Helen was brief. She told a story of desertion and forced choices, the outline essentially true, the details, all lies.

"Well," announced Rosina at the end of Helen's narrative. "With your obvious assets, and courage, there will be many men who will find you most appealing. Dr. Rogers stands confirmed."

Unfortunately, another man, not so impressed, attempted to humiliate her a few months later.

There was nothing unusual about that visit to the Park Theater. She was there two or three times every week. The play that night in June was dreadful, the actors abominable, mutilating their lines with reckless indifference. But she never tired of the upholstered seats, the decorated woodwork, the gas lit chandeliers, the ladies' lounges with handsome attendants, and the crowded food bar in the basement. Too see and be seen were enough, and a verbal contract with a customer completed a successful night.

While going up the stairs to the second tier, she dropped a ten-dollar bill and bent to pick it up. Suddenly she heard a high, slurred, obviously drunken laugh and a shouted proclamation, as if declaimed by one of the bad actors on the stage.

"Now there's a rump for the asking!" the man announced.

Before Helen could react, before she could fully register the sound of that voice and match it with a face and name, before she could think of an appropriate reply, before she could even straighten her back, he kicked her from behind, laughing even louder as she pitched forward.

Instinctively, she extended her arms to keep her head from hitting the stairs, and rolled down, the folds of her green gown and petticoats wrapping her leg and arms into twisted knots, like thick ropes. Her fall happened so quickly, she didn't have time to scream, cry out a single word, or make a sound. When she stopped rolling, she could hear the man's laughter, and she saw the stunned looks on the faces of men and women on the staircase and landing, faces frozen on dressed statues, horror and curiosity needing answers. What happened? Is she hurt? What should we do?

Helen moved to get up, and as if on cue, everyone around her knew what to do. They laughed, a chorus of sneering delight at her expense.

She was alone, her friend Lucy already upstairs in the lounge; no one moved to help, to lift her from the tangled mess of cloth and stays.

"I'm fine," she said, assuring herself and declaring her indifference to public scorn. "I am *not* hurt."

Awkwardly, Helen stood, untangling the folds of her gown, pulling and pressing them to their former splendor. She also pulled at her gloves, tightening their grip even more, delicately touched her neck to make sure her necklace was still in place, and patted the side curls of her hair. She suddenly smiled, pleased that she had removed her bonnet earlier that evening; the sight of a bonnet askew on her head, its ribbons tangled around her ears and neck, would have been *too much*, a small but jarring accent, like a red moustache on a defaced painting.

Still laughing, her assailant had run off, no doubt to brag to his friends and obtain their support and encouragement. But this tall *little boy* had made a serious miscalculation; this cowardly, drunken bore would pay for misjudging her. Lifting her skirts to ascend the stairs, and lifting her chin pointedly to mark her moral superiority in this shabby spectacle—a spectacle in which the son of a wealthy New York attorney, a supposed gentleman, kicked, no, assaulted a woman from behind and ran away like a giggling bully on a backstreet of the Bowery—Helen decided to file another complaint at the police court. She knew her rights, and poor John Laverty, an occasional customer, would have to answer to the charges. If he thought Helen Jewett would retreat to 41 Thomas Street and hide, humiliated and ashamed, he had made a terrible mistake, as only a fool prone to pranks would do. She would expose his cowardice and bad manners to all New Yorkers.

The next morning she filed her complaint at the court, but the clerk, now familiar with her legal protestations, only raised an eyebrow at the mention of her assailant's name and address.

However, she soon found an ally. A reporter left a note asking for an interview.

William Attree was a recent immigrant with an obvious English accent. He quickly explained his reason for coming.

"I read the reports every morning, like the other police reporters, looking for news items," he said, leaning forward in his chair in the parlor. "But as soon as I saw your complaint, I just *had* to see you. Your audacity is highly unusual. I knew there was more to the story than a few lines in a common list. This was an opportunity for me and the *Transcript*."

Billy Attree had a crooked nose, bright blue eyes, and crow-black hair combed back and thick with pomade. He wasn't handsome, but his bold, unequivocal ambition was attractive.

"How is this an opportunity?" asked Helen, already sensing the possibilities.

He grinned, revealing teeth yellowed from too many cigars.

"I rarely conduct interviews," he replied. "Most people are liars and tell self-serving tales. But I had to find out about you, where you came from, how you got here. I want my readers to know all about you, a woman of obvious *spunk*."

"Do you flatter often?"

"It opens doors . . . and legs."

"Are you always this vulgar with women you meet for the first time?" Helen asked, amused by her own confusion. She was both offended by his casual vulgarity and attracted to his candor. She decided to not press the matter of his character and her reaction to it. She was not going to alienate him; he was going to be useful, very useful.

"Yes," he replied. "No illusion, no disappointments, no great expectations."

"So where do we begin?"

"Tell me every detail about what happened last night at the Park Theater. Every detail."

"Then let's go upstairs to my private room," she replied, rising.

Billy hesitated, obviously startled by her invitation.

Helen smiled.

"Oh, Mr. Attree, you can be assured you'll find no evidence of carnal transaction today," she said playfully.

Billy asked, "How old are you, Miss Jewett?"

For a young woman she was remarkably poised.

"I'm twenty."

"Where were you born?"

"No more questions, Mr. Attree, until we arrive upstairs, and I'll tell you about what happened at the Park. That's what brought you here in the first place, remember?"

He followed her to her room. Books and papers littered the bed, the floor, the writing table, and the fireplace mantle. He immediately noticed a small print of Lord Byron above the pillows of her four-poster bed.

"I see you admire one of my countrymen," he observed.

"Yes, a great poet, a fearless man," she replied.

"Fearless like you," Billy said.

"Flattery again," she countered.

"Well earned," Billy replied.

"My protests in no way match his sacrifice," she said, alluding to Byron's death during the Greek war for independence from the Turks.

He leaned slightly forward and said softly, "There are different kinds of sacrifice. Please begin."

Taking her cue, Helen folded her hands in her lap, rested her back against the chair, declared, "I love the theater." She told her tale with carefully controlled but rising vehemence, and created a pointed portrait of her innocence and John Laverty's utterly crass behavior.

When Helen finished, Billy said with a slight lift of his chest, pleased by the raising of the stakes, "I will print his name in the paper, and his father's name and establishment when I find them out."

"Your bosses will allow this?" Helen asked, dubious for the first time.

"The names will sell more papers. And the louder Laverty and his friends shout, the more money the *Transcript* will make. We'll match the *Sun* soon enough."

Benjamin Day's *New York Sun* had introduced a new kind of journalism to New York, a four-sheet paper crammed with gossip, rumor, innuendo, scandal, and crime . . . especially crime. It appealed to readers in the Bowery and the Five Points, not Battery Park and Wall Street, and avoided literature and financial news. Its editorials, all written by Day, were usually rants against the political and financial establishments, and he published letters of protest letters to fuel controversy. The *Sun* was a huge success. Still in his twenties, Day was a rich man. Now other editors and journalists hungered to match or surpass his achievement. Competition was fierce.

"My reports are better than the *Sun's*," Billy concluded.

"I will be the judge of that," Helen replied. "And you will need to name *every* man who comes drunk or gets drunk and then starts breaking things and assaulting us. This is the worse it has ever been."

In the 1830s, rowdies and ruffians increasingly attacked the fancy brothels in the Fifth Ward, shouting slogans against rich men and the immoral women who served them. They usually forced entry, shouted obscenities, overturned drinks, and destroyed furniture. But by 1834 these attacks had escalated to physical assaults. In March, two men beat up Julia Brown, the mistress of the house at 64 Chapel Street.

That afternoon Helen told stories of her own encounters with unruly men at 55 Leonard, and in every one she triumphed over her assailants, wielding the power of her withering sarcasm to deflate puffed up men.

"I will not tolerate such boorish or rowdy behavior," she declared. "One of your own countrymen, a Captain Burke, discovered this recently."

"My apologies, "Billy said, knowing that she would elaborate with glorious details.

"This fat British officer came here and tried to pay for wine with a counterfeit five-dollar bill, and I challenged its authenticity. He took umbrage, puffing himself up like a giant pillow, and protested vociferously that as an officer of the crown, representing his Royal Majesty, the King, he would not *dare* to lose his honor in the presence of a common whore. I told him his presence in my room had already accomplished the loss of that honor, and that at the very least I was more honorable because I was not pretending to be someone I wasn't."

Smiling, Helen paused to make sure her tale had its desired effect.

Billy obliged, saying with grinning admiration, "Splendid."

"Indeed," she replied before continuing. "My comment so enraged him that he suddenly ran to my wardrobe and started pulling at my gowns, trying to tear them apart. But his own hands were not strong enough, and he ran about my room looking for something. Then, to my absolute horror, he found scissors on my desk and used to them to cut up my dresses. The fabrics were thick, so he could only make small slices. He then took the handles and plunged into the cloth as if he was killing a wild pig, ripping long slices in them as if flaying skin."

"Weren't you afraid that he might hurt you?" Billy asked.

Helen smirked. "I was horrified, *horrified* by what he was doing to my beautiful dresses. But he was just pathetic, so pathetic. All he could do, or would do, was attack my dresses. Some soldier, *indeed*."

"Surely, you didn't employ sarcasm at such a moment?" Billy asked.

"Mr. Attree, Mrs. Weldon counts on me at night to put fools in their place. But I was cautious enough to *not* press my luck. I only screamed for my poor dresses actually, and the captain stopped, an exhausted man defeated by wool, silk, and cotton, ribbons and lace, poor man."

He scanned her bed, where one of her green gowns rested, looked at her, and observed, "They are beautiful."

"My eyes or my dresses?" she asked.

"Both," he said. "And in my article I will call you the girl in the green dress. Now, I need your background story. No other stories, please. I appreciate the joys of delayed pleasure, but I have a deadline."

As if she had been waiting for months, if not years, for this moment, she rushed into her narrative; it seemed well rehearsed.

"I'm from Maine, from Portland," she began. "I was adopted by a distinguished family there, a family whose name I will protect, and a name you must not print, because I was treated like a daughter even though I was a servant in the household and a guardian of the small children. They made sure I had a superior education, and I frequently attended lessons with their oldest daughter at one of the best female academies, a boarding school in Boston. But my greatest education came from the library at the house; it was splendid, and when time permitted, I spent many hours there, many pleasant hours absorbing novels, history, poetry, plays."

"How idyllic," Billy said. "But, what about your *real* family?"

"The Mallorys, as I shall call them for the sake of my story, were my real family; the other one, the one from the poorest part of town, I hardly knew. My mother died when I was quite young, and my father, seeing that I had a chance for a better life, placed me in a house that offered that chance. I could work there, make an impression, and receive the benefit of being around the best people. The Mallorys heard about me, my diligence, my intelligence, my other gifts, and *asked* for my employment."

"But the good times did not last," said Billy. "You ended up *here*."

"I was seduced," said Helen solemnly, lowering her head and closing her eyes to accentuate her descent into vice. "While I was at the boarding school, the son of a merchant seduced me. He was tall and handsome, said he loved books as I did, and promised to marry me. I was young, and he took advantage by promising me that he would marry me. But once I had succumbed to his advances, I was damaged in his eyes . . . and in my own. No one would marry me. What was I thinking?"

Billy protested, "You blame *yourself* for this? What about him? Surely he is to blame for taking advantage of a young girl."

"Does it matter?" asked Helen. "I learned the ways of the world soon enough. Word got back to the Mallorys that I had fallen . . ."

"*Thanks* to him," Billy countered. "He couldn't resist boasting about his conquest. We're swine, you know. We're all swine, including me."

"Is this a warning?"

"Absolutely," Billy replied. "There is a reason I'm called Oily Attree."

"It's not just your hair?" Helen asked mischievously.

"No." Billy knew he would come to her bed soon enough, but now he pressed her to continue. "And then?"

"Mr. Mallory was devastated, wanting to protect me and knowing full well that he could not. My reputation was shattered, and so I volunteered to leave, to spare him further scandal."

"But how did your departure get you here? You left Portland. Then what? I take it that you didn't go back home to your father?"

"Of course, not," said Helen haughtily. "He heard about my fall, and he made it clear that he would not have me."

"Then you remained at the Mallorys long enough for your father to hear about it and write to you?"

For the first time he doubted a detail. Fallen women were not given days to go packing. Usually they had to leave at once.

"Yes, Mr. Mallory struggled to find some way to keep me," Helen explained quickly, "and insisted that I stay, that something could be worked out. But I knew this to be impossible."

"In a large city like Boston or New York, you could start over. Starting over: Isn't this what America's all about?"

"For you, for men, but not for us," Helen observed bitterly.

"But you don't have to accept it, just like you didn't have to accept silence when you were kicked at the Park Theater."

"Reputation is everything, at least for women. Once the word is out, it cannot be put back. It *cannot*."

"You're the victim here. One man seduced you, the other kicked you."

"I don't want your pity," Helen flashed, tightening the grip of her hands still folded in her lap.

"And you won't get or *need* it," declared Billy. "Not in the story I'm going to tell, a story of tragedy and triumph."

"Good," said Helen, rising to end the interview. "Since I am *acting* all the time, it will be a pleasure to see myself as the heroine in your play."

"Acting?" Billy asked, frowning. Was her history a carefully crafted parcel of truths, omissions, florid exaggerations, and outright lies, the perfect gift for an eager admirer?

Without answering him, she extended her hand and said warmly, an obvious diversion, "Thank you for understanding and supporting me."

Billy took her hand and said, "Thank you for your time, Miss Jewett. I hope I don't disappoint you."

"I'm counting on it," said Helen before turning to open the door. Then she stopped and turned around.

"What happened to your nose?" she asked, smiling.

"A gift from my drunk of a father. I was ten."

"Then we're both survivors," Helen said.

As promised, Billy delivered "The Fruits of Seduction." His report of the Park Theater episode included a "brief history of this young girl" so that he could convince his readers of "the misery resulting from the villainous artifices of those whose sole aim in life seems to be the seduction of a young and innocent girl, and then abandoning her to the sneers and insults of the heartless and despicable."

But Billy, preferring triumph over misery, described a pretty woman of genteel deportment who, despite her fall, became an example of courage, intelligence, sophistication, independence, and determination; hers was an especially American story, one holding lessons of hope and encouragement for other "lost" girls.

They were both fugitives.

He had escaped a drunken father and a mother who defended, excused, or ignored the rants, kicks and punches, and attacks. No one was spared; all six of the children, three brothers and three sisters lived, heard, and saw the mistreatment. They found comfort in the retelling of stories and in planning revenge.

At ten Billy started drinking. By fourteen he was taller than his father. He slapped Billy at the back of his head for some minor offense one afternoon, and Billy fought back, pummeling him in the face until his bloodied cheeks and forehead shut his father's eyes. Billy's mother screamed, but the others wrapped their arms around her like a giant sea monster with ten arms and five heads. When finally Billy stopped, exhausted by bottomless rage and horrified by the sight of his father, who no longer moved but still gasped for air, he decided to leave and never return. He knew, as surely as he knew the names of his brothers and sisters, that his father would kill him if he stayed.

Billy gathered up a few clothes, broke the lock on the moneybox under his parents' bed, grabbed a few coins, and ran out of the door, failing to say good-by and refusing to look back for fear that the sight of even one brother or sister at the door would pull him into the dark den of their squalid hovel in Brighton.

Later he managed to survive, finding work wherever muscle was needed on farms and in the small towns of southern England. Eventually, he found himself in Portsmouth, where he became a news hawker, a printer apprentice, and a crime writer. Fortunately taught to read and write by his mother before his father put a stop to it, he was good with language and received better assignments and better pay as he matured.

But Portsmouth could not be his journey's end. There countless ships unloaded travelers and goods from around the world, and there on the wharves and in the pubs and boarding houses he heard the endless talk about America, the promise of a new life, wealth for any hardworking man willing to embrace its vast open spaces or teeming cities.

He also heard about Boston, Philadelphia, Washington, Charleston, and New Orleans. But no tale of these cities could match the sheer wonder of New York—its energy, the promise of dazzling possibility, the staggering amount of uninherited riches.

Restless, Billy could see no future for himself in England, a country still gripped by tradition and privilege. He heard about changes in the north, as mills and foundries were being built in Manchester. But even there change was slow, and no one could rise to the heights scaled by immigrants to America.

He boarded the *Edmund* in 1832 with hope, ten pounds, and a bag of clothes. He regretted only the crossing. He had been warned that the North Atlantic was rough, and he vomited into his bucket day after day until he could only heave dry spasms.

But New York did not disappoint. The city was exciting, and his crime reporting work was never dull. The city had a cast of characters he'd never encountered in Bristol. Crime was universal, as were greed, lust, rage, envy, jealousy, and pride. But in America, even thieves, pimps, and prostitutes had an optimism that was irresistible. Helen Jewett was irresistible.

Chapter Thirteen

Helen became the talk of the town, and her fame was good for business; clients came eagerly to Thomas Street to talk to and sleep with the "girl in the green dress." Now she could be even more selective in her choice of customers.

Dr. Rogers, unable to resist the claims of fame, returned as well and asked for another temporary arrangement. She declined, saying sweetly, "I don't like living alone."

"May I still come to see you?"

"Of course, but fame has its rewards."

"You're raising your prices," he concluded.

"Don't you when the demand for your services increase?" she asked.

"Yes," he answered.

"Well, there you have it."

Helen always rose from bed at dawn to make sure her last client departed before the start of another business day; after a night of sex and drinking, customers often had a hard time getting up and leaving the premises before the streets filled with people. Prostitution was generally accepted, but discretion was still necessary.

Billy Attree was slow to rise. He liked to drink, downing cup after cup of whiskey and brandy, and he was a heavy sleeper, snoring like a foghorn on the East River. But he was a good customer. He did not complain about the cost of his liquor, and now twenty-five he knew how to use his body. He didn't hurry, taking his time with fingertips, lips, and tongue to explore Helen's body. When he entered her, he moved slowly and methodically, sustaining his erection for hours without coming to a climax. It was a remarkable performance, and Helen was pleased to have agreed to his request that he be her last customer for the night. Confident, even arrogant, he obviously knew what he could do when given the time. And she liked him.

She was grateful that he had written "A Woman of Spunk." But her attraction was not mere gratitude; he was attractive because he was inquisitive and never boring. Everything seemed to interest him, and he had the remarkable gift, rare among men, of giving his undivided attention.

Unfortunately, not everything went well because of Billy's work.

Ben Day of the *Sun* was not dazzled by Helen's charms, and he mocked her assault at the Park Theater. He observed in a featured editorial,

A lady of the third tier of boxes in the Park Theater named Helen—a perfect representative, no doubt, of her who caused the Trojan War—lodged a complaint at the police office against one of her admirers named Laraty who, conceiving himself to be a second Paris, indelicately assaulted the fair Helen by throwing his arms around her neck and endeavoring to perpetrate a kiss in the public lobby of the establishment. This, the fair Helen resented with becoming spirit, and gave the rude assailant an appropriate rebuke for his indelicacy toward her. This was modest and commendable, and we are pleased to find that the ladies of the third tier dare to assert their rights, and entertain so high a respect for their own character and standing, as to resent every assault calculated to cast contempt upon their virtue.

When Helen sat at her desk at dawn to write a response, she didn't expect the *Sun* to publish it, but she savored the taste of venom with every word she as she penned it, her quill almost tearing the thin paper she preferred:

Sir: You obviously have no interest in truth or accuracy. You could not manage the simple matter of spelling my assailant's name correctly. And clearly the only source of your story is John Laverty himself, who obviously wants your readers to believe that he offered only a kiss rather than a kick to a defenseless woman whose back was turned. As a matter of simple fact, he insulted me, but in your headlong rush to support him, you obviously fail to see his insult to you, his willing dupe. He counted on you to accept, without investigation, his bold lie, raising serious doubts about your credibility. And then you compound this travesty by making absurd references to the Trojan War, a tragedy of history caused by two fools in love. What happened to me at the Park Theater was not tragic. What is tragic is that a representative of the free press laughs at the pursuit of justice. And will you still laugh when, while you sleep, angry men, given virtual permission by printed winks and smirks, molest and slaughter the innocent?

She copied this letter, as she did with several deemed important or personal favorites, and read it to Billy with clipped emphasis on nouns and adjectives and a stiff index finger pinpointing key words.

But even as she dramatized her outrage, she enjoyed surprising Billy with her knowledge and opinions; his delight and sometimes shock only encouraged her to tell more, exaggerate, and pontificate.

Just a few days before she'd had to tell him about the drunken customer who brandished a gun because of a comment she made.

"I can't remember what I said—I have to say so many things to keep men in their place—but when he pulled out that gun, the sheer extremity of it, as blatant a gesture of desperation as I could imagine, I just slapped it out of his hand, and then I told the shocked fool that he was a contemptible libel on manhood. Then, to accentuate my point, I tweaked his nose, his big *fat* nose."

"Only men are supposed to do that," Attree said gravely. "Duels follow. This is the worst kind of insult. Even presidents haven't been spared."

"Pity President Jackson's nose," Helen observed.

"You know about *that?*"

"I *read*, Mr. Attree," she replied, exasperated by the apparent assumption of her civic indifference and ignorance. "I read several newspapers to keep myself informed about the issues of the day, even if I cannot vote, which one day will come to women. If women can run a business, like Ann Welden and Rosina Townsend and the other mistresses of the houses in the Fifth Ward, they can run towns and make decisions in the best interest of the citizens of New York and elsewhere. And we have proven again and again that we are as intelligent and as stupid as men. But even the most stupid *male* living in the lowest dive in the Five Points can vote. What utter nonsense!"

Billy paused, his lips parted. He clearly hadn't expected a tirade. "Who are you, Miss Jewett?" he asked, wonder and admiration in the question.

Smiling, Helen savored the moment, then teased him with her answer: "The secret granddaughter of Mary Wollstonecraft . . . the American granddaughter."

Billy laughed. "Oh, Miss Jewett, you are incorrigible."

Now it was time for her admirer to go, and she nudged him lightly at first, tapping him on the shoulder as he slept. He didn't respond, so she pushed him with both hands. Still unsuccessful, she pounded his chest with her fist. At last he sat up, the sheet falling to his lap and exposing his hairy chest.

"What the hell?" he exclaimed.

"You need to go," said Helen.

"What's the hurry?" he asked. "I was the last."

Helen pulled the sheet away, exposing his entire naked body. He had a morning erection, thick but not at full capacity. Helen smiled, pleased that her desire for him was still strong, and that he could please her immediately, if she wanted to disrupt the schedule of this Sunday morning. But no, she was not going to allow him to think *he* determined her schedule.

"Get up now," she said. "I have a busy day."

"On Sunday, the day of rest?" he pressed, grinning. "Are you going to church?"

"No," she said, unable to lie about that. She had not stepped inside a church in years, not since the Weston visits to the First Congregational Church in Augusta. "Nevertheless, I have plans for the day, and those plans do not include you. Now get up!"

He swung his long legs over to the side of the bed and jumped up, looking about for his clothes. Helen smiled at the silliness of his forgetting where he had put them in such a small room.

"Over there."

She pointed to the pile on the chair at her desk. He could have put them on the chair near his side of the bed. She suspected he'd placed his clothes on the other side so that while she waited in bed, he could pass her and show off his beautiful, naked body. He didn't bother to wear a nightshirt.

Billy dressed quickly as Helen waited, sitting on the chair and admiring his form from the back even as he covered it with layers of underwear, pantaloons, shirt, and coat.

When done, he turned and asked, "When can I see you again?"

"I will write you," she replied, adding him to her list of clients with whom she corresponded. She wrote nine or ten letters a day, and walked a mile daily to the federal post office inside the Merchant Exchange Building on Wall Street to post them and retrieve her mail.

"Let me give you one final kiss?"

"Only on the cheek," she said.

He obliged, and quickly left the room, closing the door behind him. Helen remained seated until she heard the final catch of the latch, she crossed the room to pour cold water into the bowl. She dipped her hands into the soothing water, rubbed them slightly, and patted her cheeks. Then she dampened another cloth and washed her private parts.

She planned to write a few letters, read for a while, settle her accounts with Mrs. Townsend, eat a light breakfast, write more letters, and schedule the rest of the day.

Helen's literary enticements flattered, cajoled, and teased, all of them framed to add an aura of romance, sophistication, and refinement to her relationships. Her clients loved her sexual freedom, and in bed they wanted the full dimension of vulgar abandon: no apologies and no excuses for fellatio or crouching over their faces and urinating on them. But outside of bed, they wanted sentiment, mystery, poetry, and delicate titillation. Helen liberally quoted Horace, Ovid, and the romantic poets. Occasionally she used French to punctuate her worldliness. She offered a fantasy of refined sexual congress, and her clients responded with effusive replies and gifts . . . plenty of gifts. Often Helen resorted to whining if not begging for a letter or a return visit; but to her this was only another strategy, never a debasement.

She would not write to Billy Attree for at least three or four days; she did not want him to think she was too eager. Replying to a letter received the day before from another man, she wrote:

My dear sir, allow me to say dear, for I assure you are so to me. I think of nothing but you. You alone of all the creatures of your sex, by whom I am surrounded, have evinced the least spark of real sympathy with my feelings, the least pity for my faults and misfortunes. You think I am willing to believe that a woman may cast away "the immediate jewel of her soul," without becoming fully depraved, or entirely losing the feelings and characteristics of her sex. Think, then, how anxious I must be for your society, and if you have the least spark of compassion for me, come and see as often as you can. You do not know what a pleasure your acquaintance is to me. I shall always look upon it as the brightest spot in the latter years of my existence—a single oasis in the vast desert of wretchedness, shame, guilt, blighted prospects, and perverted powers that I am compelled to call my life. Come and see me as soon as you can. I shall expect you every evening. Yours, truly and forever, if you please, Helen.

As usual, the words flowed freely. They captured just the right tone for this particular man. He needed to be her savior; she needed to play the victim. She didn't reread the letter when she finished it, so satisfied was she during its composition. She simply folded the two sheets and sealed them with wax.

She then started another letter; it was still early.

The sound of hymns coming from the street interrupted her schedule. Her room was at the front on the third floor, and she pulled back the drapery to take a look.

On the other side of the street kneeled a cluster of women dressed in black or dark grey, as if they were attending a funeral. But they sang loudly and with gusto, their eyes aimed upward to the skies, or at the very least at the top of the building across from them. All held hymnals with both hands, and they projected their words and music with clarity and the perfect blend of high and low voices, a mass of sound only possible with practice. A tall man who didn't sing or conduct stood behind them; he too looked up to the top of 41 Thomas Street, and Helen instinctively stepped back when she recognized him. She didn't want to believe it, but there he was—the Reverend John R. McDowell, surrounded by members of the New York Female Moral Reform Society, his latest venture. She remembered her encounter with him at the Park Theater and her promise to not take him so seriously.

She had heard about these visits to houses in the Point and the Hook, and was not surprised by the reception. McDowell and his associates faced threats and curses and had stopped going there, according to the *Sun*. But Helen hadn't anticipated that the better houses would be his next target. Now she felt personally affronted when she saw McDowell and his associates singing, praying, and reading scripture at her very front door. How dare they come here?

She quickly dressed, putting on a loose outfit without all the required undergarments, and went downstairs to confront them. She didn't consult Rosina or any of the other girls, or think about the possible negative ramifications. She was on a mission; she had to make them shut up and leave.

When she came out, holding a shawl over her shoulders to counter the damp air of the early morning, the group suddenly stopped and scrambled to its feet, faces stricken with wonder and revulsion, eyes bulging as if a naked woman had crossed the street.

"Just what do you think you are doing here?" Helen demanded, standing in front of the women who closed ranks as if to protect McDowell behind them. She directed her rebuke to him, glaring at those still gentle gray eyes. His slight smile enraged her even more.

"If you think your self-righteous hymns and Bible reading are going to frighten us and make us hide in our rooms, you are mistaken. We are not going to hide and quake, or be shamed into stopping what we have freely chosen to do. This is a free country, and, and, and . . ."

Helen was so angry she started to sputter. Taken aback by this rare loss of words, she stopped her tirade, feeling nakedly exposed and foolish. She took a step back and looked distractedly to the pavement.

"Miss Jewett, the constitution also grants us the freedom to protest this house," said McDowell, supremely calm and unfazed. "Today our visit is not about *you*, but about your customers. We are here to discourage *them*."

Helen suddenly recovered. His words were like cold water tossed into her face, and her entire body now seethed with anger.

"So why don't you go where true evil exists?" she yelled. "Why don't you go to Wall Street, or the harbors and the churches that support the cruel enslavement of millions? Why don't you go to City Hall, where corruption is rife, where Tammany Hall has this city in its grip, where democracy is a sickening sham? Why not *there*?"

"One evil at a time, Miss Jewett," McDowell replied, still looking directly at her. His associates had maintained their silence absolutely, as if it too had been carefully rehearsed.

Helen could feel tears of frustration come to her eyes, and before she could give him the pleasure of seeing them, she shouted, "Damn you, and damn you all," and quickly turned away to cross the street.

"God bless you, Miss Jewett," said McDowell. With that cue, the ladies returned to their knees and resumed their pious song.

Once indoors, Helen Rosina and a small group of girls who had watched the confrontation from the windows of the front room; they were all awakened by the choir, but had chosen to stay indoors.

Obviously the girls had been instructed to say nothing, and Rosina spoke only briefly.

"My dear Helen, we do not need a defense or a vulgar display of loyalty. If they return in the future, I would appreciate it if you would remain inside. I'm sure the mere sight of you confirmed their worst fears. Now let us all go about our business. It's Sunday."

As usual, her words were gently spoken and so oddly calming that Helen, usually quick to argument, could only say, "Yes, Ma'am."

Save for one, the others either returned to the parlor, walked to the back of the house, or went upstairs to their rooms. Alice Bentlow, a thin, almost frail girl who was the house's most recent acquisition, waited until everyone was out of sight, gently touched Helen's arm, and whispered, "Oh, Miss Helen, that was *extraordinary*, just extraordinary. I so admire what you did. I just had to let you know."

"Thank you," replied Helen. "But we will not mention this again, agreed?"

"Agreed," Alice said, nodding her head.

Helen started up the stairs, already planning to drop a note to Billy. She could not wait three days, as she had originally determined. He had to know about the incident on the street; and of course, he would write about it in the *Transcript*, and enhance her notoriety.

She would omit a few details, especially her incoherent loss for words and the gentle rebuke from Rosina. But the essential theme of her dramatic narrative would remain. She appointed herself as the defender of the free choice of women, and pledged, as she sat at her desk and imagined her own crusade, to oppose with absolute vigor and conviction the pious intolerance of self-righteous preachers and their duped female associates.

When she told Billy her story he listened, enraptured; and, as she had expected, he recounted it in the pages of the *Transcript*.

Then he made a request. He had a small group of friends who wanted to come see her, to receive lessons about pleasing women, and even to watch her demonstrate her skill with at least one of them.

"They would pay handsomely," Billy said.

"No," Helen replied casually, offering no explanation.

"Surely such a suggestion can't shock you? There are those who ask for all kinds of acts."

"No," she repeated.

"Business is *business*."

"You can't tell me what to do, Billy. Besides, you need me more than I need you."

"And how is that?" he asked, raising his voice. "New York would not know about you if I didn't write about you."

"Without an interesting subject, Billy, you would have nothing to write about."

"But . . ." he objected.

"You can go now, Billy. I don't have to explain everything to you, and you will never know everything there is to know about me. Secrets add to the mystery, and mystery adds to our pleasures."

"Maybe." Billy sounded petulant for the first time since she had met him.

She reached for her dressing gown, and said, "It adds to *mine.*"

She enjoyed Billy's company, but she wanted to make it clear: No man, or woman, for that matter, was going to dominate her. Certainly, no man or woman was going to tell her how she should feel, or what she should do.

No one—not Billy, not Reverend McDowell, not his female supporters, not her customers or the police or the *Sun* or the state legislature—could force her to mistrust her own thoughts and feelings. And certainly no one could force her to accept that cruel, naïve, and simplistic doctrine of moral perfection that twisted everyone's spirit and demanded a hatred for the body and sexual pleasure, as if life was a trap of endless misery.

Helen walked to the small table in the center of the room.

"To freedom," she said, raising her glass in a toast. "Billy, to freedom."

Startled, he stared at Helen, obviously waiting for clarification.

Helen smiled but refused to look away or explain.

Billy finally whispered, "To freedom," as Helen approached him with her glass.

She gave him her glass and looked directly into his eyes.

"To freedom," he said again, looking up at her and smiling as if he understood the promptings of her heart. "And to you, my friend," he added. "To you."

Gently, she kissed him. "Goodnight, Billy, dear friend."

"Goodnight," he replied, "and please accept my apology for . . ."

"I accept," she said.

McDowell and his companions never returned to 41 Thomas. But they went to other brothels, noting the names of recognized patrons and listing those names in *McDowell's Journal* editorials that branded brothels as "stagnant pools of moral filth" and called for the execution of their owners.

Customers became more discreet, but business boomed.

Chapter Fourteen

As if to accentuate the full embrace of her moral freedom, Helen was now ready to see the Five Points accompanied by her newest friend and best publicist. That indefatigable guide to his adopted city, and especially its darkest corners, would not have to wait four or five days for a letter, her usual ploy for generating hope and suspense. She would invite him that very day. She anticipated no objections to her request. Billy was a smitten man.

The tour of the Five Points came within three days. The cloudless sky shimmered like the cleanest glass and a slight breeze caressed her skin. It was a perfect day for an excursion into the very bowels of vice and corruption.

The Five Points was one of the city's most popular attractions. Tourists from Battery Park to London strolled the streets, often accompanied by an armed patrolman. Nevertheless, Lucy, now working at Rosina Townsend's after being dismissed by Ann Welden for defending Helen in the Park Theater incident, remained appalled about the planned tour. Even though a man would accompany Helen in a hired carriage, Lucy pressed her case against it.

But Rosina preferred philosophical detachment even as she had misgivings about Helen's curiosity, and she refused to offer even a hint of sympathy. As far as Rosina was concerned, Lucy was the worst kind of snob, a successful child of the slums who had stepped out of the gutter into better housing because she had gifts prized by men with money to spend. With a wry acceptance of folly and other frailties, Rosina told Helen about Lucy's interventions and asked for her indulgence: "She is a sweet girl, but snobbery is the disease she brings from Waters Street on the Eastside. Fortunately, it's *not* fatal."

At two that afternoon, the driver arrived. He was a middle-aged man with huge hands, thick arms, and a stomach bulge that pressed against his slightly soiled shirt. After he helped Helen into the carriage and before mounting his front seat, he asked Billy for the destination.

"The corner of Park and Baxter," Helen said crisply.

The driver winced, his former smile now cast in a deep scowl.

Helen bristled and exclaimed, "Sir, are you going to take us there or not?"

Billy smiled but said nothing. He was enjoying this little drama. He had hired the driver, telling him to come to the brothel without specifying other details. Drivers often refused to enter the Point unless the fee was high enough. Billy watched the exchange, eager to see how Helen would prevail. The driver hesitated, and Helen pressed on: "You will have more money than you had before arriving here. Can you afford to be so particular?"

The driver looked down and mumbled his reply. "There have been robberies there in broad daylight; those people know we sometimes have money with us."

"Then drive on when a crowd gets too close," Helen argued, so exasperated she now had a headache. She rarely had headaches, and believed them to be a mere affectation of the silly and the weak. Paulina Weston often retired to her room complaining of them when domestic life became too complicated. Surprised by the sudden pain, Helen put her hand to her forehead and closed her eyes. Finally, she exclaimed to Billy, "Say something. You hired this fool!"

"Helen, are you ill?" asked Billy, gently touching Helen on the arm.

"No!" Helen replied, her eyes still closed. "Broadway, sir. Now!"

"Yes, ma'am," said the driver, as if snapping out of a trance. He mounted his seat with alacrity and said, "We will be there shortly. We'll take Thomas going east, cross Broadway, and go south on Orange."

The ride was only a matter of three city blocks, but after crossing Broadway and passing through Center Street, they were in a neighborhood dank and dark, its rows of wooden apartments, bars, shops, and dance halls sagging from age and grime under a merciless sun that exposed every detail of rotting neglect, its streets packed with white, black, yellow, and mulatto men, women, and children who scurried from corner to corner like rats utterly oblivious to danger. Helen could not believe she was in the same city. The noise was deafening—the noise of fights between men, men and women, women and women, packs of children attacking a single adult like frenzied ants; the sickening sound of drunks vomiting into the gutters; the profane cries of public fornicators, half naked and obviously enjoying the spectacle. Street vendors peddled oysters, hot yams, and roasted peanuts; street singers shouted patriotic and obscene ditties; tumblers and jugglers, bagpipe players, and dancers eager to show off their skills thronged the streets. But what overwhelmed Helen the most was the stench.

Years of garbage tossed into the gutters, years of rain and snow mixing with horse urine and feces, and years of festering piles allowed to grow into small mountains on street corners had produced a putrid layer of muck sometimes two or three inches thick. Either caked by the sun in hot weather or distilled by rain into oozing slime, this layer touched everything and everyone, making the Five Points a gigantic cesspool.

"We can't stop here," muttered Helen, holding a cloth to her nose and mouth as she shook her head. "We need to go home."

"But we just got here," Billy protested half-heartedly.

"Please," Helen said, her eyes stricken.

"Driver, please do as the lady asked," said Billy.

"Of course, sir," said the driver, unable to hide the relief in his voice.

"We'll be back at the house soon," said Billy, surprised by Helen's anguish. He thought she was made of sterner stuff.

When they returned to Thomas Street, Helen offered only a perfunctory goodbye before leaving him at the door. She immediately went up to her room and avoided any inquiries from Rosina or the other girls who usually gathered in the rear parlor during the afternoons when they had no other plans.

What in heaven's name was I thinking? Helen thought as she rushed upstairs.

She had to take off her clothes, remove every single stitch of cloth, including her bodice and pantaloons. She had to wash herself, take a sponge and moisten her skin even under the layer of clothes that protected her from the dust and dirt and whatever else traveled in the air and possibly infiltrated the pores of her endangered flesh.

I will never go there again, she vowed. *Never.*

And I will do whatever it takes to never have to live there.

But the silent declaration was not enough; as if needing to punctuate her resolve with repeated and harder application of the wet towel to her skin, Helen rubbed herself again and again. Tears came to her eyes, tears of frustration that surprised her.

Will I ever feel clean again? she wondered. *Will I ever forget that awful smell?*

She tried to hold on to memories of her first view of the harbor and the ocean from Battery Park on an equally beautiful day with Lucy, when breezes from the south gently undulated the folds of dresses on the promenade, and seabirds flew overhead as if messengers from beyond the horizon, hovering and squawking above the heads of the men, women, and children who serenely walked below without bothering to look up and acknowledge the noisy, insistent appeals for their attention.

Everyone looked out into the harbor, smelling the salt in the air, feeling the light breeze against their skin, and shielding their eyes against the glare of the afternoon light. Even as she walked arm in arm with Lucy and took note of the furtive but appreciative glances from husbands and fathers busy with children, Helen looked to the sea, watching the rolling waves, and felt the freedom of being at the edge of the world, her back turned away from the dark wood and stone of Manhattan, the clamor of the packed thousands, the dust and mud of Broadway and Wall Street, the incessant demands of a city marching inexorably to the north and west away from where it all began with wooden ships searching for gold and a passage to India. Long ago someone had the good sense to set aside land for Battery Park, and like many New Yorkers, Helen fell in love with this narrow field of tranquility and longed to return to it whenever she began to forget the bright promise of the endless sky and sea.

The smell of the harbor was now a distant memory; only the stink of the Five Points remained, a foul reminder of an imperfect love.

Billy Attree also loved New York, but the depth of the city's hatred for colored people undermined its claims to civic greatness. He had seen enough to know that every city had its saints and sinners, fools and knaves, ugly and beautiful. But even intelligent and successful New Yorkers seemed to have a blind spot in matters of race, and from their mouths flowed utter nonsense. Billy had been reading the most recent anti Negro, anti abolitionist fulminations of James Watson Webb, the editor of the *Courier*, and wanted an answer to a fundamental question: why did successful and powerful white men fear an exploited and oppressed group, and their scattered abolitionist supporters, so much?

Ugly rumors were rampant, spreading from saloons, brothels, grog shops, dance halls, and theaters: Abolitionists were asking daughters to marry negroes. Prominent New York abolitionists—probably Arthur or Lewis Tappan, or Theodore Wright—were adopting black children. Abolitionist ministers were conducting interracial marriage and encouraging negroes to parade on Broadway, assume "airs," and dress like dandies to attract white lovers.

Billy reported all of the rumors to Helen, and she dismissed them all as "absolute nonsense." She laughingly observed, "Can you believe such preoccupations? It seems that even the most squeamish and refined of people can talk of nothing but amalgamation and promiscuous couplings. Gutter talk everywhere, even in church. Isn't it strange?"

Secretly, the rumors and the threat of violence unsettled her, her bravado a mask to hide a rising fear that her association with abolition could be exposed. A mob could suddenly appear and harm her or anyone, as a group of men had beaten Julia Brown in her brothel. Helen represented a deadly combination, prostitution and abolition, and for the first time she could not sleep soundly, her sleep interrupted by sounds of the night. The squawking of night birds, the clatter of wheels against the cobblestones, the blowing of the wind seemed to signal the calm before the fury of the storm.

From her arrival in New York, Helen used every precaution to be circumspect and anonymous about her abolitionist sympathies. She told none of the women at the houses about her opinions or her donations, and she hired a negro messenger to deliver them to his own minister who, asking no questions, then passed them on to Lewis and Arthur Tappan.

A negro servant could be trusted, but Helen was not so sure about Billy or Dr. Rogers. She regretted telling them anything about her beliefs. Still infatuated, they probably would not say anything to compromise or endanger her deliberately. But all men were prone to slips of the tongue while boasting and drinking. One slurred, drunken detail could become a rumor passing through a neighborhood like a wildfire, and one rumor was enough to feed a mob.

She waited.

The storm arrived on July fourth.

Chapter Fifteen

Only after days of fistfights, brawls, looting, arson, armed assaults, inflammatory editorials, and murder could Billy understand what was happening to his adopted city. The truth angered and saddened him, for it seemed before that hot and humid July that the bright and shining promise of America lived in New York, this remarkable island that invited the world to its shores, calling every kind of man and woman to build a city unlike any other place on earth, its foundation enriched by the differences of its people, its culture united by the pursuit of money, its packed streets humming with aspiration and ambition. The nation was divided, north and south, east and west, free and slave, city and country, but somehow, with a breathtaking display of sheer will, New York had managed to unite hope, greed, and lust in the very air its people breathed, and made everything new under the sun.

Like most immigrants, Billy had succumbed to an alluring dream, the *idea* of a New York where everything was possible, where everything was permitted. But now he realized that the spectacles he sometimes wore had partially blinded him, allowing him to see what he wanted to see and ignore what didn't fit.

He had come to accept that freedom permitted raw, undiluted hatred, but he was unprepared for the ruthless planning and organization it inspired.

After three days of rioting, flamed by anti-amalgamation rants from the *Courier's* James Watson Webb—as mobs attacked the Chatham Street Chapel during an interracial celebration of the fourth of July, assaulted negroes in City Hall Park, plundered the house of Lewis Tappan on Rose Street, and looted a Presbyterian Church on Spring Street—it became clear to Billy that the rioters, large in number, were organized, with coordinated plans and specific targets. From direct observation and personal interviews, he determined the basic facts of the urban war: First, the rioters concentrated on the houses, businesses, and churches of white abolitionists and "amalgamators." Then they attacked the churches of prominent black abolitionists. Finally, they ransacked negro quarters. Ringleaders swore oaths to create small units at night and met with larger groups at a rendezvous point, forming a square with the weaker men armed with stones in the middle and the strong men armed with clubs on the outside. Then they moved on to destroy the designated site.

Mobs were everywhere, at the Bowery Theater, the Tappan Store on Pearl Street, and the house of the Reverend Cox of Laight Street Church, City Hall Park.

Earlier in the day, organizers had sent messages that white families in the Five Points should light candles and stand at the windows so that rioters would bypass them, as the Jews in Exodus had used light to avoid the wrath of the Lord when He sent pestilence to Egypt.

With one of these handbill messages in his pocket, Billy rushed to the Five Points. Before he even entered the section, he could see the orange glow of flames and hear the sickening chorus of groans, screams, and profanity; the wailing, crying, tearing, shouting, and cursing; and the crashing of fallen brick, stone, and wood.

As planned, the houses with dark windows on Mulberry Street were sacked, burned, or torn apart. Black residents who ran into the streets were pummeled with fists or beaten with sticks. Those who could escape ran off, shouting, "The watch house!"

Billy followed the mob, moving northwest to Orange Street, where rioters broke all the windows and tore down the sign of the African-American Mutual Relief Hall. John Rollonson's porterhouse at 57 Leonard Street was next. There the mob tore down the bar, broke all of the decanters and glasses, stole money and jewelry, and broke all the furniture in the basement.

"Why aren't they fighting back?" one young man asked Billy, still the uninvolved observer. No one seemed to care that he didn't throw a single stone or break any furniture.

Billy watched but did nothing except note names, addresses, and other details for the next edition of the *Transcript*. He had a job to do.

About ready to pull down the Arcade, a saloon at 33 Orange Street, and the Swimming Bath bawdy house at Number 40, the crowd stopped after a white street inspector named McGrath spoke, assuring the men that every Negro would be out by noon the next day. The crowd gave three cheers, and some men at the front shook McGrath's hand, and then moved on to 56 Orange, where they broke all of the windows and the furniture inside, and pummeled several men.

When the mob arrived at Thomas Mooney's barbershop at 87 Orange, Mooney fired three times into the crowd, wounding one man, who slumped to the ground before his stupefied companions.

"The nigger shot a white man," said a startled young man.

For a moment, everyone froze, stunned by a vision of the impossible: A negro was fighting back when so many others had abandoned their homes and business without resistance. There was a collective intake of breath, everyone waiting for a cue to attack or retreat. The matter of race and masculinity, though unspoken, thickened the air, already rank with the smells of gunpowder, smoke, and cheap whiskey.

Then someone grumbled about "uppity niggers," and suddenly the men backed off and moved on to St. Philip's African Episcopal Church on Center Street, where they demolished the organ and almost everything else.

The police and guards never bothered to enter the area. They had been ordered by the mayor to protect more important properties elsewhere.

The sounds of looting and screaming could be heard for blocks. The glow of the fires radiated the night sky over the city, spreading fear and anxiety everywhere. Fire was everyone's deepest fear in a city of wood and brick. There had been too many disastrous fires already in Manhattan's history.

With reinforcements from Albany finally patrolling the streets, shops and stores, especially those west of Broadway and north of Houston Street, remained open; and brothels continued to do business, discreetly receiving selected rioters who, after a day of looting, had money to spend and energy to burn. Brothel doors were not open to the general public for fear that mayhem was contagious. Groups of drunken men could easily turn on other targets.

Helen entertained no customers during the riots. She stayed in her room, reading and writing letters and waiting for Billy. After days of observing and writing, he would have much to tell her.

In the meantime, the city witnessed a flood of disclaimers and summary judgments. The American Antislavery Society posted handbills throughout the city declaring that it had no desire to "promote or encourage" interracial marriage. It opposed resistance to any laws, and had no intention to dissolve the Union.

Except for the *Sun* and the *Transcript*, all of the New York newspaper denounced the abolitionists and blamed them for the riots. As usual, James Watson Webb in the *Courier* did not even try to hide his smug satisfaction with the turn of events. He wrote: "On the whole, we trust the immediate abolitionists and amalgamators will now see in the proceeding of the last few days, sufficient proof that the people of New York have determined to prevent the propagation among them of their wicked and absurd doctrines."

Billy grunted his disgust. "Can you believe the man?" he asked. "He instigated it all. What a hypocrite!"

"He hates honesty," replied Helen, trying to be light and casual, masking her growing fear.

"But all this prattle about the uprising of the people. What bullshit! The abolitionists have it right. Webb and his kind stirred up the mob. But they are wrong about who's in the mobs."

"I hear that all the gangs of New York—the Bowery Boys, the Atlantic Guard, the True Blue Americans, all of them—roamed the streets looking for colored people," Helen said earnestly, trying to make sense of the chaos. "There aren't enough jobs, and white laborers don't want the competition."

"I was *there*, remember? And I covered the police courts as well," Billy replied, peeved by her assumption of labor competition. "Damn, I was tired, running around to see what was happening, and then having to get to the court early in the morning to check on the arrests. And standing there before the court judge were clerks, bankers, lawyers, merchants, shopkeepers, and politicians, gentlemen of property or standing hardly threatened by draymen, stevedores, or cooks. And all the masons and bakers arrested had nothing to fear either; none of those jobs will ever be open to colored people. Hardly rabble, or scum. But what's most galling to me is that so many were arrested but not booked. Even some who posted bail *never* had trials. And many of the names I had never got listed in the papers, certainly not in the *Courier*, not even in my own. So many got away with destroying colored homes and shops."

"Did anyone die?" asked Helen.

"No. It could have happened, but the real message was clear: We want your balls. They didn't *need* to kill anybody. They just wanted to destroy any sign of success or independence. Damn, I hate the injustice, the lying, the corruption, the bribery. Isn't there enough money for everybody? Do you have to be rich and also a lout?"

"Arthur and Lewis Tappan are rich, and they are not louts."

Helen immediately regretted her comment. Billy knew her abolitionist sympathies, but she had never directly linked them to the Tappans, who were still receiving her anonymous donations. Even a name, mentioned only once, could now ignite a mob.

"Do you *know* them?" asked Billy, his eyes bright with curiosity.

"No," said Helen, shaking her head to punctuate her denial. She had never met them. "I know about them only by what I read. Even so, I was horrified when people attacked Mr. Tappan's house and his brother's store."

"Fortunately, Lewis Tappan sent his family to Brooklyn, and his brother armed his clerks at the store. Webb was there, egging them on. But I'm going to make sure that people read about what really happened to those poor people in the Five Points. Many fled the city. Others were left with *nothing*."

"I'm moving," Helen suddenly announced.

Reminded that she had to avoid the danger of destitution at all costs, she had to find refuge at a safer brothel, a brothel further removed from the violence, even by a block or two. It didn't make sense, she knew. But somehow the thought of change reduced the pressure of her unreasonable fear and, for now, that was all that mattered. Besides, the same men who frequented 41 Thomas could and would do business at another address.

"I know your self-regard defines you, but this is *all* you have to say after hearing of the suffering of others?" Billy asked.

Billy had a way of provoking her, and she replied hotly, "The suffering is real, but I don't need to hear about true suffering in a haze of journalistic sentimentality. And please, spare me any claim to the literary gifts or charms of the *Transcript* or any other penny paper for that matter. These are penny papers only, just penny papers, not Addison and Steele, or Doctor Johnson."

"I know that," said Billy, "and your tongue cuts as deeply as the best in our business."

"Oh never mind." Helen was bothered by the look of hurt in his face; even cynics like Billy Attree, all disappointed idealists, apparently had professional pride. "I will be going to Madame De Berry's at 128 Duane. Philadelphia House she calls it."

"But why are you moving?" Billy insisted.

"I just have to," said Helen, not wanting to explain what seemed foolish, irrational. The effort would be utterly useless.

"I will follow you there," Billy said. "To Mrs. Berry's, not to Philadelphia," he added with a slight shudder, his snobbery deeper than any native's. New York was the greater city, of course.

"I should hope so," replied Helen.

"Will Mrs. Townsend react poorly? You don't need another incident like the one with Mrs. Welden."

"I don't think so. Mrs. Townsend is agreeably pleasant about almost everything."

"Even with the loss of profit?"

"From the beginning, she didn't demand that I stay or make any promises. I am committed to leaving, no matter what her opinion. This is not indentured servitude."

When Helen informed Rosina about her decision, Rosina only smiled and said, "Helen, my dear, you are a girl on the rise. Remember, I didn't hold you to empty promises, and Mrs. De Berry's house is a fine one. Not as fine as mine, of course. But perhaps you will find happiness there at Philadelphia House, where, as far as I know, *brotherly* love does not flourish."

Chapter Sixteen

Philadelphia House was not as grand as 41 Thomas Street, but Helen found other satisfactions there and never regretted her move.

A narrow Federal-style house, it stood in a row on the south side of Duane between Chapel and Church. To the east, near Broadway, was a brewery; to the west, the African primary school, where many of the children living in the Fifth Ward on Thomas and Hudson Streets received their education; and across the street, a bar room run by an Englishman was a favorite spot for the "sporting men about town." Just one block to the west on Duane, near a small triangular park, stood the house of John Livingston, the wealthy owner of land and brothels throughout the city, adding luster to the compact and integrated neighborhood.

Although Thomas Blakely owned Number 128, the nameplate next to the front door said, "Mrs. Berry." An Englishwoman, Mary Berry called herself the "Duchess de Berry," or simply "the Duchess," and assumed airs that only the most pretentious could sustain. She spoke grandly, as if every pronouncement were for the ages, and cast her lifted double chin as for profiles on coins of a future realm. Helen liked her anyway. Mary's condescension was so wide in scope, she invited everyone to what she named "the party of my life," and she openly enjoyed the company of the women, no matter their age, who worked for her or came to visit. Jealousy never consumed her time or energy, so supreme was her lofty self-satisfaction. Her receptions and parties, large and small, attracted visitors who only had to pretend to be calling on a duchess in an imaginary chateau. It was a game, and Mary Berry enjoyed playing it with a zest so free of strain or longing that hundreds, including Helen, agreed to the rules.

Fantasy had its rewards, especially after a summer and fall of riots. The upheavals of July did not return, but race riots continued throughout the country. And because the Tappan brothers would not back down, the threat of violence hung in the air like white smoke that could turn at any moment into billowing black clouds.

Helen tried to dismiss all the blather and fulminations, but she continued to worry, fearing a conflagration that could sweep away the innocent, the guilty, the unsuspecting, and the ignorant with stunning indifference. Her fears were somewhat assuaged by the constant presence of Frank Berry, who was the only man known to live full time in a New York house of prostitution. He was not Mary Berry's legal husband, but she maintained him as guard, protector, solicitor, escort and pimp, and he was always ready to intervene when a customer became too loud and too drunk. Frank was a big man, tall and thick in the shoulders and chest, his ready grin both charming and deceiving. When confronting a lout, he smiled and spoke softly as he asked for calm and a quick departure; but with the first sign of resistance, Frank Berry unleashed his arms and legs like a giant engulfing his hapless victim. He was an indispensable man.

Mary Berry took his name, loved and respected him, but Frank Berry was never invited to Mary's annual Christmas Eve dinner, an extravagant affair she scheduled for only her "girls."

On Christmas Day the Duchess opened Philadelphia House to all, receiving visitors, men and women, from the neighborhood and brothels throughout the city, with one exception: Even the most successful black madams could not attend. Their presence disturbed the holiday spirit of too many. Mary called on her negro colleagues on New Year's Day.

But on Christmas Eve, the girls of Philadelphia House were expected to wear their finest gowns and bedeck themselves with their best jewelry. The house was illumined by hundreds of candles, and decorated with ribbons, candies, and red berry clusters. The Duchess hired two violinists and a pianist who had the opportunity to play an imported harpsichord available only once a year and rolled out by hired servants with a solemnity worthy of an ancient idol. Mary beamed as she carefully monitored the reactions on the faces of her girls, nodding her satisfaction when she noticed sufficient awe and delight.

Helen studied the others closely, calibrating the degree of her smile and refusing to simper. But she couldn't resist a spontaneous outburst of applause on seeing the instrument, and the other girls turned, surprised and curious, openly wondering if a line had been crossed. The Duchess signaled her pleasure, applauding too, and the other girls joined them. They didn't have to wait until after dinner to hear the musicians, as was custom. To Mary Berry, a concert before dinner, a selection of five carefully selected pieces, was the essential overture to the evening's central event—a grand dinner highlighted by her own toast and summative remarks about the past year.

This dinner was no glutton's paradise, with mounds of oysters, fish, chicken, potatoes, and slabs of mutton. The portions were small, cut into thin slices garnished with buttery sauces, nuts, onions, and berries. The veterans duly explained the Duchess' strategy: There would be no heavy meats and starches to dull the mind's receptivity to her holiday opinions. The ringing of a small bell would signal her call for everyone's absolute, undivided attention.

Maria Stevens, a veteran of three years at Philadelphia House, reported the shifting and unchanging character of Mary's address; it was an annual report with specific references to the year's major events and issues.

The year in review needed no melodramatic enhancements. The details were all too familiar, depressing, almost numbing, as the facts of riots, disease, political corruption, and protests accumulated.

Then the Duchess de Berry lifted her wine glass and declared, as she looked into the faces of the woman before her, personalizing her comments in the most direct way possible when speaking to a group: "You are my *girls*, my family of special *girls*, and I wish for you only the best that the coming year can bring. But the best must be firmly based on the lessons, however hard and pressing, of the past year. And 1834 was hard, indeed. But oh, the promises of 1835 can only surpass the year before, because progress is in the air, on the wind, pressing upward to unparalleled heights of achievement. To those whose eyes and ears are open, we are the wise and prudent women of a special island, our island, Manhattan, founded by men but sustained by women, whose toil supported the blood and tears of tested and tired hucksters and hustlers who had to find solace and comfort in our arms. *We* are the foundation of civilization itself. Our aims are equal to the claims of religion and the Merchant exchange. *We* are the engine greater than the steam marshaled by Mr. Fulton, for it is passion, the passion we celebrate in our rooms above, that comforts and then reinforces the economic, political, and social energies that compel men to do what they must do: make money and wage war. Whatever might be our indirect involvement in these pursuits, our involvements are limited by the restrictions imposed by men who are afraid of our intelligence and moral superiority, our compassion and endurance. The closure of the ballot box, and restriction on claims to personal property are their carefully chosen weapons. Nevertheless, and this is the essential and absolute exception, *we* are the true sisters of Gotham, our Manhattan, our promised land. *We* are the true goddesses, the royalty of the New World, as old as the services offered to man since the beginning, and as new as the youngest among you. Never forget this, my dear, sweet girls; whatever may be said about me and about you, no one—not the preachers from the heights of the highest pulpits, not the editors from the lowest penny papers, not the merchants from the toniest parlors of the mansions facing City Hall Park—no one can touch the core of our integrity. *We* are true to ourselves. We know why we are here, and there is honor is this splendid truth. And we celebrate our knowledge that integrity, believed to be the domain of only men, is our greatest prize, our highest virtue."

Helen could not believe her ears and instinctively looked around the table to see who might first respond with embarrassed gulps for air, tittering laughter, and then peels of cascading ridicule. But suddenly she knew that could never happen. She was sitting at a table of disciples and, once she recovered from the shock of her utter isolation, she wanted desperately to belong, to silence absolutely her critical contempt, to stifle the impulse to raise questions and find incongruities, to be just another girl in the all-encompassing embrace of the sisters of Philadelphia House. In a flash, she capitulated. And Helen felt, for the first time in her memory, a deep serenity. She looked to Mary Berry and to the girls to her right and left, and then to Maria across the table, and found tears and smiles, as if they all had heard the promptings of her heart and granted a silent invitation and benediction.

"You may applaud now," intoned the Duchess and everyone, including Helen, dutifully obeyed, their hands clapping with light, delicate taps as only the hands of true ladies could do.

———•———

When not performing upstairs in her room, writing letters to her favorite customers, or reading, Helen spent more time with her companions in Philadelphia House than she ever had with the women at her previous houses. The weather that winter was cold and forbidding, forcing most people to stay indoors and entertain themselves with games, gossip, singing, shared reading, and theatricals. Helen won accolades by reciting scenes from Shakespeare, assuming the voices of Rosalind, Juliet, Cleopatra, and Portia. She never boasted, and smiled delicately as she took her subtle bows, a nod of the head, and a deep but quick curtsey.

When it stopped snowing and the Battery and Broadway were cleared for pedestrians, Helen, Maria, and others promenaded on the streets in groups of two or three, arm to arm, looking into shop windows, buying clothes and trinkets, and attracting attention everywhere they went. Though men leered and women glared, Helen and her friends ignored them all, for they were not soliciting or trying to antagonize. The pleasure of each other's company was their only goal during these excursions. Trips to the Park and Bowery Theaters were also frequent; and on some occasions, determined in advance, the women transacted no business and gave their undivided attentions to the entertainments below. When Helen wanted to visit a museum and see an exhibit without the distractions of friendly gossip and comparing notes about handsome men, Helen she would ask Frank to escort her into places that barred unaccompanied women, it being assumed that women without male escorts had only sex for sale in mind. When Helen had to see the Chinese lady with the incredibly small bound feet, and reflect on the suppression of women, she asked the Duchess for permission to ask Frank. She readily consented.

"Of course, you're one of *my* girls," Mary said, repeating a declaration she made to every girl in the house again and again.

The highlight of the season was the Duchess de Berry's annual ball, one of several sponsored by prominent madams in the city to entertain and attract clients. But the Berrys' was the most publicized and the best attended. The Duchess had gifts for self-promotion unmatched by Rosina Townsend or Ann Welden. She even invited the city press, but only the *Transcript* dared to send a reporter, and Billy Attree came determined to give his readers every salacious detail and another glowing report on the charms of Helen Jewett.

Sitting on a raised chair in the front salon, the Duchess received Billy as an ambassador to an exotic kingdom, extending her hand for him to kiss and giving him a chance to bow his head. He knew what to do; he had done his research, and he stood at attention, silently waiting for her address. He grinned.

"Welcome, Mr. Attree, to our revels," said the Duchess solemnly. "I am counting on you to use your eyes and pen to our great advantage."

"Of that you can be assured," he replied.

"Some have suggested that, given the spirit of the times, I should have canceled this affair. But in dark times the sun is needed more than ever."

"All hail to the sun," Billy said, looking directly to her eyes.

"Of course, Mr. Attree, I am beyond blushing, but even I am not impervious to compliments."

"I don't flatter easily," Billy lied.

"Your praises, then, are even more valuable. And you will duly offer them in your paper, true?"

"How can I not?" he asked, looking aside through the side doors to the chandeliered salon filled with beautiful women and well-dressed men, and the sounds of quadrilles, the waltz and cotillion. "May I have the next dance?"

The Duchess arched her eyebrows. This request was clearly a violation of protocol.

"Mr. Attree, this is *not* my common practice."

Billy never stopped smiling, even at this apparent rejection, and replied, "But royalty has the prerogative of breaking the rules, and making new ones."

"I will be the talk of the town," she said, her voice soft with consent.

"And so will I," replied Billy, extending his arm.

They walked into the back salon, and all eyes turned to them. The music of a waltz stopped for an instant, and the Duchess raised her hand as a signal for the music to continue as she and Billy moved to the center of the floor.

"Spare no details," intoned the Duchess, as they moved to the rhythm of three-quarter time. "Your readers must *see* the red satin, the white watered silk, the embroidered pink with blond trimmings, the black and white lace. They will want to *see* my girls."

"They will see," promised Billy.

The lilting music continued, its strains filling the warm hall. At the end of the last chord, the Duchess thanked him for the dance, and said, "*All* of my girls have special charms, Mr. Attree. Remember this."

As if she had read his mind.

He protested gently, "Of course."

From the beginning he had intended to celebrate the charms of Helen, and give only a passing nod to the rest.

He nodded again and escorted the Duchess back to her throne in the front parlor, where she received more guests. He returned to the main salon, looking for Helen. He found her quickly; she stood out, dressed in a satin gown the color of emeralds, trimmed in white down, its low and tight bodice accentuating her breasts and the blue pendent jewel that rested on them. The contrast of her flawless white skin, the black hair pulled into a swirl of ringlets to the side and back, and the tint of her gown and jewelry made a breathtaking portrait, and Billy gasped, surprised by the survival of even a hint of wonder.

When she noticed Billy approaching, Helen immediately excused herself from her male companion, an older man of obvious wealth and standing in the community, and came directly to Billy, whispering, "You've made quite an impression for yourself, Mr. Attree. But please, I beg you to not use this occasion to mention me, or highlight me, or make me the one person that matters in your account of this ball. Do you understand?"

Now annoyed by another women reading his mind, he asked coldly, "What makes you think that among all this splendor, you should indeed stand out? Don't flatter yourself so brazenly, my friend."

"You don't understand," insisted Helen, drawing at his arm to emphasize her confidential confession. "We work together here, and there is only one standout— the Duchess. I am happy here, and don't want anything to spoil my relationship with Mrs. Berry or the girls. What you wrote before was a good thing for my reputation, and for developing my clients, but this ball can't be about that. Don't do it, please."

"What's this all about?" he asked, almost laughing at this desperate plea for restraint. "*You*, who scan rooms and streets for advantages like a predator for prey?"

Helen pulled her hand back, as if the skin of his arm had suddenly scorched her.

"That was cruel, truly cruel for you to say, Billy."

"I'm no judge or critic here, Helen, just another hunter, you and me, brother and sister."

"Don't say that."

"Incest repels you?"

"Have you no limits?" she asked, shocked by him for the very first time.

"I am dedicated to pushing them," he declared. "And my band of brothers, my club, will push the limits with me."

"Then I will charge accordingly," Helen replied, scanning the room again. "There will be no group rate."

Billy laughed and put out his arm at the sound of a delicate Ländler waltz.

"You see, Helen, we're alike. So let's celebrate our affinity, you and I, hunters together."

Helen took his arm, and replied with firm insistence, "I agreed to your request, and you will agree to mine. Do not mention me at this ball. Do not."

"Very well," he said, and they took the floor, smiling broadly and nodding their heads ever so slightly toward those who acknowledged the handsome couple. He kept his promise and didn't write about her *this* time.

Fortunately, Helen's career continued providing material for his press pieces. Whenever *The Transcript* reported more confrontations with unruly customers and the filing of charges against them in the police court, described her visits to city sites and cultural events, or even mentioned her sharp opinions about a variety of subjects, the issues sold out.

Then Billy went too far, and an aggrieved reader confronted him with a knife.

Chapter Seventeen

When Helen heard the news she rushed to New York Hospital, where Billy had been taken after a hasty crossing of the Hudson River.

When she saw his bandaged faced, she groaned and said again and again, "Oh my God, oh my God. What did they do to you? Oh, my God."

"My condition is grave," said Billy, sounding unfazed. "But I will recover. My doctors promise."

"What happened?" Helen asked,

"You remember John Boyd?"

"How could I forget? You made fun of him in *the Transcript* for having a working wife, and she was only my hairdresser. I warned you about taking on a Chichester gang member.'"

"He followed me on the Hoboken Ferry," said Billy slowly; the effort to talk caused obvious pain, but he persisted. "Can you believe it? John Boyd followed me to the Ferry after I passed his barbershop on the way to the caves in the palisades."

"Who was with you?" asked Helen, feeling a pang of jealousy. "Handsome single men don't go to parks alone, unless they intend to find someone there."

"Does it matter?" replied Billy, "Thank goodness it wasn't you. It was a romantic fling, and you wouldn't be found dead there anyway. Not your taste."

"Don't joke," Helen insisted. "Not now. He could have killed you!"

"It was a beautiful day. The view of the city was spectacular."

"Get to the point," Helen said grimly. Billy was unusually discursive. Was reliving that moment just too painful?

"He could have killed me, but he didn't," he replied." He was hiding behind one of the columns, and leaped at me from behind. I fell, and he kicked me and stomped me in the head and on the chest. He pulled that knife out of his jacket and made sure that I saw it, holding my face. Then he sliced it. He passed the blade through the left side of my nose, and I heard people scream. I felt this sharp pain and warm blood. I was screaming too: My face! My face!. There was a lot of blood. My companion ran out and came back with some other men. Boyd had run off by then. They carried me to a public house nearby. Doctors were brought in and did what they could to stop the bleeding. The first doctor said I had been stabbed in the brain, but I never lost consciousness in New Jersey. Here I fainted, thank goodness. Doctors are supposed to help, but the pain was too much, even for me, when they started working on my face. I screamed bloody murder again. I think I was louder here than before."

Helen reached for his hand, pressed it lightly, and asked, "Will there be scars?"

Billy's chest rose in an effort to laugh, but he couldn't. The pain in his face was too great. "Appearances always matter, don't they?"

"I didn't mean to suggest . . ." Helen withdrew her hand.

"I have the highest hopes that I will not *repulse* you."

"You can *never* do that," assured Helen, pressing his hand again.

"I have other charms," Billy asserted.

"Indeed," Helen replied.

"And from now on I'll wear a pistol for self defense," he continued. "So don't be disturbed when I start taking off my clothes and you see it."

"You have every right to carry one."

"He's now in jail but he'll get out, and I will be prepared. He'll never get close to me again, he nor anyone else."

"No one will ever get close enough to hurt you," Helen asserted, trying to bolster her own confidence.

Now Billy pressed his hand over hers, and added, "But close enough for other matters. I can still get hard."

Helen kissed him on the top of his head, and said, "Vulgar, as always. I will let you rest now. I will come again. We have so much to talk about."

"My recovery must be swift," Billy replied. "So much is going on, and I want you to meet someone."

"Another one of your sporting club members? So many of you are forming or joining clubs these days."

"Yes, but he's different."

"How different?" Helen asked.

"*Very* different. You'll see," Billy replied and said nothing more.

———

Richard Robison came to Philadelphia House with an introductory note from Billy, and when Helen saw him for the first time, she gasped. He was more than beautiful; he was exquisite, with fine porcelain skin and sapphire blue eyes. She wanted to see him without clothes as soon as possible. Surely his naked body would surpass the best ancient Greek statues.

Billy's note was characteristically brief. "Please accept my new friend, Richard

Robinson, arrived from Durham, Conn. As a member of my club, he knows of your charms."

"A friend of Billy's is a friend of mine," said Helen, sitting down in the parlor on a hot June afternoon.

"It's terrible, what happened to Billy," said Robinson, his voice soft, almost feminine in its lilting timbre.

"His doctors are amazed by the speed of his recovery. Soon you'll all be making the rounds."

"I have so much to see and explore," Robinson replied, his smile revealing even, white teeth.

Somehow the very word *explore* and the unwavering, direct look of his blue eyes stirred her longing. For all she knew, he could have been referring to the Battery, Trinity Church, Broadway, or the grog shops in the Bowery, but there was a leering hint of solicitation that only experience and context could explain. He was in a brothel, and men came there to conduct, eventually, only one kind of business. Given what he already knew, he surely understood the circumstances: He was not there to select her, she was there to select *him*.

That she'd made that selection the moment he came into the room was a problem. She could never appear that susceptible or so eager. Men were arrogant enough, and surely a young man from the country didn't need a bigger head made possible by easy capitulation; she wasn't a slut.

"Mr. Attree will be a splendid guide," she replied carefully. "Like most reporters, he knows all the right places to see."

"And all the *wrong* places," he added.

That one word, *wrong*, left a knot in her stomach. She shifted in her chair, trying to get more comfortable. The humidity of the afternoon didn't help, but she knew the difference between perspiration and the moisture between her legs. *Who is this man?* she thought. *How can anyone have this affect on me?*

She immediately stood, as if it to break some kind of spell. Robinson stood as well, and expressed his regret, "Oh, I'm so sorry that our time together has ended so abruptly. I hope I haven't offended you, or . . ."

Helen returned to her seat, shaking her head, and clarified her position. "Oh no, Mr. Robinson, you've not offended me at all. I was just so uncomfortable with the heat. New York in June is absolutely unbearable."

"Perhaps we should go for a walk," said Robinson.

"Oh no," said Helen, "We can't do that. The haze is so thick and gray, and the smell is ghastly. I hear that horses are dropping dead in the streets."

"Then we'll stay, if you will have me," Robinson replied.

Have me? Helen felt like she was about to scream. *Just stop talking. Please be quiet, at least for a moment!*

Reaching into his coat pocket, Robinson said, "Oh, I should not forget to give you this."

He pulled out a single, pressed rose, and whispered a line from Shakespeare as he presented it to her, "The rose looks fair. But fairer we it deem for that sweet odor which doth in it live."

Taken aback, Helen could only stare at the bud until she saw the dismay on Robinson's face and he said, lowering the stem, "I know it's only a single rose, and it's already wilting." And then he added quickly, quoting another line, "Would that I have some flowers of the spring that might become your time of day."

"Oh no, Mr. Robinson, no," Helen replied, shaking her head. "I was just surprised you know the Sonnets. I don't know anyone who knows . . ."

He interrupted, shaking his head, "I know only a few."

"But then you added a line from "The Winter's Tale"—would that I had some flowers. Hardly anyone knows "The Winter's Tale," Helen said, delighted but still incredulous.

"It's beautiful," he said.

"Like you," Helen replied.

Richard waited, sitting erect in his chair with his hands on both knees, and never looked away, a model of masculine patience. This gesture endeared him even more to Helen; but she did *not* want to make an absolute fool of herself.

"Where are you working? Who's your employer?"

"I clerk for Mr. Hoxie, on Maiden Lane."

"And where do you live?"

"In a boarding house, on Dey Street, Number 42."

"And your family? Do you have brothers or sisters?"

"My father owns land, several acres, and I'm his first son and eighth child, out of twelve."

"Twelve!" Helen cried. "Your poor mother!"

"Father had two wives. His first wife had six daughters, and she died. Then he married my mother, and had three sons and three more daughters. My full name is Richard Parmalee Robinson, Richard for my father and Parmalee for my mother."

"Her given name?"

"Cynthia, Cynthia Parmalee."

"Lovely," said Helen. "They must be a handsome couple."

"Why do you say that?" he asked.

She immediately regretted the compliment. It was another unavoidable reference to his beauty, and he *knew* it. Damn it, he was just another narcissist and expected her to praise him. Nevertheless, she found herself making an offering.

"It's obvious."

"A blessing and a curse," he observed. "Lord Byron understood."

She started. "Did Billy tell you about my interests?"

"Yes, he did," Robinson replied, "and *all* relationships are helped by common interests. I, too, admire Lord Byron. In fact, my journal, dedicated to my mother, opens with a quote from *Manfred*."

"What does it say?" she asked, testing the seriousness of that interest.

"'When these eyes shall be closed in death, the heiress of this book is my mother.'"

"Yes, that's from *Manfred*," said Helen, seeing the line in her mind's eye. "But why make a reference to death when you are so young? How old are you?"

"Eighteen."

"You have your life ahead of you." She was trying to align an apparently cheerful, confident position with his grim expectations; and he looked even younger than eighteen, like an adolescent in full flower, fifteen or sixteen at most. The eyes, though, seemed to age him—cobalt blue, intense, unblinking, they suggested the clear, cold pools of too many winters. "My dear boy . . ."

Robinson's face suddenly hardened, his voice thickened.

"Don't use that word. Don't *ever* use that word."

Stunned by this boy giving orders, she protested, "What word? *What* are you talking about?"

"*Don't* call me a boy," he answered, still with the tone of an affronted, powerful man.

Helen rose.

"Just *who* do you think you are?" she asked, looking beyond him to the door.

As if suddenly awakened from sleep, he started and stood up before dropping to his knees before her, a desperate supplicant unable to look at her critical face.

"Oh, I'm so sorry, Miss Helen. I didn't mean to offend you. You mean so much to me. I would never insult you. That word just burns somehow. Please understand. Please."

"Please get up Mr. Robinson. This is *so* unnecessary."

"I won't get up until you forgive me," he pleaded, his head still down.

"Mr. Robinson, you need to *stop* making demands, " she said, softening her tone. She was charmed by his juvenile devotion. "I forgive you."

He rose and returned to his chair.

"Thank you, thank you, Miss Helen. My life is vastly improved by you being in it." He grinned, the stress of the last few minutes disappearing in an instant.

Needing to end the interview, she offered her hand and said, "I will write to you." She always left the beginning of relationships to an exchange of letters when she chose a favorite. He was now on that short list. He was not at the top, of course . . . not yet.

"I am going out of town briefly," he said, standing. "My brother is ill, and I need to see him."

"I hope it isn't too serious," Helen replied, genuinely concerned, even as she wanted his undivided attention.

"We shall see," was all that he said about his brother's condition.

"I too will be traveling, to Philadelphia with the Duchess de Berry, and I hope to find your letters waiting for me. I will write, and you will have no excuse but to answer."

Suddenly mortified by her imperious tone, she winced. But she had to retain command, establish the rules, stay in control.

"I will write. I promise," he replied.

"I will see you on my return," she added, turning toward the door of the parlor. And then she heard the whispered words of Lord Byron coming from the thin, delicate mouth of that beautiful boy:

"She walks in beauty like the night/of cloudless climes and starry skies/and all that's best of dark and bright/meet in her aspect and her eyes."

"Oh, Mr. Robinson," she said, turning to him with her most open smile of the day, "You are shameless, absolutely shameless."

"When I'm going about town I will go by the name Frank Rivers," he said. "I prefer it, as a precaution. I don't want my father to hear about *everything* I do. People talk."

He said nothing more, nodded, and left the room. Staring at the door, Helen made another decision: She had promised to write, but she would not write first. Although smitten by the man, she had her pride. She would wait for him.

She didn't have to wait long. It was a brief note, saying hardly anything about her, more about the health of his brother. But it was sufficient proof of his interest, and she responded immediately, not waiting until the morning. She wrote by candlelight:

> *My dear Friend—You were truly kind to write on Monday morning, when your feelings must have been of a very painful nature, owing to the intelligence of your brother's illness. I sincerely hope he may recover, for you who are so kind and good do not deserve to be afflicted, and when I see you I really trust I may learn that he is convalescent. If you get in town and my letter in season, you will have arrived most opportunely, for then we may expect the pleasure of your company. However, if you do not, of course I shall see you immediately on your return, and you do not know how much I want to see you. Believe me, I think your acquaintance a very valuable acquisition, and should dispense with your visits with much reluctance and regret; and shall never voluntarily do anything that may render me unworthy of your confidence and esteem. Affectionately, Helen.*

Solicitous, but not preening. And the phrase "valuable acquisition" implied with sufficient delicacy her ultimate power.

He answered, scribbling on a rough sheet of paper an incomplete line from Keats: "Sweet hope, ethereal balm upon me shed . . . Yours, Frank."

A few days later, Helen wrote again, the rush of emotion inspiring her to use the word "love" for the first time:

I know not, my dear Frank, what your idea of this chequered life may be, but to me the current of existence would be but a black and sluggish stream, if love did not gild its surface and impel its tide. I anticipate that a further acquaintance with you will throw an additional charm over my time, and make the sands of life run more gaily before me. There is so much sweetness in that voice, so much intelligence in that eye, and so much luxuriance in that form, I cannot fail to love you. The pleasure I feel in your presence and your smile, speak of hours and nights of joy. I long to see you, to hear your conversations animate your features once again, but I must defer that pleasure to your next visit. I must now bid you an affectionate adieu.

As soon as he returned to town, he came to her and took her into his arms in the parlor, casting aside discretion and possible interruption.

"I am the happiest person you've ever met," he whispered.

She was thrilled by his exuberance, this young need to please her. However, she was startled by the size of his erection, apparent through the thin cloth of his trousers. It was huge . . . unbelievably huge. She was an experienced woman, but this was a shock.

"You deserve this," she said, enjoying the warmth of his arms, the press of his narrow chest against hers.

He kissed her deeply, then he stepped away, saying, "I want to see you tonight. I *have* to see you. When shall I come? I *need* to come."

"Come tonight," Helen said, smiling. "You'll be first, and the others will pale by comparison."

He laughed at the reference, throwing his head back as a triumphant accent to the obvious. "I can't wait," he said. "But I'll have to."

He rushed off.

That night he was patient, almost tender, as he prepared her for receiving him. She marveled at the size of his organ, but marveled more about his solicitude. He seemed to care about her comfort and sheepishly thanked her for not expressing concerns about potential pain. She closed her eyes, hoping that he would gently suck the nipples of her breasts, stroke the skin of her arms, and whisper just one endearment without asking. He didn't.

Instead, he offered a brief, perfunctory kiss before the delicate exploration of his fingers enhanced her receptivity. Penetration was slow and deep, and she waited for a reaction more powerful than curiosity—a sudden rush of overwhelming warmth, a stronger beating of her heart, an intimation of joy in the quick intake of breath, the sweat of her skin. She expected to be swept away, but instead she tolerated another juvenile performance, all thrusts and grunts and the usual blasphemies. Only *his* needs mattered.

Her silence alerted him, and he apologized. "I am sorry for not being the best. I'll try harder the next time."

"No," she said, amused by the allusion. She made sure her voice was light and uncritical. "*That* won't be necessary."

"Then what was it?" he asked earnestly.

"You never asked me what I wanted. You just assumed that . . ."

"I know what *I* want," he replied. "That's why we all come here."

She almost sat up, astounded by his brutal candor and yet still disappointed. Their meeting, surely, was not a transaction.

"Then what about love?" she asked.

He gasped and said plaintively, "I am such a stupid fool." He repeated the word "fool" four times and shook his head, accenting his displeasure. "Will you forgive me?"

"Of course, my dear . . ."

She caught herself before saying the hated word. But it was too late. He pulled his body away by no more than an inch, but he'd made his point, and now it was Helen's turn to apologize. "I'm sorry. It's a bad habit, and it won't happen again."

"Good," he said at once, then added with an impish smile, "Now what is it you want me to do? Teach me, and I promise to be the perfect student. Learning from the best can only increase my bliss . . . our bliss."

Helen appreciated the correction, now enjoying his adaptability. He could change in an instant.

"Let me show you what I prefer," she said, sitting up in bed and cupping her breasts with both hands. "Now suck, gently, delicately with your tongue."

Robinson responded eagerly, openly grateful that she had guided him, repeating his thanks again and again. Although she could not forget her initial disappointment, she enjoyed her new role.

Later they sipped wine and recited favorite lines from Shelley, Keats, Shakespeare, and Byron, alternating passages in a seamless invocation to love and its place in a universe where God had no dominion or even place and only passion mattered.

At last, Helen had found a partner, a true partner who understood the essential nature of love and devotion. He believed. He acted. And he quoted!

After he had departed that night, only a lengthy letter could adequately express her satisfaction:

My dearest Frank: You are one of the happy persons gifted with so pleasing a disposition that you seem born for the purpose of commanding love. Your graceful ease of manner renders you welcome in any society. You are so obliging that you always interest yourself in what others are saying to you; indeed, you forget yourself in order to oblige others.

I have met very few persons who could share in all my feelings so largely as _____, who was my earliest companion. When I walked, read, or conversed with him, I whispered to my heart, *If I could find one like him how much I should love him.* These are my earliest impressions. Lately, there has been in me a romantic feeling that wished for, but quite despaired of ever finding a beau ideal, until I met you. I feel that if devoted love or deep tenderness could make my heart happy, I was capable of imparting it, yet with all these ideas I did not entertain the thought that there could be found a living being who could love me, and now that I feel quite assured of being loved by the only one whom I value, I feel no scruple of pride in acknowledging it.

The greatest kindness you have ever conferred upon me is permitting me to have your miniature. It is ever before me, and as the representative of one so dear to me, I prize it. In my selfishness I could say to you, do not forget me for a moment, and believe me, as in truth, I am, devotedly yours, Helen.

After all these years, she had never mentioned Harlow Spaulding to anyone, but he had remained with her, a romantic ideal waiting for reincarnation. At last, she had found him. Even so, she had to protect Harlow, carefully withholding his name. Mail security was precarious, and exposure would surely humiliate him after all these years. He was probably married with children by now, and he could not afford any association, however old, with a well-known New York prostitute.

However, she may have ever felt about Harlow Spaulding or Frederick Fuller, her passion for Richard Robinson was consuming her, and she reveled in it. She was alive, truly alive, and the taste of life was intoxicating and very sweet.

And Billy, now fully recovered, wanted to know all the details.

"He's read all your letters to me," Billy said, opening with casual understatement in the privacy of her bedroom. She was receiving no customers that night; she was tired, wanted a break, and had to give Billy her undivided attention, surely deserved after his ordeal.

"Those letters are *private*, meant for him, and him alone," she replied, trying to suppress her disappointment at this violation of trust.

"He didn't think so. So how was it? What was it like?" he asked.

"What in heaven's name do you mean?" she replied casually. She looked to a letter on the nearby table, a calculated distraction.

Billy smirked. "You know *exactly* what I mean."

"Why didn't you tell me before?"

"I wanted you to have the same shock I had."

"You've *seen* it? When did you see it?"

"He had to show it for the club, as part of our initiation."

"Initiation?" Helen's voice rose. "For heaven's sake, you're not a Mason or a Templar!"

"What do you know about such things? These are *secret* organizations, for men only."

"There are no secrets, you should know that. Men talk, especially in this room. Just like you are doing now."

"I have to make sure all my club members are clean and without problems that could cause difficulties as we go about town. He says his endowment is a blessing and his curse."

Helen frowned. "As is his face and figure, his entire being, a point he never fails to make."

"But you *were* surprised? It's long even when soft, almost halfway down his leg, and he's cut like a Jew!"

Helen sighed, exasperated by Billy's unflagging vulgarity. He was incapable of refinement, sensitivity, or discretion, and embraced his ignorance with eager, almost malicious, glee. He liked to rattle her, as if on a mission. He hated pretense and putting on airs, and he seemed to enjoy making her a target. And yet, she could not help liking him. Yes, he was gross and unrefined; but he made her laugh, especially when describing crime, political corruption, and the entertainments of the backstreets and alleys of the city he obviously loved. His zest for New York and his own life, however difficult and dangerous, was beguiling, standing in stark contrast to the studied artificiality of her life in a "palace of love." Here was a man without illusions or pretense.

"Yes," she replied, knowing full well that Billy would elaborate with graphic details.

"First he told me his father gave up his foreskin to God as a sign of thanks, so impressed was he at the size of it, even when he was an infant," Billy said, grinning. "Then he told me his father had the foreskin cut off, to shorten it because it was too long, too ugly, obscene for a mere child to have such an appendage. He changes his stories. Sometimes I don't know *what* he is really about."

"But he is welcome in your group anyway?"

"Why, of course. He's charming, eager to please, and he raises the eyebrows of all the ladies. My word, he has this thin, boyish body, and he's hung like a horse! The ladies cry out sometimes, 'Oh, no, no, no, I'm not taking that in. Not me. Find someone else.' And then there are the proud, the curious, who say, 'I can take it. I like them big.'"

"Aren't you envious? Doesn't he make all the rest of you feel small?"

He had a ready answer. "It's just another difference, another detail, like height, hair color, the size of the ears or nose. Women are different, too, in countless ways; the more differences, the more interests."

"But *you* wanted to know how it felt to have him with me. *You* had to know. It matters, so don't pretend it doesn't. You are actually making him into the calling card for your little sporting club. For once, I think you have a blind spot, and you don't like to admit it. As for me, and for most of us, the heart matters more, *far* more. When he gave me his portrait, I cried."

He leaned forward, and Helen leaned back ever so slightly; she had gone too far, and for the first time, she was afraid that he might strike her.

He was her friend, but she now realized that anger coursed through the blood of *all* men. Even Jesus had turned over tables and forced the money changers out of the Temple.

Billy had stopped smiling and said, taking a deep breath, "Well, well, well. Aren't you all high and mighty now that Richard Robinson and love have entered your life? You read poetry together and quote Lord Byron back and forth, all the while pretending that you are so refined, so pure, so rarified, like spirits lost in some kind of dark cave trying to get out. Well let me remind you, dear friend, I know what it's all about. It's cock and balls, cock and pussy, lots of pussy, some games, some gambling, some drinking, and my cock up your ass, and don't you forget it."

Helen stood and pointed to the door. She was careful to not raise her voice, fearing that he would hear her absolute disgust.

"Billy, you may leave now."

He stood too, but he remained unappeased.

"There are other whores in this town," he shouted. "Don't you *ever* think I need you like you *need* him!"

Chapter Eighteen

Billy sent flowers to Helen two days later and asked her to join him on a trip to Niblo's Garden, an oasis of transplanted large trees, hanging cages full of birds, flower beds with strange but beautiful plants, winding pathways lined with statues and glowing glass lanterns above. On an entire city block patrons strolled through the grounds for fifty cents, or ate and drank at tables in latticed boxes surrounded by lush shrubs, petunias in riotous profusion, and deeply green, thick-leafed plants and flowering trees.

Billy regretted his earlier outburst, and he hoped that a promenade in the garden and a visit to the Joice Heth exhibit would help to restore their fractured friendship. His note to Helen directly apologized. "I am sorry for what I said, most sorry."

He could not admit his jealousy, or forget the scar on his face.

"Yes, come see me. I need to speak with you about *him*," she replied in her brief note.

Robinson had been sharing the letters Helen had written him. They seemed desperate, almost hysterical, as if love had deranged her. Billy didn't doubt her sincerity, even as she demanded Robinson's submission. But how could he tell her that Robinson received her letters with an odd, disturbing ambivalence? He seemed flattered, annoyed, triumphant, anxious, and skeptical as he read them to Billy, and declared his unworthiness and entitlement.

"She loves me," he told Billy, his eyes wide with wonder, "and I love being loved."

But he never said he loved her.

Robinson had intrigued him from the very beginning.

Walking into a saloon directly across the street from Philadelphia House on Duane Street, Billy had immediately noticed the handsome young man sitting at a table alone. He was drinking and smoking, as most men did in bars, saloons, clubs, and dives throughout the city. But these habits seemed odd and inappropriate for a beautiful boy dressed as a man in a dimly lit room reeking of tobacco, beer, and spit in overflowing spittoons.

Billy had introduced himself, extending his hand. "Billy Attree of the *Transcript*, police reporter and guide to New York's pleasures."

Robinson didn't hesitate taking Billy's hand. He smiled and asked, "Are you a confidence man? My father warned me of men like you. He even gave me a book to advise me."

"Mr. Alcott's *Young Man's Guide*, no doubt," Billy replied, pleased to be judged a threat. "It's selling quite well."

"Richard Robinson," he answered. "Richard Parmalee Robinson, and you didn't answer my question."

Billy had already formed his sporting club, and he was seeking a few more members. This boy could be the perfect calling card for group activities. *The ladies will swoon at the mere sight of him*, he thought.

"The city's being overrun by young, single men, and they need guides. I will leave it to you decide if I am your seducer," Billy said, enjoying his turn as the villain in a melodrama even the new *Herald* had noticed. "Welcome to the city of desire."

Robinson grinned and replied, "My father always said I was a devil. I eagerly anticipate a tour."

Billy ignored the almost childish attempt at baiting him with this casual reference to the "devil," and pursued another line of clarification.

"Including the Five Points?" he asked, testing Robinson's possible interest in its squalid pleasures—interracial sex, raucous dance halls, dog fights, boxing matches, and gambling and drinking until dawn.

"Of course," Robinson had replied, not once averting his eyes, a startling blue, crystalline and cold. "Everyone's heard about it."

"How long will you be in town?" asked Billy.

"My father sent me here. I need to grow up, improve my prospects, he said, even though I'll inherit thousands of acres in Connecticut when he dies. I'm the oldest son. But I've found a position with Mr. Hoxie in Maiden Lane. When Mr. Hoxie reports about the success of my prospects, I am expected to return. But," he said, grinning slyly, "I have no intention of returning. I will triumph here, as anyone with my obvious *assets* can do. I don't need my father's money . . . not here."

Billy started. He could swear the boy had become the seducer, his beautiful face a lascivious portrait of dangerous invitation. Billy was an experienced man, and this was the practiced look of child prostitutes, that unsettling attempt to integrate sexuality with the unblemished face of youth and innocence. City Hall Park had boys like him. Robinson was cleaner and better dressed, but the visual impression was unmistakable. Robinson was *not* innocent. At this point Billy could only manage a weak response, "I see," a sure sign of his fascination.

Then Robinson learned forward and asked, "Do you know the girl in the green dress?"

Surprised, Billy turned to look at Number 128 Duane through the front window.

"Yes, I do," he said turning back to face Robinson. "We're acquainted."

He'd almost said, "We're friends," but thought better of it. Full disclosure could wait.

"I want to meet her. I have been watching her. I even followed her once on Broadway. I hear she's *highly* selective."

"Yes, she chooses her clients carefully," observed Billy.

"I want to be more than just another client," said Robinson, his voice hardening, as if affronted by the mere suggestion of being ordinary. "I hear she has favorites, but I will prove to be irresistible, and her absolute favorite."

"What?" Billy felt his anger rising.

This virtual stranger, new to the city, had the audacity to presume Helen's favor. He could tolerate bravado; it was the common response of insecure young men eager to hide their fears. But Robinson's presumption was too much. Nobody could presume Helen Jewett's favor, not even Billy Attree.

As if slapped and suddenly awakened from a walking dream state, Robinson exclaimed, "Oh, oh. I'm so sorry. I didn't mean whatever I said. Sometimes I just get carried away, excited, and you know . . ."

He sputtered now, sounding mortified and remorseful, and shook his head again and again. "I shouldn't have said that. I *shouldn't* have. I shouldn't have."

He seemed like a boy suddenly caught dressing up in his father's best clothes, but Billy didn't know if he should chastise Robinson or forgive him. So he sought some kind of middle ground between outrage and fascination, saying, "Just be more careful. Some people will not tolerate or forgive such outbursts, especially Helen. So be careful."

"Thank you, sir," Robinson replied, eager and relieved. "I cannot thank you enough. Are you still willing to introduce me to her?"

Billy laughed, his anger suddenly evaporated by Robinson's eagerness to make a dream come true. Like a child promised a toy, Robinson could not forget his desire and would not relent.

For a moment, Billy withheld consent to prolong Robinson's agonies. But finally, he said, "Yes."

"Thank you, sir. Thank you," replied Robinson offering his hand. "You will not regret your generosity, and I won't forget it."

"You're welcome," Billy replied graciously.

"When will you introduce me?"

"Soon."

"How soon?"

"I will write a note within a day or so," said Billy, his tone sharpening as Robinson's demanding arrogance returned as quickly as it had disappeared moments before. "Come to my apartment and I will give it to you then. There you will meet some of my friends."

"Very well," Robinson replied, backing off.

"She likes poetry," said Billy, wanting to secure Robinson's gratitude and loyalty before introducing him to his club and its ambitious sexual agenda. "She reads it, recites, loves others reading favorites to her."

"Who is her favorite?" Robinson asked, his voice cold, as if he recognized Billy's ploy.

"Bryon," Billy replied, "Lord Byron."

"May I buy you a drink?"

"Certainly," said Billy, refusing to reciprocate. He needed to have the upper hand. There could be no gestures of equality.

Now that Helen had fallen for the boy with astonishing speed, Billy recalled that first encounter again and again, and he found justification for concern with every word spoken by the both of them.

Billy especially didn't like his own confusion. He took pride in his understanding of character, but Robinson baffled him. He had to get a handle on the younger man and force his unqualified submission. But his own need dismayed him. Clearly, he had advantages over Robinson, despite the boy's stunning beauty and family background. Billy had knowledge and experience, an obvious worldliness that Robinson admired and needed, especially in an environment as exciting, tense, and dangerous as New York's. Guide, teacher, club president, unofficial pimp, the opener of closed doors, friend of madams and the police, a keeper of city secrets, a constant threat to the powerful, a voice of the free press, this he was, and more. And yet Robinson stirred a disturbing unease. Robinson was beautiful and ugly, delicate and hard. His blue eyes told more than even Billy wanted to know.

How could he explain this to Helen, especially now that she was in love with the boy? What would be the point of telling her? Robinson was her favorite now. But soon he would be cast aside as just another failed john, and she would move on in her futile search for the perfect love. There was no such thing, but how do you say that to a woman as strong-willed as Helen Jewett?

Billy decided the best strategy was to wait and see what Helen had to say. He hoped that she could be distracted by other pleasures—the return of a friend, the latest news, a walk in a beautiful garden, and a visit to a popular exhibit.

But first Helen had to gently chastise him, and Billy accepted this as the price of readmission to her favors.

"What you said was *cruel*," she said, her smile a signal to Billy that she didn't mean to wound him. "Some wounds to the heart cannot be forgotten. Forgiven, but not forgotten."

"I understand," he said, nodding his head once, and moved on to his plans for the day. "I rented a carriage to get there."

"I'm not sure I will like it, the Heth exhibit that is," Helen said, putting on her gloves.

"Everyone in town is going, and you want to be able talk about it. You like a good show," Billy replied.

"This is more than an entertainment. Those posters make her out to be some kind of freak or monster."

Woodcut posters of Joice Heth were plastered all over town. Wearing a lacey bonnet and a simple dress, she had a deeply wrinkled, black face and nearly closed eyes, so closed they seemed white slits with a dot in the middle. Her thick right arm rested oddly across her chest, as though its weight had to be supported by her bosom. At the end of her arm was a hand with long fingers and nails like talons. The posters announced in bold letters that she was, "The greatest natural and national curiosity in the world."

"Do you believe she was really George Washington's nurse, as Mr. Barnum claims?" Helen asked, dubious and yet intrigued. "She would have to be really old."

"We'll go and judge for ourselves. We won't have to rely on hearsay," Billy replied. "And if we don't like what we see, we can leave and enjoy the rest of the gardens. Have you ever seen them?"

"No. No one has ever asked me. Men are so stupid. Can you imagine the amount of money Mr. Niblo would make if women, alone or in groups, could spend money there?"

"Yes, you're right, as usual," said Billy, enjoying again her sharp tongue and her tendency to cast aspersions against entire groups that irritated her. He had missed her company.

"But promise me we won't talk about *him* until after we see the exhibit and walk the gardens. I refuse to give *him* sway over my entire day. It's so beautiful today, isn't it?" Helen was determined to not utter even his name, as if it had the power to rend the humid air asunder.

On the road they talked of other matters, the fire on Fulton Street, the play about Mathias the Prophet at the Bowery Theater, and local politics. The election riots and the triumph of the Tammany Hall Democrats with a mere one hundred and eighty votes now inspired constant talk about corruption and political conspiracy.

When they arrived at the gardens, they proceeded immediately to the Heth exhibit. Helen didn't want to linger over the exotic flowers and delay her anticipated displeasure. She just wanted to get it over with.

Joice Heth sat in a chair on a raised platform in the main hall still filling with people.

"I want to get a close look," said Billy. "I don' think she's as old as that Barnum says."

Helen, holding him by the arm, hesitated. "I'm not sure that is necessary. No one is *that* old."

"We can hear what she has to say. I've heard she tells interesting stories about President Washington."

They pressed forward and found an obviously old woman, her dark skin lined like paper crumpled in a fist. Her eyes had almost disappeared, so deeply sunken were the eyeballs in her sockets. She had no teeth, obvious from her closed mouth and sunken cheeks. But her bushy grey hair was thick and made the bonnet, unable to contain it, seem silly and useless. Her right arm, supported by a delicate sling, lay across her almost flat bosom and seemed abnormally long, as her thick, dark fingers sported four- to five-inch brown nails.

Before the program started, before she even spoke, Joice elicited laughter and pointed fingers. Some children giggled and made disparaging remarks.

"Look at that black thing!"

"Boy, is she ugly, old and ugly."

"A black monster in a dress!"

Suddenly, Joice shouted, "Be away! Clear out, or I'll come after."

The children laughed even more but stayed to hear her tell her story about George Washington and the peach tree.

"And I raised him," she proclaimed in a high, strong voice, "and his truth is my truth, and he be raised by me to tell it. And it was peaches—no cherries, peaches."

At the mention of the president's name, silence fell and everyone listened intently, including the children, nudged and pulled by their parents as if in church. She was there in the garden, a witness to the cutting of the famous tree and young George "standin' up like a man and telling de truth." At the end of the story, everyone applauded.

Then Joice spoke to the nurse who accompanied her when she was before the public.

"I want somethin' t' eat," she said.

"Yes, Joice. I will give you a fine piece of boiled mutton."

"Stop," Joice exclaimed, "Mutton is de devil, and fit for nothin' but de dogs."

"I know, Joice, mutton isn't that good. But it will do for you."

Her voice thick with offense, Joice replied, "I am *Lady* Washington, and I want as good as anybody else gits."

The audience roared, delighted by Joice's spirited response and the reference to her title.

Helen was not amused and turned to Billy. "This in *not* right."

"What do you mean?" he asked, following her as she turned away.

"It's like we're at a slave market, just like the ones described by Mr. Garrison. This is no different."

"She's making a living, like the rest of us."

"She' s a slave."

"Not in New York. There are laws, and besides what is the difference between this and the annual balls where you all stand around to be ogled by potential clients, and arrangements finalized? What's the difference?"

"Look at these people." Helen waved a hand at the crowd. "They are here to stare, and laugh, and point, and feel superior. She is *not* a dog! She is a human being. And fifty cents, a bargain for the cost of humiliation."

"How do you know that? How do you know what *she* feels? She seems to be enjoying herself."

"It's a mask; she's putting on a show. She's hiding the truth, I am sure. And some of us would be surprised if she revealed her true feelings. I'm sure those so-called masters in Virginia were surprised when Nat Turner woke them up at night."

"Helen, it's not wise mentioning that name around here, even now."

"You, urging caution? *You?*"

"I just want to protect you. I can't help it."

"I don't need your protection."

"Please, Helen, let's not ruin the day with an argument. No more arguments. As you said, it's a beautiful day."

"You didn't ruin the day. Mr. Niblo and Mr. Barnum did that, and all these hateful people. What kind of people are we when we come to enjoy something like *this?*"

"Who is feeling superior now, Helen?"

"There are high and low rides, and we are on one of the lowest now. I want off."

"Very well."

"And I need to talk to you about Robinson. Let's sit down at one of the tables so we can have some privacy. I don't want to wait until we get back to town."

He hesitated, then said, "I think the numbered waiters will offend you and cause more agitation."

"What are you talking about?"

He explained the system, knowing full well that she would object. Earlier in the season Mr. Niblo had told a group of reporters, "At my ivy-covered boxes you can take a rest and have wine, coffee, cake, and sandwiches there; and my waiters are all the best. But if, by any remote chance, one of our waiters offends our customers, all our customers have to do is write down his badge number on his white apron, and pass that on to my dear wife. We have to make sure that our waiters, all black of course, are respectable and accommodating to the letter at all times. One complaint, and he is dismissed. You know some people are offended by the mere sight of negroes, so this little system assures them that we will respond to the slightest provocation, and keep our patrons happy and returning with lots of cash."

"Those numbers *are* offensive," protested Helen. "These men have *names*, for heaven's sake. Couldn't they bother to write their *names?*"

"Let's sit on a bench on one of the walkways. We'll have privacy, and the waiters won't be around." He moved toward one without taking her hand. She followed him.

Billy took a deep breath and said, "Our last conversation didn't go well. Perhaps you should talk to one of the ladies at the house, another woman who will understand. We men have brutish feelings, and our interests *are* limited."

"I don't understand," Helen said, reaching into her reticule for a letter. "After all that I have said, confessed, how could he write a letter like this?"

Helen handed the letter to him, and Billy read quickly:

> Dearest Nelly, I have but one sheet of ragged paper to figure out before me. Here I sit, now almost noon, just out of bed, fresh from heavenly dreams of you. Nell, how pleasant it is to dream, be where you will and as hungry as you will, how supremely happy is one in a little world of our creation. At best we but live one little hour, strut at our own conceit, and die. At last we arrive at our journey's end, but not without marks of old age and trials, beloved by all. But Nell, I never expect to see that number of years. Although I am seemingly so happy and cheerful with all around, I am not without my bitter moments of dismal misery, when I loathed all, myself, and everything on earth. Ah! Many's the time when alone at dead of night, on my knees, and with arms outstretched to Heaven, and heart sick, I've called on my heavenly father to take me away, and I would bless all, bless everything, friends and enemies—the storm passes away, again I am happy, contented and cheerful. Nell, I am in one point your physician (doctor) and you must obey me. Did Cashier come to see you after I left?

"I don't understand him," Helen repeated when Billy had finished reading the letter. "I don't understand him *at all.*"

Billy felt touched and relieved. Although reacting more intensely, Helen was just as bewildered and confused about Richard Robinson as he was, and now they shared another common bond.

Here was documented proof that Robinson was unstable and unpredictable, a man who veered with astonishing speed from declarations of love with exaggerated romantic flourishes and clumsy clichés to morbid confessions about death and dying, from flights of romantic fantasy to rancid religiosity. That reference to his "one point" could not be more crude and shocking after all that talk about God, death, and the transports of love. *I am vulgar*, thought Billy, *but this is crass obscenity.*

The letter raised as many questions as it answered, but Billy thought it best to focus on the opening declarations about love. "He says he loves you right there in the letter, and hopes for better days."

Helen flashed, snatching the letter from his hands. "Not once has he *told* me that he loves me. Not once has he *told* me. Writing it is not enough. He needs to *say* it."

Billy made a mental note to tell Robinson: Appease her, calm her fears, tell her what she wants to hear, say it as if quoting Byron. It will have the same effect. This current agitation did not appeal to Billy. He'd thought Helen was made of stronger stuff.

But there was more to it than the absence of a stated word.

"I think he is seeing someone else," Helen said, looking down as if ashamed that anyone could possibly prefer another.

"Oh, Helen, of course he sees other women," Billy replied, with a light laugh. "He's a young man. This is what we do before marriage. You know that."

"Why does he care about this man, Cashier? Why make his name the last thing he says in a letter to me? Why is he interested in what happens with another man? I am not some kind of go between."

"I don't know," Billy confessed.

"He's given his heart to someone else. I don't give a damn who gets that cock, but the heart is mine. Mine!"

Shocked by this outburst, Billy looked around to see if anyone heard her.

"Helen, please. We're in public."

"I knew you wouldn't understand."

"But I do, Helen. I assure you." He had a true measure of the depth of her rage and despair; she had used a word never uttered before in his presence. She always chastised him for his "gutter mouth" and challenged him to use more elegant words for intercourse and sexual parts. "Shakespeare had more variety," she'd once announced proudly.

But now with the use of just one word, she had revealed her disgust with Robinson's organ and unknowingly realized Robinson's greatest fear—that he was just a freak, a beautiful boy with a huge, circumcised penis, a freak Barnum could never display but one that was currently opening doors and spreading legs all over town, the butt of jokes, the object of envious scorn. Billy was certainly not going to reveal to Helen his plans for Robinson. Some gentlemen had expressed an interest in more exotic pleasures.

"Do you know who she is?" Helen asked coldly, as if hate for this unknown person could extract a confession.

"No, I don't," Billy replied, truthfully. "And if I did know, I would not tell for fear for her safety."

"I knew this reconciliation would not work," Helen said, looking into her lap.

"So you only meant to *use* me? And fool that I am, I thought we were friends."

Billy stood suddenly, to emphasize his displeasure.

Helen reached out and took his hand, saying warmly, "You are my friend, and friends *use* each other in the best ways."

"Then how can I help you without betraying his trust?" he asked, sitting down again.

"His *trust?*" Helen drew back ever so slightly. "What has he done to earn *that?* Surely gambling and drinking together don't do that."

"Our club. We swore an oath."

"What is it?"

"I can't tell you."

"You *won't* tell me."

"No, I won't. Some things are meant for men only. You perhaps know too much already."

"But surely you can advise him about his relationships if he is to be successful?"

"Yes, so what do you want me to do, or say?"

"Tell him I love him, but ask him if he wants to know how much I can come to hate him."

"Helen this kind of threat doesn't work with men. You will drive him away if you are not careful."

"He is already moving away. I can see it, hear it in his letters."

"Then wait, say less and write less, and that void will create a hunger for your company."

"He has my company," Helen insisted. "But I want more. I *need* more."

"Be patient," he lied. "He will come around."

She would learn the truth soon enough. Richard Robinson couldn't love her, or anybody else. It was all a game for him, nothing more.

Chapter Nineteen

"I love you." Robinson sat in Helen's room, smiling at her. He had arrived at eight, and they would talk before going to her bed.

"I have waited so long for you to say that," she replied, taking his hand. "It means so much for me to hear those words come from your lips, the sweetest sound from the sweetest lips."

"And when I leave tonight, I want to say what Keats said about the end of the day. But I can't remember the lines rights now."

Still pressing his hand and looking into his eyes, Helen quoted with tender recollection, "The day is gone, and all its sweets are gone! Sweet voice, sweet lips, soft hand, and softer breast."

She took his hand and pressed it against her bosom.

"Do you know *every* line of *every* poem?" he asked, gently pulling his hand away.

Instantly the spell was broken, and she was on the defensive once more.

"No, I don't. I have favorites."

"And you have so *many*," Robinson replied, his reproach playful and casual.

But Helen heard accusation and breathed a deep sigh before taking her next step. She had to recover the magic of just of few moments before, the magic the words had created. She turned to her strongest and greatest weapon.

"I want us to read the balcony scene from 'Romeo and Juliet.'"

"Now?" he asked, turning his head to the bed, his true point of interest.

"Yes," Helen replied, "The perfect love, described with the most perfect words, a fitting prelude to our *bliss*."

She almost winced at the choice of the word; it seemed overwrought, extreme even for her.

She walked to the table and retrieved sheets of paper with the entire scene recopied in her elegant script. Standing, she handed the sheets to him. He looked at them, his lines underlined in red ink, and then looked at her, his face showing surprise and curiosity.

"I've been waiting for this moment," she explained. "I knew it would come, eventually. Our love is here, on these pages."

"But do we *need* them?"

"Yes, yes," Helen replied, her voice rising.

"How long will this take?" Robinson asked, looking again to the bed.

"Not long, not long at all," she replied. "It's not the entire scene, just key lines that I want us to say, for us to hear."

He looked down at his opening lines and began, "But soft! What light through yonder window breaks? It is the East, and Juliet is the sun. Arise, fair sun and kill the envious moon . . ."

Helen was so moved by the care of his unhurried recitation, the emphasis on exactly the rights words, as if he were an experienced actor, she interrupted him, clutching the text to her chest. "Splendid, just splendid," she murmured.

Robinson grinned and asked, "May I continue?"

"Of course."

He read with intense concentration, and the words flowed as if he were indeed a seasoned actor skilled at reading lines. When he ended with his last lines, "Sleep dwell upon thine eyes, peace in thy breast! Would I were to sleep and peace, so sweet to rest," Helen took a deep breath and said, "I am ready for you."

She began to unbutton her bodice, and he pulled at his cravat and stood to undress more quickly. When he pulled down his trousers and fully revealed himself, Helen could only say, "Yes."

He declared the obvious. "I'm ready, too."

He was a familiar sight by now, of course, but she remained astonished by the contrast between his thin frame and the thick mass jutting out from his groin. He was the embodiment of those illustrations in Judge Weston's special collection, no mere figment of a lustful imagination. But now his physical dimensions did not matter. He was no longer a Satyr or Priapus, his weapons an engorged organ and mockery in his eyes. He was her love, the man who could inspire a passion that kept her up at night, tossing in bed, yearning to be with him as soon as possible, and rising out of bed in the middle of the night to scribble letters by candlelight so that he could know how much he mattered, how much she wanted to see him.

Afterward, as she lay luxuriating in the warmth of her body and its heightened sensitivities, she suppressed the impulse to giggle. This was a night of exceptions. She had thoroughly enjoyed the sex and didn't feel the need to disentangle herself and pull apart, giving herself space to breathe freely and forget the man beside her.

"That was the best," she heard him say.

She started. The words were true. Yet if there was a time for silence, this was the moment. She waited, hoping he would understand her signal, but even as she waited, she could hear the silent demand for affirmation and approval. The magic of the hour had dissipated completely, and Helen struggled to cast another spell for its return.

"I love you," she whispered.

"I love you too," he replied. "And I can hardly wait to come see you again."

Her letters had urged him to come see her, to not delay, to give no excuses for giving her the time she needed. He was saying exactly what she'd wanted to hear, according to her letters, a barrage of desperate appeals delivered two and three times a day. But now the promise to come again seemed empty and manipulative, another trite offering of appeasement and dismissal.

She sat up and stared straight ahead. "It's time to go."

"What?" he asked, perplexed.

"It's time to go," she insisted. "There are others."

"Do you *have* to mention them now?"

She didn't regret the reference. Jealousy enhanced the distinctive nature of their relationship. He needed to be reminded of the others, so that his special place was affirmed.

"You can love me *despite* them," she replied, turning to look into his face. She thought she saw incipient tears. Those incredible blue eyes were inviting pools, and she turned away, resisting total submersion. He had to go; she had more work to do.

"I love you," he whispered, reaching out to touch her back. His hands were soft and smooth, the hands of a man not made for work in fields and mills.

She left the bed, stepping away without any effort to cover her nakedness.

"Come again soon," she said, not looking at him. "I'll send a note giving the exact time and day."

"As always I can count on your explicit directions, " he said, his mockery unmistakable but light and gentle; he was amused by her habit. "And we can talk about what's happening in town, especially the news of those discoveries on the moon, those moon bats and all. Aren't they amazing?"

The *Sun* had published a series about life on the moon that began with descriptions of flora and fauna, mountains and valleys, and culminated with descriptions of flying "bat men." The original issues sold out, multiple issues followed. The series was reprinted as a pamphlet with illustrations, and it sold out as well. The *Sun* was now the most popular newspaper in town. Ben Day was a wealthy man, and the city roiled over talk about life on other planets, the existence of God, and the place of deception and fraud in American life.

Already irritated by his making a joke of her incessant letter writing, she lashed out without raising her voice. "Do you really *believe* such absolute nonsense? The *Sun* made it all up."

"How do you know that?" he asked hotly.

"I just know," she replied. Billy had told her that Richard Locke, the Englishman fired by Webb and hired immediately by Ben Day, had done a brilliant job. But even Locke was careless. "If you read closely, you can see the inconsistencies. The *Sun* made claims about sources that didn't even exist when it said it did."

"Why do you have to be always superior?" Robinson asked coldly.

"What do you mean?"

He thickened his voice. "Why do you always have to *show* me how much more you know, and how limited I am in my knowledge, my experience—you, the worldly lady in town and me, the country bumpkin. Perhaps I need to be with someone who will accept me for what I am?"

"I accept you," Helen said, reaching for her chemise.

"As long as I play a part, the part in some play. Romeo in that play, or some character in your own, the one you are always writing with *me* in it. God, I hate what you're doing to me."

This self-pity was unbecoming and infuriating. She exclaimed, "What I am doing to *you*? Get out now. After all I have done for you, this is what I get in return?"

"Done for *me*? Just what have you done?"

"You have a special place in my affections; you are there."

"*Put* there by you," he sneered. "Always in command, *assigning* places."

"Get out," she cried. "Go find someone who will tolerate your cruelty."

"I will," he promised, rising from bed.

"You probably have already, and you're just lying to me *again*."

"By tomorrow it won't matter. You will have *pushed* me into her arms."

"You can't make *me* the cause. You will do it all on your own."

"At least she will be *grateful*," he said, pulling up his trousers as if to accent his point.

"You bastard," she said with soft vehemence.

"I have proof of my birth condition. Do *you*?"

She raised her hand to slap him, but he grabbed it, holding it tightly before her face.

"You're hurting me," she said, suddenly immobilized by pressure at her wrist and the seething hatred in his eyes.

"Don't *ever* think you can slap me, and not suffer for it," he said. "Others have paid the price."

He frightened her now, and Helen recoiled, turning away from a face she no longer recognized, every feature cast in white stone, cold and pure like marble in a cemetery. She was incredulous. How could he change so quickly? Or had he been acting all along, and this face was his true face? Why couldn't she see it before? Was love that blinding?

She didn't know what to say, so she simply waited.

Robinson softened his grip and then released her hand. She thought she heard a suggestion of regret when he spoke again. But she wasn't sure. He had an amazing capacity to instill doubt and insecurity, and she felt adrift in unfamiliar territory.

"I'm sorry. I'm leaving now," he whispered.

He gathered up the rest of his clothes and left, his shirt half buttoned, no cravat, hat on his head, shoes in his hand, and the jacket loose around his shoulders.

Helen stared at the door. *What do I do now?*

She turned to her desk. She would do what she always did when she needed to make sense of her experience, clarify her thoughts, and determine her next steps.

Then she heard a knock at the door.

"Miss Helen, Mr. Easy is waiting for you," the servant girl said.

"Tell him he will have to wait. I have something I must take care of. Don't send him away. Just tell him to wait, and I will send for him to come up."

Command had returned to her voice. Tom Easy would, of course, wait. He was proud and grateful to be another one of Helen's favorites, and would wait all night if she required it.

She reached for paper and pen, and began to write:

"My dearest Frank . . ."

For the next two months letters and notes poured from her, and her daily walks to the post office were a familiar sight on the streets. Occasionally she would hire a carrier, but on most days she preferred carrying the letters, the touch of the paper stock adding to the weight of her sentiments, which ranged from declarations of eternal love and desperate appeals for reciprocity to protests and denunciations, often in the same letter. She would not openly admit it, but her daily deliveries were a literary barrage, an incessant call for obedience.

What did Robinson have to do to demonstrate his undying devotion? It seemed to vary from letter to letter, if not from line to line. At the beginning of their relationship, Helen often reread her letters. But now she didn't reread them, hoping that the accumulation of pages alone would clarify her expectations and desires. Unfortunately, his answers would show that he did not see and feel what she wanted him to see and feel, and so she would resume the campaign.

He didn't write as often, and he seemed to stay away to heighten her expectations for his return. He spent his days at Mr. Hoxie's, and obviously spent many of his nights carousing with Billy Attree and other single men.

But he could, at the very least, reply with a line, answer *every* note to show that he had received it and thought about what she was trying to say. Yet when he did respond, he only frustrated her more. He evaded, prevaricated, even lied outright.

But it was the silences that most pained her. Days went by, and he would send nothing. It frustrated her that she could only demand replies. Worse, she could not command his presence and find him at Philadelphia House at precisely the identified time. Instead, *she* had to wait.

Finally, he would appear and, after recriminations and explanations, apologies and declarations of eternal devotion, they would climb into bed and behave like mindless animals. Sometimes he would just appear, and before a word was even spoken, they were grabbing at ribbons, buckles, and stays, stripping themselves half naked before falling to the bed and consummating their passion. He was gentle, then wild, as if released by a fear of giving discomfort or pain. And, for a few moments, consumed by the pleasure of knowing that this boy belonged to her and knew how to satisfy her need, her skin seemed to burn and her eyes could not bear even the dimmest candlelight.

Then, inevitably, he would say something wrong, make an odd reference, or ask an insulting question, and the recriminations would begin again, followed by an argument, an abrupt departure, and more letters.

Sometimes she wondered if they both preferred writing letters than seeing each other.

Despite her misgivings, the letters continued, revealing an almost anguished need to communicate every emotion. He replied less and less, and his letters showed a gradual withdrawal from her burning intensity.

Now her powerful memory pained and exhausted her, as lines from their letters accumulated in her brain like dialogue in a fast-paced play at the Park or Bowery Theaters:

Helen: Do you feel today as if you have been floored last night, or not; for my part, I feel literally *used up.*

Robinson: I must now, again, beg your pardon. I know I was acting wrong, in trifling with feeling such as yours, but yet I could not help it.

Helen: Jealousy has often made me unhappy and I have vainly tried to cover it. There are very few men who understand. Women only can understand a woman's heart.

Robinson: I have the book you asked for.

Helen: I cannot sleep. Let me, for heaven's sake, hear from you soon.

Robinson: I'm sorry.

Helen: When I think of you as the only being on earth I really love, I feel the more inclined to weep. Alas, you know now what it costs me to reproach you, but I have never, since I have known you, had but one hope, one wish, which is that long after you had ceased to see me, you would think of me as not utterly beneath the herd with whom I have been obliged to associate.

Robinson: I'm sorry.

Helen: You cannot be ignorant of the power you possess over me, and you must not betray it. I should not say you must not, but rather why, why have you done so?

Robinson didn't answer this last question, or reply to most of her letters. He was too busy visiting Adelia Phantom at Julia Brown's on Chapel, a younger girl named Emma Chancellor at Number 171 Reade Street, and many others around town. He loved seduction and conquest, and women wanted his body and his money. Sometimes he didn't even have to pay. He preferred Number 41 Thomas Street, the most splendid brothel he had ever entered, calling it "Whore Heaven." He also preferred Helen above all the rest. He once confessed to Billy that when he was inside her, he was in heaven itself. Nevertheless, he had to explore other lands, fill other holes, and cultivate as many gardens as possible. They needed him, and how could he resist their call?

Chapter Twenty

Usually the women at Philadelphia House gathered in the back parlor in the early afternoon to talk. They planned excursions to the theaters, stores, and parks; they discussed the vagaries of fashion, comparing dresses and jewelry; and they complained about their customers, who invariably proved the gross insensitivity of men in general.

Men were good for sex, money, and gifts, and little else, the women usually concluded. And as possible husbands, they were sure to cheat, betray, and disappoint. Female friendship was far more reliable, and the women at Number 128 Duane spent hours cultivating it. There were jealousies, of course, especially when someone went too far in extolling her own abilities, or boasted about gifts she had received. But in general, the women at the Duchess de Berry's had a comfortable, supportive home.

Even so, Helen was not able to turn to the Duchess, or bring her misgivings and anxieties about Richard Robinson to the group. Her emotions were too raw, her confusions too unsettling for exposure in the light of the afternoon parlor. Her vulnerability had wounded her pride, and she couldn't bear the prospect of showing her weakness.

But she had to talk to someone, and it had to be a woman. Only a woman could possibly understand.

Finally, she turned to Maria Stevens, who had carefully described and explained the culture of the de Berry house when Helen first arrived there. A year older than Helen, she seemed younger because she was so quiet, gentle, and reserved. Many men liked this about her. She wasn't terribly exciting, but she never expressed disappointment or relief. She had a job to do, and she performed it without expectations or complaint. Some people judged her as reliable and dull, and Helen had originally thought she could not possibly like her. But soon she'd found Maria to be a sweet and uncritical listener. Helen needed these qualities, especially now.

The two sat in Helen's room, where they could be sure of privacy.

Helen read two of Richard's letters, and at the end of the second, she observed, "I'm in love with him."

"He is a charming man," said Maria, smiling. "I can see why. He quotes poetry, and . . ."

Helen interrupted her, "He quotes the *same* passages over and over again."

Maria frowned, but she maintained her lightness of tone and continued, "You are so well read and know so much."

In their world, no one knew more. Many of the women could read only their own names. Helen's literary gifts gave her prestige and power.

Helen waved her hand, deflecting the comment as irrelevant. Yes, she was well read and knew hundreds of poems by heart, but Robinson was only interested in repeating the same tired lines, as if she didn't notice. It apparently never occurred to him that she would count the number of the poems in his repertoire of seduction and manipulation.

"I see his faults, and yet I cannot but love him, "Helen confessed.

"We are *all* imperfect," said Maria, "and we hope for love."

"And I have given it, and he mistreats me nonetheless."

"Do you think he suspects disappointment?"

Defensively, Helen leaned forward. "What do you mean?"

"I regret the question, Helen. I was only trying to help. I will ask no more questions. I have no solutions. I don't know the kind of love you have for him."

"Have you ever been in love?"

"Yes, a long time ago, before I came to New York. But I was young, very young and naïve."

"Do you think it wise to fall in love with a customer?"

"Please don't ask me that. If I say it is unwise, then you might think I am judging you as foolish, and if I say otherwise, then my support could hurt you if things don't turn out well."

"Then you do think this will end badly?"

"I can't predict what will happen," said Maria. "I only want your happiness."

"I am not happy," said Helen.

Maria waited, as if to say silently, *I can face the truth, whatever it is.* And, as she expected, Helen could not bear the silence of waiting. Helen had to talk, to explain. Helen had to write letters to explain even more. Words and words and more words. Could someone drown in them? Was Richard Robinson, in his own way, struggling for air?

"I thought that true love, when it finally came, would be strong and unassailable," Helen said. "Outer forces might batter it, but the core would remain strong. Romeo and Juliet, Anthony and Cleopatra—their love was like the sun, even behind the clouds of death itself. That is what I had hoped for. That is what love *should* be."

"But you did say once, in one of your readings, and I remember it so well because when we heard them, we all applauded, 'The course of true love,' you said, 'never did run smooth.'"

"*That* was a comedy," said Helen sourly.

"I should have taken a lighter touch, back then when I fell in love. We are all so serious when we're young."

"Are you saying I'm too serious?"

Maria winced, and spoke carefully. "Helen, everything I say is meant as the cause for thought. I am *not* drawing any conclusions. I am not in a position to make judgments, and I won't, for the sake of our friendship."

"That's the coward's way."

"No, it's the *friend's* way. We must bite our tongues now and then, if love is more important than being right."

"Then you are biting your tongue now. You are *refusing* to be honest."

Maria stood and said sadly, "There is nothing I can say that will make you feel better. If I said you are mad for loving him, that he is unworthy of you, you would hate me for not appreciating him. And if I said your love is all that love should be, you would accuse me of not seeing him clearly. If you come to me again, and I hope you will because I want to always be available to you, I will hold you in my arms and cry with you, or I will hold your hands and laugh with you. We will *talk* about everything and anything except this. Please understand."

She left the room, and Helen sat at the table perfectly still.

Was there anyone who could understand what she was going through? Maria was a convenient target for her frustration, but Helen chafed under the weight of it. Nothing seemed to make sense. Her neatly constructed universe of cause and effect, a solid structure of rational insight and wise observation, a heady mixture of irony balanced with emotional truth, was being undone by a boy with the reckless indifference of a child toppling over blocks. He was sorry and dutifully apologized. But there was no denying the pleasure he took in his destruction of her carefully built creation.

They fought now every time they saw each other, and every fight was followed by apologies and more recriminations.

His letters confirmed that she was not insane; he at least could recognize his own cruelty and instability:

My dearest Nelly, You were offended Wednesday evening at my language. I do not wonder that you were. It was harsh—very harsh, but I could not help it. No one can love you more than I do, dear Nelly; yet how strange, whenever I meet you I cannot treat you even with respect. You must think it very strange that I profess to love you so much and yet always treat you so harshly. Yet I have told you over and over again, that loving you as I do and not being able to see you, it makes me most crazy, and I have no control over my feelings, but Nelly you must forgive me. I hope to God it will not be always thus. For one thing, dearest Nelly, I can never reward you sufficiently. You have promised me your miniature; what can I give you in return? Nothing, but my repeated vows of unutterable affection. But I will always wear it next to my heart, and forever guard it as a sacred treasure. I know my letter cannot be very interesting to you. I suppose you think us all alike. But Nelly, for God's sake, don't forget me. Frank

Even though she was no innocent, at times she found his *need* insufferable.

One evening that fall Robinson rushed into the house unannounced, sweating and eager to see her, interrupting her conversation with a group of men in the parlor. He obviously expected her to drop everything just for him, her previous plans not mattering one bit.

She snapped at him in front of her three male companions, asking imperiously, "What did you come up here for, to put me to the *trouble* of going upstairs?"

This oversexed boy obviously thought his mere appearance would so inflame her she could do nothing but run upstairs, rip off her clothes, and fornicate like a dog.

Robinson's face turned white and his thin lips trembled. Helen could see the tightening of his fists, but she knew he was more mortified than angry.

"Very well," he said simply, and turned to leave. When had he closed the door, Helen laughed loudly, loud enough for Robinson to hear her, and the other men joined in.

She observed to her companions, "At least you gentlemen *know* your place."

They laughed again, and Helen selected then and there the man she would take up to her room. One of them had a rich and mocking laugh, and on that night she found this quite attractive. It was carefree, joyous, and deeply masculine. His powerful jaw and the thick thighs that completely filled his trousers added to his allure. He was a man, not a boy.

For only a moment, Helen felt badly about her treatment of Robinson, but she suppressed thinking about it because she wanted to focus on her more immediate, income-generating pleasures. However, her remorse deepened when she received a letter from Robinson the following day.

My mind was made up in a moment not to trouble you, but as I walked out, and after I got out, I could hear your *loud laugh*. I was not always thus, Nelly. There was a time when the trouble of going upstairs was compensated by the pleasure my visit occasioned you, but I have recently had occasion to think that you have got tired of me, and that I am now in your estimation placed on a par with all the others. I know I have treated you harshly now and then, but I have always suffered for it. Lately, I had resolved to treat you kindly, and hoped that nothing would again mar my feelings toward you. 'Tis useless for me to tell you how I love you, for you now make it an object of sport. Nelly, if you have ceased to love me, tell me so—if you still love me, why did you drive me away from you last evening? You saw I was going. You might have even asked me to stop—but my exit only occasioned mirth from you. You may say you did it only for fun. If it was fun to you, it was cruelty to me. Do you think I am entirely devoid of feeling that I can be driven from your door, by you, and not feel it, and sensibly too?

At this point, Helen could almost see herself putting on a shawl and running to his boarding house on Dey Street. But her heart felt an immediate chill as she continued reading:

I have acknowledged that I have often suffered intensely by allowing myself to think of you. I will never acknowledge so much again. By God, I love you, but unless I am loved in return *as much as ever*, I never shall enjoy myself with you as I have done. I never can bear to have your love for me diminish one atom. For God's sake let me know soon the cause of your treating me as you did last night, and when I can again visit you without being too much *trouble* to you. From one who loves you, Frank.

Here he was, indeed, declaring his love. But he was *commanding* her to love him in return . . . or else. *I won't enjoy myself as much if you don't love me like I love you. I can't have my love diminished one atom.*

He didn't care about her at all. She was simply a receptacle for his pleasure, and love was a word he used as casually and as commonly as a vulgar street laborer.

She deserved better, and she decided then and there to ask for the return of her portrait miniature. This request in her next letter would not mark an absolute and unrecoverable severance in their relationship. But some measure of control had to be restored, and Richard Robinson had to be reminded that he was not in charge of *her* feelings.

She would, of course, tell Billy.

Chapter Twenty-One

Now Billy wished he had been more honest with Helen about Richard Robinson.

Even so, truth had its limits. He could never admit to her that he envied Robinson's physical advantages, despite his casual dismissal of distinctions made significant by so many others. In fact, he resented Robinson for generating an almost irrational jealousy, even as he exploited him as his club's most impressive member.

But Billy also knew that envy, the true child of invidious comparison, could not explain the constant churning of his bowels when he was in the same room with Richard Robinson.

He tried to deny the cause, but he knew.

It was a dangerous mix of fear and desire.

He had invited Robinson to his modest but well-kept rooms on High Street. Unlike many single men in town, Billy lived alone rather than in a boarding house. The extra expense had definite advantages. He could write in peace and have visitors without interruption.

Billy originally intended to push the boundaries with Robinson, just to see how far the boy would go to please him.

Sitting in a chair facing his guest, Billy leaned forward and said evenly, "You're going to pleasure yourself in front of me, and I don't want to hear any shit about you going mad. We've all been doing this ever since we could get hard, and we never went mad despite all the warnings. I'm sure you've done this before on the farm in Connecticut, and proudly so."

"Yes, sir," Robinson replied without hesitation.

"About what?" Billy replied.

"Both matters," Robinson said, a slight smile on his face.

That was all he needed to know. Robinson would do anything he asked. Billy's control was absolute. Robinson's expression didn't change; that soft, delicate smile remained, and his blue eyes never wavered in giving Billy their complete attention, as if he were an object of adoration.

Or so he thought.

"Just why did your father send you here?" Billy asked abruptly.

He wanted to break rules, laws, and commandments, but he needed to pause for just a moment more. Absolute freedom thrilled and frightened him in equal measure.

Robinson did not miss a beat, saying simply, "He was afraid of me. I was doing things."

"What things?"

"Starting small fires; killing bugs and small animals. I like destroying things."

"You hunt."

"Too loud and too messy. Traps, and then fires while they're still alive."

"You can't be serious?" asked Billy.

"I also lie," said Robinson, now grinning.

Robinson's attempt at humor was surprising, awkward, almost obscene. There was nothing funny at all about fires and the torture of animals. Even Washington Irving could not transmute such material into a laughing matter.

"Don't ever lie to me again," said Billy. "*Ever.*"

As if slapped in the face, Robinson sat back in his chair, cringing like a chastised child. He was now again the boy eager to please after making a serious mistake. "I'm sorry, sir. I didn't mean to offend you. I was telling you the truth, about my lying and all. My father tired of it, and said he didn't want me around anymore."

"Just don't lie to me. You understand?"

"You will believe me, then, if I tell you something really bad."

"What?"

"I had to kill Emma Chancellor, that prostitute you wrote about in the paper.".

Startled again, Billy asked, "Is this another unfortunate attempt at humor?"

"No."

Despite Robinson's promise, Billy suspected he was lying again, but he decided to go along to see what he would reveal. "What did you have to hide by killing her?"

"I steal money at work."

"So why did you tell her."

"To impress her."

"You could have lied again."

"She laughed at me."

"About what?"

"She said I was stupid for telling her."

"That was unwise. You can't be sure about women though. They love to talk."

"I can't have exposure. If anyone exposed me, I would blow her brains out, " said Robinson. His face was blank, emotionless. This announcement was as casual as a remark about crossing the room.

"For stealing, or for stupidity?" asked Billy, deepening the chill in his voice.

As if the question made no impression, Robinson grinned and asked, "Is there anything else you want me to do for you?"

Billy's heart pounded, a sharp beat that made him close his eyes. The moment had come, the realization of a dream he had night after night: dropping to his knees and taking Robinson into his mouth. Billy leaned back in his chair, his honest admission bringing relief to his aching muscles for the first time in days. Enjoying the relaxing calm, he kept his eyes closed for almost a minute, but when he opened them, he found Robinson fully exposed before him.

Billy smiled, now amused by the boy's arrogant offering of spread legs, open trousers, and both hands around his massive organ.

"Some other time," Billy finally said, gently dismissive with a wave of his hand. "You can do this for someone else. Now dress yourself."

"Will I get into trouble?" asked Robinson earnestly as he stood pushing his shirt into his trousers and buttoning his trousers.

"Not if you do as I say, and keep quiet."

"I can't have exposure," Robinson said again, with a hint of fear now.

"Of course," Billy observed, struggling to harmonize the two contrasting images of Richard Robinson before him, the eager boy willing to do anything for his club leader, and this cold, calculating young man who could lie and then talk about torture and murder with astonishing ease. Billy could not make sense of him, and said cheerfully, masking his discomfort, "Well, we won't have to worry about anything, shall we? Let's have some drinks and then go out. The night is young, and I have some specific men I want you to meet. These gentlemen will pay well, very well for your services."

"My father won't answer to any more of my appeals. New York is expensive, and I need the money."

Looking back, Billy found these early encounters with Richard Robinson simple compared to all the drama and tribulation associated with Robinson's relationship with Helen, the highs and lows, the arguments, denunciation, and apologies, the declarations of love, and the complaints about deception and betrayal.

Both of them asserted that this emotional mess was true love. Billy concluded that if this were so, he would have nothing to do with it. Billy actually missed the days when he and Robinson could just drink, gamble, and fuck without worrying about Helen.

He appreciated Robinson's devotion and cooperation as a member of the Lion's Club, but he now wished that he had never introduced him to Helen.

In fact, he now wished that he had never met Robinson at all.

There was something sick and dangerous about him.

Billy had hoped that he could have had the best of both worlds: sex and interesting conversation in Helen's room, and dangerous but always stimulating excursions into the darker corners of the city's streets, a band of brothers on the prowl without concern about the feelings of overly sensitive women, a band of brothers even willing to turn to each other for pleasure.

He still could do as he wished, but he would do so without Robinson.

He could always simply exclude the boy from the club, but there was the problem of Helen.

Robinson and Helen were tangled in a complicated web, and Billy was tired of it. He couldn't wait for his upcoming trip. He'd been assigned some out-of-town reporting for the *Transcript*, and he hoped for a final breakup between Helen and Richard by the time he returned to the city.

Both of them were acting like absolute fools and needed to go their separate ways. He hoped that 1836 would be a better year for everybody.

Before he left town, he wrote a quick note: "Dear Helen. When can I see you alone again? We have so much to talk about, now that the city has run that British abolitionist out of town. Can you promise me that you will not mention Robinson during our next time together?"

Even as he wrote, he knew the absolute futility of this request.

———•———

Mary Berry claimed that all of "her girls" at Philadelphia House were equal sisters, but she revealed her favoritism when she announced her decision to send Helen to Philadelphia in December to inspect her house there and review its procedures and accounts.

The Duchess told everyone at Sunday supper. As far as she was concerned, this was a family gathering, where news and gossip were shared and decisions proclaimed. The credibility of news stories could be discussed and debated, but house decisions were *not* open to analysis or debate. Even the beneficiaries of her favors, always surprised, were expected to raise no questions or ask for explanations. The Duchess only required a beaming smile of gratitude.

Unsolicited, the Duchess portentously explained to the group at the table, "Although the time for such an eventuality is far off, and this announcement is in no way a final declaration of an ultimate decision, one must prepare for the continued existence and financial success of this enterprise by thinking of the inevitable, and train those who have revealed through their intelligence and diligence that they can continue the work, if they choose to remain loyal to us and remain in the precincts of our regard."

Helen was delighted to be chosen, but she had no illusions. She could not be bribed into staying with the Duchess. Nevertheless, she appreciated the recognition and the opportunity, as well as the distraction a trip planned for mid-December could provide. Gowns and jewelry had to be selected, letters written, accounts reviewed, and her usual customers prepared for her absence.

She was actually relieved when Robinson wrote that his involvement in the seasonal inventory would keep him away for a while. She was exhausted by the arguments and predictable appeals for understanding and reconciliation, the constant bickering, the tears, recriminations, and excuses.

Helen also found the attentions of another favorite, the seventeen-year-old George P. Marston, who called himself "Tom Easy," to be more satisfying, at least at first.

The oldest son of an elite family from Newburyport, Massachusetts, Tom Easy was handsome and eager to please. Unlike Robinson, he made no demands and did not need constant affirmations of his worth. He was grateful for Helen's interest in him, and counted any meeting, however intermittent, as an occasion for muted celebration. Devoted, cooperative, quiet, gentle, kind, and good in bed—the perfect acolyte.

But he was dull and admitted his own stupidity.

Tom had difficulties with Helen's moodiness, and confessed his struggles with recognizing it, writing to her:

> Dearest Helen, I know I am a dull and stupid fellow, and that I have a blockhead. That accounts I suppose for my not having observed your ill humor on Thursday evening. But though that escaped my notice, my thick and stupid head observed with pain that you were unhappy, and it guessed the cause. Helen, if I could but restore that man to your affections, if I could but remove the cause of your unhappiness, if I could but dispel the mist and uncertainty in which you are involved, in one word if I could but make you happy, I should ever experience the liveliest joy, in knowing my endeavors to render myself of some service to you had not been wholly fruitless, and that I had been the humble cause of many happy hours.

Here was true devotion. Tom was willing to restore Robinson, "that man," if that could make her happy; and he was willing to remove him as well, although he was vague about his intended methods. That Tom and Robinson were also friends who met regularly for drinks at Clark and Brown's added a measure of poignancy to Tom's adoration. Or was he simply confused, knowing only to muddle through and hope for the best, unlike Robinson, whose every move was calculated to defeat her?

Years before, Judge Weston had taught Helen how to play chess, and she eventually learned how to win, watching him and planning her strategy for victory with each and every move of the pieces on the board. Her most enjoyable contests were those when the outcome was in doubt until the very end. A masterful player and teacher, the judge took pleasure in seeing his pupil challenge and sometimes defeat him. But Helen felt no joy in combating Robinson. Every letter she sent was answered with more provocations and insinuations. He acted as if they were equals, ruthless competitors determined to checkmate, and this made her resentful and even desperate.

There were no such tensions with Tom Easy. His pseudonym was a perfect reflection of his temperament, and in the fall of 1835 she needed easy.

But all too soon, she found Tom unsatisfying. In bed he remained solicitous and responsive, but in social settings he was slow. He couldn't read rooms quickly enough and take the appropriate action. Most of the time, he simply stood, a beautiful statue in a crowded parlor or theater, adding nothing to the conversation, making no comments, a mere accessory.

Recently they'd stood together in the main staircase of the Bowery Theater during intermission, his arm around her. A friend had approached, and Tom left them to talk. He walked up the stairs and noticed another friend, whom he followed down the stairs, passing Helen on his way. He came up in five minutes, and Helen went down. He waited for her to return, but after a few moments, he went looking for her. Her found her at the door, and she immediately reprimanded him. He was her escort and he'd abandoned her in a crowded theater without comment, passing her not once but *twice* without saying a single word or indicating the slightest interest in her interactions with others. When others had approached her, he retreated, slinking away like a shy, awkward boy at his first ball. And when she protested, he said nothing, asked no questions, offered no rejoinders, made no claims for a contrary point of view. She *wanted* an argument.

Instead Tom wrote a letter later that evening. After reviewing the events, he observed,

> When I met you at the door to find out that you were angry with me, I knew not what to make of it. There were many people looking at us, and I knew it. That entry was too public a place for any explanation. Therefore I went upstairs, expecting, if you cared anything about it one way or the other, that you would shortly follow me up—but I saw nothing after. Please write me and let me know how I have offended, and if you consider me still your friend and welcome to your house. I would cut off my arm sooner than go more than once where I knew I was not wanted.

After reading this letter, she groaned and then tossed it to the end of her desk, almost tipping over her small inkbottle.

She was admittedly a moody woman, subject to sudden emotional shifts, and Tom Easy had witnessed these shifts often enough. But every time he witnessed a change, he expressed surprise and befuddlement, as if experiencing it for the first time. Every incident brought the same response—a blank smile and the plaintive hope for an explanation. He could not give her what she enjoyed—a good argument, an exciting disagreement. She had to admit that her arguments with Robinson were frustrating and exhausting, but they were also exciting, engaging, and energizing. She felt *more* alive with him, and now missed the thrill of the intellectual and emotional contest.

Or so she thought—until she received Robinson's letter of November fourteenth. It was his longest ever, and it began with the salutation, "Miss Maria." Immediately infuriated, she stared at the old pseudonym she'd abandoned before coming to New York, and suppressed the urge to crumple the letter and toss it across the room. "Damn him," she said. What could be his reason for mentioning that name *now*? Was he yearning for some imagined past, when she was younger, new to town, and more agreeable? She found no answers to these questions in the body of the letter, but what she found astounded her:

I think our intimacy is now old enough for both of us to speak plain. I don't know on what footing I sand with you. Any deviation from the line of conduct which you think I ought to pursue, and I am blown. All of your *professions, oaths and assurances* are set aside to accommodate your new feelings towards me. Even this very letter will be used as a witness against me, to avenge a fancied insult received at my hands. Poor Frank, has indeed, a thousand insurmountable difficulties to encounter. Bandied about like a *dog,* who as he becomes useless is cast aside, no longer worthy of a singe thought, except to be cursed. No sooner extricated from one difficulty than he is plunged into ruin and disgrace by one he had confidence in; one who professed attachment more sincere that any other, who swore to be true and faithful, she who would be my friend till death parted us! Oh, has it come to this, and she the first to forsake me, whom I so ardently endeavored to gain her lasting regard and love. He has but two wishes left, either of which he would embrace, and than his Heavenly Father *with all the ardor of his soul: death* or a complete alteration. After reflecting on our situation all night, I arose this morning feverish and almost undecided, and so ill as to be able to attend to but a portion of my business of the day. I have, however, come to this conclusion, that it is best for us both to dissolve all connection. I hope you will coincide in this opinion; for you well know, that our meetings are far from being as sweet and as pleasant as they once were, and moreover I concluded from the terms of your last note that you would not regret such a step. I am afraid it will be the only way for me to pursue a gentlemanly course of conduct. In *my opinion,* my conduct the last time I was at your house was far from being gentlemanly or respectful. I behaved myself, as I should never do again, let the circumstances be what they might, even if I had to prevent it by never setting in your house again. I was very sorry for it, and now beg your pardon. I have done to you as I have never done to anybody else, (in the case where other gentlemen are concerned). This I hope will be forgiven, as there is no harm done, and let the circumstances justify the act. H----, as we are about to part allow me to tell you the truth of my sentiments---I have always made it a point to study your character and *disposition*. I admired it *more than any other female I ever knew*, and so deep an impression has it made on my heart, that never will the name and kindness of Maria G. Benson be forgotten by me. But for the present, we must be as strangers. I have only to say, do not betray me; but forget me. I am no longer worthy of you. *Me ex memoria amitte et ero tuus servus*, Respectfully, Frank.

Every underscored word and phrase were like slaps in the face; their utter selfishness, preening hypocrisy, morbid sensitivity, gross sentimentality, vulgar religiosity, and flagrant pretentiousness forced her to close her eyes and try to soften the pounding in her head. For a fleeting moment, she almost laughed at his Latin closing, but she was compelled to read the letter again and her headache deepened. He had managed to out maneuver her, initiating their breakup with a maddening serenity. "No," she declared aloud. This was *not* how it was supposed to happen. She had created the relationship; she would end it too.

But when she read the letter for the third time, she recognized the opportunity now before her. She could prove her superiority with unparalleled grace and equanimity, and demonstrate her gratitude for the end of a tawdry melodrama. It was time to move on, especially now that she leaving town. Her business mission for Mary Berry could mark a definite and clear break.

However, she didn't want to return his miniature. Year after year she intended to show off this trophy, proof that she had as her lover the most handsome man in New York. It surpassed the other miniature portraits in her collection. Fearing incrimination, most of her regular customers asked for their return, but enough simply walked away, hoping for the best. She would keep the prize. Forget him? Never.

Recalling her earlier Latin lessons while living with the Dillinghams, she was able to decode the closing words of the letter *Leave me out of your memory, and I will be your servant*, it declared, and Helen snickered, amused by its sheer absurdity.. Richard Parmalee Robinson could not serve anyone except himself. Serving others was constitutionally impossible.

Nevertheless, Helen would receive him as requested, accept her miniature and make no comment. If he tried to bait her, saying something provocative or suggestive, she would not reply. But she would *not offer* to return his portrait. He would have to ask for it.

Robinson came the next day, and she didn't inquire about his health or his plans, or seek any explanation about comments he'd made in his letter.

When he returned her portrait, she said, "Thank you," and nothing more.

And he didn't ask for his portrait, even though he's said he would. At least one part of his letter had proven true. He had indeed studied her disposition and came to the right conclusion: nothing more needed to be done. He smiled, nodded his head, thanked her with two words, and departed.

Helen could now leave the city with at least some important business resolved.

But she could not stop writing letters to Robinson. It was a habit that helped to pass the time. She now crafted them more carefully, avoiding spontaneous expression of feeling, and made them shorter, with only a few sheets. Her letters were now the letters of a friend, not a lover. She avoided the word "love," and mentioned in passing the "kindness and attention of a gentlemen" encountered in the train car. "If it weren't for him," she said, "I never should have got along."

As she traveled toward Philadelphia, the physical and emotional distance calmed her nerves and made the casual sharing of news and gossip possible and enjoyable.

Then devastating news came from New York.

Chapter Twenty-Two

By the time Helen learned of the fire, it had burned out after another night and day. Fortunately, the fire had not reached Duane Street or the other brothels in the neighborhood. But the glow of the conflagration could be seen as far away as Philadelphia.

Nevertheless, Helen was eager to return to see the damage for herself and to make sure the lives of those she knew had not been unduly disrupted. Did smoke and ruins now permanently scar the city she had come to love? Could the realization of everyone's worst fear—a destructive fire of unimaginable scale—diminish the city's vibrant spirit, its almost breathtaking commitment to the demands of commerce and entertainment, the proud displays of wealth, the open and eager pursuit of fabulous dreams, the noise of preachers, hawkers, hookers, singers, and politicians, all seeking their place in the light of a sun blocked by the towers, steeples, and cupolas of Manhattan? If almost six hundred buildings had burned, many of them in the financial district, did this mean that some of her wealthiest clients now faced financial ruin and could no longer afford the indulgence of brothel visits and the gifts that resulted from them?

And then Mary Berry informed Helen in a letter that Robinson had come to Number 128 Duane Street and asked for service from another girl!

This visit was an outrageous violation of house etiquette, and was dealt with swiftly. As the Duchess explained,

Dear Helen: An incident which took place last evening obliges me to write to you this morning. Your Frank came about nine o'clock, enquired for Maria, and said he should see her. She was then upstairs with a gentleman. I asked her downstairs, but judge my surprise when he told me he wanted to remain with her. I told him he should not, but he tried to insist upon doing so, but again I told him I would not suffer such a thing. I asked him in my front room. Maria came in so I should hear what passed. He wanted Maria to consent then, or to meet him next Thursday night at the theater. I waited to hear her reply. She, in a very ladylike and candid manner, told him she would not, and rejected his offer with becoming dignity, so he went away just as he came. He had another gentleman with him. Tom Easy is very anxious to see you. I wish you to come home as soon as possible; be assured all things shall be right until you return.

Helen returned to New York a few days before Christmas. She was vexed by the news that the Duchess had allowed Tom Easy and a friend to relax and drink in her private room while she was gone. The Duchess had even built a fire for them. But she would deal with this later.

She wrote a curt note to Robinson:

Tuesday afternoon. I have returned to town, and wish to see you this evening without fail. I am back thus soon on your account, so you will please sacrifice an hour of your time on mine. It may be for your interest to accede to this request. Yours, etc. Helen.

Anxious and needing distraction, Helen in the meantime went downtown with Maria Stevens to survey the burned ruins and decided not to say a word about Robinson's overtures as Maria had done the right thing in declining him.

For at least that afternoon he was forgotten. They walked among hundreds of residents and tourists who came to gawk, shake their heads, point, and speculate about the future of their city. Helen had read both the *Sun* and *Herald*, and stared at the illustrations, trying to comprehend what had happened. But nothing had prepared her for the devastation. Entire blocks were reduced to smoldering rubble, consumed by raging balls of red and yellow flames described by one observer as giant, insatiable monsters with long, twisted orange arms and fingers impervious to the bitter cold that December night. Water had frozen in the hydrants, wells, and cisterns, and a desperate effort to crack the ice of the East River and get water proved futile. The water froze in the engine hoses, and firemen watched helpless, as the fire danced in quick and high steps down Pearl Street to Wall Street and to the river. To the west, Exchange, Williams, Baker, and Stone streets were incinerated, and only the marble facade of the Merchant Exchange on Wall Street remained after the fire destroyed the rest of the building. Its magnificent sixty-foot dome had collapsed, destroying the statue of Alexander Hamilton, finished only eight months before.

Having passed the Exchange many times during her walks, and always resenting her inability to enter it, Helen now stood silent before the broken remnants of this symbol of the city's economic pride and wondered how the city could recover. The entire southern tip of Manhattan smoldered in the afternoon light, and spiraling columns of smoke punctuated the already grey skies. Helen and Maria had to cover their mouths with gloves to prevent gagging in public.

Despite the fire's scale, however, Helen remained optimistic. About its recovery she had no doubt, even though the fire had consumed thirteen acres and looters, shouting anti-rich slogans, had emptied scores of mansions, piling high mounds of furniture, clothing, and dishes in the streets. Fortunately, only twenty had died that night; the toll could have been far worst. And no matter the circumstances, Helen believed that dreams and effort guaranteed positive results. Like most New Yorkers, she knew the city would recreate itself and become even greater.

The stock exchange had resumed trading, the flagship store of the Tappan brothers had reopened, and the Merchants' Exchange Company had solicited plans for a new Merchant's Exchange. Along Wall Street, banks and offices were partially or fully demolished, but the word was out that the Greek revival style would dominate the neighborhood. The Federal style of red brick facades, fan light doorways, and dormers was now old fashioned, and anyone who could afford to move was moving north. Rumor had it that John Jacob Astor, the city's richest man, would build a new and more opulent hotel on upper Broadway near City Hall Park. Of course, its wealthy patrons would desire the company of only the most fashionable "ladies" in the best houses of the Fifth Ward and in other houses sure to open nearby.

However, Helen's mood soured on her return to the house, finding Robinson's reply waiting for her.

> My dearest Nell—forgive me, forgive me! Though things may look against me, I can easily explain and, I think, to your satisfaction. Your language is cruel—bitter, but I can forgive it on the grounds of the apparent cause you have for it. I will be at your house at eight without fail. Yours ever, Frank.

Neither the salutation nor the appeals for forgiveness impressed Helen. The note was as self-centered as ever. "But I can forgive it," was especially galling, as if coming from a man in a position to dispense favors, like a corrupt Catholic priest offering forgiveness in a darkened confessional.

A note she received that same afternoon from Tom Easy deepened her sour disposition. She knew he and Robinson were friends, or at least drinking companions, but clearly Robinson was too arrogant to see Bill as a legitimate rival, or even suspect he would try to undermine him. But Tom told her,

I was taking a lunch and a glass of porter with Frank, and it was then he informed me you had got back. I supposed he's been to see you but he said he had not. Ah, Helen, may I hope that. I am not so fond of *change* as a certain gentleman named Frank of my acquaintance.

But Robinson did not come to see her, as she had demanded; and later she learned the reason.

The Duchess had barred his entrance, and never told Helen about it. She learned about it from Robinson after he had mentioned it in another letter.

On the day after Christmas he wrote,

Dear Nelly, You have maintained silence longer than I expected. You know that I never shall go into that house again, therefore I could not come to you, but expected you would tell me where I could see you. You have done me an injustice but once, when you believed what Mrs. B stated in her letter. You might and ought to have disbelieved it. Still I don't know that you can be blamed, for I once deceived you and others sadly. But my days of deception are over and I hope we can at least be friends. Monday night perhaps you will be at the park, and then I shall see you. Burn this if you please. I hope you had a merry Christmas.

Helen's heart softened. He seemed truly contrite, and the spirit of the holiday season moved her to reconsider her attitude. He had disappointed her, but was disappointment that important? And what human being could be spared from it? Even Jesus felt it in the Garden of Gethsemane.

Trying to be more open and less judgmental after a needed separation, she replied,

My dear Frank, You are perfectly aware of the disappointment I felt at not seeing you, also my anxiety to do so, but dearest, you know I can forgive you anything. I think your account will be quite square when we meet tonight. I am at a loss to know what you mean by "if Mrs. Berry will admit you," for heaven's sake tell me, for if you have been refused, I will vacate the premises immediately.

They met that night at City Hall Park, and he told her what had happened. She apologized for the incident but said nothing about what she would do about it. He apologized for deficiencies of character, but did not elaborate.

The night was cold, and they could not stay outside for long, but they word-lessly made an effort to protect the restored warmth between them. Robinson recounted his story with a few words, and Helen reacted with a word or two: "Yes" and "I see," little more. They avoided the danger of too many words, in-stinctively knowing that lengthy sentences and protracted explanations could obliterate tender mercies in a flash. They had walked into this dangerous territory too many times before and had become acutely aware of every ditch, alley and dead end there. Instead, they held hands, smiled, and listened to the sounds of the city as it shimmered in the dim light of the gas lamps around the park and on nearby streets.

"We're still friends," he said after a long pause, looking up into the star-lit skies.

"And Happy New Year," Helen replied.

At last, there could be peace between them, and she needed to savor it on a cold night in a virtually empty park.

But there could be no peace back at 128 Duane.

Helen confronted Mary Berry for excluding Richard from the house.

"You have no *right* determining which men I can or cannot see," she said the following day in the parlor. "And I did not appreciate you allowing gentlemen into my private room while I was gone."

"Of course I have the right," replied Mrs. Berry, amused by Helen's presumption. "This is *my* establishment, and I make the rules and can break them at my pleasure. You know my rules. That young man is too quarrelsome and too young. The combination of immaturity and obnoxious arrogance is absolutely intolerable. He is not welcome here anymore, and he will not be allowed to enter this house again."

"Then I will have to leave. I will find another place to live," declared Helen.

Mrs. Berry said solemnly, "You *are* an ingrate, just as Ann Welden told me."

"She spoke to you about *me?*" Helen asked, surprised.

"Why of course she spoke about you. We talk to each other just as you girls talk about *us.* I had hoped that you would be different, but in the end you are *not*, even after all that I have done for you. I am so disappointed that you would choose a foolish boy over me. You should know that boys like him will hurt you in the end, and you will curse the day you ever met him."

"I cannot stay here," Helen insisted.

Mary Berry slowly rose from her chair, absolute control in her lifted jaw, her tightly closed lips, her narrowed eyes, and the hands that gripped her crossed arms as she held them just below her bosom.

"Very well," she declared in the imperious tone she usually assumed for only the most important occasions. "You will *remove* yourself immediately after the New Year, and darken our days no more."

Mrs. Berry left the parlor, closing the door behind her. Only after she heard the clicking of the door did Helen allow the tears to fill her eyes. She regretted the rupture between them. Mrs. Berry had indeed been kind to her, and the stay at her house held many good memories. But the charge of ingratitude hurt most profoundly because it was true.

She had to get away. There was no turning back. She rushed up to her room before anyone could see her tears or notice her pain. She immediately began to pack, even though there was sufficient time for more leisurely preparations, and Tom Easy and a friend were coming that very evening

And then, Helen made a decision. It came suddenly and provided a small measure of relief because it was so simple. She would *not* tell Richard Robinson when she was leaving or where she was going. Some friends didn't have to know *everything.*

Chapter Twenty-Three

Helen stared at the unsealed note dated January twelfth; apparently written in haste, it said:

Dear Nelly,—Thinking you had entirely forgotten me, I think it high time to enquire what has become of you. Hearing you had left Mrs. B's; I am astonished that you don't inform me. Is it that the name of Frank has no power to please you any longer? Is it true that you have made up your mind to forget me, to DENOUNCE ME to those you most sacredly most promised not to? Am I not debased enough when I deserve to be forgotten by you, but that you must still go further and betray me? Nelly, Nelly, pause ere you go further; think of how we were once situated, and if you can convince yourself that you are acting a noble part in cutting my throat, go on, is all I have to say. My course will be short and sweet! No bitter, bitter, as well you know. Since our acquaintance commenced, what an eventful one. Can you look back on it without pleasure and pain? I cannot. Frank.

She read the letter again and again, trying to make sense of it, the pervasive fear of denunciation, the references to cutting his throat, the implied pleasure she would receive in hurting him. Was he *mad*? What did he think she knew about him? What were his other activities? And why would he say such things in an unsealed letter subject to the prying eyes of the carrier or anyone else?

Had she done something to so agitate him? Moving to another house without telling him was certainly an insufficient cause. She racked her brain for the probable cause, but could not determine anything she had said or done that could incite such dread.

She wrote a quick reply, promising that she would never betray him "under any circumstances." That promise he could count on no matter what others might say, she insisted.

However, she was not ready to see him privately in her new rooms at Mrs. Cunningham's at Number 3 Franklin Street. His anger concerned her, and so she asked him to meet her at eight o'clock on the corner of Chapel and Franklin, near Tom Reilly's Hotel. "Be punctual," she ordered at the end of the note.

"Why didn't you tell me you moved?" Robinson immediately asked, his voice accusing, his eyes piercing even in the dim gaslight.

Lamely, she replied, "I needed time, some distance between us."

"What are you afraid of?" he asked. "Me?"

"No, I can't count on myself," Helen said.

"For what?"

"I am stronger when you are *not* around," she admitted, surprised that she'd told the truth.

"Then you *are* afraid of me," he exclaimed, his triumph muted but unmistakable.

"No," Helen protested, shaking her head. "I am not afraid of you, or of anyone else. I've been through enough and I've seen enough to know that you can *never* truly frighten me."

"Don't underestimate me," he said.

"What do you mean? Surely, you are not threatening me!"

"No, I am not," he replied quickly, softening his tone. "I mean that I *can* be someone to fear. My father is afraid of me."

"Why?"

"He says I'm evil," said Robinson.

Helen laughed lightly, "How *melodramatic*! And why does he believe that?"

"I started fires, small fires near the house."

"What is it with boys and young men? Tom Easy got arrested for starting a fire. He even spent some time in jail for it. Foolish certainly, and you can see what fires can do. Evil? I don't think so."

"Don't mention Tom."

"But you are friends," Helen protested.

"Don't mention him in front of me," he insisted.

"Don't speak to me in that tone of voice," she replied. "I *hate* that tone of voice, that tone as if you had some command over me, as if I was a maid in your father's house. I hate it, do you understand? I hate it, and you promised in your letters that you would not behave this way. You *promised*, but I think you can't help yourself, and I can't help myself in getting angry and upset. There are all kinds of people around me, and I can laugh at their mistakes and annoying habits. But I can't laugh at myself around you. I have no sense of humor around you, and I despise myself for taking you so seriously."

"Then what do you want me to do? Never come back?"

"No," she said. He seemed hurt. But she wasn't sure; he was a good actor.

"As I said, I need some time to think. We'll write, of course, and see each other for dinner and even the theater. But I need some time, a separation of sorts."

"Very well," he said. "I only hope you will answer my letters. I *need* them."

"I will write," she said. "You can be assured of at least that."

"May I accompany you back to your house?" he asked.

"No," she said evenly.

"But it's dark and dangerous!" he protested.

"I came alone, and it was dark then as it is now. I am not afraid of the dark. I am not afraid. Good night."

"Good night," he said, standing still as she walked away.

He was not done for the evening, and as he walked the streets he wondered which brothel he should visit. He needed to mount some whore, find immediate release from the tension building up inside him.

Usually he ignored the streetwalkers who invariably teased him with their leering eyes, a lift of their skirts, a caress of their breasts. But tonight he would not waste time. He would not participate in the protracted ritual of talk and drinks in a brothel parlor, the game of whore seduction practiced by Helen Jewett and her kind, the elegant phrases, the coy delays, the pretense of romance.

He needed a hole to fill, and he needed one now.

He noticed a girl at the corner standing under the gaslight. He knew immediately why she was there. No lady would be on the streets alone at night. It was cold, but she was ready for business.

He approached her, and the young woman smiled. She wasn't pretty, but she wasn't ugly and had all of her front teeth.

"May I be of service to you, sir?" she asked.

"Yes," he said, "and be quick."

"A dollar, sir."

"Fine," he said.

"My room is nearby."

"No."

"But it's cold, sir."

"Then I'll find someone else who's not so particular."

"Don't you bother sir. I'll do what you want."

"Just find a recess and lift your skirt, and I'll take you from the rear. That's what I want."

"Yes, sir."

As if she had a favored spot nearby, she led him to a recessed alcove, its steps leading to a basement apartment. Fortunately, the enclosure protected them from the cold air, and there was a small fire.

Quickly and with great efficiency, she pulled up her dress and petticoats and exposed herself to him, leaning against the windowsill for balance.

Robinson unbuttoned his trousers and pulled out his penis. Without saying a word, without giving her any warning, he rammed into her.

"Ah," she said, startled. Instinctively, she turned her head to take a look, saying, almost plaintively, "Sir?"

"Shut up," he snapped. "Just shut the fuck up!"

"Yes, sir," she replied, turning her head away.

"Can't you women just shut up?" he repeated, his voice raw as he tried to pound his groin against her buttocks. "Damn it," he added.

He was too big.

"What's wrong, sir?" she asked, worry in her voice. Or was it fear?

"I said shut up, you fucking bitch. I said shut up!"

Within seconds, he was done. He made no effort to spill himself on her buttocks or on the ground. If she became pregnant, that was her problem. She knew the risks of the trade.

He stepped away and started to button up. His fingers felt cold for the first time.

"My dollar, sir," she said, turning to him, her dress falling to the ground in a swoop of cheap wool and cotton.

He slapped her face, enraged by her cool demeanor.

"This should be free," he said, "and you should be *grateful* for getting what no other man in this town can give you."

She put her hand to her cheek and replied, unfazed, "One dollar, sir."

Her eyes told him everything. She was not afraid of him.

"I could just walk away," he said. "Or . . . I could kill you."

"Then do it," she said, both weary and defiant.

He reached into his waistcoat pocket and retrieved the dollar coin. The prostitute put out her hand, but Robinson dropped the coin to the ground, smiling as it clattered against the stones.

She surprised him. She did not bend over to get her money. She didn't move at all. She waited.

"Cunt," he said.

Tears suddenly filled her eyes, and she moaned as if wounded. But she still didn't move. Two thin stream of tears flowed down her cheeks.

Suddenly, he whispered, "I'm sorry. I shouldn't have said that. I know better. " He took a step, pressing his case. "You're doing only what you have to do. I'm sorry."

"No you're not," she said, matter of fact.

Robinson froze, his anger returning as quickly as it had evaporated. "You fucking cunt."

"That's better," she replied. "Honest."

He could see a dim smile, and he resolved to return on another night, when he would kill her for trying to humiliate him.

If he could find her.

But he was still not ready to go home. He needed a drink, so he headed toward a tavern popular with clerks on Clarke Street. He thought of Helen and decided to follow through with her suggestion and take her to the theatre. They would go see that new play at the Bowery, *Norman Leslie*. It was a hit, filling the house night after night. The play, based on a book by a reporter from the *New York Mirror*, told the story of a young girl murdered by her lover in 1799, his arrest, and the trial at a City Hall courtroom. Reviews had made particular note of the two hundred people on the stage for a carnival scene in the last act. Robinson had to see that.

At the Clark Street tavern his companions, already drunk after countless rounds of whiskey, shared their adventures of sexual conquest, citing names of prostitutes, times, places, and results, all of them always triumphant, all of them always reflecting on their astounding prowess. Nevertheless, there was always one preeminent hero in these predictable tales, and that title belonged to Frank Rivers, whose sheer stamina no one could match. He could perform for hours, exhausting his partners. But he never seemed to find satisfaction, always needing more women, like a drunk with an unquenchable thirst.

His companions never boasted about intimacies with Helen before Robinson, even though some had been her customers. But they invariably interspersed news and gossip about the sex trade among their tales, and enjoyed tales about the game he and his roomate, James Tew, played at brothels, both men calling themselves "Frank Rivers" and creating their own comedy of errors. "We are alike in every way, except one," Robinson had observed. His listeners managed to grin with admiring sympathy, but no one mentioned the rumors about his endowment, fearing that envy might be misconstrued for unnatural desire.

It was from this group that he learned three days later that Helen had fallen ill. Her unnamed illness wasn't serious, his companions averred, probably a cold.

Nevertheless, Robinson felt compelled to find a moment, perhaps during a break at work, to write her.

Finding that moment, he composed his most honest letter to date:

> *My Dear Nelly, Nelly, for God's sake, write me soon and tell me how you are getting along! It is hard to me to know that you are sick, and not be able to assist you—not to see you, and even not to hear from you. But if it is too much of an effort for you to write, I beg of you not to. I had rather not hear from you than have you make yourself sick by overexerting yourself to gratify me.*

I wish I could see you this evening, Nelly, but it cannot be. By heaven! You are in my thoughts day and night all the time. If I knew you thought half as much of me as I do of you, it seems as though I should be most happy. But, Nelly, you must not forget me, though I do treat you cold sometimes—do not be angry with me. I know you think me a strange being, yet cold and insensible as I sometimes appear, I have feelings over which I have no control, and which, if trifled with in any way, would make me unhappy and almost crazy. I am called away; excuse me and the one-thousand-and-one mistakes. Forever yours, Frank.

Robinson had to wait another week before he and Helen could meet at the Bowery Theater. Dressed in resplendent green, Helen looked fully recovered. Her eyes sparkled and danced as they surveyed the rooms, and she moved her full skirts with a slight but accentuated thrust from side to side to emphasize the pleasure of her return before her many admirers.

She could not quell her excitement about the play. She had read the novel on which it was based, and eagerly related details of the story to Robinson, despite his protestations. He liked surprise and suspense, but she dismissed his avowal with a wave of her hand, saying, "This is history, New York history."

Julia Sands had been murdered, according to the police, by her fiancé, Levi Weeks, who was defended in court by the remarkable and influential legal team of Alexander Hamilton, Aaron Burr, and Brockholst Livingston in March of 1800. The play showed Weeks in Bridewell, the city jail, and dramatized his three-day trial at the City Hall courtroom, where he was finally acquitted.

When Helen and Robinson finally sat in their seats, other men made a point of getting her attention, and she acknowledged them as they leaned over to get a look or stared at her from boxes throughout the theater.

Several of her customers, including Tom Easy, had approached her before the rise of the curtain for the first act, and expressed their hope to see her again soon. Robinson fell silent, fuming that he had to witness these exchanges. Helen would be in bed with some of these men soon enough.

Robinson tried to be philosophical. After all, he knew she was a popular prostitute. What did he expect? Jealousy seemed absurd.

Nevertheless, his despondency deepened as the evening went on, and Helen's indifference to his mood particularly wounded him. She never asked, "What's wrong?" She never tried to assuage or comfort him. During intermission, he didn't raise any objections, so she found others with whom to talk, saying courteously, "I'll be back. There are people I must see. I'll meet you at our seats."

Helen thoroughly enjoyed the play, particularly the sets and the crowd scenes, applauding vigorously at the end. But she never asked for Robinson's opinion. She thanked him for accompanying her, although he seemed incidental to her enjoyment, and allowed him to hail a cab for her return to Mrs. Cunningham's.

"Good night," she said, looking at him but without extending her gloved hand.

"Good night," he replied coldly, seething. And that was that, until a note arrived for him the following day. Helen said she had noticed he was unhappy at the theater. She didn't ask for an explanation, but her comment gave him the opportunity to explain:

> *Dearest Nelly, Your letter was received at two o'clock, and I thank you for it. You were right in thinking me unhappy last evening. If I had not been, believe me I should not have treated you as I did. I know I did not treat you as I ought, I knew it at the time, yet I could not help it. Did you ever know me to appear happy a whole evening when with you at the theater? I don't believe you have, at any rate, not lately. I have told you often, I believe, that when I am with you, I want to be alone, where no one can see us. Can you think it is in my power to sit at your side a whole evening, your friend watching you and you him, and feel happy? Those who do not feel as interested as I do might, but Nelly, I cannot. I cannot sit with you in the presence of one who has purchased you as his; do you really think I can? I repeat. I cannot. I am glad to see you, yet I am never more unhappy than when I am with you at the theater.*

Reading the note, Helen shuddered.

He should be grateful she'd even *bothered* to have him in her presence, in her bedroom, at the theater, or anywhere else. He was a clerk from the country whom she favored. He needed to be more grateful that she had condescended to give him her time and attention. Enough was enough. He had to adapt. Her days of concession, adaptation, and compromise were over.

She would set the rules, and he would have to abide by them. When she wanted him, he had to appear. No more invitations. He would be *summoned* instead.

Her notes proliferated, one after another, a cascade of threats, appeals, invocations, and demands sent at least one a day, often more.

What started as a campaign of submission became a cry of desperation when he refused to come see her. She wanted control, but he was not having any of it, not now, not ever.

Helen now resorted to self-pity, writing,

On Saturday last I wrote you a note, which you have not yet replied to, and I am sure I don't deserve to be treated so cavalierly, and I must see you before another night has elapsed or I shall be half crazy, beside which I have something very particular to tell you which I cannot well postpone.

He still didn't reply.

She began to echo back Richard's emotional barrages, even using the words he had used earlier:

If, my dearest Frank, you have ever tolerated for one day the painful suspense I yesterday endured, then you will pardon me for writing you a harsh, cold letter. I feel amazingly like blowing you up, if I dared—not with powder.

At last, he promised to write in a quickly scribbled note. He wasn't specific about when he would write, and after a two-day lapse, Helen jumped into the breach:

My dear Frank, You have passed your promise by two nights, and yet you have not thought proper to send me a single line, even in the shape of an excuse. Do you think I will endure this? Shall I who have rejected abundance for your sake, sit contented under treatment which seems invented for my mortification; nay, for my destruction. Pause, Frank, pause, ere you drive me to madness. Come see me tonight or tomorrow night. Come and see me and tell me how we may renew the sweetness of our earlier acquaintance, and forget all of our past unhappiness in future joy. Slight me no more. Trample me no further. Even the worm will turn under the heel. I have love, but do not, oh do not provoke the experiment of seeing how I can hate. But in hate or in love, I am your Helen.

This grabbed his attention, and he replied the next day:

I have read your note with pain. I ought to say displeasure; nay, anger. Women are never so foolish as when they threaten. Keep quiet until I come on Saturday night. Then, we will see if we cannot be better friends hereafter. Do not tell any I shall come. Yours, Frank.

Their meeting was calm and without accusation, as if all of their energies had been spent in writing their letters. They apologized without being specific; they feared the details would again ruin the possibilities for immediate pleasure.

"I want you," he said truthfully.

"I want you," she admitted.

"I love you," he lied.

"I love you," she replied, the words now a mockery of the sweet emotions of the previous summer, when excitement and infatuation had made everything seem possible, when if there was no innocence, there was at least a kind of splendor. And they both made promises they could not possibly keep.

"We'll always love each other," she said.

"We'll tell the truth."

"We'll not allow jealousy to poison us."

"We'll not deliberately hurt each other's feelings."

"We'll do no harm."

"We'll be happy."

Chapter Twenty-Four

Helen missed Billy.

He was still traveling out west and sent letters about his adventures. They reminded her of the value of his friendship—direct, uncomplicated, and honest. He and Helen were not lovers with intense longings and needs; they were just friends who had sex now and then.

A constant reader of the city newspapers, Helen stayed informed, but nothing compared to Billy's take on city crime, politics, and social life. His gossip was especially rich because it was free of the resentment so obvious when women typically gathered in parlors to admire and complain. And his letters actually described people and events, providing rich details for those who were not there. He was a true reporter. Thanks to him, Helen lost any inclination to travel west after he reported how his mail stage overturned four times on his way to Louisville, where a brother lived.

Unfortunately, separation made him sentimental, and he extolled the variant of her name, preferring "Ellen" because of the noble character in Scott's *Lady of the Lake*, a mutual favorite. For the first time he admitted to not liking the name Helen, because it referred to "that slut who cuckolded her husband" before the Trojan War. He then compared her to a swan "that is compelled to pass, in the course of its career, through and across some devilish and impure stream (as well as very many translucent ones), yet the instant she is freed from immediate contact with them, she simply 'shakes her feathers,' stretches her noble pinions, and her plumage resumes its pristine purity and beauty."

Earlier, he had declared her a "woman of spunk." Now she was a swan shaking her plumage for a return to her original purity after an occasional dip in the unavoidable filth. Was he now claiming she was the storied prostitute with a heart of gold burdened by her unfortunate circumstances? *What is it with men and their encounter with the open spaces beyond the Hudson River?* she wondered. Was Billy Attree destined to become another *true* American, shedding his English skin for Indian feathers and a hatchet?

Billy asked her about the activities of Frank and Tom Easy. But he could not resist his honest insensitivity, even when paying her a compliment. He observed,

"Oh my soul, Ellen, I never knew but two women whose society I thought worthy of accepting on a journey. Jane Price was the one, and your self is the second. You must believe me, for I cannot remember to have ever behaved so like a scoundrel or a barber's clerk as to have flattered you."

From Texas, after nursing a young woman back to health with medicines from his brother, he declared,

God bless you, Ellen. I long to see and talk to you, for I have seen such sights—but yet I have not yet transgressed with an Indian girl, no, nor with any other kind since I left New York. But this is not virtue, for I wish, oh, how I wish I had you with me this very night.

Helen appreciated both his reticence and his desire, and eagerly anticipated his return in late February. But she needed more immediate satisfactions, especially the satisfaction of scintillating and challenging conversation. Bored with Tom Easy, frustrated by Robinson, and missing Billy, she summoned David Rogers, her old suiter, and he came almost immediately, a true gentleman.

Dr. Roger's voice still stirred her like no other, and she had long ago forgiven him for his crude self-indulgences. Without specifically naming the offending events, he had apologized in a brief note; and he said in another that if she ever wanted to see him again, he would gladly oblige for an "evening's entertainment." No more "arrangements" at his home, he added. "Too complicated."

They had a variety of other matters to talk about. He was actually interested in her opinions about recent events: Benjamin Day reprinting pages of *Maria Monk*, a novel about sex between nuns and priests and infanticide, inciting mobs at his office; Joice Heth's return to New York; and Jamie Bennett being attacked with a walking stick by James Watson Webb on Broadway. Since the recent inception of the Bennett's New York Herald, Helen read his newpaper with great interest. He attacked the police, politicians, prostitutes, actors, bankers, and his press competitors most of all, sparing no one. A known hot head, Webb finally had enough of the printed abuse and confronted Bennett in broad daylight and beat him until he was unconscious.

At the mere mention of Bennett's name, Helen observed, "He got what he deserved. What did Webb call him? The lowest species of scurrility?"

"You? Defending James Watson Webb, of all people?" replied Rogers, amused. "The man is a coward, knocking Bennett from behind"

"Bennett's time was long overdue," she insisted.

"And what about freedom of speech and of the press, Miss Jewett?" Rogers asked, his tone good-natured even as he taunted her.

"I am not condoning assaults like this one. Mr. Webb is a coward, indeed. I am only admitting my satisfaction with what happened."

"He wasn't harmed, unfortunately. It could have been much worse."

"Mr. Bennett seems amused by the incident. His account in the *Herald* laughs it off. Did you see it? He is shameless."

Before he could answer, she reached for her book of clippings and began to read: "The fellow, no doubt, wanted to let out the never failing supply of good humor and wit, which has created such a reputation for the *Herald*, and appropriate content to supply the emptiness of his own thick skull."

"Well, it worked," said Rogers, once she stopped reading. "He sold nine thousand copies. People can't get enough of this kind of news, and Mr. Bennett clearly knows how to promote himself."

"I predict other attacks," said Helen, amused too.

"And he will rise to embrace his near martyrdom; after all, he compared himself to Zoroaster, Moses, Socrates, Seneca, and Martin Luther just a little while ago."

"But even so arrogant a man can't believe this?"

"If he tells us enough times, we'll believe it. I'm great, my paper is great—the claptrap of politicians and hucksters since time immemorial. He and Barnum are just alike. Advertising is all, even if it is a lie."

"Joice Heth was a lie," said Helen. "Not her condition, her age. I hate what Barnum did to her."

"Of course you know she just died?"

"Yes, I saw the notice in the papers, and everyone is calling for an autopsy."

"I asked for one this summer, and Barnum agreed that it could happen once she passed away."

Startled, Helen exclaimed, "But why? He knows you will find out he's been lying."

"His recent plans say everything. It will be public, and huge. Tickets will be sold."

Helen shuddered. "How can you participate in such a spectacle? This is outrageous."

"But not unprecedented. Have you ever heard of the Hottentot Venus?"

"No," Helen lied, her cheeks reddening slightly. She'd seen prints of her in Nathan Weston's private collection. As seen from the side, the black Venus had huge buttocks, massive balls protruding from her back like boulders about to drop to the ground. Her breasts fell like long tubes with bulbous tips over her belly, but a small, triangular, beaded cloth covered her pubic area. There was no attached background information explaining her history.

"She was a South African woman who had *steatopygia*," Rogers explained. "It's an excess of fatty tissue that enlarged her buttocks and distended the lips of her private parts."

"How unfortunate," Helen whispered, looking away. His clinical references to female body parts still embarrassed her.

"She was in an exhibit that traveled all over Europe," he continued. "In London, for an extra charge, people could poke her buttocks. In Paris, she was part of an animal show. When she died in 1815, a French zoologist dissected her and presented her cut out genitals in a jar to French scientists before sending her skin to England, where it was stuffed and put on display."

Helen shuddered and moved slightly away from the table where they were sitting. Then she said passionately, "It's the fate of women everywhere, every time."

"No, it was more than that. Dr. Curvier wanted to show that the Hottentots, her people, were closer to animals than Europeans."

"To make his case, he could have used *a man* if it was only a matter of racial difference," Helen replied, her voice rising. "There is something especially hateful about the treatment of women here and everywhere. If Mr. Day had published a novel about *priests* cavorting about, no one would notice or care. Priests have been doing the unspeakable for centuries. How else do you explain the Reformation? But a novel about cavorting nuns, now that's news!"

"Women are not supposed to be sexual beings," Rogers replied, always matter of fact.

"We know that's not true," said Helen, a light tease in her voice.

"Mr. Day will have even more news when I am done, because I am giving his new editor, my friend Richard Adams Locke, exclusive right to observe and report the autopsy proceedings."

"*You* have a reporter friend?"

He smiled wryly. "Why should that surprise you?"

"No one signs anything, the cowards."

"As usual, you are too harsh. But with the Moon Series, I had to meet the author."

"Mr. Day *claims* to be reprinting some Scot's work."

"You don't believe him?"

"Of course not. He's a liar, a hopeless liar," Helen asserted, again grateful for Billy Attree's confidences.

"Nevertheless, I had to meet the brilliant liar who wrote those pieces. The scientific knowledge, its sheer scope, in astronomy, biology, physics, and anatomy, was astounding, even in a fiction."

Helen sniffed, emphasizing her point. "Scientific fiction . . . how helpful."

"At first, Mr. Locke maintained the lie. After all, the *Sun* made a great deal of money. But he had a need to tell. He needed someone to know he is an amazing writer. I think he's a genius. After a few drinks, he confessed. I promised not to tell."

"You tricked the trickster."

"His powers of observation will help me in making my case about Mrs. Heth."

"So you too belong to the camp of Bennett haters," Helen said, smiling again.

"The army expands, but my opinion of Mr. Bennett, who deserves my scorn and a thorough repudiation, is not my primary motive."

"Then what is it?"

"I will settle the fact of Mrs. Heth's humanity, once and for all."

"Have you become an *abolitionist*, Dr. Rogers?" asked Helen, still trying to be light even though she could tell he was absolutely serious.

"Yes," he answered after a pause, "but *not* as you think. I'm not signing any petitions, or going to any meetings. But recent events—the riots, the attack on the U.S. mails, the mass meetings, and all the rest—have convinced me that we are profoundly ignorant and must be forced to *see* what cannot be denied."

Helen was surprised by his idealism, or was it naiveté? She sighed, and spoke carefully, not wanting to offend him. He was essentially a decent man.

"We can hope," she said, "But I suspect the autopsy will make no difference to those who insist on her inferiority. It certainly didn't change your French doctor's mind. Mrs. Heth may be granted *humanity* in 1836, perhaps, but nothing more. There will be those who will insist on her inferiority . . . and on mine. They can have it no other way. It's pathetic really, and says more about the beholder than anything about Jocie Heth, or me, and all the rest of us put down by men. So many are *pathetic* really."

"So, do you consider killers of prostitutes pathetic?" Rogers asked. "You've heard about what's happening, haven't you, in the past few months?"

"Yes, I've heard rumors and seen short items in the papers about bodies and missing women. But that's happening to streetwalkers and prostitutes in *low* houses, not in respectable houses."

"Ah, you remain a snob, Miss Jewett, and you talk about these women like the men you despise."

She flushed.

"No, that's *not* true," she said, hotly. "That makes the murderers even more pathetic, killing poor, desperate women, don't you agree?"

"Just remain discriminating, Miss Jewett, and be careful. Most of us are louts."

"There are exceptions," Helen said, reaching to touch his hand.

"And may I benefit?" he asked. "Is it time?"

"Yes," she said, wanting to be closer to him, to feel his warmth, to accept his embrace, to bridge whatever gaps remained between them. "Yes, indeed."

The amphitheater of the city saloon on Broadway was packed. Fifteen hundred men—medical students, clergymen, physicians, and the merely curious—had paid fifty cents each to see the widely advertised "anatomical examination" on Thursday, February twenty-fifth. The room was hot and smelled of sweat, damp wool, and cigars extinguished at the doors. The heated arguments about Joice Heth continued until the very last minute, creating a rising buzz in the hall stopped only by the sight of a mahogany coffin carried into the hall at exactly noon.

There was a sudden, collective intake of breath, and then absolute silence. Six burly men carried the small coffin, followed by a solemn P.T. Barnum, very tall and awkward in his cheap, tight-fitting clothes, and his associate, Levi Lyman, half his size and even more confident. David Rogers waited at a large table at the front, and behind him stood Locke, ready to report every detail of the autopsy to readers of the *Sun*. Dr. Rogers's surgical tool case was open nearby. The blades of the scalpels and knives gleamed in the lamplight.

The carriers lowered the coffin to the floor, opened it, raising the lid carefully and putting it to the side as the sound of handled wood penetrated the furthest reaches of the hall. Then they lifted the wrapped body and placed it on the table. The men stepped away from the table, as directed by Mr. Barnum, and Dr. Rogers came to the front to explain how scientific evidence would settle the controversy about Joice Heth's age.

Using the deepest register of his dark voice, its authority unmistakable and beyond reproach, he explained the fact of ossification, the conversion of body parts into bone.

"It is the surest evidence of extreme age," he explained, "especially in the major arteries."

He told the crowd about an autopsy he'd performed in Italy on a woman who died at one hundred fifteen years of age.

"Her heart was almost completely ossified, the entire organ," he declared. "Today we will take a look and see if Mrs. Heth has organs with similar character."

Rogers turned to his surgical case and lifted a scalpel, showing it above his shoulders so everyone could see it. Then he turned to the body, lifted the sheet covering the abdomen, and made his first incision, cutting across it. He reached into the cavity with his ungloved hands and probed around the organs. Observing closely, Locke forced himself to not gag and turn away, even as the sound of fingers pushing and prodding viscera repelled him. One man in the front row bolted from the hall.

"The abdominal organs have a perfectly natural and healthy appearance," Rogers declared. "The liver is the proper size and, by indications, shows no signs of disease."

Except for Rogers' work and Locke's scribbling behind him, there was perfect stillness in the hall, no words of dissent or confirmation, no nods or shaking of heads.

"Now the heart," Rogers announced before exchanging the scalpel for a handsaw.

Now groans could be heard, as men unfamiliar with autopsies anticipated the sound of metal against bone, the hissing, wrenching, and tearing. When he began, some in the audience covered their ears, and when Rogers finished his cut of the sternum and pried apart the ribs, several men turned away. Another man in the front row vomited into a napkin and was quickly escorted from the hall.

Rogers delicately cut into the heart and took a close look at the valves, bending over as his fingers continued to explore and calibrate. He whispered his findings to Locke and then turned to the audience and noted the absence of ossification of the valves. "There is only the slightest evidence of ossification at the arch of the aorta," he added.

"Now the lungs," he announced, and turned again, examining this organ for what seemed a long time. "There are many tubercles in the left lobe, a sure sign of tuberculosis. This was the immediate cause of death, not a cold, as previously reported."

He wiped his hands on a cloth and returned to his instrument table for another handsaw.

"Now the brain," he said, "the center of reasoning and general intelligence. Mrs. Heth was a great talker, and had a memory for great details of her past, and the nation's past as well. I am sure that I will find a normal and healthy brain."

At the sound of the sawing of the skull, several men covered their ears, and when Rogers lifted the brain from its cavity, hundreds turned away at first, then returned to gawk at the compact folds that made thinking and feeling possible. Its small dimensions moved Locke, who had never seen a human brain before. That something so small could produce such wonders of creativity and discovery only reinforced his deep sense of the mysteries of creation. For just a moment, Rogers' pronouncement about Jocie Heth's age was anticlimactic.

"Joice Heth could not have been more than seventy-five," Rogers declared, his voice projected to the end of the hall, "or at the utmost, eighty years of age!"

Locke turned to Barnum and his assistant, as if to accentuate the final denial of their claims, but they stood absolutely still as commotion now racked the hall. Some men stood up, shouting and gesticulating; others remained seated, but argued their point. The autopsy may have settled Joice Heth's age, but conflict and controversy continued. Barnum smiled nervously; his name and motives were being bandied about, and the chatter of "humbug" filled the air.

"Remove the body," ordered Rogers, although he had no authority to issue such an order. The carriers hesitated, and he said, irritated, "Use the back door. There is no point in waiting for the hall to empty."

They obliged, moving quickly, reminding Rogers that ends are always faster than beginnings. Within minutes, the amphitheatre was empty, except for Barnum, Lyman, Locke, and himself.

An awkward silence ensued. Then Locke broke it, saying with a cheer that seemed to his friend out of place, "My report will be in *Sun* tomorrow morning, and we'll of course sell out."

"First things first," said Barnum, his pompous arrogance fully restored.

"You understand our priorities, sir," said Locke, gathering his papers and pen. "And thank you, David, I mean Dr. Rogers, for your work. I know we all learned something."

"Indeed, we *must*," Rogers replied, turning his head pointedly to Barnum, whose body filled his clothes like a glove. He was fit, not fat, and he projected confidence as only a professional huckster could.

Barnum obviously expected Locke to leave, but Locke didn't. Barnum then approached Rogers as he gathered up his things.

"You know, Dr. Rogers," said Barnum at his most unctuous, "I engaged Mrs. Heth in good faith. I relied on her appearance, and everyone will acknowledge that she *looked* very, very old. And I believed in the documents in her possession as much as I believe the Declaration of Independence."

Rogers saw no need to gloat, and replied graciously, "Indeed, she looked much older than her age, and looks can deceive. I actually expected to spoil at least a half-dozen knives to sever the ossification in the arteries around her heart and chest."

Lyman then joked, "Perhaps the medical profession can't decide with precision on cases such as this one."

"Sir," said Rogers lifting his chest and chin, "after today's solemn work, I am *not* amused." He took the arm of Locke, and departed.

As promised, the *Sun* on the following day had its account of the autopsy; it started with its final conclusion:

Dissection of Joice Heth—Precious Humbug Exposed.

The anatomical examination of the body of Joice Heth yesterday resulted in the exposure of one of the most precious humbugs that was ever imposed upon a credulous community.

A debate on the nature and value of "humbug" ensued. Some claimed that only the truth mattered. Others said truth was immaterial, that glitter and entertainment mattered far more."Did you get your money's worth?" was the essential question asked by supporters of hoaxes and humbugs. "Relish a joke," urged Horace Greeley, who informed his readers of a false report of victory given by a Greek soldier. When confronted, the soldier had asked, "Am I worthy of punishment for having given you a day of happiness?"

And in that spirit, Levi Lyman went to Jamie Bennett's office and told him that he and Barnum had humbugged Dr. Rogers, passing off another Negro as Joice Heth. Joice was actually still alive and on exhibit in Connecticut!

Eager to expose the *Sun* for all of its offenses—refusing to hire him, printing the Moon Series, outselling his own newspaper—Bennett eagerly took Lyman at his word, overlooking the fact that Lyman had approached him months earlier with a bribe to print advertisements for the first Heth showing. Bennett had refused, and when he saw the advertisements in the *Sun*, the *Courier*, and virtually every newspaper in town except his, he had swelled with the pride of his moral superiority. That pride carried him through his wars with Webb, Day, and all the rest.

Now he had another battlefront. He issued his next bombardment with obvious relish on February twenty-seventh:

Another Hoax!

Annexed is a long rigmarole account of the dissection of Joice Heth, extracted from yesterday's *Sun*, which is nothing more or less than a complete hoax from beginning to end. *Joice Heth is not dead.* On Wednesday last, we have learned from the best authority, she was living at Hebron, in Connecticut, where she then was. The subject on which Doctor Rogers and the Medical Facility at Barclay Street have been exercising their knife and their ingenuity, is the remains of a respectable old Negress called Aunt Nelly, who has lived many years in a small house herself, in Harlem.

He agreed with Rogers that the woman was about eighty years old, but then Bennett recklessly pressed on, unable to restrain the missiles of slander and libel. "Are you not sir, the real author of the Lunar Hoax?" Bennett asked, the first of the "few plain questions" he meant to ask the doctor. "Did you not furnish Locke with most of that humbug? Did he not, at *your* request, undertake to pass for the author of the work? Is it not known to you that he is incapable of writing the scientific portion of that hoax?"

David Rogers never answered Bennett's charges, although he had grounds to file a libel suit and join the ranks of the many others who filed against newspapers with less serious complaints.

He stated his position to Helen, lying in her arms during the quiet comforts of sexual satisfaction after a rapid but heated coupling.

"I'll buy a special stick for Webb, for the next time he pummels Bennett on the streets. You know there will be a next time. And we'll toast the bastard for beating the other bastard. True justice will be served, and I'll be a grateful contributor. Do you want to make a donation?"

"Absolutely," she replied, and they both laughed.

Chapter Twenty-Five

"You can't be serious?" she asked Billy, finally back in town. "You heard me correctly. I'm going back to Texas to fight for Texas independence with Sam Houston and Stephen Austin."

"But Texas," cried Helen. "Texas?"

"All who love liberty should come to Texas and fight. They need men, and each volunteer will get paid a salary, rations, and six hundred and forty acres of land."

"Six hundred acres of wasteland," cried Helen. "Desert."

"You've never seen desert, Helen, so how would you know? But it's safe for women and children. I was traveling near San Felipe with four men and seven women, all under twenty-five, thirteen children, and several dogs. Why don't you come with me, Helen? We can start a new life there."

"Not if you die out there," said Helen grimly. "People die in wars, remember?"

"Oh, I won't die. Besides, the Texans are fighting for something . . . for freedom, for independence. And the Mexicans are fat, lazy, and have more land than they know what to do with. They don't *need* Texas, when they have almost everything out west, California and the rest."

"If you have to fight for it, the Mexicans want it badly enough," Helen objected. "And we don't need another slave state. I'm sick of people prattling on and on about freedom, all while they want slaves to serve them on plantations."

"You don't understand," Billy said. "But you would if you could see what I've seen."

"You've changed. Billy," said Helen, recognizing the futility of argument. He was determined to go, and meant to leave in early March, with or without her. She was certain that he never seriously thought she would abandon New York and go with him or anyone else. Her life was in New York. It was all she knew, all she wanted to know.

"I know I have changed, and I'm glad for it. I saw people who had *dreams*— dreams for themselves, dreams for their children and their grandchildren. They're committed to believing in and fighting for something bigger than themselves. They have a cause."

"You came from England looking for a better way of life, more freedom than what you could find there. Didn't you find it here?"

"Yes, I did," he replied, smiling for the first time. "This country is so much more open, with more opportunities than in England. Back there, the rich control everything and the land is only yours if you inherited it from generations back. Here you can make your own life, or so I thought. But Wall Street, Battery Park, the Livingstone's and all their kind are duplicating London. Tammany Hall is no better than Parliament, and the Five Points can match Church Lane in London any day. But out west there is open space and the chance to start again, to build a different kind of land, different cities."

"When they first landed, I'm sure the pilgrims and planters all thought the same thing when they saw the forests hugging the coast," Helen replied, both touched and irritated by his passion. "New York was forest once, and the Dutch came with that same sense of wonder you have and built Manhattan on the backs of the Indians. Your Mexicans are the Indians, same story, same history. And those Texans, if they manage to break away from Mexico, and that is highly unlikely, will take, burn, and destroy to build their own cities. Just wait and see."

"But I want to be a part of that creation, to be a part of building something. New York is finished."

"New York will *never* be finished," Helen asserted.

"I've seen enough. In Texas, there are fewer people, less crime, less of everything."

"It sounds *boring* to me," she said.

"You're too comfortable, Helen; and it's only when you're forced to see the sky from the ground and eat food by the river, that you can truly feel the beauty of the natural world, the wonder of it."

"How soon you have forgotten the overturned coaches on the way to St. Louis."

"But the Mississippi River and New Orleans and the Ohio Valley are wonders to behold."

"You've become a silly romantic," she observed wryly. "What have you been drinking?"

"From one romantic to another, I've had time to think about my life, what it means, and what contribution I can make to it. I want more than *this*."

At the word the word "this" he waved his arm above his head and to the four corners of Helen's cramped room.

"And you will die for it," she said.

"Then I will at least die for something worthwhile. But let's not talk about death. This is all about a new life, a new beginning."

"What about your friends?"

"I have no friends, except you."

"What about your club, your young lions, and Robinson?"

"They represent the worst, when I cared about nothing but my basest pleasures and inclinations. I started it, and I can end it just as easily."

"What about your sworn oaths of loyalty and secrecy?"

"Empty oaths, meaningless promises. Once my club is gone, they will join others, if they want to. We're joiners, we men."

"Your army is another club," said Helen.

"Dedicated to a higher purpose than gambling all night and fucking whores and . . ." He stopped, catching himself when Helen flinched at the reference to her work.

"I'm sorry, I didn't mean to offend you, or disparage what you've chosen to do. Please, if we are to part, let it not be on a note of dissention or violent disagreement. I want to have a fond memory of you. Thoughts of you sustained me while I was away, and will sustain me when I leave again. I only meant to separate myself from behaviors and practices I no longer can defend."

"What behaviors?" she asked. Billy was lost to her, but there was still a chance to manage Robinson through information she might gain from Billy.

"Oh Helen, just be careful. Robinson can't be relied upon, and I'm not sure about the way he thinks about things. He's a *strange* one."

"Why do you say that?" she pressed.

Billy hesitated for a moment, and then he said, as if liberated from any obligation to Robinson, "I thought I was introducing some young country lad to the ways of the world. Well, he knows *more* about the world than I know. I see it in his eyes. He has done things, terrible things, and I don' think you should see him anymore."

"What things?" Helen repeated, her heart beating rapidly.

"Fires, torturing and killing animals. He likes doing risky things, going to Battery Park and finding men to suck him. And he might be involved in some kind of embezzlement with Mr. Hoxie, working with that Cashier fellow. And, worst, of all, he told me he killed a girl."

"That's a lie," Helen exclaimed, almost shouting. "You can't believe that! He likes to lie, to shock. Surely, you don't believe he could do such a thing?"

"I don't know if he did it," Billy acknowledged. "He has lied to me before, and this might just be another lie. But he *enjoyed* telling me the lie, and that is what's so sickening. I *don't* like him, and you should stay away from him."

"Well, if you think by telling me this that I will reject him, no longer love him, you're mistaken," Helen declared.

"I have no such illusion," he answered. "I have seen some of your letters, and no matter what he says or does, you forgive him. Love is a mysterious force.

I wish some days you loved me that way, with such passion, with such *blind* devotion."

"I'm *not* blind. I see perhaps all too clearly. Our love will end, as has your love of New York and our way of life. Everything ends, eventually."

Billy caressed her hand.

"Please be careful," he said. "End it gracefully, as carefully as you can, as I am trying to do and failing miserably. End it well, and let him move on to somebody else. There will be someone else. For men like him, there always is."

"I never thought you could be jealous," she said.

"Well, there you have it. I *am* jealous. I'm jealous of his extraordinary looks, his extraordinary endowment, and most of all, his ability to obtain a love I have never known, and perhaps will never know. He is so *unworthy* of your love, because your love is so much grander than he could ever conceive. But none of this matters anymore. He is out of my life for good, and I will not miss him. But I will miss you, dearest Helen, and I want you to be happy."

"I thought you didn't like the name Helen," she replied, tears in her eyes.

"Oh that," said Billy, rolling his eyes. "Just another moment of romantic silliness, that letter about Helen of Troy and all. Helen isn't your real name anyway. What is it? You never told me."

"Dorcas," she whispered. But she didn't look away, as if ashamed. She still didn't like it, but she needed to see directly Billy's reaction to the truth. This evening was an evening of truths. "Dorcas Doyen."

"I don't like that name either," he said.

They giggled like children.

———•———

Helen decided to move again. Billy's departure unsettled her, and she thought a change would be a fitting end and beginning, a bridge between the loss of Billy and her reconciliation with Robinson. She wrote a note to Rosina Townsend, and asked for permission to return to 41 Thomas Street.

Rosina responded quickly. "By all means. We must talk. Come on Saturday around four before afternoon tea. You can't have your old room. Someone else has it. You'll be in the rear upstairs."

Helen understood the benefits of her return for Rosina. Helen could command the highest prices for an hour of entertainment. For a full night of pleasure, the profits to the house could be substantial. Nevertheless, she felt she was returning home. Number 41 Thomas Street represented the best in New York brothel life. The furnishings were of the highest quality and the clients were the most discriminating and generous. Although she didn't know all of the girls, she knew at least Elizabeth Salters and Maria Stevens, who had departed Mrs. Berry's soon after Helen did.

And by all accounts, the other girls got along well. Rosina Townsend would not have the gossip, backbiting, and jealousies of other houses. She established her weekly Saturday afternoon teas as the essential vehicle for maintaining domestic harmony. But unlike the Duchess, Rosina Townsend seemed truly interested in the welfare of her girls and the perpetuation of domestic tranquility. She had no interest in vulgar display and vain attempts at recapturing the splendors of soirees in the Petit Trianon. She would leave mere shows to Barnum, Niblo, and other hucksters.

"Thank you for receiving me." Helen sat down across from Rosina in the parlor, where the others in the house would soon gather.

"Of course," said Rosina, smiling broadly. "I was sorry that you left us, but I remained hopeful that you would return. After all, we are *incomparable*." Rosina quickly but delicately scanned the room to reinforce her point.

"I have one condition," said Helen, maintaining an even, pleasant tone of voice. Rosina's smile immediately disappeared. She knitted her eyebrows and Helen responded quickly. She didn't mean to offend or affront Rosina, who waited for an explanation, her face now a rigid and silent rebuke. Even with all of her success, Helen Jewett was in no position to impose conditions.

"I found a young helper," Helen said softly. "I want to bring her with me. She cleaned my room so well, and helped me dress in the most efficient and yet sensitive way. Of course, you know how important it is to have the best help, with all the stays, eyelet closures, buttons, the pinning of sleeves. She is small, but she has strong arms for pulling the strings of a corset, and yet she is gentle, too. She is a find, and I want her here. Her name is Sarah, Sarah Dunscombe."

Even before her arrival in New York, Helen had planned to have a negro maid, one whom she could trust with her anonymous donations to the abolitionists. But such a girl also had to meet her high standards for domestic service, and finding such a maid was not easy. She tried one girl after another, causing some to wonder why she was so particular. Nevertheless, Helen continued to hope for that perfect combination of industry and discretion, and eventually she found Sarah, recommended by another prostitute at the Park Theater who said pointedly, "She knows how to keep secrets. Most negroes do."

"By all means," answered Rosina, her eyebrows knitting together. "I understand the importance of having that kind of help. This cannot be a problem."

"She is a negro," said Helen quickly.

"That is not a problem," replied Rosina.

"Thank you for agreeing to my request," said Helen.

"It was *not* a request," corrected Rosina. "It was a condition. What would you have done if I had said no?"

"I would not come back," replied Helen.

"Your loyalty is impressive."

"She has earned it."

Helen relaxed now that her condition had been met. And yet she remained guarded, not sure where the conversation would take her. She was still not ready to tell Rosina about her donations to the abolitionists, and she doubted she ever would. It was just too dangerous, given the times.

"If she were white, I would still want her," Helen added. "She just *happens* to be a negro."

"One day this will not matter, but *not* in our lifetimes. Is there anything else you need to tell me?"

"I have some favorites who will come regularly to see me. My friend Tom Easy will come every Saturday. Another one is Frank Rivers. You will especially notice him. He is most handsome."

"Your favorites do *not* interest me," said Rosina, her tone hardening once more. "As long as they pay and mind their manners when they are here, I don't care who merits your special favors. Anything else?"

"No," said Helen.

But then Rosina smiled, and said, leaning forward, "Helen, I am so pleased that you will be with us. Your intelligence, wit, and interests will enliven our times together when we are not doing business. When you first came to me, I was all business. But that has changed. Although how we earn our living makes everything else possible, I am now more interested in how we spend our time between our entertainments. Men are *not* that interesting. When they come here, they are interested in only a few moments of pleasure, everything else is prologue and epilogue, and they can barely hide their impatience and indifference. We'll have to enrich our days between times in our rooms."

"Will the mention of customers be forbidden?" asked Helen.

"Oh, of course not, my dear," said Rosina, warming to the conversation. "We must discuss them as we discuss the latest purchases at A.T. Stewart's. We will compare notes and describe qualities—all, of course, with discretion, tact, and good taste. We can never be vulgar. This is not that kind of house, as you well know. Thankfully, we have not had attacks here from the uncouth. Is your tongue as sharp as ever?"

"Yes," said Helen.

"Good," said Rosina. "It will be useful if the time comes, I am sure."

"I will do what I can to help," Helen replied, smiling.

Rosina reached for the small bell on the table and rang it twice. The interview had come to an end, and the others girls of the house could now enter the parlor and greet the house's newest member. They were all delighted to meet Helen or renew their acquaintance, embracing her in turn, offering their names, and making promises of lasting friendship.

Once they were all in the room, sitting in chairs around the small table at the center, Rosina thanked them for their reception, and then asked, "What shall we talk about today? What interests you? Shall we talk about the play at the Bowery, *Norman Leslie*, or Mr. Barnum and Joice Heth, or politics? We could even discuss the bank wars. Now *that* will shock men, that we even know who Nicholas Biddle is! We are not supposed to know, and some of them think we're not true ladies when we show an interest or knowledge about money. But aren't they foolish? We are in the business of making money, and building a life based on its acquisition. Our service is as old as time, but our goals are the same. So what shall it be?"

Helen waited for the selection, vowing to simply listen and withhold her opinions for another day.

She moved into Number 41 on March eighteenth.

————•————

The first two weeks went well. Robinson came on three occasions, and there were no accusations or recriminations; his stays were not lengthy, but they were relaxed and efficient. Talk, sex, talk, and then more sex before he left for the night, returning to his boarding house. He couldn't afford the rate for spending the night, or so he said. He was just a clerk.

But on March twenty-ninth, discord erupted again.

His request came without warning. Robinson sat down at Helen's table, and said, "I'm here to have you return my letters."

"What?" she asked, dumbfounded. "What do you mean?"

"You know exactly what I mean," he said coldly. "I want you to give them back."

"No, this is not how it is supposed to happen. No, I'm the one to ask for the return of mine *first*."

He laughed lightly. "But that is not how it happened, is it? You can't change that fact."

Abruptly, she stood. Her hands were now tight balls of raging skin and bone. "Get out!"

He looked up and said, his voice still calm and obliging, "When I get what I have asked for, and I did ask for what are mine."

"There is someone else."

"The letters are mine."

"I knew it would come to this, you betraying *me*."

He laughed again. "Betrayal only comes when there is a promise of fidelity. I made no such promise."

"You said you loved me."

"So I did, but we were not engaged, and certainly not married."

"But there are promises of the heart; they don't need to be spoken."

"I've heard yours all too clearly. They are loud. Indeed, they are deafening, and I've heard enough!"

"Billy was right. You are a liar!" Helen cried, her eyes wide with the recognition of the truth. Billy had left town on March sixth, and she'd cried for hours, desolate to lose a friend who always had her best interest in mind. She needed him now more than ever.

"How convenient for you to refer to a man who abandoned all of us for some foolish pipedream, his wilderness fantasy."

"You have no right to scoff. He at least believes in *something*. What do you believe in? What do you hold dear besides yourself?"

"There is nothing *but* the self. Everything else is a lie made by the weak and the stupid."

"You can't love anything or anyone," said Helen, astounded that he could be so utterly clear and comfortable with his selfishness.

"Then returning my letters should pose no difficulties for you, should it? Why should you keep the letters of someone you abhor?"

"Because they are mine to dispose of as I like."

"As I am now engaged," he said, enunciating each word for emphasis, "my letters to you could prove . . . embarrassing. I want them back, to eliminate possible *complications*."

"What are you talking about?" she asked. "Engaged? How can you be engaged? You are not even twenty yet. You may have prospects, but I can't imagine any respectable woman *settling* on you at this stage of your career."

Robinson stood now and said with soft but deep anger, "There is no *settling* on me. I'm as good as it gets."

Helen was so struck by the absurdity of the remark, she threw her head back as she laughed. "You cannot be serious. You can't."

"I don't have to convince you," he snarled. "Your opinion doesn't matter to me."

"Of course it does, or you wouldn't have come here to get your letters and *explain* yourself. You could have just stopped coming."

"And continue receiving a barrage of your pleading, whining, insistent, argumentative letters? No, thank you! I'm *sick* of them, and the only way I knew for you to get the message that I don't want them anymore is to come here and tell you to give mine back. I knew the request would shock you, and I hoped it would so shock you that you would shut up once and for all. Damn, I am *sick* of you."

"So the mask falls away at last," she said.

"And so it has. Are you happy now? Is this what you want?"

"I never wanted this kind of ugliness," she said sadly.

He chuckled. "Oh, I can get even uglier, if you push me."

"I'm not afraid of you," she said. "I know all about you, what you have been doing. Billy told me *everything*."

"And what of it? The mask is off, and you can see me fully, directly. What difference does it make now anyway?"

"*I* now control what the world sees," she hissed. "I can put the mask back on, or keep it down on the ground. All I have to do is write a note, and once your fiancé, whoever she is, knows what I know, it will be *all* over for you. There will be no marriage, no prospects."

"I told you not to threaten me. I warned you."

"I'm sure she would *not* be happy to hear that you sport with men in Battery Park, that you spend your time in brothels with other men who come to watch you in bed with me. The scandal would be too much to bear."

Suddenly, he was at her throat, his right hand pressing against her neck and his left pulling the curls at the back of her head.

"You had better keep your damned mouth shut. Do you understand? I am warning you. Don't take your chances with *me*. Now give me those damn letters, or I will break your fucking neck."

She couldn't speak, he was pressing so hard. Realizing this, he relaxed his grip, and she said hoarsely, "I'll get them for you now."

"Good, very good," he said. "That's all I wanted in the first place. Do you want yours?"

"No," she said, struggling to maintain her composure. "You may keep them as a reminder of someone who loved you once, before her eyes could see clearly."

"You are such a cunt," he said, drawing back as if scalded by the touch of her skin. "All alike, you women."

"Congratulations on your engagement, and unhappy marriage," said Helen.

He slapped her across the face.

"Oh," she said lightly, not altogether surprised. But she made sure her eyes remained cold and unyielding.

"Now give me those damn letters."

She went to her dresser drawer and pulled them out. She looked up to her portrait of Lord Byron, and thought of how Lady Caroline Lamb had described him: "He's bad, mad, and dangerous to know." She almost giggled, thinking of how her relationship with Robinson began with a quotation from Byron. Now it ended with another.

She handed the letters to Robinson, saying, as if he could hear her inner reflection, "At least he was a poet."

"Fuck you," said Robinson. "At least my fiancé is not a bitch."

"Your language has deteriorated. Won't she be surprised?"

"*You* won't be telling her. I'll make sure of that," he said, turning away. He stopped at the door, his hand on the doorknob, and turned to face her. "How could I ever think that you were anything but a good fuck?"

Chapter Twenty-Six

She had to see him again.

A demand for the return of letters was usually the sign of an irreparable breach, but she had absolute confidence in her powers of persuasion. She would write to him, ask him to come see her. She would offer forgiveness, accept him into her arms and bed, assure him of her devotion. Then, when the time was exactly and exquisitely right, she would demand the return of her letters, terminating their relationship and reaffirming her control once and for all.

That end could be years away, if she so willed it.

Helen wrote him every day for a week, sending Sarah, her maid, to his boarding house. He was never home when she came, and so she left Helen's letters with the proprietor. Robinson sent no reply until Saturday, when he asked for a brief opportunity to speak with her on Sunday.

She consented, and he came to the house promptly at four in the afternoon. She received him in the main parlor, and they retreated to the side parlor for greater privacy. Helen intended to delay an invitation to go up to her rooms until she could tell he was completely within her power.

Robinson was dressed in his Sunday finest, a well-tailored jacket that emphasized his narrow frame, accentuated his youth, and declared the absence of excess and indulgence. Most men had too much flesh in the waist and hips, the consequence of overzealous consumption of slabs of beef and pork and too many rounds of whiskey, brandy, and beer. But not her Robinson. He was the ideal man about town, slim, handsome, intelligent, fascinating, provocative, and sensual.

He certainly was not her wealthiest client. After all, he was only a clerk at Hoxie's on Canal Street. And yet he had money for good clothes, meals at Delmonico's, tickets at the Park and Bowery Theaters, and gifts for her. Although she was usually inquisitive about sources of income, making sure that her clients could afford her fees and fulfill her expectations for gifts and other indulgences, she did not pursue these inquiries with him, knowing his father had money.

Her reticence and the resulting mystery only enhanced his allure. His sexual prowess was a delightful surprise. On the surface, he seemed delicate and slight, too fastidious for romps in the bed of prostitutes. His anatomical endowment made him unique; she had never seen a man so big. But after minimal instruction he was deferential, patient, and sensitive to her needs, and carefully used his physical gift to arouse receptivity so intense she often gasped. Nevertheless, his words mattered more. The memory of lines he'd written in letter after letter reinforced her ardor, her need to be with him, to hear him speak, to do and say things that would force him to write more words. Words were ultimately the engine of her desire.

He was the only man she knew who could match her in the generation of letters, declarations of emotion, and the raising of questions. Only he could make her read scribbled lines in the middle of the night, to decipher them by candlelight, and immediately try to craft the appropriate reply, all the while leaving some measure of ambiguity and uncertainly so that he would continue to probe and question, and write another letter. Helen did not drink much, and no one at Number 41 or at Mrs. Berry's had ever seen her drunk. But these letters, his as well as her own, were her very own elixir. She needed them to stimulate her, create that stupor that warmed the blood and lightened her head. Helen knew she was silly, and occasionally felt she was no better than the opium eater Thomas De Quincy, whose diary she had read in Judge Weston's secret collection. But she was not eroding her body, she decided; she was only reinvigorating her heart and mind. She felt more alive when she wrote letters and received them. What harm could come of it?

When he sat down at the table across from her that Sunday afternoon, he looked directly into her eyes, and said warmly, "I am so sorry, although I know no apology can ever match the depth of my vulgarity and ingratitude. I was not a gentleman that day, and you have every reason to despise me and not receive me. So I am especially grateful for today. Once more I am reminded of your generosity of spirit, and realize I always want your friendship."

Helen waited, carefully crafting her response. She had to maintain a delicate balance between dignity and delight. She was still thrilled to see him, and was certainly ready to forgive him. But she could not let him believe that she was a toy he could dispose of because he was frustrated, bored, or eager to play with another.

"What do you need?" she asked, her words flat, unthreatening.

"I want your forgiveness."

"You have it," she replied.

His face brightened, and he said, leaning forward, "Thank you. Thank you."

"What else?"

"Can we remain friends?"

"Just friends?"

"More than friends."

"What about your future wife?"

"We can be discreet, like the other husbands who come here."

"Then you'll remain my favorite?"

"As long as you wish."

"And you'll return your letters?"

"If you want them."

"Yes, and will you answer my future letters?"

"Yes, but please, draw no conclusions if you do not hear from me as frequently as you write them. Please."

"I will not insist that you reply to each and everyone one."

"Thank you for understanding."

"When can I see you in my room?"

"May I come this Saturday, the ninth? I will bring the letters."

Helen was careful to not convey disappointment. Why wait? Why not come up to her room now, or earlier in the week? Besides, she usually saw Tom Easy on Saturday nights. Saturday was *his* day. But she deferred. Robinson had his reasons for asking, and she did not want to create any cause for disagreement. Everything was going so well.

She replied, offering a slight smile, "Yes. Come on Saturday at nine. Can you spend the night?"

"Yes," he said.

"Good," she said, and then rose, extending her hand.

He looked down at it, then raised it to his lips. "Thank you so much for giving me another chance," he whispered after kissing her hand.

"We'll read Byron to celebrate," she replied.

He looked up, his bright eyes suggesting either curiosity or confusion. Helen couldn't be sure. But no matter, he was coming to *her*, and together they would read some of her favorite lyrics, their yearning beauty sure to deepen his devotion. She momentarily considered a quote from *Don Juan*, but feared its mockery might inflict a wound. Unlike Billy, Robinson could not laugh at himself.

"As you wish," he said, sounding resigned.

Helen felt the urge to rebuke him, but she held her tongue, having achieved most of what she wanted. Though her heart had skipped a beat when he agreed somewhat reluctantly to read Byron, she counted on Byron to weave a spell again.

"Until Saturday," she said, making sure her voice and smile were soft and free of any hint of criticism or disappointment. "Goodbye."

Helen could not remain silent until Saturday. She wrote him three letters that week, declaring her love, expressing her high hopes for that day, reiterating his standing as her absolute favorite, and suggesting possible activities they could do together. She made sure not to mention the theater. He could not abide the attention she received there, and she saw no need to irritate him. Of course, she would continue her weekly appearances there, but she would not go with him again under any circumstances. Even if he asked, she would find some reason for declining.

Saturday, she rose early, washed her face, and sat at her desk to write another letter, one he would receive before he arrived that night.

When her maid arrived to restart the fire, clean the room, and help Helen to dress for the day, the thin eighteen-old-year smiled and said, "Miss Helen, you are happy today, really happy."

"He's coming tonight, Sarah. My Frank is coming, and tonight will mark, I assure you, a new beginning for both of us."

Sarah suddenly stopped her dusting and turned to face Helen. "It's been hard for you, Miss Helen."

When Helen first hired her, Sarah had been unnerved by her intimate disclosures, and there was the obvious fact of racial difference and the emotional dangers in any kind of interracial friendship. Servants were especially vulnerable, and Sarah knew all too well what could happen when young white women, even prostitutes, realized what power they had over negroes. Black maids could be fired immediately, but that usually happened only after days or weeks of cutting remarks, slaps to the face, a push to the back, kicks in the legs. Jobs were scarce, and these white girls knew that black girls needed the work and would tolerate cruelty and suffer silently.

But Miss Helen was different. She appreciated having a good maid, and Sarah knew she was good—hardworking, thorough, fast, careful, and very private. Whatever she heard or saw, she kept to herself. When the time came, Helen even asked for her help in making sure that her donations made their way, discreetly, to the coffers of the antislavery society. For one who was always explaining her reactions to men, and especially her feelings about Frank Rivers, she didn't say much to Sarah about race or racial politics. She was direct and to the point one day, and that was that.

"It's just not *right*," she said to Sarah. "Slavery is unjust, and bigotry is contemptible."

Sarah wished that Helen's opinions and feelings about Frank Rivers were as clear and simple. Instead, they simmered and boiled, then turned as cold as ice water, and as quickly burst into flame. Fire and ice, a mystery to Sarah, but unmistakably real when she heard Helen's words and watched the shifting faces of a girl only a few years older than she.

"Yes, things have been difficult lately, and I have been sore pressed to make things right between us," Helen explained. "But I think I have found the answer."

"Is there anything I can do today to make things better?"

"Yes, take my note to Mr. Easy. And make sure to tell him that he is *not* to come tonight. He will not ask about it, as you well know. He is most obliging in his dim way."

"Yes, Miss Helen. Will you be going out today?"

"Yes, Miss Salters and I will be taking a walk to A.T. Stewarts this afternoon, and then we will be taking tea with Mrs. Townsend and Miss Stevens. Mr. Rivers will be coming around nine, so I will need for you to come back at your usual time tonight to prepare the room after I entertain some other gentlemen earlier in the day."

"Some old friends, or new friends?" asked Sarah.

"New friends during the day, and an old friend tonight," Helen replied.

"What will you be wearing?"

"One of my simpler green dresses. It is still quite cold outside, and my coat will cover most of it, but we will have to pay special attention to my hat, jewelry, and gloves so I can still dazzle through a restricted window my obvious charms."

Helen giggled, and Sarah replied, "Yes, Miss Helen. Just tell me when you're ready for help with your corset, ruffles, and stays."

"Oh Sarah, sometimes I wish I could just walk the streets stark naked. It takes two people to get dressed for any occasion, no matter what!"

"Miss Helen!" exclaimed Sarah, embarrassed but not surprised. Helen Jewett was so bold!

"I'm just joking, Sarah, of course. But it is tiresome to endure the pull of corset strings, the ear curls, the final attachment of ruffles. What we must do for beauty's sake! Still, I must be grateful for not having to stay fully dressed until I go to bed."

"Yes, Miss Helen," Sarah replied, turning away to continue the dusting.

"I'll write a few letters," said Helen. "Then I'll be ready."

"Yes, Miss Helen," Sarah said. Then she noticed a miniature on the dresser drawer. She had seen Helen wear it around her neck.

"My, my," Sarah whispered.

"That's Mr. Rivers," said Helen. "He's beautiful, isn't he? In person he's even more extraordinary. Maybe one day you'll see him, but he never comes when you're here."

"He is handsome, Miss Helen, and I can just imagine how he makes you feel when he's here."

"You may look at it as long as you like, Sarah, but when you're done, give it a dusting and put it back into the drawer."

Sarah flinched, looking up from the miniature like a child caught taking a piece of candy from a forbidden jar.

"Oh, I'm sorry," she said. "I have better things to do."

"You can't help yourself," Helen said, uncritically. "He has that affect on every-body. And *that* is just a picture."

Sarah wiped the miniature quickly, returned it to its Moroccan leather case, and put it in the bureau drawer.

"Someday you might be fortunate enough to get a good look at him," Helen said. "Then you'll understand."

That afternoon Sarah returned at five to prepare the room for the night. She went to the cellar to get hickory wood for the fireplace, and when she returned she found Helen with a young clerk from A.T. Stewart's. Fully dressed, she was sitting in his lap and said, "Sarah, this is Mr. Strong. He will be here for a while, but you continue with your work. Be sure to bring a pitcher of water, and I will need some clothes for tonight."

Sarah nodded, but said nothing, staying busy. Usually, she was alone when cleaning Helen's room in the late afternoon. But sometimes Helen had company and expected Sarah to simply carry on. Only when absolute privacy was required would Helen excuse Sarah, and send her home.

Tonight was one of those nights. Sarah dusted and polished, went out for water, and returned with fresh bedding, tightened sheets and coverlets, smoothed out pillows, and ignored the animated conversation between Helen and Strong. They ignored her too, as if she were invisible.

Finally, Helen, delighted to show her generosity before company, said, "You can go home early, Sarah. I won't need you for the rest of the evening. I will see you tomorrow. Good night, and again, thank you for doing such excellent work. I was a maid once, long ago, and you are *far* superior."

"Thank you, Miss Helen," Sarah replied.

"And don't forget to put my favorite handkerchief on my pillow," she said, beaming.

"Yes, Ma'am," said Sarah, making sure that she didn't mention Mr. Easy, who had given her this expensive gift and was not coming as usual that night.

Later, Helen continued to be cheerful, expressing her hopes at tea table that evening with Rosina, Elizabeth Salters, Maria Stevens, and Emma French, all of whom had troubled histories with men. They listened sympathetically to her past travails, and all hoped for the best.

Helen had a specific request for Rosina.

"Frank will be coming at nine, and I have asked Tom Easy *not* to come tonight. As you know, this is his usual night. But please, if he comes, don't let him in."

Rosina's room was at the front of the house, facing the street, and she usually checked to see who came knocking at the door.

Rosina agreed. "Don't worry, my dear. I don't want anything to ruin your special night."

At nine fifteen, Rosina heard a knock at the locked front door and a request for Helen.

"Miss Jewett, please?" the man asked politely.

Rosina asked him to repeat his request. She had to be sure the voice did not belong to Tom Easy. The man repeated it, and she unlocked the door. As soon as she opened it, the man raised his cloak to the top of nose, exposing only his eyes and forehead. He wore a cap. The attempt at disguise was silly and unnecessary; she recognized Frank Rivers, thanks to the globe lamp hanging behind her in the entry way.

Now silent, he proceeded down the hallway toward the parlor, where Helen awaited him. Rosina hurried beyond him to open the partly closed door to announce his arrival.

He had already turned around to go up the right staircase and waited at the landing. Helen went up to meet him there.

She plucked at his cloak and said, loudly enough for Rosina to hear, "My dear Frank, I am glad you have come."

They entered her room, and Rosina didn't see them again until eleven, when Helen came downstairs in her nightgown, knocked on Rosina's door, and asked for champagne. Rosina went to the cupboard in the side parlor, discovered that it was empty, and volunteered to go down to the basement to get more.

"I can get it," Helen whispered.

"No," said Rosina. She never gave her keys to the basement pantry to anyone, assuring tight control of her inventory. "You go back up, and I'll bring the champagne to you and your guest."

The basement was cold and damp, and she retrieved a bottle quickly, placed it on a tray from the parlor pantry, and went up to Helen's room.

She knocked before entering, and when she opened the door, she found Helen standing there, smiling broadly.

"Mrs. Townsend, please join us for a drink. To celebrate a birthday, Frank's birthday."

Rosina could see Robinson lying on the bed, his back against the backboard, his body covered to his shoulders by a sheet as he leaned against his elbow and read a book illumined by a candle on a small table placed near him. He did not turn to acknowledge her or speak.

"Thank you, my dear," said Rosina, "But I need to return to my guest."

"Then we can celebrate tomorrow," Helen replied.

"Yes," said Rosina. "Tomorrow. Goodnight."

"Goodnight," whispered Helen, stepping back into her room and closing the door.

"Now you can be mine," she said.

And he replied, "Yes, now and forever."

PART 3

Chapter Twenty-Seven

When David Rogers heard the news, he cried out, "Oh no! Oh no!" He felt sick to his stomach, but not surprised. Too many prostitutes had been killed in the city in the last few months, and he had never believed that prostitutes in even the most elite houses were immune to madmen.

He had hoped that Helen, a smart woman, would be especially careful and circumspect. But obviously, from what information he had already, someone she knew, perhaps someone she trusted, had killed her.

And he was sure that her emotional and physical condition in the last few weeks had compromised her judgment and weakened her prudence.

Helen had come to see him in his office just two weeks before, after sending a brief note that said, "I must see you, and I cannot wait until you call again at the house. Please."

He replied immediately, and she came two days later, dressed in simple green with no adornments, no ribbons, no jewelry, no rouge, and no powder. She had thin lines under eyes clouded by tears, apprehension, and lack of sleep.

"I'm not well," she said needlessly. "But it's not my head, or my limbs, or any other part of my body. I'm sick at heart, and I can't sleep because I am so worried. Can you give me something so I can at least sleep."

"Of course I can, but why can't you sleep? Your answer is important for me to decide what to give and how much."

"I told you. I'm worried." She didn't elaborate.

"About what?" When she didn't answer, he answered for her. "It's him, isn't it? It's always him."

"What do you know?" she asked, her tone desperate, as if he had refused her request. "I don't talk about my customers to other customers. That's rude, impolite, and indiscreet. You know that, and you have never asked before."

"But you came to me as your doctor and, besides, I hear things. My patients talk. You should know that."

"They talk about me?" she cried. "How dare they do that! We're supposed to protect each other's privacy."

"And to protect that privacy, I am not going to tell you who said what. I only know that you are not happy, and Frank Rivers is the cause."

"You cannot know that for certain unless I tell you specifically, and I won't."

"You don't have to. You said yourself that you were sick at heart. That is enough for me to know you're talking about the vagaries of love. How unfortunate for you. You love one of your customers. I'm sure you have been warned about this."

"Are you going to help me or not?" she asked. "If I wanted a lecture, I could have gone to Trinity Church."

"Of course I will help you," he replied. "I'm going to give you a light dosage of this sleeping drought, and you'll let me know if it's strong enough. If it isn't, I will strengthen it."

Helen almost jumped from her chair. Smiling broadly, she embraced him and whispered again and again her gratitude and relief. "Thank you, thank you, thank you. I don't know how to thank you."

That was his last conversation with her. She didn't come back, and he had been too busy with his lectures and surgeries to wonder about her. He was scheduled to return to Rosina Townsend's at the end of the month.

Now he had a note from the city coroner, William Schureman, who asked him to perform an autopsy, along with his colleague, James Kassam, at Rosina Townsend's.

How can I do this? I have done hundreds, and I have performed autopsies on the bodies of people I have known, but I have never performed an autopsy on the body of a friend, someone I have known intimately.

His right hand began to shake.

Perhaps I should decline, he thought. *Let someone else go. It doesn't matter who does it. The cause of death can be determined by any number of people.*

Rogers knew the reasons he had been summoned.

He was the city's best surgeon and most reputable anatomist, even though everyone knew he'd developed his skills through autopsies, as in the Joice Heth case, and from the dissection of the bodies of criminals and unclaimed indigents snatched from graveyards. Additionally, Rogers lived just three short blocks to the south of Thomas Street on Chambers, and he had treated the women at Number 41.

Now he had to cut the body of his friend and occasional lover.

He could accept the fact of her death. She was gone, and there was nothing he could do about that. But the prospect of slicing her from the neck to the lower abdomen seemed such a violation.

This vibrant, vivacious, beautiful, and intelligent young woman was now a collection of organs—a heart, lungs, liver, stomach, intestines covered with blood, her spirit reduced to the elements of a mystery. How did she die? Who killed her?

His right hand still shaking, Rogers went to his nightstand and dipped both hands into a bowl of water. He dabbed his face, especially around the eyes. He had to be fully alert. As usual, he had been up late, reading, taking notes, preparing for his next series of lectures.

Steeling himself for what he must do, and trying to forget the sweet moments he'd shared with Helen, he walked to Thomas Street and arrived at nine o'clock. Already a line of men and boys stood outside the house waiting to see the body, as was the custom. Dr. Kassam arrived five minutes later.

By then the parlor was full of people, Mrs. Townsend and seven remaining girls, the coroner, seven watchmen, the city's highest ranking police magistrate, and two other brothel mistresses—Mary Berry and Mary Gallagher.

The police had conducted interviews and a search of the rooms and the grounds. A hatchet and cloak had been found in the backyard, and a young man whose name was Richard Robinson, but who people kept calling Frank Rivers, had been arrested for the crime.

The arresting officers, Noble and Brink, had taken Robinson upstairs to see the body, and everyone was still talking about Robinson's calm demeanor and casual claims of innocence even when he saw Helen. One comment had so shocked the listeners that it was now quoted repeatedly, becoming a chorus of moral outrage and incredulity. When Mrs. Gallagher, assuming his guilt, asked Robinson why he'd killed Helen, the young man replied, "Do you think I would blast my brilliant prospects by so ridiculous an act? I am a young man with brilliant prospects."

The phrase "brilliant prospects" was tossed now from mouth to mouth like a curse.

It was time to go up to Helen's room.

"I'm ready," Rogers said to Kassam, more for his own resolve than as a signal to begin their work. They walked up the wide staircase.

Helen's room was on the right at the rear of the house, and the door was already open. The smell of smoke was pungent, and Rogers suppressed the urge to cough. The killer had started a fire, which had consumed part of the bedding and singed Helen's lower legs. Fortunately, a night watchman was nearby and had summoned the firemen, who prevented a conflagration. Memories of the devastating December fire were still fresh in everyone's mind.

But Rogers couldn't be distracted now. He had to face Helen as an unfeeling representative of the city of New York with a job to perform. He could not feel grief, regret, love, or even resignation. He could only feel the sensation of cold skin and blood, the information gained from muscle, sinew, and slippery viscera.

Dressed in her nightgown, Helen lay on the bed with her back slightly turned away. As if hearing a command from a distance, Rogers heard Kassam say, "Let's put her on the floor."

Immediately, Rogers said, "I'll take her feet."

He knew instantly he had not reached the depths of cold indifference. He wanted to avoid touching her bloodied head for at least another moment.

The men put their arms underneath Helen's shoulders and hips and lifted her from the bed to the floor.

"Let's begin," Kassam said, exploring the wounds to the forehead.

This is not Helen, Rogers repeated to himself. *This is not Helen. She is gone. This is just a shell of who she was. She used this body to make a living, but this did not define her. She was not this, not this.*

He was losing concentration, and then suddenly, the thoughts were purged from his mind. He had a reputation to sustain; his expert opinion had to be validated. His job *did* define him. He was a doctor, and doctors had to do this work. He and Kassam talked briefly, deciding that three blows to the head had killed her, and she had died in her sleep.

To accentuate his resolve, Rogers said, "I'll perform the incision."

"By all means," Kassam agreed.

Rogers opened his case and retrieved a scalpel while Kassam cut away Helen's nightclothes, exposing her torso now flat on the floor. Rogers poised the scalpel and then penetrated the skin. He gently but quickly pulled the scalpel through the skin, and blood flowed freely, filling the chest cavity and spilling on to the floor. Neither man made an effort to prevent stains or absorb pools of blood around them. They only used a few cloths and sheets to improve the clarity of what they needed to see.

Rogers cut into the lungs and pulled back folds of the organ for Kassam's inspection. Kassam declared it, "Clear and healthy."

Rogers cut around the heart, making incisions so that it could be lifted for closer inspection. He didn't intend to take it out of the cavity; that would take too long. They only wanted to determine the absence of disease, and eliminate it as a possible cause of death.

Her stomach was half full of partially digested food. Her uterus was without issue.

"Unimpregnated," Kassam concluded.

However, their explorations did reveal evidence of on old disease.

"I wonder what was the cause?" Kassam asked.

"Let's discuss our conclusions," Rogers said, moving on to avoid disclosure or needless speculation.

They discussed their findings and concluded that, based on the body's position on the bed and the serenity of her face, Helen had died "without a struggle" from a blow to the head while she was sleeping. Death can be a merciful intruder on occasion. The burns came later.

"We'll need to close the body," said Kassam, looking down at their remaining work. "Since you made the incisions, I'll finish. Do you mind?"

"No, I don't mind," said Rogers, relieved. "I'll help, of course. You'll sew, and I'll press the flesh together."

"Are you sure?" asked Kassam.

"What do you mean? Of course I'm sure, and I'll write the report."

"Let's be done with this business," Kassam replied. "I'm sure the coroner has a jury by now."

The two men finished their sewing and covered the body with a sheet before going downstairs. Rogers asked for a place where he could write his report, and Rosina obliged him, offering the desk in her bedroom.

The jury of twelve—men rounded up from the crowd directly outside the house, as was usual in cases of suspicious death—sat in the rear parlor. The ten witnesses waited outside in the hallway. Rosina told her story about the discovery after admitting Richard Robinson to the house earlier in the evening. Elizabeth Salters and Emma French testified to seeing Robinson arrive on Saturday night. Maria Stevens and other women in the house had not seen him, as they were otherwise engaged. Mary Berry confirmed that Robinson was called Frank Rivers, and that he had come to see Helen regularly at Number 128 Duane. Officer Dennis Brink described the arrest after two watchmen described the discovery of the cloak and hatchet. Rogers read his report.

The jury came to its conclusion quickly, taking less than fifteen minutes to deliberate. There was no surprise. The foreman officiously read the jury's finding: "It is the opinion of this jury from the evidence before them that Helen Jewett came to her death by a blow or blows inflicted on the head with a hatchet, by the hand of Richard P. Robinson."

It was now midday. A large crowd had formed outside, and an officer had been posted to maintain order. Rosina had returned to her parlor to tell her story again to anyone who was interested. There was a hint of self-dramatization in her narrative, but she had experienced a terrible shock, and talking was, in David Rogers' opinion, a legitimate way to reduce the pain.

He walked home alone. Suddenly, his eyes stung and tears flowed down his cheeks. He did not wipe his face.

Chapter Twenty-Eight

James Gordon Bennett's day had begun with mere routine. After washing his face and having his usual breakfast, he'd left his room on Nassau Street and walked to his dank office, once a coal cellar, in Ann Street near lower Broadway. He'd edited copy at his desk, two wide planks supported by two barrels, and waited restlessly to hear from his assistant, who prowled the streets for breaking news. It was Sunday, April tenth, and no papers published on the Sabbath. But Bennett had to be ready for Monday, and he needed a good story.

He wanted something more exciting than another report on the extraordinary weather of that winter. True, snow remained on the streets for three solid months, breaking records; and the Hudson River had been frozen since December, making it possible for New Yorkers to walk on the ice to Hoboken. But that was old news. And he couldn't get excited about the latest scandal coming out of Albany. All politicians were corrupt anyway, and their predictable greed so bored him that no words of his could bring such banality to life.

His *Herald* was less than a year old, and the city barely noticed the first editions. No one cared that he printed the very first article about Wall Street finance, and only a few praised his detailed account of the December fire. The *New York Sun's* success, especially after the Moon Series, seemed to mock his failure.

Bennett hated negroes, Indians, Irishmen, Italians, Germans, Jews, foreigners, politicians, bankers—anyone who held opposing views or who slighted him in any way. But most of all, he despised the *Sun's* editor, the younger Benjamin Day, loathing his youth, good looks, early success, fame, and reputation. He hated Day with the cold ruthlessness of a priest burning a heretic at the stake.

Bennett dreamed of ending Day's career with one dazzling issue of the *Herald*, its profits so overwhelming and embarrassing to Day that he would immediately close his doors and sell the *Sun*. As Shakespeare was the great genius of the drama, Scott of the novel, Milton and Byron of the poem, Bennett meant to be the genius of the newspaper.

He missed the irony of his obsession, justifying his focus on the *Sun* as essential preparation for the decisive but short press war to come. He had no time or inclination for paradox or ambiguity.

His twelve-year old-assistant, rapped at the door: "Murder, Mr. Bennett, a *good* murder."

Bruce didn't know much, but when he entered, his wide blue eyes and the sputtered words, "Hatchet, fire, and whorehouse," were enough for Bennett to brave the city streets, still slick with the melting snow of another spring storm, and head for the crime scene on a Sunday afternoon. Bad news was good news.

But Bennett didn't hurry, confident in his assumption that the other editors and reporters would go instead to Bridewell, the city jail, for information. He stepped carefully, avoiding the horse turds and garbage on the cobblestones, even as he walked with his hatless head pitched into the slight wind and recalled the girl in the green dress who had lived and died at Number 41 Thomas Street.

He had never purchased her services, but he'd read stories about her in the other penny papers. He especially remembered the article that called her "A Woman of Spunk," and described her shameless, daily walks to the post office, parading in fancy green gowns and expensive jewelry, smiling but carefully avoiding any suggestion of solicitation, and refusing to hide in her house just because she was a well-known prostitute.

Even dead she attracted attention.

Crowds usually gathered outside crime scenes to see the corpse before it was removed for burial. But the lines outside 41 Thomas Street were especially long that afternoon.

Bypassing the men in line, Bennett could hear the speculation about possible suspects for the murder. Maybe a customer killed her after she pressed charges at the police court for disorderly conduct? Maybe another prostitute jealous of her fame and fortune killed her in a rage, and then burned her body to avoid detection?

At six feet, Bennett stood over most men in town, but he was glad to see the giant Mulberry standing guard at the steps of the brothel. A massive man with shoulder and arm muscles no coat or jacket could hide, Mulberry only had to spread his arms like an eagle and coldly stare at the men and boys below him to keep them from breaking ranks to push their way inside. When he noticed Bennett, who passed those in line and ignored their grumbling displeasure, Mulberry smiled broadly and announced for all to hear, "Ah, here's Mr. Bennett on public business. Come in, sir!"

"Thank you, sir," replied Bennett who enjoyed bringing a smile to Mulberry's face. Flattery never seemed to fail with pretentious men wielding a little power and, like all the other Irishmen Bennett had encountered, Mulberry was crude and easily duped. A Scot immigrant himself, Bennett had no affection for the latest wave of immigrants flooding New York. And who would be next, the Turks?

Turning his head toward the man closest to the front door, Mulberry said, "Brighton can give you all the background, sir. It's been a busy day. The poor girl has been dead for less than a day, and the vultures are picking."

"So tell me, Officer Brighton, what's happened so far?" Bennett whispered as he turned his back to Mulberry and the men in line, as if becoming a conspirator.

"Sir, the morning . . ."

But Bennett interrupted him, raising his arm immediately when he felt a gust of chilled wind.

"Let's go inside and continue there," he said, eager to see the interior of the four-story row house. He could not afford the prices at 41 Thomas, and preferred frequenting houses in New Jersey and Brooklyn, where he could enjoy inexpensive liaisons. Now he could enter the front door of a famous whorehouse and see its notorious interior free of charge.

The main hallway, with open French doors to the parlor at the rear and two flights of stairs on the right and left, was somewhat dark, despite the skylight above. Bennett heard voices coming from the back parlor and silently turned to Brighton for an explanation. Brighton immediately explained, "That's Mrs. Townsend, the house madam, telling her story. She has been doing that all day, telling it over and over again, to anyone who will listen. She discovered the body. Seems to enjoy the attention."

"Good," Bennett replied." I'll interview her later."

He walked down the hall to glance into the back parlor before going up to Helen's room. The parlor was opulent and elegant, with gilded mirrors on each wall, large paintings of wilderness scenes, sofas, ottomans, and expensive mahogany tables and chairs. Before a large group of young men in chairs and on the floor Mrs. Townsend sat, already in black and holding her fat hand and a small white linen cloth to her ample bosom, as she retold her tale.

"Poor, poor Helen," she moaned, too absorbed by her grief to notice Bennett and Brighton. "And the horror, the horror!"

Bennett turned away, now more eager to go upstairs and see for himself. Without any coaxing, Brighton provided background information, whispering as they ascended the staircase. At the landing he described the basic events of the day, repeatedly looking down to the hall below.

Outside Helen's room, Bennett paused, allowing Brighton to elaborate his tale. Bennett, steeling himself with deep but subtle intakes of breath, needed the additional time before going in. Dead bodies were not new to him; investigation often led him to the city morgue, and death marched through the fields and streets of America and Scotland with relentless indifference. But this death, he knew, was going to be different. It could make him famous. It could get him out of the cellar on Nassau Street.

Once they were inside, the police officer pulled back the cloth covering Helen's body, and Bennett closed his eyes. Then he stared, stunned by the white, marble-like skin, the bronzed burns on her legs, the deep gashes on her head, the blood thick, hardened eruptions. The crude stitches of the autopsy and the small puckered folds of the earlier peeled back flesh turned his stomach.

Helen's face was still beautiful, delicate, its features showing no signs of stress or struggle. At the very least, Bennett thought, she never knew what happened. He closed his eyes again.

Then he heard Brighton.

"This is the blow that did it." Brighton pointed to the gash.

Annoyed by the gratuitous comment, Bennett turned away, whispering, "I'm more interested in her things."

He scanned the room, first noticing the picture of Lord Byron on the wall above her bed. Posters of theatrical productions with advertisements of players were pinned above the mantel to the left. Two large mirrors hung on both sides of the bed, obviously meant to give unencumbered views of the room's essential activity.

Now forty, Bennett still didn't like to see his own image. He was imposing enough. His height and slumped shoulders, the rail thin body, the long face with its hooked nose, the wavy dark black hair all suggested austere authority. But he avoided any reminder of the inward turn of his steel grey eyes. He attributed his condition to excessive reading, but he remembered hating his crossed eyes before he learned to read. *Strabismus*, the doctor called it. How he loathed that word.

He inspected the room. Near the wall stood a small table piled with books by Bryon, Edward Bulwer-Lytton, Sir Walter Scott, Fielding and Richardson, Alexander Pope, and Dryden, along with recent copies of the *Knickerbocker* and other literary periodicals. In a nearby corner sat a work table covered with pens and expensive stationary, and on this pile rested a large scrapbook filled with copied poems and passages from Shakespeare, the Bible, Samuel Johnson, Gibbon, and others.

Turning the pages of the album, Bennett exclaimed, "Who was this girl? A whore with taste? Remarkable."

"And she was some letter writer," replied Brighton, nodding his head. "We found two trunks with over a hundred letters, more books, clothing, and other albums."

"*Letters?*" Jamie asked, thrilled at the possibility of reading and then publishing them.

"We took the trunks to police court as evidence," Brighton explained, a deepened voice and a lift of the head to mark the officious note.

"I need to see them," Bennett said, perhaps too forcefully. Surely he would find details of the sex business in them—prices, rules, and the names of customers.

Brighton's eyes widened. "Well, sir," he said in a conciliatory tone, "You'll have to ask Captain Noble. He just might let an important man like yourself see them."

"More than see," Bennett insisted, implying that he had influence with the police. He had none, but he needed to sound important today.

Brighton's thin smile faded from his face, and he asked, "Are we done here, sir? I can take you down and introduce you to the mistress of the house. She *wants* to talk to the press."

"Yes, I am done here. Introduce me, but I will make an appointment to speak with her on another day, and at length, about her discoveries."

They left the room, descended the stairs quickly, and managed the introductions and scheduling for the interview with peremptory speed. Obviously ready to consume Bennett's time that afternoon, Rosina expressed her disappointment: "Oh, I see, Mr. Bennett. You are so busy that you can't hear today the travails of the sole witness to a most terrible crime."

"On Tuesday, Mrs. Townsend. You'll have your chance to tell me *everything.*"

He nodded his head and departed without acknowledging or thanking anyone. He had to get back to his desk. The words for tomorrow's lead article filled his head, and he had to put pen to paper before he forgot them.

Bennett knew what would be his angle. Under the title, "Visit to the Scene," he would describe his discovery of Helen's body and give New Yorkers the eyes to see every detail of murder in a famous sex den.

When he arrived at his office, the words flowed freely. His description of Helen's body came in one heady rush of inspiration. When he was done, he wondered again how anyone could kill so beautiful a girl in such a brutal way. But he had to leave the answer to this question to another day; he had papers to sell. And, knowing his readers, he also knew he would have to ignore some details. The autopsy cut would be too distracting, too disturbing. A beautiful dead body should not have an incision like *that.*

Bennett could barely restrain his excitement.

———◦———

When he heard the news, Benjamin Day *could* have taken a hansom cab to the old city jail on Broadway. He could afford it, after all. But he loved to walk, even in winter, the crackling of the snow and ice under his boot and the bite of the wind on his cheek stirring memories of the roads and fields of his hometown in Massachusetts. He was a New Yorker now, and he loved the sounds of the city, the peeling church bells, the vendors on the streets, the clatter of hooves on the cobblestones, the high-pitched talk of street corner prophets and politicians. He walked everywhere.

Usually he sent his editor to see the Bridewell parade of crime for possible stories to print. But yesterday he'd granted his editor Richard Adams Locke permission to stay home with his wife and family on Sunday. Locke was a tireless worker and needed the rest.

The crumbling jail, scheduled for demolition, was now just a way station for suspects facing indictment. The high-ranking police officers could usually be found at the police office on Chambers Street. But on this Sunday afternoon, Day found the two arresting officers—Dennis Brink, the constable of the Fifth Ward, and George Noble, the assistant captain of the watch at City Hall Park—receiving reporters and answering questions about the murder and an already notorious arrest. The small reception room was packed. Reporters shouted questions and conclusions that made Brink's and Nobles' answers difficult to hear or understand.

Day would have none of this. He was not going to make comments or ask questions in a raucous crowd agitated by the details of the murder. Only twenty-six, he was the city's most successful publisher, and he would demand the officers' undivided attention later that day or the next. As he left the reception room, he hissed "Robinson!" to another officer standing by the door, and the officer turned to his right without comment and led Day down the hall to a cell.

Robinson was sitting on a chair, smoking a cigar. Only one other reporter, from the *New York Post*, stood before the cell. He turned to Day and shook his head, saying sarcastically, "This is a waste of time. What rot!"

The other reporter departed, leaving Day to observe the accused murderer alone. Dressed in a tightly fitted, dark blue frock coat, white shirt, and black cravat, Robinson had a slight build, with narrow shoulders and small, delicate hands. He looked even younger than his nineteen years, like a prematurely tall adolescent who'd just entered puberty. But his handsome face was extraordinary. Day could not deny its beauty; there was no other word for it. His facial features made him as comely as any Renaissance Madonna. Only the thinning blonde hair, cut short just below the ears and revealing part of his scalp, prevented perfection.

"Mr. Robinson," Day began, introducing himself at the cell bars. "I am the owner of the *New York Sun.*"

"I'm innocent," Robinson replied softly. "I didn't do it. I have prospects. Such a crime is unworthy of a man with such prospects."

"I am interested in what you have to say," Day said, gently pressing the younger man.

Robinson stood, repeating his refrain again and again. "I'm innocent, a man of prospects, *glorious* prospects."

"I see," Day concluded reluctantly.

He was not going to get more. Robinson was either beautiful and stupid or beautiful and deceiving, the truth well hidden by a mask of alluring white skin and a line repeated with unwavering conviction.

Robinson smiled then, revealing flawless white teeth, a jarring sight in a man who smoked cigars.

"*Tell* your readers of my innocence," he said, his tone insistent.

"Your *innocence*, sir, is not for me to determine," Day said, annoyed by Robinson's presumption. "A jury will decide that."

"Theirs will be an easy decision, sir. I am young and *look* innocent."

Day turned away, saying nothing more. He needed more information about Robinson, and he knew he could get it from Officer Resolvat Stevens. For a small price, Stevens had proven himself to be an invaluable source in the past; and today he would no doubt appreciate Day giving even more for his services. Officers were underpaid and times were hard.

Day found Stevens standing at the back of the room where Noble and Brink still faced a barrage of questions from insatiable reporters. He said only, "Come with me," and Stevens immediately obliged, following him into the hallway.

"We need a private place," Day whispered.

"Yes, sir."

Stevens was old enough to be Day's father. But his wary eyes, the unctuous tone in his voice, and a slight stoop revealed his subservience. He did not wear a uniform, only a copper badge on his coat. Most officers resisted the idea of wearing anything that made them look like "livered lackeys." Even in 1836, New York City had no official police department. City aldermen hired volunteers for a dollar twenty-five as night or day watchmen. And, having their own private armies, the aldermen resisted uniting them into a single force. Citizens feared this consolidation of power as well, as police work attracted far too many gangsters, ruffians, and toughs of all kinds. Better for them to fight each other than fight the rest.

Stevens found an office nearby. He opened the door and Day quickly passed by him, entering a small, windowless space with only a narrow table and two chairs on opposite sides. Rank with the sweat of fear, the room was perfect for interviews and police intimidation.

Day sat in the chair on the other side of the table, facing the heavy door and its small window. Police interrogators always sat there, and Day meant to reinforce his dominance at once.

"So what do you know about the arrest?" he asked after both men were seated. He sat rigidly in his chair, refusing to lean forward to suggest intimacy or conspiracy.

Stevens began to relate the facts of the discovered body, but Day interrupted him, saying emphatically, "No, I'm not interested in *her*. I'm interested in *him*, the arrest, what he said when the police arrived, and what happened *after it*."

"Brink and Noble can tell you more, sir. They were there," replied Stevens, now defensive.

"I *know* that, but you heard them today, and I don't have time to wait until they are free."

"Yes, sir."

Day could hear sarcasm, a favorite weapon of the servile, and he silently calibrated his tone of voice. He reminded himself that he *needed* Stevens, even as he loathed the idea. "And . . . ?"

"They found him in his room at a boarding house," Stevens continued, his tone official, his grey eyes unwavering. He had the upper hand, at least for the moment. "And what was most odd, they said, was that he was so calm. He didn't even react when he was told of Helen Jewett's death. They confiscated his journal."

"What?" Day asked, finally leaning forward. "He kept a *journal?*"

"Yes, sir. It's locked away as evidence, along with his cloak they found in the yard behind the house."

"I have to see the journal," said Day, excited by the prospect of access to the thoughts and feelings of the enigmatic prisoner. "I must."

"That won't be possible, sir," Stevens said.

"And why *not?*" asked Day, leaning further forward, a carefully calibrated inch.

"We have our orders," replied Stevens.

"For a price," said Day, lightly introducing the matter of bribes.

"Not today," Stevens replied without missing a beat.

"Then *when?*"

"When things have calmed down, when reporters are no longer interested in the murder, when . . ."

"You will *not* be the one to determine *that*, Stevens," interjected Day, assuming the upper hand again after a lapse in control. For a fleeting moment, Stevens had found a measure of authority, even after accepting a bribe, and this new and surprising position had to be squelched once and for all. "After I speak with Noble and Brink, I will be back, and I *will* take a look."

Stevens lowered his eyes. "Yes, sir."

For added emphasis, Day declared, "And you will *not* share that journal with Jamie Bennett under any circumstances."

Steven's entire face became animated, as if the very mention of Bennett's name had ignited a fire under his skin and behind the whites of his eyes. "It will be a cold day in hell before *he* sees *anything.*"

"So you too have the misfortune of knowing the man," Day observed.

"He has no *respect*," said Stevens, as if Bennett had personally attacked him.

Bennett was an unrelenting critic of the police force, but he reserved his venom for its leaders. Stevens, the perfect sycophant, had aspirations for higher office. He defended his superiors, unlike other policemen who openly enjoyed the press attacks. At a time when pay was low and the public had little respect for the police, loyalty had little value with the rank and file. Steven was an exception.

Day now rose, satisfied that he had what he needed.

"Let Brink and Noble know I will be coming to see them tomorrow afternoon around one for a *private* interview," he said.

"Yes, sir," Stevens said.

Day was ready to spend the rest of the afternoon and evening with his wife and two children. He planned to jot a few notes for Locke, but the April eleventh issue was already printed. April twelfth would be soon enough to describe his visit to Bridewell and the more detailed reports from Noble and Brink.

The next morning, Richard Adams Locke dropped a copy of Bennett's *Herald* on Day's desk.

As soon as he began reading, Day started shouting, "Damn it! Damn it! Damn it! I can't believe this! James Gordon Bennett wants to *fuck* a dead girl."

He threw the paper to the ground.

"Fuck Jamie Bennett," he shouted. "Fuck him till kingdom come!"

Locke waited silently for his boss to calm down.

Finally, Day asked softly, "It's selling, isn't it?"

"Yes, sir. Sold out already, I believe."

"I have to give the old man credit," Day said. "A stroke of genius to go to Thomas Street first and then describe his *own* discovery of Helen's Jewett's body."

Locke said nothing; even agreement was dangerous. Easily provoked by incompetence, opposition, or a mere hint of superiority in the work of others, Day would launch rants against offenders, especially subordinates. He could not keep employees. But Locke was willing to stay. Thirty-six and married with two small children, he needed the work; and more importantly, he had helped Day make a great deal of money by writing the Moon Series. Nevertheless, Locke remained cautious. Already shy, awkward and self-conscious about his face, deeply pitted by small pox in childhood, and a slight stutter, Locke feared another barrage of insults. Day always aimed with merciless accuracy.

"But . . . I have you."

Day smiled for the first time. In his mind's eye James Gordon Bennett was a buzzing fly in a cramped room. All Day had to do was listen carefully, follow the noise, and swat Bennett down with the brilliant pen of Richard Adams Locke.

"Thank you, sir," replied Locke.

"Bennett can have his love affair with a dead girl," observed Day, suddenly in a smug, less combative mood. "We'll focus on Robinson, that beautiful little bug with alabaster skin and cold, cold eyes. I know people, and he's the one. I am *sure* of it."

"Yes, sir," Locke replied.

"And we will *prove* it. But first we will suggest it seems unlikely that a gentleman of such breeding could commit so heinous a crime," Day continued. "We will flatter the prejudices of those so willing to give the wealthy the benefit of the doubt. *Then* we'll show how he has *duped* them all."

"Yes, sir," repeated Locke.

"My gut instincts are *always* right. The evidence will *prove* me right."

"Yes, sir."

Ben Day grinned now, adding, "And while I was at the station yesterday, my dear friend, Officer Resolvat Stevens told me that Mr. Robinson kept a journal. Yes, the bastard kept a journal. When I get my hands on *that*, I will have final proof. And when I'm done, we'll sell papers by the thousands, far more than the *Herald*. Mr. Locke, we will kick Mr. Bennett's impudent ass down Wall Street and back. Our readers will be far more interested in the murderer than the victim. After all, Helen Jewett was a prostitute. Not just *any* prostitute, of course. You remember that letter she wrote to me after her fall at the Park? Intelligent. Literate. Presumptuous. But still just a high-priced whore."

Chapter Twenty-Nine

On the day of Helen's burial, rain pounded the streets, discouraging everyone but the most resolute to venture outside. It was a convenient excuse for most of the women at Number 41 Thomas Street to avoid St. John's Burying Ground.

Rosina did not try to persuade them, making no comment on their excuses about appointments and other plans or the need to keep their clothes dry for the day's business. Even when Elizabeth Salters said they all needed to protect the house from the stink of drying clothes, Rosina only shook her head, saddened by the triumph of vanity over loyalty and common decency. *Will it end like this for me?* she wondered. *Buried on a dark day with heaven spitting on my grave?*

At least Helen would lie in peace in her beloved New York. Five years earlier the city had passed an edict forbidding any new internments in the popular churchyards of Trinity and Saint Paul's. These yards were overfilled, and Rosina had to go a mile north to the corners of Clarkson, Hudson, Varick, and Leroy to pay six dollars for a plot.

Rosina didn't object to the gravesite broker's decision to designate Helen as a widow. After she told him the basic facts of Helen's life and death, he informed her that he had only four choices in his ledger: girls, married women, single women, and widows. Of course, he knew about the murder—didn't everybody? But rules, procedures, and traditions had to be followed, he said, "to keep the hounds of hell at bay after major violations of the commandments."

In the "Report of Interments" he finally listed Helen's name, her age, the state of Maine as her place of birth, Thomas Street (without the house number) as the address, and the cause of death as "Homicide." Rosina didn't press for more. There were details enough in the local papers to satisfy the depraved or the merely curious.

Ah, such is death's sway over the facts of life, Rosina thought. *First come the lies in ledgers and on tombstones. Then families and friends repeat stories that ignore the inconvenient and embarrassing facts. And then a whole life, with all of its maddening and exhilarating messiness, is reduced to a few spoken lines.*

Of course, it was the written lines that were worrisome.

Rosina was sure that flames in fireplaces all over town were consuming Helen's letters. Few men, especially among the city's most prominent, wanted to leave behind documentary proof of their relationship with a murdered prostitute.

Rosina had never written many letters. Her position required discretion.

Now she regretted that decision. What once seemed wise now seemed foolish. She had actually consented to erase herself, undocumented and childless, eventually to be forgotten. Who would care to remember an old brothel madam, if she were fortunate enough to live a long life?

She was not accustomed to such reflections. Self-pity was bad for the skin and bad for business. But Helen's death was so brutal and unexpected, and the public exposure so naked, Rosina was forced to confront her unexamined assumptions and face her dormant fears. During the ride back to Thomas Street, she had time to think about these matters, but she realized as well that making arrangements for Helen's burial had provided distraction and a measure of relief.

Once Rosina returned to the house, only Sarah was willing and prepared to return to St. John's for the burial. She had come on Monday morning to do her usual work in Helen's room, empty the chamber pot, rekindle the fire, dust and lay out Miss Helen's morning clothes. Sarah was usually not allowed in the parlor. She was a room maid only, so she knew immediately something was terribly wrong when she was invited into the room. She even dared to ask, "What is it, Miss Rosina? What is it?"

When Rosina finally answered her, Sarah had screamed and then fainted, falling to the floor.

It took only a few seconds to revive her with the smelling salts Rosina always kept on hand.

"It can't be true," Sarah pleaded. "It can't be. I just saw her. She said she would see me tomorrow. Oh, my Lord, why did this happen? Who could do this?"

When Rosina told her about the arrest of Frank Rivers, Sarah shook her head. "That can't be. She loved him so. They had their disagreements but . . ."

She suddenly stopped, her eyes wide with the shock of recognition. She was talking openly with Mrs. Townsend, the white madam of the house. What was she thinking? She could get into trouble, serious trouble.

Rosina gently pulled her up and led her to a chair. Pulling back ever so slightly, Sarah said, "I can't. It's not my place to sit in here."

"This is my house, and you will sit down," Rosina insisted.

Sarah complied at once, but she kept her head down, too afraid to look directly into Rosina's face.

"You need to listen, and listen carefully." Rosina took Sarah's hands. "You were one of the last people to see Helen alive, you and me, and there will be questions, many questions. If there is a trial, you will be called to testify, to tell what you know, in front of all of those people."

"Oh, no, I can't do that. I've never been in a courtroom. I can't talk in front of all those people, in front of *white* people. I can't do it!"

"You'll have to. You need to be brave, for Miss Helen. Someone she knew did this terrible thing to her, and we must help the police punish him."

"How?" Sarah pleaded.

"By telling the truth, by telling exactly what you know down to the last detail. You'll have to remember everything. And so will I. It started already, and until it's over, the police, the reporters, they all will be asking and talking. You will need to be strong."

"Yes, Ma'am," mumbled Sarah, tears streaming down her face.

"You can do this, and I will be here to help you in any way I can. I promise."

"Thank you, Miss Rosina. Do I need to clean up Miss Helen's room?"

"Oh, no dear, at least not yet. The killer tried to burn the house down, and the room smells of smoke. You'll have lots of work, but not right now. People keep coming and looking for things that might tell about what happened. I'll let you know when it's time."

"Will I still have my job?" Sarah asked plaintively. "She brought me here to work for her, and now she's gone, I don't know what's going to happen."

"Oh, don't worry about that now. Miss Helen spoke highly of you, and I'm sure we can find work for you here. There's always a need for good help."

Later that morning Sarah stood in the entryway, her black clothes soaked from the storm outside.

"Thank you for coming," said Rosina. "You'll be riding in the carriage with me."

"Will there be room for the others?" Sarah asked.

"There are no others," Rosina said wearily. "Just you and me, I'm afraid. We're her only friends. Come."

They didn't speak on the way to the burial site, and Rosina had the carriage wait for them when they arrived. Any formalities would be brief. A formal service had not been planned, and no minister was willing to read scriptures or offer any benediction. It was only deemed a Christian burial because the shrouded body was going into consecrated ground, for a price.

The rector of St. John, dressed in a black suit and top hat, said the words, "Ashes to ashes, dust to dust," threw a handful of mud on the shrouded body, and announced through tight lips, "And that is *that*."

Rosina stood absolutely still under her umbrella. She had anticipated brevity, but the curt dismissal from a rector who seemed only annoyed by the intemperate weather was too much to suffer in silence.

"The dead *deserve* more respect," she said.

"You got your money's worth," he replied. "Do you want to watch the diggers fill the grave?"

"Do you work for God or Mammon?" Rosina asked, but then she turned away, taking Sarah by the arm.

"Come," she said. "We'll drink a toast to Helen back at the house."

"Oh, Miss Rosina, I can't drink on a work day."

"Today's not a work day. Helen deserves something better than *this*," said Rosina. "It will be our little secret."

"You won't tell my mother?"

"Of course not."

"No, she would not like it."

"Very well," said Rosina. "Now let's get back to a warm fire."

When they returned to the house, Rosina took Sarah into the rear parlor, where Elizabeth Salters, Emma French, and Maria Stevens waited for an account of the outing.

They all stood as Rosina entered the room, and Elizabeth asked, "What happened? We regret not being able to go, but we can show our respects by our interest in . . ."

Rosina said coldly, "You may leave this room at once. You may return once I and Miss Dunscombe are finished using it."

Maria started to leave, but Elizabeth reached out to stop her. "But wait. You are asking *us* to leave, and a maid can stay?"

"Yes," said Rosina, her voice icy.

Elizabeth faltered, looking down to avoid Rosina's remorseless stare.

"And if any of you dare to mention her skin color, this will be your last day here. Do you understand?"

The three women were avoiding eye contact and did not reply.

"Do you understand?" repeated Rosina, hardening her tone even more.

Their heads still bowed, they all whispered, "Yes."

"Now leave us," said Rosina.

They hurried from the room.

"And they considered themselves Helen's friends. Some friends."

Sarah did not know what to say, having never seen such an open disagreement between Mrs. Townsend and her girls. She couldn't wait to get home to tell her mother about the unusual scene.

Rosina smiled and took Sarah by the arm.

"Now let's get warm before we have our drink. For once I will serve you, because you were the only one who cared enough to go with me, the only one. If Helen can see this, I am sure she is most pleased."

Rosina had not entered a church in years, and she harbored serious doubts about heaven and the cruel God of her Calvinist upbringing. But occasionally she grabbed at the thinning rope of hope like a desperate swimmer in a tumultuous river. The idea of heaven softened the pain of loss and regret. Maybe, just maybe, Helen lived on somehow, and death and all of his disciples did not have the final victory.

———·———

Two days ago Rosina discovered Helen's body and ran screaming from her room. Now she had to relive the nightmare, having agreed to an interview with James Gordon Bennett, the editor of the *New York Herald* who had visited Helen's room that Sunday, and described her furniture, possessions, and corpse with an unseemly attention to detail.

When she entered the front parlor that Tuesday morning, she found Bennett and his companion looking at the painting, "The Death of Jane McCrea," by John Vanderlyn. Rosina immediately regretted its prominent place in the house.

Two Indians with rippling muscles held a kneeling white woman by her hand and hair as they readied to scalp her with hatchets. Details were meant to titillate. The victim was fully dressed, but the bodice of her dress was cut low and revealed the nipple of her right breast, and the flowing fabric of her gown accentuated the left thigh and her crotch covered by a cloth too obvious to ignore—a soft triangle covering the flesh about to be violated by half-naked savages.

The coincidence was painful. Helen's murderer had killed her with three blows to the head with a small hatchet found in the backyard of the property.

Hoping her soft tone could suppress any hint of dismay, Rosina asked, "Gentlemen?" and they turned. Immediately she smiled when she noted the handsome face of the young man who extended his hand, saying, "Thank you for receiving us."

Although dressed all in black, her dark hair pulled back severely into a bun highlighted by delicate streaks of grey, Rosina was sure that her mature and lasting beauty had impressed him. She still received high-paying customers.

"This is my colleague, Mr. Thomas Wilder of Chambers Street," Bennett said, The older, tall man stood erect , his clenched hands at his side, his steel grey eyes severe, with annoyance. "He's a lawyer, and lawyers write excellent letters for getting the attention of those with information."

"I'll cooperate with the press," Rosina replied. "Letters won't be necessary."

She pointed to the sitting area on the right. "Please, take a seat," she said, dabbing at her eyes with a lice trimmed with cloth. They were still settling into their chairs when she continued, "We just buried the poor girl yesterday morning.

What a sad affair. Only her servant and I were there in the rain. Not even my girls here wanted to go. After all the good she did. She helped the sick. She gave to charities."

"Which charities?" Bennett asked, unmoved. The girl was dead, and her tawdry burial, hastily arranged and noted briefly in the papers without specifics of time or place, mattered not at all. There was nothing Bennett could do about *that*.

"She didn't tell me," Rosina replied, her tone matter of fact, her dark eyes now slits of disdain. "She said she didn't want to embarrass them because of her . . . profession. She gave without acknowledgment."

"How do you know this?" Wilder pressed.

"She told me," Rosina replied.

"Girls usually lie about their pasts; she could have lied about this and . . ."

Rosina interrupted him, his face now discounted. Wilder was just like every other lawyer, cold, relentless, and arrogant. "Have you no respect for the dead?"

"Tell us what happened the night of the murder," said Bennett, brutally curt. Wilder was not helping.

"From the beginning," added Wilder, quickly taking his cue and leaning forward. "And spare no details, because you surely will be asked about them before the Grand Jury. I will be taking some notes. You *are* a crucial witness."

Rosina began her tale at once, as if the beginning was carefully rehearsed: " It all began in the middle of the night with a knock at my bedroom door. I'm at the front of the house. A man asked if I could let him out of the locked front door. I was annoyed at being awakened, so I yelled out to him to get his woman to let him out. The house has its rules. I lock the front door around midnight, and if a customer leaves before morning, he must be escorted out after a girl gets the key from me. But no one came, so I went back to sleep."

"Were you alone?" asked Wilder.

"No, but the noise was so slight, he didn't wake up."

"Who was he?" asked Wilder.

"I cannot say," Rosina replied.

"The police will get the names of all of the customers at the house that night; they are *all* witnesses," Wilder observed.

"I *must* protect my customers," Rosina replied.

"Sentiment is irrelevant," sniffed Wilder.

"Would you be so dismissive if you were here that night? They all left anyway, before the police arrived."

"I am asking the questions, Mrs. Townsend. And these are nothing compared to what you will face."

"I must protect my income," clarified Rosina. "Now may I continue?"

Without waiting for a reply, she continued, as if she had stopped in mid-sentence: "I went back to sleep, only to be awakened again by another knock at the front door, a louder knock. My companion heard the noise too, and rose with me. This time I checked the clock on my mantel. It was three in the morning. I peeked out my window, and I could see it was one of Elizabeth's regular customers . . . Elizabeth Salters, on the second floor. I put on my robe, lit a lamp, and opened the door. He went upstairs, and when I looked down the hall, I noticed a lighted globe lamp on the table in the parlor. It didn't belong there. I have only two of them, and both belong upstairs."

"What did you do about it?" Wilder asked.

"I went down to the parlor, and saw that the French doors to the backyard were open, and the bar I use to lock them was on the floor. I don't have a key for those doors. You can only leave from the inside by removing that bar."

"What did you make of that?"

"I thought perhaps someone went outside to use the privy, but I wondered why anyone would go outside in such horrible weather when we have chamber pots in the rooms. And no customers can exit the house from the back since there is no direct access to the streets behind the house."

"So what did you do?"

"I went back to my room and fell asleep. I dozed off in my chair, actually. But I didn't sleep long, because I was bothered by the open door, and I didn't hear anyone reenter the house. So I went back to the parlor and called out into the yard several times, "Who's there?" No answer. I barred the door and went upstairs to check out which room had the missing lamp. And that's when I discovered Helen."

"If the rooms are locked on the inside by the girls with customers, how could you enter a room to find out about a lamp, or anything else for that matter?"

Unfazed, Rosina replied, "I tried Maria Stevens' door at the back. It was locked, and then I went to Helen's room, and the door was unlatched. When I pushed the door open, smoke rolled out. I ran for help, frightened that Helen and her customer—I knew she had one that night—had suffocated in there. I pounded on Caroline Stewart's door, and she and her customer came out, and we all screamed, "Fire!" Everyone got up, yelling and screaming and running around."

"Did you return to Helen's room then?"

"No. I went downstairs to my room to call for help from the front window, hoping to get the attention of the watchman at the corner of Thomas and Chapel. Then I went back upstairs to go into the room."

"Were you alone?"

"No. I went in with Maria, hoping to save Helen and her friend, and what we found so horrified us we ran out of the room screaming."

"What did you find?"

"Smoke came from the smoldering sheets, and poor Helen's nightgown was now ashes. Her body was burned on one side, charred like crusted wood, and she lay in the burned bed with three gashes to her head and a pool of blood soaking the pillow."

Bennett watched Rosina, trying to detect calculation behind the emotionless narrative—every verb and noun seemed carefully chosen, their impact heightened by Rosina's chalky skin. Only her eyes hinted at the horror her words described. The tears had long since disappeared, but her black eyes glistened with fierce attention. Rosina knew she was riveting.

"When did the police arrive?" Bennett finally asked.

"About four in the morning. Officers Noble and Brink. They searched the yard and found a hatchet and cloak. They asked several questions. I identified Helen and told them about her visitor for Saturday night. She usually had a caller named Tom Easy come on Saturday nights, but she told me not to let him in that night. She was expecting someone else."

"And when did that someone arrive?" asked Wilder.

"He came between nine and ten. And even though he covered his face with a cloak, I knew who he was. The slight build, the soft voice, the delicate hands—I knew it was Richard Robinson who went up to Helens' room at once. He was still here at eleven, when Helen asked for champagne and I took it up to her."

"You, the mistress of the house, went up there with champagne like some kind of servant?" Bennett asked.

Again unfazed, Rosina replied, "It's my way of checking on my girls. I went up with champagne and two glasses, and when Helen unlocked her door, I placed them on the table near the door and saw Robinson lying on the bed, at the foot, reading something to Helen."

"Did you see his face?" asked Wilder.

"No, I didn't. But I could see the back of his head, the thin blond hair covering his bald spot. It's such a pity, a man so young and so handsome, having *that* to mar such fine features."

Bennett suddenly rose, now more interested in returning to Helen's room. He would leave the rest of the inquiry to Wilder.

"Mr. Wilder will continue his questioning about the discovery of the weapon. And if you don't mind, Mrs. Townsend, I will return to Helen's room to reaffirm my first impressions, and determine others for my readers."

He didn't wait for a reply, rising from his chair and walking to the door.

"You will need a key, Mr. Bennett," declared Rosina, her cold, imperious tone meant to remind him that she was still the mistress of this house and an authority to be reckoned with.

Bennett stopped suddenly and waited before turning around. "Of course," he said, now extending his arm and offering his upturned palm.

With the key still in her pocket, she also waited, wanting Bennett to stand there and look foolish. He didn't move, as if suddenly cast in stone. But she understood: to lower his hand would be a small but significant gesture of defeat.

No one spoke. The air seemed thin, and the room, once magnified by mirrors, now felt smaller, its walls closing in like the walls of a magic box. Wilder was forgotten.

But Rosina finally reached into her pocket and handed the key to Bennett. She had made her point. Bennett left without comment.

"Well," said Wilder, recovering his voice, " Mr. Bennett knows how to provoke." He grinned, and Rosina once more succumbed to his charms. Of course, she would not invite him to her bed—that would be unseemly under current circumstances--but she quickly wondered about caressing the contours of his cleft chin, a marvel of chiseled perfection, with one hand and gently holding his manhood in the other. If later he asked for time in her room, she might, she just might consent.

"Please tell me more about Miss Jewett's background," asked Wilder, still cheerful. "Where did she come from? Who were her parents?"

Startled, Rosina asked, "Excuse me?" She heard his question, but needed time to recover her poise now compromised by guilt. Remember Helen, she thought, chiding herself. This is not about your pleasure or income.

Wilder repeated his question.

"Helen's real name was Dorcas Doyen," said Rosina softly, underscoring Helen's dislike for it with a slight shudder.

"Enough of a reason to change it, "said Wilder, shaking his head. "Dorcas, what a shame."

"She was born in Maine, and worked for a prominent family there, virtually being raised as a ward while being a servant."

Rosina repeated the lies and half-truths told to her and Billy Attree in the *Transcript*. She now didn't mind Helen's elaborate, self- serving stories; they added to her charm.

Wilder seemed captivated. He virtually stopped asking questions.

Then Bennett returned and demanded answers. "Where did she come from? Who were her parents? How did she get those books? I need to know!"

"Mr. Wilder can tell you," Rosina replied.

"Answer them again," Bennett said, turning to Wilder for reinforcement.

Wilder leaned forward and smiled, his dimples doing their needed work. "Just repeat your tale, please."

"Very well," Rosina said. "But all this talk is so exhausting. As I said before, Helen was from Maine and served in the household of Judge Nathan Weston."

"The Chief Justice of the Maine Supreme Court?" Bennett asked, startled.

"Yes," said Wilder.

"I don't know that much, actually," Rosina continued, choosing carefully her words. "She became the playmate of the judge's children, but then had to leave Augusta for Portland, where she began working as a girl of the town. When she moved to New York, she lived and worked at other houses before coming here. She moved out, but came back just a month ago, and then, and then this terrible thing happens to her. Poor Helen, poor, poor Helen."

Bennett turned to Wilder and declared, "You will prepare a letter to Judge Weston making inquiries about his connection to a notorious prostitute. Be respectful but firm. I can just see him sweating in his black robes, trembling at the prospect of scandal. I do wonder how he will explain the messing details of his once private life."

His eyes brightened, and he smiled for the very first time, cracking that marble face. The coming press war was personal.

Rosina had been dismissed, and she was not having it. "And when will my interview be published?" she asked.

"You will have your day, Mrs. Townsend, and soon," Bennett intoned. "But now there are more important stories than your discoveries and bereavement. Come, Mr. Wilder, there is more work to be done."

He said nothing else, refusing to even nod his head, a simple and minimal courtesy in polite society. But Rosina made sure she had the final word: "And good day to you, sir."

The interview issue, containing the most explicit details about the sex trade in the history of the New York press, sold out, and now she was the most famous brothel madam in town. But four days later, Rosina heard more horrible news.

———•———

Her eyes filled with thick tears that obscured her sight and flowed down her cheeks.

She had cried earlier in the week, but those tears were more communal than personal. She was *supposed* to cry, given the place of Helen in her affections and the enormity of the crime perpetrated against her. She had also cried at Helen's burial, but then she was too angry to shed legitimate tears.

But now she grieved, truly grieved, feeling irreparable loss and the absolute cruelty of the universe.

Medical students had gone to St. John's Burial Ground armed with pickaxes and spades and had dug up Helen's body. They removed it in a bag and took to the College of Physicians and Surgeons on Barclay Street, where they dissected it for medical study.

Jamie Bennett reported in the *Herald* that her "elegant and classic" skeleton now hung in a cabinet. He sounded almost gleeful.

Rosina consigned him to the hell she doubted but needed to exist. *Men are such pigs*, she thought. *Damn them all.*

She saved the threatening letters she received.

One anonymous writer warned her that if she offered testimony against Richard Robinson before the Grand Jury, she would meet "a fate similar to the melancholy and untoward one which befell the unfortunate Helen Jewett."

Another said she would not live three days after the trial.

Incensed rather than frightened, Rosina gave the letters to the district attorney, and the police posted a guard at Number 41, where crowds had gathered to gape and point fingers.

Four of her girls had already moved out, seeking safer quarters in the Fifth Ward, and customers simply stopped coming. Even the most reliable ones, the regulars who came virtually every week, were conspicuously absent, failing to make appointments and not responding to discreet inquiries from girls whose names were now in the papers.

The bright glare of notoriety was too much for even the boldest, unmarried men.

Now the twisted lips, the rolling eyes burning with contempt, the raw hatred in the ugly chant, "Whore, whore, whore," from citizens on the streets and other public places confirmed for Rosina what had to be done. She was finished, her business ruined. She would schedule an auction of the furniture for the day after her testimony. There was no time for sentiment, foolish pride, or naïve hopes for a sudden reversal of fortune. The brothel business was subject to the same rules of supply and demand; if customers were no longer buying, then the end was that simple. No money, no house.

There was another harsh reality.

The owner of Number 41 Thomas Street, the rich and powerful John Livingstone, had maintained a conspicuous silence about his business affairs, which seemed to shroud the entire city in a sleep. It was clear to Rosina now that she only had influence because Livingstone and her customers had consented to give it; when that consent was suddenly withdrawn, she had nothing left except her pride and the will to start again, somewhere, somehow.

She would leave New York.

But that would have to wait until another day. First, she had to get through her testimony before the Grand Jury.

But when the Grand Jury met on April eighteenth, even larger crowds gathered outside the court chambers to jeer and hoot as she and the other girls entered the room. Rosina accentuated the lift of her chin to maintain her composure and hide the cold dread coursing through her body.

Escorted into the chamber by police officers, Rosina and the others were questioned repeatedly about the details of April ninth and tenth, as expected. But the insistent questions seemed aimed to challenge their credibility.

After two days of testimony, which included the depositions of Richard Robinson's roommates and coworkers, the jury indicted Robinson for murder. Rosina was not surprised. He was the last man to be seen with Helen, and clothes linked to him were found at the crime scene. A guilty verdict at the trial, scheduled for early June, was sure to follow.

In the meantime, Rosina had to organize the sale of the house furniture. Although she leased the house on Thomas Street, the furnishings were her own, the results of gifts, discreet investments, the high prices for the sexual services offered at Number 41, and the careful saving of income.

She hired Dennis Brink and another police officer to stand guard during the auction, and from the window she watched young men pay up to four times the original cost of already expensive furniture.

Someone called out, "Come, boys, let's have some relic of the departed's."

After the purchase of the charred footboard of Helen's sleigh bed, the young man pulled out a hatchet and hacked the board into pieces. He then deposited the splintered pieces into the hands of scores of other young men who stared and bowed their heads as if receiving pieces of the true cross. But their leering grins betrayed their true feelings; if they couldn't have Helen's body, they could at least have a piece of her bed. Disgusted, Rosina shook her head.

Nevertheless, the sale went well, and Rosina planned to use the proceeds to start another house in another town, if she could free herself from her association with a notorious murder.

Time would tell.

Then in May, as she waited for the trial, calamity visited again.

Maria Stevens, who had lived and worked in the upstairs room adjacent to Helen's, suddenly died from chills and extreme fever.

Perhaps death had come as a relief, sparing Maria the agony of a constant memory, the smell of smoke, a brief but unforgettable sight of blood and a burned body. Now she could no longer hear the rumors and read the speculations about her involvement in the crime.

Maria had told the coroner's jury and the Grand Jury that she didn't know much. That night she had entertained two men at once, and could not hear anything in the next room. She repeated her story to Rosina and anyone else who asked about that night. Nevertheless, from the beginning, she was considered a suspect—even after Robinson's arrest. Jamie Bennett had suggested that a woman consumed by jealousy could have committed the crime. He didn't name Maria, but he indicated that her proximity to Helen's room gave her opportunity.

And how could she *not* hear so brutal a murder, the sound of a hatchet pounding a skull, the screams? Clearly, she was lying.

Or maybe, she knew too much. Maybe she could name the *true* killer, and was murdered to insure her silence.

Maria's funeral was brief and spare, but even the solemnity of a funeral could not keep people from reviewing the speculations about the murder in the New York press.

And there was no end to the mud and scum spewing out of the press pot. *The dead have no defenses*, Rosina thought. Helen and Maria were mere ingredients used by cooks making swill. And now, cannibals all, they intended to toss in the living for the good of the stinking feast.

Jamie Bennett was the worst offender.

At first, he wrote that Rosina "united under the same flashing eye, the manners of a lady, the elegance of a Lais, the passion of a Fury, and the cunning of a serpent. Rosina Townsend stands at the head of her caste."

Faint praise from a self-righteous hater of women, but at least she was the best madam in town.

But finally Bennett revealed his true self in a prurient poem. Rosina would never forgive him for the doggerel he printed about her, an attempt at poetry unworthy of print anywhere. But its sting still burned her:

"Rosina's parts for all mankind
Were open, rare, and unconfined.
Like some free port of trade
Merchants unloaded their freight,
And agents from each foreign state
Here first their entry made."

It pleased her to hear that James Watson Webb had flogged him again on the streets in broad daylight on lower Broadway that May, knocking him down and beating him over the head with a stick, as he had done in January. Whatever the offence, Bennett surely got what he deserved. Rosina hoped there was even more blood the second time.

As the city waited for the trial, the press wars continued. Rosina wanted to ignore them, but she couldn't resist. Like most New Yorkers, she had an appetite for scum, especially after the *Sun* printed extracts from Robinson's diary.

Day assured his readers that nothing in it *proved* guilt. But he wondered, after reading it, about Robinson's *capacity* for it.

Rosina understood men and took pride in her bemused assessment of their petty pride and silly needs. But Robinson's diary shocked her.

After dedicating his diary *to his mother*, he could still write:

Most youths at seventeen or eighteen years of age take a pride in boasting of their amours, of their dissipations, and of their wild exploits. I have, however, no taste for such exposures. If I had, I could mention things that would make my old granny, and even wiser folks, stare, notwithstanding that I am young, and look very innocent.

Rosina had met far too many young men with such foolish pride, but she had never read words that chilled her more:

No mind is strictly sane while under the undue influence of any passion; for passion always distorts the intellectual vision. We are perhaps more sane in the morning than in the evening. Sometimes, at the dead hour of midnight, a thought is roused up from the deep caverns of the mind, like a startled maniac, which all the energy of reason can scarcely re-cage.

This was not a confession, but indeed it was proof that the beautiful boy feared his darkest thoughts and feelings. And his father feared them too, saying in a letter Robinson had inserted in the diary,

I dislike the idea of your going to New York to reside, nor will I attempt to disguise the reasons. I fear that your moral character may suffer. You will there be ensnared by a thousand temptations, which I fear you have not the strength of principal to resist. I know your self-confidence; but I also know your weakness, my son. Even where you are, I tremble for you. Indeed, indeed, you are, I fear, a child of the devil.

How could any sane, good man *keep* such a letter?

These revelations, however, did not deter Robinson's supporters, who now formed Robinson Clubs. Members dressed like him, wearing tight-fitting plum-colored dress coats with black velvet collars, black neck scarves, and floppy caps. They assembled below his jail cell, waiting to catch a glimpse of him and receive the notes he dropped through the bars of the window, all with the same message, "A man of such prospects, I am innocent." They harassed prostitutes on the streets, and hissed and booed reformers at public meetings convened to denounce the sins of prostitution.

Then artists began making lithographs for sale in stalls and bookshops on Broadway. One picture showed Helen carrying a letter in her small hand as she walked on the street in her usual green silk dress, gloves, bonnet, and parasol. For a mere pittance the buyer could see her large eyes and confident smile, and never know that the tiny feet and hands were only symbols of refinement in 1836. Helen was beautiful, but she was not demure. She always thought her feet were too big, and she never liked her long fingers. They made her look like a farm girl, she once told Rosina.

The lithographs sold out. Buyers *had* to have pictures of the city's most famous prostitute.

Another picture had Helen dead in her bed, her shoulders and breasts fully exposed, the nipples clearly defined, her thigh and calves half covered by burned blankets. There was no blood, no gashes, no evidence of Dr. Roger's autopsy. The *Sun* could not deny the lithograph's erotic power, saying, "It is sufficiently indecent to render it attractive to persons of depraved taste." Day added that the artist had "murdered her far more than Richard P. Robinson did."

The real Helen had disappeared. "The press is endeavoring to give her an apotheosis," complained one paper. Another sneered, "It has become really amusing to read the first attractive fictions in which the life and character of the wretched Helen Jewett have been dressed by the penny press. Here was a girl who could play the harp, guitar, piano, and speak Italian, French, and Spanish. Next we will hear she knew the Augustan classics."

But there was one consolation.

The editorial and prints represented what most people in town assumed: Robinson was guilty of murder, and only a fool or dupe could believe otherwise.

Rosina hoped that Helen's confiscated letters might provide answers to unanswered questions, as if Helen could now speak to everyone from beyond the grave.

Chapter Thirty

The trial would begin in five days, and a crime reporter would need a clear head. But today Billy would drink whiskey until he killed the pain of regret and remorse and could sleep without guilt twisting his body.

He stared at the almost empty bottle, the moisture on the glass reminding him of the sweat that soaked his skin that night, and silently acknowledged the futility of his hopes. His friend was dead, and he blamed himself for her murder.

He had not killed Helen, of course. Nonetheless, Billy felt the cord of terrible probabilities thicken around his neck as he recalled the past two years. She might still be alive if he had not written that article, "A Woman of Spunk," for the *New York Transcript*. Perhaps she would still be alive if he had not introduced her to Richard Robinson, now in prison since April. Did Robinson kill her, or was he innocent, as he claimed to the press at every opportunity?

Maybe Helen would still be alive if Billy had not left for Texas, pursuing a romantic dream and abandoning her as she struggled to control an unreliable and wayward nineteen-year-old lover. He should have stayed and protected her somehow.

Billy sighed, thinking again of the way Helen died and was now imagined in prints hawked on street corners all over town. Seeking distraction, he remembered better days, and then he drank until he could remember nothing.

When the day of the trial finally arrived, more than six thousand people showed up in a downpour, waiting to fill a courtroom on the second floor of City Hall that could hold only a thousand. The boisterous crowd, almost all men, packed the marble staircase and the downstairs lobby, and flowed into the park outside under a dark gray sky and windy rain. At least it was no longer cold. After months of winter, with another snowstorm falling in mid-April, spring had arrived at last.

The courtroom doors opened at ten, and those at the front surged forward, filling every seat and the space for standees at the back. At one front table before the judge sat Robinson's defense team—Ogden Hoffman, William Price, and William Maxwell.

Hired by Robinson's employer, Hoffman was the best money could buy. He'd served as the city's district attorney for six years, and had returned to private practice just six months ago, a successful attorney best known for charming juries.

His two- and three-hour summations were so captivating, even reporters would stop taking notes and just listen, spellbound. At the end of a trial he earned tears from the jurors and applause from the crowds in packed courtrooms.

Maxwell and Price were his assistants, mere appendages to an imposing presence belied by Hoffman's slight build and short stature.

Behind them sat Robinson's father and uncle.

At the other front table sat the lawyers for the prosecution—Thomas Phoenix, a sickly man who seemed distracted most of the time, and William Morris, a lawyer unable to earn any listing in the legal directories printed every year.

Twenty editors and reporters had been allowed earlier that morning to enter the room by a rear entrance and sit near the front of the courtroom, so they could take notes. There were no official transcripts of trials. Court-appointed scribes usually wrote brief summary notes for coroner reports, Grand Jury testimony, and depositions. For notorious cases, the public had to depend on reporters, once barred from taking notes until the Supreme Court had overruled the ban, to provide as many details of the proceedings as humanly possible. Like theater critics, these reporters needed vibrant characters, dramatic exchanges, great speeches, and a climax befitting a well-told tale. Accuracy was not required or expected. Dull reporting was unforgivable.

Ben Day was not going to miss a single day of the trial, and he appreciated his good fortune in having Locke with him in the courtroom. With Locke at his side taking shorthand notes, and his brother-in-law back in the office assuming more and more of the management of the paper, Day could focus his undivided attention on the men before him, especially Hoffman and the presiding judge, Ogden Edwards, grandson of the great preacher Jonathan Edwards, son of a federal judge who had served in the Continental Congress during the Revolution, a member of the state legislature, and a judge in the Circuit Court for twenty years. His recent conviction of twenty journeymen tailors who were charged with price fixing and conspiracy to strike suggested a prejudice against common workers of all kinds. He wore snobbery like a badge on his black robe and could not hide his contempt for Day and all his scribbling kind.

There were two other presiding judges; they sat on either side of Edwards, silent and stone faced, reflecting what everyone knew: this was Judge Edwards' court, and they were mere appendages.

Day and Locke sat as far away from Jamie Bennett as possible. Even so, Bennett never missed the opportunity to glower and sneer, accentuating his disdain for everyone else in his profession. His great enemy, James Watson Webb, stayed away, sending his police reporter instead because he could not abide, he said, "the stink of crowds in closed spaces." His refusal to appear disappointed those eager to see a reprisal of the May brawl between him and Bennett. Even after a second assault, Bennett took the opportunity on the city's now most prominent stage to show gladly that he wore his recent injuries. His left hand, used again to deflect Webb's cane, had long since healed, but he kept it wrapped in a fresh white bandage, large enough for the back rows to see.

Reporting for the *Transcript* again, Billy sat at the table with Day and Locke. Seeing their good fortune in his timely return, his editors had immediately re-hired him. "You have the best eyes and ears, and you'll keep it clear and simple, unlike that Locke fellow."

Billy wished he could take notes as quickly as Locke, a rare shorthand master. He had heard that Locke was drinking heavily these days. Was the guilt from writing the Moon Series too much? Would the drinking and his frustrated dream of starting his own newspaper affect the quality of his work?

Billy didn't know.

But Billy was sure of one thing; he would be sober throughout the trial. Four days had passed without a drop of liquor.

He had to have a clear head to learn more about Robinson; that he kept a journal without telling Billy was still a shock. Thankfully, Billy and his friends were not incriminated as debauched rakes. Robinson was only interested in talking about himself.

The other city commercial and mercantile papers sent no one to the court-room, refusing to sanction so sordid a case with their official presence. Whatever needed to be said would be reprinted briefly and without acknowledgment from other sources. The penny press would have this trial all to itself.

The noise in the courtroom was almost deafening as men argued about guilt and innocence, recited known facts, repeated rumors, and retold gossip. Dressed in their caps and tight-fitting blue jackets, Robinson's supporters sat in clusters throughout the courtroom, hooting and laughing. Judge Edwards pounded his gavel, but it silenced no one.

Then Robison, escorted by the keeper of the Bellevue Prison, entered the room, and silence prevailed. Wearing a new blue suit and a curly, light brown wig, and walking steadily to a table near the jury box, he appeared unfazed by the crowd. There'd been rumors that after his arrest so much of Robinson's hair had fallen out because of frayed nerves that he had to have his head shaved. Even so, he held his head up and smiled, his wide blue eyes looking ahead with unwavering focus. He twirled the dangling cloth cap in his hands constantly, but Day could not tell if this was a mere habit or a show of nerves.

Robinson had to remain standing, as protocol required, as the jurors, to be paid twelve cents a day, were selected.

Jury selection took five hours that first day.

Fifty-nine men were summoned to the proceedings, but only twenty-one bothered to appear. Of those twenty-one, only seven were selected for the jury after the judge dismissed four for cause, and ten were excused after Hoffman's peremptory challenges. The prosecution didn't challenge a single man.

Scowling, Judge Edwards explained to the lawyers that he would have to use the ancient practice of Talesman. Under British and American law, he could randomly draft jurors from in or about the courtroom. But he had decided that the huge and unruly crowd had no impartial or disinterested members. Instead, he would send court officers to find Talesmen from neighborhood streets and stores.

A few in the courtroom shouted their displeasure, smelling class prejudice. "Aren't we *good* enough?" asked a self-appointed leader, who received approving nods and shouts of "yes" from supporters. Judge Edwards only stared out into the courtroom until the officers returned with three-dozen rounded up men.

The winnowing process began again, and after three more hours, Judge Edwards had his jury of twelve men: a druggist, a shoemaker, a store keeper, an insurance company secretary, a clothier, a coal dealer, two grocers, and four merchants—all white and sufficiently respectable, of course.

Once the jurors were seated and sworn in, the judge read the indictment: one count of "willful and deliberate murder." Although brief, Edwards' slow, almost ponderous reading suggested the full weight and solemnity of the law. The projection of his deep voice to the very back of the courtroom compelled a grudging respect. Clearly, violators of the law would pay, and pay dearly.

Still standing, Robinson did not move. Unsmiling, he looked straight ahead. He stopped twirling his cap.

The district attorney offered a brief opening statement, characterizing the offense for which the prisoner stood charged as "the most atrocious and diabolical" he had ever presented to a jury. Murder and the aggravated crime of arson made this case particularly egregious, Phoenix said, and although the evidence against the prisoner was "almost exclusively circumstantial," it was so strong and clear and conclusive that it rendered the "situation of the unfortunate accused" as perilous and awful.

Incredulous, Billy shook his head. By openly admitting that the people's case was founded on circumstantial evidence, Phoenix had made possible the introduction of "reasonable doubt." And then he had characterized Robinson as "unfortunate," giving jury members the opportunity to indulge feelings of sympathy for Hoffman's client. Could a district attorney declare his incompetence and stupidity this early?

Phoenix called his first witness for the prosecution—Rosina Townsend. Billy took careful note of her bearing.

Rosina was led into the courtroom by police officers whose job was to escort her and her associates, one by one, from the Grand Jury room in the building behind City Hall, and then take them back again.

Rosina dressed simply; her dark blue gown was form fitting, as current fashion required, but the lace on the bodice and sleeves was dark, delicate, and minimal. She wore no jewelry, and her bonnet was small and without flower or fruit clusters. A single silk ribbon, dark yet shimmering in the light as it fell from the bonnet across her shoulders, was the only suggestion of luxury. Her mature beauty could not be denied, and she maintained her dignity throughout the five hours of direct and cross-examination.

Led by Phoenix's questions, Rosina repeated the testimony she had given in earlier depositions before the coroner's jury and the Grand Jury about the night of the murder, reiterating the certainty of her recognition of Robinson by noting the side look of his face and his thinning hair.

She then described the discovery of Helen's body four hours later, at three in the morning. Her narrative was detailed and dry, as if drained of emotion by constant repetition, even as she said, "One side of Helen's body was burnt; when I first saw her she was lying on her back, with her left side very much burnt, and large gash on the side of her head. When Miss Stevens first got to the bed, she brought some of the ashes of the burnt clothes, and remarked that they must all be burnt up."

The crowd listened with rapt attention, almost everyone straining neck and back to hear every word in the courtroom.

Then Hoffmann began the cross-examination, starting with questions about Rosina's past. She reported her age as thirty-nine, her status as married. Her husband was not dead, but Rosina had not seen him since he abandoned her for another woman in Cincinnati eleven years earlier. She came to New York in 1825, worked first as a seamstress, then as a chambermaid, and then a prostitute in a "house of assignation."

The narrated details of her work history—and particularly the details of those last weeks at 41 Thomas Street, when Robinson came to see Helen about six times, all at night—had the desired effect on the men in the crowd. Disturbed more by details of the prostitution business than about the details of murder and arson, they groaned and jeered as Rosina related her story. Her tale was no descent into horror, with the required melodrama of shame and remorse, no wringing of hands, no invocations to God and the fear of divine judgment. As she told it, her biography was only a series of career choices, and Richard Robinson was just another customer.

The men in the courtroom wanted a morally depraved whore, and Rosina was not a willing performer. Prostitution was a business, and nothing more.

"My God," shouted an outraged citizen, and hundreds erupted, repeating the phrase throughout the courtroom like a chorus in a morality play.

"Silence in the court," said Judge Edwards, his voice tentative, almost subdued. Day was sure Edwards agreed with the dissatisfied men.

Then Rosina revealed that there were *two* men who bore the name Frank Rivers when they came to her house, and the courtroom erupted again. The men hooted and yelled, raised their fists, and started to chant insults and derogatory slogans. The suggestion of a sordid game of duplicity and seduction was too much.

"Whore! Whore! Whore!" they cried.

"Love for money, and money for love!"

"Shame, shame, shame!"

Judge Edwards pounded his gavel again and again, but he allowed the demonstration to continue for almost five minutes. The outraged men only stopped when he threatened to jail them all for contempt of court. It was getting late in the day.

Once order was restored, Hoffmann continued his cross-examination, searching for inconsistencies and discrepancies.

"You said there were *two* Frank Rivers. Who was the other man, and how could you tell them apart?"

"The other man who also called himself Frank Rivers was Mr. Robinson's friend and roommate, James Tew."

"Now why did they both go by the same name?"

"I don't know," said Rosina honestly. "I only know that men play all kinds of games, pretending and assuming roles according to rules of their own making. I don't care about the specifics, as long as my customers pay and my girls are not hurt."

"Objection," said Phoenix, rising. As if oblivious to the explosive nature of Rosina's revelation, Phoenix only said, "She is in no position to know their minds. Conjecture only."

"Sustained," said the judge.

Unfazed, Hoffman continued: "On the night of April ninth. how did you recognize Mr. Robinson?

"I do remember Robinson standing near the casement, and the lamp light on his face."

"Did you see his *full* face?"

"No, he covered it with his cloak."

"Did you see his *full* face when you saw him in the upstairs room?"

"No, I only saw his side face."

"Why?"

"Robinson was on the bed lying on his stomach with his bedclothes near up to the shoulders."

" If you didn't see his face, then what did you see?" Hoffman inquired.

"His bald spot," she replied, generating light laughter in the courtroom. "I don't understand why," Phoenix observed.

"Sir?" asked Elizabeth.

"Thank you," said Phoenix, turning away quickly.

"How many other men do you know have bald spots?"

"Several, but I don't know exactly how many for sure."

"Are there *other* details of which you *cannot* be certain?" he asked, turning to the jury with a mocking smile.

"After the horrible discovery of the murder, I can scarcely say what took place." As soon as she spoke, she regretted it. But it was too late.

Billy scanned the faces of the jury. Hoffman's questions were producing the desired effect. Rosina was not a witness to the crime. She was too busy doing her own job to be a legitimate witness. Hoffman and his team wanted the jurors to not remember any detailed descriptions of his client, who was admittedly there that night. They wanted the jurors to see far more clearly, even if imagined, the details of Rosina Townsend spreading her legs for paying gentlemen.

Rosina never lost her poise, but her admission of uncertainty was progressively undermining the prosecutor's case, Billy believed.

"Were there other gentlemen at the house that night?" Hoffman asked.

"Yes."

"How many?"

"I don't know. All the men made their escape before the coroner came to hold the inquest."

"Did you know them?"

"The majority I did not know. May I have a glass of water?"

As she waited, a juror had a question. Jurors were allowed to ask questions.

"Did you see the prisoner at the coroner's inquest, or at the police office, and if you did, did he have his hat on when you saw him?"

Rosina could not hide the scorn in the roll of her eyes.. Why did Robinson's hat matter, she wondered? What difference did it make? No one denies that he was at the house that night. The juror's implied suggestion that she couldn't identify him because he wore a hat was absurd. It was absolutely astonishing what a juror could become obsessed about. Forget the body burning in the bed, and remember the hat.

Forget the hatchet and the cloak Robinson was wearing, and remember the bald spot!

She took a sip of water from the glass that had been found. It was then handed over to a juror who had discreetly asked for a glass of water, too. Cups and glasses were shared throughout the city, as most citizens drank from public wells and backyard cisterns, so no one raised an eyebrow at the passing of a common glass. But everyone noticed when the juror declined Rosina's glass, shaking his head vigorously. His point was clear: He would not pollute himself by sharing a glass with Rosina Townsend. Hoffman turned around silently, making sure the reporters had noted this priceless gift to the defense.

At half past eight the Judge Edwards excused Rosina, and she rose from her chair, her head high, the luster of her eyes undimmed by exhaustion or embarrassment. Billy had to admit his growing admiration. Rosina had considerable presence, and it was no surprise to him that she was a success in her own world. Yes, as she had confessed in court, she had been "frequently subjected to rude and brutal treatment from ruffians and others."

But Billy could tell, as she told her story, that such abuse had never entered her heart or poisoned its self-regard. She was a strong, ambitious, and intelligent woman, and she did not suffer fools. Her rise, against all odds, surpassed the achievement of most men in New York. Despite her sex and chosen work, Rosina had lived the American dream. Of one thing Billy was now certain: If Rosina Townsend were the district attorney, she would prosecute with calm but ruthless dispatch, a methodical and efficient practitioner, all business.

If only Thomas Phoenix could be more like her.

It was getting late, and some men in the crowd had departed for the night, going home for dinner and time with family. But the courtroom was still packed; for every man who departed, another immediately filled his space.

The district attorney continued his call of witnesses for the prosecution. Their testimony was a numbing recitation of already known facts, all circumstantial, as Phoenix readily admitted. Hoffman could not hide his impatience. Billy, too, wanted to go home, eat some bread and cheese, and then find a whore for a quick and joyless coupling before going to sleep.

A brief exchange grabbed his attention, however.

"Did Mrs. Townsend ask you to go searching the backyard?" asked Maxwell during cross-examination of the watchman who had found the hatchet.

"No, I took my own course in searching. Mrs. Townsend did not tell me where to go," he replied.

Then Maxwell asked, "Do you think it possible that the hatchet might have been thrown to the place where you found it by some of the girls who were standing about the yard?"

The watchman arched his eyebrows, but Phoenix raised no objection to the introduction of another possibility—a female murderer, one of Helen's associates.

"It's improbable, but not impossible, I guess," the watchman replied.

It was now ten o'clock, and Judge Edwards ordered the court's adjournment. A seed had been planted. Someone other than Robinson could have murdered Helen Jewett. The sound of the resonating syllables of that most elegant and slippery of legal phrases, reasonable doubt, although unspoken, could be heard throughout the courtroom.

Chapter Thirty-One

Rain fell with blustery winds on Friday, June third, but the weather did not deter the thousands who arrived at City Hall Park as early as seven o'clock and created an impenetrable mass of packed humanity by eight. In a crowd larger than the day before's, the frustrated jostled for position, pushed and shoved, and cursed the courts for ineptitude, inconvenience, hostility to democracy, and a multitude of moral offenses. Chants and profane slogans punctuated the rising din.

By ten o'clock the courtroom doors were opened, and men scrambled in, rushing to available seats, creating a near riot. Finally, after much pounding of the gavel and shouted imprecations from the bench, the excited men settled down.

Phoenix resumed his call of witnesses for the prosecution, devoting his attention to a narrow range of physical evidence—the interior and exterior of Number 41 Thomas Street, a cloak and hatchet found in the yard, a string attached to the hatchet and the cloak, and a smudge of whitewash on Robinson's pantaloons. All of the witnesses—both police officers and watchmen—verified the objects and had to answer questions again and again about their size, shape, cost, and past history, as if repetition alone could build a solid case.

The jurors listened impassively, their eyes blank with obvious boredom, until Hoffmann cross-examined the arresting officer, Dennis Brink, badgering him with questions about his relationship to Rosina Townsend and the other prostitutes at the brothel across the street from his own residence.

Brink was a big man, his chest filling his coat and a lifted chin projecting confidence. But under cross-examination, he seemed to deflate.

Brink had served process papers at Number 41 Thomas Street against servants and sometimes against girls in the house. He had been hired to protect the house from rioters, and to protect the property during the sale of furniture and other items. But he *never* was a customer there, and he *never* knew Helen, he asserted, officious and obsequious in the same breath.

Nevertheless, Brink damaged his own credibility.

He was far too familiar with Rosina Townsend, Helen Jewett, and all that messy brothel business. Billy understood jurors. They were both fascinated and appalled by it all, but in the end they would default to self-righteousness and, proving their moral superiority, stand against Rosina and *all* of her acquaintances. Guilt by association was a marvelous thing. For now the crime under consideration was *not* murder, it was depravity, and the stink of it was rank indeed.

The testimony of Elizabeth Salters, whose room at Number 41 was across the landing from Helen's, fulfilled high hopes for more sordid details about the sex trade.

Elizabeth was blond and beautiful, with exquisite skin and high but soft cheekbones accentuating hazel eyes that could only be called alluring. All theThe men in the courtroom watched and listened without the background groans, hoots, sneers, and hisses that had accompanied Rosina Townsend's testimony.

"How did you know the prisoner, and for how long?" asked Phoenix, also unable to keep his eyes off her.

"I knew him before Helen was killed. I met him about seven weeks before at Mrs. Townsend's. He used to come and see me there."

The courtroom stirred and Phoenix smiled, having achieved the desired effect. "To see *you* there?"

"Yes," she replied.

"I see. Did you know or hear of a quarrel between Helen and the other girls at the house?"

"I never knew or heard of her having a quarrel with anyone in the house, or out of it for that matter," Elizabeth replied, smiling sweetly as if her personal statement alone, offered with such benign assurance, would put the matter of female jealousy to rest, even though prostitutes occasionally saw the same clients.

"Were you at the house at the time of the murder?" continued Phoenix.

"Yes, I was there, and toward morning a gentleman came to see me."

"When?"

"He came in a quarter of an hour before I heard the alarm."

"Did you expect him?"

"Yes."

"Did you hear him come into the house?"

"No, I didn't. I didn't hear him until he came to my room."

"What was his condition when the alarm was given?"

"He was undressed when we heard the alarm," she said, startled by the nervous laughter in the courtroom.

"I don't understand why," observed Phoenix.

"Thank you," said Phoenix, turning away quickly; he was done with her.

Hoffman now approached Elizabeth and asked questions about her background. She informed him and the courtroom that she was nineteen and had lived at the house of Mrs. Brown, another madam, before moving to Rosina Townsend's. Hoffman then returned to the night of the murder.

"How many were in the house on the night of the murder?"

"I can't say. There were several persons in the parlor, but I cannot say how many, or who they were."

"Did Helen Jewett know that you were seeing Robinson before you moved to Mrs. Townsend's?"

"I don't know."

"Did he come to see you at Mrs. Townsend's?"

"Yes, he did, and the other Frank Rivers came to see me. too. They have both been in my room at the same time, and they used to dress a good deal alike."

Her casually revealed statement ignited the courtroom, its indulgence exploding in an instant. The shouting and yelling, a near universal chorus of indignation and disgust, was so loud Judge Edwards had to pound his gavel multiple times and demand order.

Hoffman smiled. Of all of the day's images, this would be the most memorable: a beautiful and naked Elizabeth Salter entertaining *two* men who used the same name and dressed alike when they arrived. Did they watch each other, one pair and then another, or did they perform as a trio, touching and exploring simultaneously? If a constant sifter of the meaning of testimony and evidence could barely keep the scene out of his mind, what could the common men of the jury do?

Hoffman returned to the alarm on the night of the murder. "What did you do once the alarm was called?"

"I ran out of my room in only my nightclothes," she said, turning suddenly to the sounds of tittering disapproval. "I didn't have time to dress."

"Did you see other men in the hall?"

"I cannot say how many. I was too frightened."

"Did you see any of them try to escape?"

"No, I didn't. But when the doors were opened to let the watchmen in, they *did* get away."

"Did you see a person in Helen Jewett's room when the alarm was given?"

"No."

"Did you see him when he came that night?"

"No. We were in the parlor when he came, and Helen told us that her dear Frank had come."

"How was he dressed?"

"I don't know."

"Did you know about Mr. Robinson's bald spot?" asked Hoffman.

Elizabeth started for a fleeting moment, and then replied, "Mrs. Townsend told me last week of the particular bald mark she had observed. She told me it was a curious bald place on the crown of his head. Before she told me that, I never knew anything of it."

"Knowing Mr. Robinson as you did, how could you miss it?"

Annoyed, Elizabeth said peevishly, "I have more than once seen the prisoner with his clothes off, and so exposed that I should think I could have observed the place upon his head about which Mrs. Townsend spoke. It must be a *recent* development."

Another uproar in the courtroom forced Judge Edwards to pound his gavel and demand order again.

Hoffman returned to the theme of female jealousy, and asked, "Was there any ill feeling between you and Helen Jewett because of Frank Rivers leaving you to visit her?"

"I never said anything to her about his visiting me."

"Did your secret behavior with the prisoner *bother* you?"

"I thought she had *most* right to him, as I understood from him that she had known him intimately for a long time."

Hoffman frowned and asked, "*Most* right? What do you mean by that?"

She began her reply, saying "I . . .," but Hoffman cut her off and asked, "Did Miss Jewett have a regular customer for Saturday nights?"

"Yes," replied Elizabeth, her mouth tight, her eyes now slits of irritation and disdain.

"Who was it?"

"He went by the name of Tom Easy. That's how I knew him. That's what everyone knew him by."

"Thank you. You may step down."

"Is that all?" asked Elizabeth. Her moment on the stage had come to an abrupt end, and she was not ready for this kind of exit.

"Yes, thank you," he repeated, and turned away.

Elizabeth Salters sat still for a moment, looked around as if seeking options, and then stepped down, making sure that all eyes were on her. As a final gesture, she bestowed on Robinson a mischievous smile before the guard took her out with a slight touch of his hand to her elbow.

Robinson did not smile back. Even when she had mentioned him and the details of their relationship, he never turned his face toward her. For hours he sat at the defense table saying nothing to his father or the lawyers. He never acknowledged the hostile witnesses or reacted to their testimony. He looked straight ahead, as if they were not there, his face serene and blank. Only once did he acknowledge his supporters, turning to them with a brief wave of his hand when pandemonium broke out during the testimony of Rosina Townsend. Surrounded by hundreds, he sat in his own world.

And the men who'd been at Rosina Townsend's house that awful night remained in theirs. They were never identified or called to the witness stand.

Chapter Thirty-Two

Early Saturday morning, all the entry gates of the hall were closed. Guards stood at all the entrances, restricting business at City Hall to the trial and allowing only members of the bar, reporters, and witnesses to enter the courtroom. The behavior of the mob at the opening of yesterday's session was "absolutely unacceptable," pronounced Judge Edward. Exclusion would teach the unruly masses a lesson and guarantee better public manners the next day.

Soon after ten o'clock, Robinson entered the courtroom. He went directly to his chair and sat down, saying nothing to his family, lawyers, or employer. He looked blankly at the three judges before him as if they were part of the stark wall behind them.

Phoenix began the proceedings by calling Sarah Dunscombe to the stand. His perfunctory questions led her to calmly describing the rudiments of her daily schedule.

The defense team crossed-examined her to reduce her already compromised credibility. After all, she was young, female, black, and worked in a whorehouse. Yes, she was one of the last people to see Helen alive, but she didn't see a crime. Maxwell and Hoffman alternated their interrogation, asking questions about her service that Saturday night and exposing her ignorance about Robinson. She didn't know him, and what she heard was hearsay and therefore inadmissible.

During the interrogation she looked down and rubbed her hands repeatedly,

"Are you frightened?" asked Hoffman pointedly, as if her confession would disqualify her testimony.

"Yes," she replied.

"Why?"

"I'm not used to bein' in public."

"Nothing further," he said, unable to hide the annoyance in his voice.

Hoffmann was eager to begin his defense, and still the prosecution had not rested its case. Murder trials didn't usually take this long, and given what Hoffman had to do, he was now certain that the trial would last for five days at least, surpassing the record established by the trial of Levi Weeks in 1800. Silently,

Hoffman cursed Phoenix and Morris. Indefatigable plodders, they were the culprits, dragging before the jury maids, clerks, and prostitutes who could prove nothing but the banal details of their banal lives.

But when Oliver Lownds began to testify, Hoffman took notice. As he listened to the police magistrate's story, Hoffman began passing quickly scribbled notes to his assistant for the first time during the trial.

Lownds reported that after Robinson's arrestd he had opened Robinson's locked trunks and a chest of drawers brought by Dennis Brink to the police office, and had found a wallet stuffed with large numbers of bills of exchange. The courtroom stirred.

But Phoenix asked no questions about the wallet, demonstrating once again the triumph of stupidity over curiosity. Hoffman could hear the obvious questions in everyone else's mind: What was a poorly paid clerk doing with a fat wallet filled with bank notes to his boss? Where did the money come from? Was Robinson an embezzler?

Once Phoenix had finished questioning Lownds,Maxwell asked him a distracting line of questions about the fences and exits at Number 41 Thomas Street and the alleys around it. The inquiries were so detailed, so boring that all the reporters in the room stopped taking notes. The strategy worked. The wallet was not mentioned again.

Hoffman and Maxwell could barely hide their glee. Thomas Phoenix was more incompetent than they had realized. His case was incoherent. There was no structure to his lineup of witnesses, and no powerful conclusion seemed to be in the offing. True, there were interesting details about brothel life, but so far nothing in the testimony could solidly link Robinson to murder.

After a brief recess, the prosecution tried other approaches. William Morris called Joseph Hoxie to the stand and asked about Robinson's terms of employment. Hoffman objected, saying that questions about salary "had no bearing on the case." The judge agreed, but Morris approached the bench to argue his position.

"Following the money is an age-old, but wise admonition, sir," he said firmly.

"You have laid no groundwork for such an inquiry, Mr. Morris," the judge replied, "and you certainly may *not* ask anything about possible suspicion."

"But, sir. . ."

"Stand back. I'm done," the judge snapped.

Morris then pursued questions about Robinson's handwriting. Joseph Hoxie reported promoting Robinson to assistant bookkeeper and had seen him copy letters. Morris then showed samples of Robinson's writing in a manuscript book and fifteen letters. On both occasions Hoxie declared that he could not swear to a positive identification.

"I cannot see any writing that I could venture to swear positively was his," he concluded.

Avoiding another scowl from Judge Edwards, Day scribbled a note to Locke, asking, "What's going on? He promotes R.R. as a bookkeeper and can't swear to his *writing?*"

But then Phoenix and Morris pulled out a surprise. They called to the stand a man named Frederick W. Gourgouns, who worked as a clerk in an apothecary shop on Broadway.

A receipt made out to a "Mr. Douglass," found in Robinson's trunk, had led the police to the shop, which was owned by a Doctor Chabert, who was known for treating prostitutes in the back room of his store. Tall and skinny, Gourgouns towered over most men. But his greasy hair and pimpled face diminished his stature, and he spoke with a clipped, sharp tone, as if only his words mattered anyway. With smug awareness of their power, he silenced the room as if he had fired a musket, and waited patiently for a pigeon to drop dead from the sky.

"He called himself Douglass when he came into the store several times, but I remember Robinson coming in early April after dark and asking for *arsenic*. For killing rats, he said."

He obviously enjoyed the ensuing consternation. No one in the press had heard this before; there had certainly been no mention of this in the newspapers. Bennett and Day looked at each other with equal befuddlement. Day whispered, "Well, I'll be damned."

"Are you certain he is the person, the prisoner at the bar?" asked Phoenix, pleased by his explosive surprise.

"Yes, I think he is. I believe the prisoner at the bar, to the best of my knowledge, is the same person who called himself by the name Douglass."

"Did you sell any poison to him?"

"We are not in the habit of selling it to anybody," Gourgouns replied, "and especially not to *strangers*."

Maxwell whispered to Hoffman, "Let me have him."

Stating his case for the inadmissibility of Gourgon's testimony, Maxwell declared with a voice high and assured, "The circumstances of the prisoner's attempting to obtain poison for the purpose of killing Helen Jewett, or any other woman, are not proper evidence under this indictment. Helen Jewett was killed with a hatchet. Evidence about arsenic is immaterial."

The judge agreed.

The defense team, accepting yet another defeat with no apparent disappointment, returned to the identification of Robinson's handwriting, calling on another coworker to verify the handwriting in Robinson's diary. The witness looked carefully over the leaves of the journal, one by one, and marked with a pencil twelve authentic pages. But he was not asked a single question about the diary's content. And when he was shown seventeen letters, he identified them as written by Robinson but was not asked a single question about *what* Robinson said in those letters.

Billy surmised the Phoenix strategy. Having proven that Robinson wrote the letters, Phoenix would now read the letters written to Helen and admit them as evidence, establishing a motive for murder.

But Hoffmann immediately objected. And then, as if his strategic preparations mattered not at all, Phoenix immediately capitulated, declaring, "I have some *doubts* as to the legality of their admission as testimony for the prosecution against the accused. At this stage of the proceedings, I should rest the prosecution."

"*What?*" asked Billy, so startled that he forced Judge Edwards to turn his head and look with a fierce scowl.

In all of his days attending trials and following cases, Billy had never heard a case for the prosecution end so abruptly, without warning, without fanfare, without sufficient reference to the crime and the demands of justice. And to end it all with a confession of doubt about the admissibility of his evidence was simply flabbergasting.

Shocked, too, Hoffman was speechless, a rare event. But he quickly found his voice.

"Your honor," he announced, extending his arms to dramatize his outrage as he offered a premature summary of his position, "this is *final* proof of the prosecution's pathetic position, having made a case on a stack of weak playing cards."

He then denounced the reputation and character of the witnesses for the prosecution, and accused most New York newspapers of trying to turn the tide of public prejudice against his client by resorting to "the most trifling and minute circumstances."

He condemned specifically the *Sun* for mentioning the prisoner's shaved head, denouncing it as a "mean subterfuge" and a "contemptible distraction." On the other hand, he praised the *Herald* as an honorable and worthy exception to the "culpable conduct" of the other city newspapers, and he promised to exculpate his client by providing the testimony of a respectable tradesman whose "positive alibi" would show that the prisoner was elsewhere on the night of April ninth, a full mile and a half away from Rosina Townsend's house.

In one brief speech, Hoffman managed to upend the already teetering scaffold of the prosecution's case. The courtroom stirred like a buzzing bee hive. Judge

Edwards frowned, but did not call for order. And Bennett slowly turned his head toward Benjamin Day to gloat, with a wide, triumphant grin.

Day faced Bennett with contemptuous, damning eyes, his rage pure and cold as winter ice. Billy noticed this exchange and wondered if Day, well known for his temper, would be Bennett's next attacker.

Hoffman then called "his respectable tradesman," Mr. Robert Furlong, to the stand, and asked for a brief description of his background. A man of medium build and an undistinguished face, Furlong told the court that he was the owner of a small family grocery store at the corner of Liberty and Nassau, where Robinson bought and smoked cigars. He didn't know Robinson's name or occupation, but he knew the prisoner by sight since he had been in the store "often."

When asked to describe his encounter with the prisoner on Saturday night, August ninth, Furlong reported, "He came there about half past nine o'clock. He bought a bundle of cigars, twenty-five, lighted one and took a seat on a barrel, and smoked there until ten o'clock. Before then he read a newspaper and jokingly dropped ashes on our sleeping porter, whose head was laid back and his mouth wide open." Furlong grinned.

"How did you know the time?" Hoffmann asked.

Furlong replied, "When the store clock struck ten, my partner said, 'There's ten o'clock, and it's time to shut up.' The prisoner took out his watch, a small silver one, expensive looking, and said it was one minute past ten o'clock. I took out my watch and compared my watch with his. That was our usual time, and the porter went out to put up the shutters."

"What was the prisoner doing?"

"He remained seated, smoking all the time, and by the time the porter was done, the prisoner nearly got through with his second cigar."

"Did he say anything?"

"He remarked that he was encroaching on my time, but I replied, 'Oh no, not at all.' And just before he went away, he stood a short time on the stoop, and said, "I believe I'll go home. I'm tired," and bade me goodnight."

"What time was it?"

"It was ten or fifteen minutes after ten."

"How far is your store from Thomas Street?"

"A full mile, sir. A *full* mile."

Under cross-examination, Furlong gave even more details about Robinson. He read the *Evening Post* that night. He commented on the unpleasant weather. He wore dark clothes, a coat, vest, and pantaloons.

"Did he wear a cloak?" Morris asked.

"No, sir. A coat."

After a few more questions, the defense recalled Joseph Hoxie, Sr., who confirmed that the watch mentioned in Furlong's testimony was one that Hoxie had bought for Robinson.

Hearing this, Billy, Day, and Locke again turned to each other, silently asking the question no one else seemed interested in answering: Why would Hoxie give Robinson a watch? Billy could see a pattern—promotion, gifts, support for an expensive lawyer, sitting beside the accused at a notorious trial. Why did Hoxie *favor* Robinson?

It was now ten o'clock at night. Judge Edwards called for adjournment, and almost every one hurried out of the courtroom to get to bed.

Hoffman sat absolutely still, reflecting on the day and thinking of his future.

Now there were in the record two conflicting accounts of Robinson's movements on the night of April ninth.

He knew the jury's preference, and he was confident that his strategy for Monday—a call of witnesses to muddy the narrative told by Rosina and her "ladies"—could only deepen the jury's hunger for the clarity that could only come in the closing arguments of a great summation on Tuesday. Before that important time, he and his partner would ask a stupefying number of questions with the absolute assurance that only the reporters in the courtroom would remember or care about the questions and their answers.

But a great speech would make a lasting impression. After all, who remembered the details of the Compromise of 1820, or the Nullification Crisis of 1832? A few pedants and some musty historians who wrote books no one read. But people still talked about the powerful impact of the speeches of Daniel Webster, Henry Clay, and John C. Calhoun. Truth didn't matter; only eloquence mattered.

Hoffman smiled. The coming of the Sabbath day was most convenient. His body needed the comforts of a bed, but his brain would not rest. It had to get ready for possibly the greatest moment of his legal career.

Silently, he thanked Helen Jewett for her timely demise.

Chapter Thirty-Three

By Monday, June sixth, the rain had stopped and the streets were stinking rivers of mud and sewage. No one could escape the splattering sludge; even ladies and gentleman found dark and repugnant streaks and clumps on expensive silk gowns and freshly polished boots. But after five days of heavy rain, people crowded the streets. Sick of confinement, New Yorkers returned to the shops, stores, and restaurants eager to spend money, and filled parks, street corners, and theaters ready to argue about the latest news.

The crowd around City Hall was the largest since the Robinson trial began, but the thousands who arrived early that day were calm and orderly. The word was out. At the slightest danger of violence, the doors of the building would be sealed, and only jurors, witnesses, lawyers, and reporters would be allowed inside. The earliest arrivals now received numbered tickets and were told that a ticket would allow entrance into the courtroom until every seat, up to a thousand, was filled.

The trial began promptly at ten o'clock. The proceedings still generated great excitement, especially after Saturday's dramatic testimony from Furlong, and the heat and sound of arguments about witnesses and conflicting evidence thickened the air. The smell of mud and sweat was pungent, but few complained, not even the fastidious Ogden Hoffman, who had no love for the democratic masses. For the forthcoming climax of the trial, the masses would play an essential role. As witnesses, they would serve as the largest audience in the history of New York trials. They would be *his* audience and at *his* feet.

But first Hoffman had to distract, confuse, and exhaust their appointed representatives, the men of the jury, with a long line of defense witnesses.

Richard Robinson would not be one of them.

The young man's bottomless vanity had served him well, producing an expressionless mask that could inspire adoration. Hoffman counted on the men of the jury to resist envy and resentment, the inevitable consequences of invidious comparison, and cling to the cultural association of beauty with innocence. Richard Robinson was certainly no saint, and no line of questioning or objections could obscure the fact of his rampant seductions. But Hoffman counted on more than the rules of evidence to win his cases; and this case especially needed the comforting solace of prejudice and presumption. Staring at this attractive, well-dressed, and self-possessed young gentleman, the jurors should assume that he was unworthy of a brutal murder. He didn't *look* the part. And Hoffman made sure that Robinson did nothing to dispel this impression. Robinson must remain silent throughout the trial, answering no questions at the witness chair, providing no testimony on his own behalf.

Instead, he would maintain silence. Golden silence.

Hoffman recalled Rosina Townsend.

"Did you know the colored girl named Sarah Dunscombe?" asked Hoffman.

"Yes," replied Rosina.

"What did she tell you about Frank Rivers' visit that week before the murder?"

"She told me that Frank Rivers had been in Helen's room on the Thursday preceding the murder."

"Did you, and I emphasize, *you*, say positively that Frank Rivers was at the house on that Thursday?"

"I do not believe that I said positively he was there on Thursday. I think I said it was on the Wednesday or the Thursday. But if Sarah said it was Thursday, I should be inclined to believe her. But I am not certain."

Then came another sudden shift in the interrogation.

"Where was Maria Stevens' room in your house?" asked Maxwell.

"Her room adjoined Helen's."

"And when did Maria Stevens die?"

"She died on Wednesday of last week at the house of Mrs. Gallagher."

Hoffman suddenly changed the subject again, and Rosina's eyes began to blink. *Why is this happening?* they seemed to implore. She looked to Judge Edwards, as if expecting an answer, but he was impervious to her.

"Where were you last Thursday, Friday, and Saturday during the trial?"

She answered coldly, revealing a dismissive irritation that no ordinary man could tolerate. "I spend the principal part of my time in the Grand Jury room in the building across the park."

"Who was with you?"

"I was in company with the ladies there—*Miss* Salter, *Miss* French, *Miss* Caroline Steward, *Miss* Elliott, *Miss* Brown, and *Miss* Johns."

"Was the colored girl, Sarah Dunscumbe, also there?"

"Yes, Sarah was there."

"Were you all *together* for meals?"

"The girls and I have dined together every day except one during the progress of this trial."

"Together?" he asked, looking toward the jury. "You and the *colored* girl?"

"Yes."

Under cross-examination by Phoenix, Rosina confirmed that she had been asked not to hold conversations with anyone in reference to the trial. She then added, "I have invariably observed the injunction, and when the girls spoke to me, I begged them *not* to do so."

This was Rosina's lowest moment, Billy concluded. She was now willing to exonerate herself at the expense of the others.

Now Hoffman called James Tew to the stand. Tew swore he'd found Robinson in bed beside him when he woke up between one and two on Sunday morning, April tenth. When he woke up again between three and four, Robinson was still there. When he rose at daybreak, he discovered that it was raining and talked with Robinson about canceling their plans for horseback riding. They agreed not to go, returned to bed, and an hour later heard police knocking at the door.

There was absolute silence in the courtroom as Tew described the morning of Robinson's arrest. His testimony was delivered confidently, showing no emotion or concern.

"The officers told him that they had something to say to him, and he asked them if they could not say what they had to say while he was in bed. One of them replied that he wished to see him in private. He got up, partly dressed himself, and went into the hall from the room. Robinson returned to the room and finished dressing. He told me that the men wanted him to go with them, and he asked me to go with him. I replied that I would; he then asked the men if I might go, and they had no objections. I asked him in a whisper what was the matter, and he said he did not know."

"Did he saying anything to you privately? Anything that no one else could hear?" asked Hoffman.

"No."

"Did you notice any emotion or confusion on the part of the accused?"

"No. From the time I first woke him to the time we went out, I did not notice any confusion or emotion in him different from anything I have always noticed in his conduct."

"Did you talk about anything in the carriage?"

"Robinson and I talked about the weather. It was raining very hard, and I said that the rain would clear the ice out of the river."

"Did you notice any indications of guilt in his conduct?"

"No. Up to the time of our arrival at Mrs. Townsend's, I witnessed nothing in his conduct indicative of guilt."

"How long were you at the house?"

"Until about twelve o'clock."

"Did you see him go upstairs to see the body?"

"I believe he was taken up to the room, but I am not certain."

"Did you see him immediately after he saw the body?"

"No, I did not."

Surprising everyone, Judge Edwards leaned forward, furrowed his brow, and asked, "Was Robinson asleep when the officers came to your room?"

"Sir?" asked Tew.

"You heard me," snapped the judge.

"I think Robinson was asleep when the officers came," Tew replied.

Judge Edwards now had more questions. No other witness had stirred such interest. But Tew seemed to glow under the gaze of Edwards' stern demeanor, for surely his questions gave weight to his testimony.

"Were you awake when the prisoner came in on Saturday night?"

"No, nor did he wake me."

"Do you know the hour, positively the hour, when you awoke and spoke to the prisoner?"

"No, I don't know. But I did ask him what time he came in?"

"What time did he say?"

"He replied between eleven and twelve."

Tew smiled as he waited for more questions from his eminent interrogator, but Edwards only announced to Phoenix, "Your cross."

More animated than he had been in days, Phoenix now pressed his questions as if every detail of Tew's answers fundamentally mattered.

Under cross-examination, Tew revealed that Robinson had a night key that allowed him to get into the house at any time he pleased. He also told the court that Robinson often came home after Tew and others went to bed. When asked about Robinson's pantaloons, he said he didn't know what sort he had on that night.

Then Judge Edwards asked, "Did you observe on Saturday night that Robinson had any paint or whitewash upon his pantaloons?"

Tew smiled broadly and replied with smug satisfaction, "No, I did not."

"Did you see anything of the kind before you arrived at Mrs. Townsend's?"

"No, but at the house Mr. Brink asked Robinson, 'What is that on your pantaloons? Is it whitewash?' It was then my attention was called to it."

"What happened?"

"When Mr. Brink called Robinson's attention to his pantaloons, I saw a white mark on the left side of the right leg, below the knee."

The judge directed Phoenix to continue his cross-examination, and with questions in no apparent order, he got Tew to admit that he had never seen Helen

Jewett that night, or asked for her. He saw no cloak in his room on the morning Robinson was arrested that matched the cloak he usually wore. Robinson smoked multiple cigars in his room before he left for the evening. He had seen Robinson write, but he was not familiar with his handwriting. He also could not say exactly whether Robinson kept a journal.

Hoffmann and Maxwell conferred discreetly, exchanging notes and a few words as Tew testified. Tew's credibility now seemed to be under a severe strain. How could he live with a friend and not recognize his handwriting, and not know if he kept a journal?

It was obvious that the prosecution was trying to introduce letters and journals as evidence, and Maxwell objected: "Objection, sir. Irrelevant."

Phoenix bowed slightly and said respectfully, "If it displeases the gentlemen— and rather than they should think that their client had not had a fair trial, and had been illiberally dealt with—I will forgo any interrogations in reference to these matters."

Billy could not believe his ears. Phoenix had allowed matters between "gentlemen" to take precedence of matters of allowable evidence. Forever the gentleman, Phoenix seemed to care more about his opponent coming to the wrong conclusion about *his* motives than undermining the credibility of a defense witness. Phoenix apparently didn't want his opponent to think that his client was not having a fair trial!

Billy could only pity the state for having the prosecution of criminals in the civil hands of Thomas Phoenix. He might as well have been sitting at the defense table beside Ogden Hoffman, given all the accommodations he continued to make.

"Your honor, the defense rests," said Maxwell.

Judge Edwards called for an hour break, and Day and Locke reviewed the day's testimony in the hallway, away from Bennett and any other Robinson supporters. Day was too agitated to care that Billy was standing nearby.

"The prosecution's case is an absolute *disgrace*," hissed Day, looking around so as not to be overheard and failing at the attempt. He paced a brief space like a mouse trapped in a cage. "Phoenix should have his license revoked. Something *must* be done!"

What had once seem inevitable was now unraveling before their very eyes.

"It's not in our hands, sir," said Locke. "We're only reporters."

Day continued to pace, shaking his head and cursing under his breath.

"Damn," he declared. "Damn, damn, damn."

"Yes, sir," Locke dutifully answered as Day's pacing slowed.

When break was over, Phoenix began the prosecution's rebuttal, suddenly announcing, "I propose to read four letters that were found in Helen Jewett's room, and proved to be written by the prisoner at the bar to the deceased. Two of them were dated August 1835, one without a date, and one dated in November."

"Objection!" shouted Hoffman, looking to the judge for agreement. He had never been so vociferous.

But Judge Edwards overruled the objection.

An incredulous Hoffman could only utter a befuddled, "Sir?"

After all this time, Judge Edwards was now interested in what the letters had to say?

Hoffman pulled at the lapels of his jackets, as if signaling the return of his studied poise, and observed, "The obvious intent of submitting the letters as evidence against the prisoner is to show that he had at some distant period entertained malignant feelings toward the deceased, and had, on one or two occasions, threatened her with injury. If such threats and such letters were not written immediately before the murder, they ought not be used to prejudice the mind of the jury against the unfortunate accused. I appeal to the well-known magnanimous and benevolent feelings of the district attorney, and to his mercy and sense of justice, to withdraw the proposition he has made."

He bowed his head toward Phoenix, as if to match Phoenix's courtly manner.

Phoenix smiled, nodded his head, and replied graciously, "It is my sense of public justice and obedience to the oath I have taken as attorney for the people that induce me to urge the proposition. I do so with feelings toward the unhappy prisoner at the bar that are far from harsh, unfriendly, or unkind. However, as there are some circumstances detailed in the letters which relate to other persons entirely unconnected with the prisoner, and an exposure of which would do some real injury, I submit them to the court for their erasure of any particulars that should be deemed as irrelevant and not pertinent to the issues at trial."

Hoffman objected again. "I oppose their admissibility as testimony against the accused on the grounds that they are calculated to prejudice his general character in the estimation of the jury when *no* attempt has been made by his counsel to sustain his good character and reputation."

"Submit them to me *now*," ordered Judge Edwards, leaning forward as he extended his hand to receive them.

Phoenix handed over the four letters and returned to the prosecution table.

Edwards quickly read the letters, as everyone in the courtroom waited silently. Everyone knew this was a crucial decision. Would Helen Jewett, now dead, have a voice in court?

No one in the courtroom, still full at nine fifteen in the evening, said a word.

"The letters are *inadmissible*," Edwards finally declared, "and this court is adjourned until tomorrow at ten."

Chapter Thirty-Four

Despite the ruling, Phoenix had more to say.

With frequent nods and bowing at the waist, he respectfully argued the next morning, "I am firmly and decidedly of the impression, with all due deference to the opinion of the court, that the decision which had been given was founded on misapprehension or error."

As people whispered and the judges said nothing, Phoenix pressed his case.

"One of the letters, dated November fourteenth, 1835, is of the utmost importance as regards its connection with some material evidence that has been already adduced for the prosecution. I beg the court, therefore, to reconsider the proposition that was made and deliberated on, and permit me, at all events, to introduce this *one* document."

Hoffman replied suavely, "To obviate any further difficulties in reference to his proffered testimony, and to avoid further discussion, I will, on behalf of the prisoner, consent to the reading of the letter which the gentleman deems to be so important, if the gentleman will on his part stipulate that he will not offer or read any other letters, and will permit the counsel for the defense to make use of the other three letters if we should deem it necessary or proper."

"I willingly consent to the proposition of the learned gentleman," Phoenix agreed.

"Very well," said Judge Edwards, "you may read the letter."

With absolute silence in the courtroom, Phoenix read the November fourteenth letter addressed to "Miss Maria," the letter that called for the end of Robinson's relationship with Helen and asked for the return of his miniature. Phoenix read the letter with a dull monotone until the very end, when he read emphatically the letter's last sentences: "Now I have only thing to say, do not *betray me*, but forget me. I am no longer worthy of you."

After reading Robinson's Latin inscription, "*Ne ex memoria amitte et ero tuss servus*," and then the closing "Respectfully, Frank," and finally the date, Phoenix handed the letter over to the reporters for copying.

Silence.

There were no questions, no reflections, no attempts at clarification or interpretation, as if all tongues had been tied. Gloating, Phoenix sat down and waited for a signal from the bench for the continuance of the day's proceedings, as if the letter spoke for itself and settled the issue most ignored at the trial—motivation for murder.

But Judge Edwards said only, "Continue," and Phoenix casually replied, as if offering an afterthought, "If it pleases the court, I wish to prove that the prisoner, when brought before the police magistrate, refused to give answer at all to any questions put to him."

This time Judge Edwards rolled his eyes before saying, "Such testimony is altogether inadmissible."

Phoenix insisted gently, "I was under the impression, if it pleases your honor, that I had a strict legal right to introduce this fact to the jury."

Even as he objected, Hoffman remained courteous, saying, "If it pleases your honor, if the refusal on the part of my client to answer any questions that were put to him at the police office be a crime, it may be justly chargeable to *me*, for he acted entirely under my direction and advice."

Phoenix's face flushed. Apparently embarrassed by this reminder of the client's fundamental right to remain silent, he immediately changed the subject, pointing out another detail: Some witnesses who had been subpoenaed on the part of the prosecution at the early part of the trial, and whose testimony would be very material, could not now be found. He paused ever so slightly and added, "I therefore am under the necessity of *resting* the case for the people."

Phoenix sat down, looked straight ahead, saying nothing to his associate and never giving any specifics about the missing witnesses. He waited.

At last, what everyone had wanted to hear would finally come. Now it was time for the two teams to make meaning out of five days of contradictory testimony, bring order to information chaos, and clearly define the issues before the jury and the courtroom.

Billy liked a good speech as much as anyone, but he was not prepared to hear *each* lawyer on both teams give summations—five lawyers giving *five* summations! Given Hoffman's reputation, Billy expected an impressive showing, but he was not prepared for a three-hour speech *after* Hoffman's associates, Price and Maxwell, had spoken.

After an already long day, Billy's buttocks ached in his hard chair, but he found a measure of comfort in the knowledge that Locke had promised to share his notes. His shorthand made it possible for him to capture most if not all what was said. By the end of the day, everyone agreed that ten and half hours of speech-making were too much; it was much easier to write down questions and answers.

Day five of the trial didn't end until after midnight.

Price, who'd had little to say throughout the trial, opened for the defense. He was the quintessential clerk, obsessed with detail, accumulating facts like rocks piled on the chest board of a tortured man. He spoke softly, with the calm certitude of the zealot but without passion. Now his virtual silence for five days made sense. He had prepared for this moment, methodically mastering a mountain of testimony, fact upon fact upon fact, until he could stand at the very top of it and describe the panoramic view for those too lazy or too stupid to make the ascent and clearly *see*. He would be their eyes and tell the clear truth: The prosecution had no case against his client.

He appealed to the jury: "Gentlemen, he is one of yourselves. Does he seem like an old convict who would go into a house and commit murder and arson? Why would he foolishly leave the hatchet and cloak behind? What could be the motive, the plunder of her jewels?"

After dismissing the significance of a hatchet, white paint, a cloak, and trivial comments made by multiple witnesses, Price came to his main point—an attack on Rosina Townsend made more devastating because it was delivered with quiet but cold dispatch, like a swift assassin.

"Mrs. Townsend's *debased* character renders her word worthless. She is little better than a criminal herself, murdering the souls of beautiful girls and breaking the hearts of their grieving parents. Since our courts cannot take any convicted criminal's word, why should it take Mrs. Townsend's? When it comes to Helen Jewett's killer, it is reasonable to presume that Rosina Townsend is the killer."

Applause erupted throughout the courtroom. This clear reflection of popular sentiment made Price smile for the only time during his summation. On his mountain of fact and opinion, the true flag had been unfurled. Then he added, as a grace note, "Mr. Furlong's testimony is *conclusive*. He came here without knowing the prisoner or his people, on behalf of the young man."

Robert Morris' two-hour summation for the prosecution was a meandering rehearsal of the circumstantial evidence based on the cloak and the hatchet. The lunch break came as a relief for Day and many others, but it did nothing for Morris, who continued his aimless wandering, repeating often the conflicting viewpoints about the evidence without declaring the prosecution's preference. He too appealed to the good judgment of the jury, saying, "Gentlemen, if you think the prisoner is innocent, you have a right to acquit him. If the cloak was not his, he is not guilty. If it was his, he still may *not* be guilty."

Again Billy shook his head. Morris had been called in to help Phoenix because Phoenix was suffering from some unnamed ailment. But Phoenix didn't need this kind of help. Morris was another drowning, outclassed incompetent.

The rambling continued until Morris read Robinson's November fourteenth letter. At its conclusion, Morris addressed the issue of motive: "There is an evident secret here, that she had a knowledge that could betray, a secret that could affect his standing in life."

Then he dropped the issue of motive as quickly as he had introduced it, and returned to specific points of discrepancy in the evidence from the defense: Robert Furlong, an honest man, was confused and mistaken. If Robinson had visited Furlong's store frequently, how could Furlong know with certainty that he had been there the night of the murder? One witness had said that Robinson wore his cloak at eight that evening. If so, what had Robinson done with it if he came to Furlong's in a coat at nine-thirty? James Tew didn't know the time when Robinson returned to their room. When he was awakened by Robinson's arrival and asked what time it was, Robinson had lied, saying it was earlier, when he had actually arrived between three and four a.m. after the murder.

He characterized Robinson as a "cool young man" who had only one moment of "trepidation" when he dropped the hatchet and cloak. Then Morris invited the jury to acquit Robinson if they could "account for the cloak, hatchet, and miniature without believing that the prisoner participated in carrying them there," or if they had doubts. But if they had no doubts, then they must convict, "no matter what your own feeling."

This irresolute conclusion was the unintentional but perfect setup for a vibrant Ogden Hoffman, who rose from the table and established his theme for the entire speech: His "poor boy" was innocent and could not have committed so heinous a crime. He made sure to call Robinson "the boy" throughout his summation, and he gave credit where credit was due. The police behaved properly and the district attorney had shown great magnanimity as a mediator between the prisoner and the people.

Then he attacked, skillfully wielding his verbal knife against Rosina Townsend: "It is she who has sworn against him; it is she who would erect gallows for that boy; it is she who would send him to an early grave. There is a foul conspiracy in this matter."

He swiftly reviewed the salient points of her unreliable testimony. Dennis Brink had told her about Robinson's bald spot, and she then claimed she saw it on April ninth, when actually his hair had fallen out from stress *after* his arrest. Rosina had tampered with Sarah Dunscombe's testimony, talking with her to coordinate dates. She had conspired with Elizabeth Salters and another prostitute to determine a mutually agreeable time for Robinson's arrival. He called this a "deep and a damnable perjury between them," and then asked with special emphasis the obvious question: Why would the women conspire to frame Robinson?

Hoffman had his answer in a blistering characterization of Rosina Townsend and the motives of women.

"I am not going to say that a prostitute's oath is not legal in a court of justice, but I am going to say that eminent judges have held it very doubtful as to the credit that should belong to it. Can a juror go with his oath based on the polluted declarations of a common prostitute? Does she care for human life, she who has seen victims every day in her house, who has seen with pleasure the plague spot on his cheek and knew that corruption was his work? What was it to Rosina Townsend that a father's hopes lay buried there? What was it to Rosina Townsend that a mother's hopes are destroyed?"

At first he had posed his answers as rhetorical, even saying that "maybe" Rosina started the fire to collect fire insurance. She lit the fire but extinguished it in time so as to not to destroy the whole house but still receive coverage for the damage to Helen's room.

But then he was unequivocal in his answer, saying with a flourishing wave of his arm, "A woman's pride, once wounded, a woman never forgets—a prostitute, when once her pride is injured, will pursue her victim to the grave. Eliza Salters has sworn that she had no feelings of unkindness at being deserted, but do you believe her? Is it contrary to woman's character, to bear such a thing without feelings of revenge?"

Hoffman had his answer: Whoever killed Helen Jewett, it was *not* Robinson. "How could this boy commit this crime?" he asked.

He carefully explained why Robinson could not be the killer. He showed no signs of guilt the following day. He did not wake his bed partner with heavy breathing during the night. He did not blanch when the police came to the door in the morning. No one was able to impeach the testimony of the honest man, Robert Furlong. Hoffman admitted that Robinson "felt love and passion for *that* woman" and feared that Jewett would betray the secret of his immoral life with prostitutes. Then Hoffman asked a provocative question and offered an unanswerable challenge to the prosecution: If there were any secrets, why did the prosecution *not* bring them out?

He took a short break, needing refreshment with a cup of coffee and some biscuits, and then resumed his dismantling of the evidence for the prosecution. The prosecution's hatchet was one of thousands in town. The condition of the tassel on Robinson's cloak was based on the word of a prostitute.

Then Hoffman came to his peroration, addressing the jury directly, making sure that he could be heard from the very back of the courtroom:

"This boy's poor, sick mother, a mother who dotes on him, might die if her boy is convicted; and his father surely would live a blighted life. But gentlemen, you will not allow it. You will not come the stern executioner, you will come the messenger of peace. You will wipe the tears away from their eyes. They will say our son has been lost is found. But if that verdict shall be death, I cannot answer for the result. May God, in his mercy, guide you in your decision."

It was eight-thirty, and there were tears in the courtroom. Hoffman smiled, his triumph complete, and he nodded his head specifically at the one weeping man on the jury before he sat down. He turned to Maxwell, giving him the chance to bring down the curtain.

Fortunately, Hugh Maxwell was brief. He read passages from Blackstone, keeping the focus on the rules and limitations of circumstantial evidence.

"Gentlemen of the jury, a conviction requires that all reasonable doubt be allayed," he said dispassionately. He repeated the phrase "reasonable doubt" and observed that while a chain of circumstances might be probable grounds for presuming guilt, it could not support a conviction.

At nine o'clock, Thomas Phoenix rose to speak. He moved slowly, but his voice was strong and assertive. "I have come to the conclusion that the person who owned the cloak and hatchet was the one who committed the murder. I wish I could think that prisoner at the bar had not committed the murder. I would be the first man to shield him. But he is guilty. Guilty."

Phoenix recounted the night of the murder, describing how Robinson crept down the stairs after striking Helen Jewett and igniting her bed, dropped the hatchet and cloak as he fled through the back door and scaled the wall, which left its fresh paint on his pantaloons.

Now Phoenix became his namesake, rising from the ashes of his courteous conciliations, and attacked Robinson with passionate vehemence even as he maintained control of his voice during the remarkable denunciation.

Robinson's composure was not, he said, a sign of innocence. It was the unnatural and deeply troubling reaction of an extraordinary young man who could not show emotion even when he learned of his lover's death and saw her corpse. This was for the woman with whom he had been so long in intimacy, with whom he had been a few hours before probably mingling in caresses! Why, gentlemen, even a *dog* would have howled forth his lamentations. Will it be told that this was his coolness? It looks like a man who made up his mind to act. His appearance in this case seemed unnatural, and the next thing to his manner would have been to eat a portion of her flesh and drink a portion of her blood. No wonder there is an excitement in this community. Gentlemen, before you is a *monster*, a true monster."

There was no movement in the courtroom, and Phoenix looked out to the courtroom as if to make sure he had hit his mark. He smiled slightly and returned to the jury with his customary civil tone, pulling back from the precipice of his own making.

"Gentlemen, he has a tongue in his head. He can, as you have found, write a superior letter, could employ counsel, and yet, on the morning of his arrest, could say *not* a word of where he had been on the previous night. But consider this: What secret did Helen Jewett hold over Robinson? Read his letter in the jury room, gentlemen, and the more you read it the more you will find there a *cause* of murder. You will find in it a threat, and that he crouched as no man of spirit should crouch to a prostitute because she possessed a secret he was afraid would be exposed. That secret could *not* have been his immoral life. He went to the theater with Miss Jewett and was seen in public with her. It was, said Mr. Hoffman, only a small peccadillo. No, gentlemen, there was *more*. But I can say no more, having been overruled by the court."

Phoenix was done.

At eleven o'clock Edwards began his summary of the case before giving final instructions to the jury. As expected, he reminded everyone that in order to convict, the jury had to agree "beyond all reasonable doubt."

He urged the jury to weigh the character of all the witnesses, but then he characterized the weight of some of the witnesses.

"Prostitutes are not to be entitled to credit unless their testimony is corroborated by others, drawn from *better* sources," he said solemnly. "Testimony derived wholly from persons of this description, without other testimony, is not to be received."

Flabbergasted, the reporters looked at each other.

Judge Edward had just told the jury to acquit Robinson.

But the judge did more. He began to speculate openly about the evidence, suggesting possibilities, and even drawing conclusions.

Perhaps Robinson had gone to the brothel earlier on the day of April ninth and left his cloak there. Maybe he took his hatchet there too, as young men are well advised to arm themselves when visiting brothels. Then he'd gone to Furlong's store, leaving the hatchet at 41 Thomas Street, where someone else used it. Sarah Dunscombe's testimony should be disregarded because she was an attendant in the brothel "stew." The Robinson letter was irrelevant because it was written months before the murder.

Oddly, he even mentioned Helen Jewett's feelings, saying Helen "seemed to feel much affection toward him" and would have returned Robinson's miniature if he had asked. No one during the trial had ever mentioned or discussed Helen's emotions or feelings about anything, so the reference was surprising. For five days Helen Jewett had been only the victim, a mere name, a reference point. As a human being with an interior life, she didn't exist, until now.

But this hint of sensitivity disappeared as quickly as it emerged from Ogden Edward's thin lips, and he reminded the jury once more of the great divide between honorable witnesses and improper people.

"Gentlemen of the jury, be calm and firm," he intoned. "Attend to *honorable* witnesses but not improper people, and convict if you feel it is beyond reasonable doubt, but acquit so as to not immolate an innocent victim."

It was half past midnight when the case went to the jury. The men rose from the chairs and started toward the exit. Then they stopped, formed a tight cluster, and sent word asking the judge if the court would remain in session while they deliberated.

"Yes," the judge replied.

Another shock reverberated throughout the courtroom as men whispered this surprising turn of events and leaned forward, trying to overhear any deliberations. Judge Edwards made no attempt to silence the low buzzing of a hornet's nest, its menacing threat about to explode. The jury then left the courtroom.

Billy was too disturbed to speak. Any pretence of careful deliberation had fallen away, its raw exposure more shocking because it came as a surprise. Even now, after so much had transpired in the past five days, Billy felt like an absolute fool.

Of course the jury did not need to waste its time. After all, the facts clearly spoke for themselves. There were no ambiguities, no shades of grey.

Justice was blind no longer. More than her customary veil had been stripped away; she was stark naked before an incredulous and grateful multitude.

The crowd only had to wait eight minutes.

The jury filed back in, the foreman turned over the handwritten verdict to Judge Edwards, who directed the prisoner to rise and announced, "Not guilty."

The courtroom erupted with applause and shouts of approval. The judge pounded his gavel and called for order repeatedly, but even he could not suppress the crowd's jubilation.

"Yes, yes!" cried Jamie Bennett. "There is *true* justice!"

Robinson cried as he turned to the receiving arms of his grateful father.

Billy and Ben Day sat absolutely still.

Chapter Thirty-Five

Every editor and reporter who covered the Robinson trial, and many of those who didn't, gathered the next day after work at the Windust. Over coffee or whiskey, almost all of the men in the crowded main room discussed the trial and expressed surprise and outrage at the verdict. From the beginning they had assumed Robinson's guilt and expected the court to agree swiftly with opinions proclaimed for weeks in newspapers and drawing rooms. However, as the days of the trial went by, many could see that the court was disposed to favor Robinson, especially with the number of defense objections supported by Judge Edwards. Already there was a joke going about town that opened with the statement, "Robinson won," and the question, "How do you figure?" The answer invariably inspired raucous and cynical laughter: "Well, he had *six* lawyers: Price, Maxwell, and Hoffmann, and Judge Edwards, Phoenix, and Morris."

Ben Day already planned to expose the trial in a series of articles in the *Sun* for at least a week, and maybe more after a careful examination of Locke's notes. Billy was already pursuing his own investigations. Now that the trial was over and the verdict in, the *Transcript* was no longer interested, and Billy intended to share his discoveries with Day to strengthen Day's case. Billy was sure that in waging his renewed war against corruption, Day would overlook professional jealousy, forgive Billy for working for traitorous former employees, and gladly accept the fruits of his labor—for a price, of course. Billy accepted the essential truth: They were both whores.

That very morning Billy went to Furlong's store, because Furlong's testimony had been so important. He found a porter there, a Mr. McDermott, who said he had worked the night of April ninth and didn't remember seeing Robinson there.

He also found a Mr. Kyle at the Park Theater who said that representatives of Mr. Hoffmann asked him to swear falsely that Robinson was with him between nine and ten on April ninth at the Shakespeare Rectory on Park Row, a favorite eatery for theater folk.

Sitting at a full table in the Windust, Billy listened carefully to speculations and considered how he would pursue his investigations. Several journalists openly accused Edwards of corruption. He'd received a bribe from Hoxie, declared one reporter, and most at the table nodded their heads, pounded the table, and shouted their assent with no concern about accusations of slander. Nothing was sacred at the Windust, and no one was subject to censure if he said it there. Freedom of speech was absolute, and only the printed word could get you hauled into court. Even then you were subject to fine or imprisonment only if you claimed a truth; there were no limits on questions and speculation. The possibilities were endless, and the men on Park Row, like boys at a yard game, had fun naming alternative realities.

The district attorney was protecting important people.

The men at Townsend's that night knew what happened but were allowed to get out by the magistrates who came that early morning.

The men of the jury were all personal friends of the prisoner, having met him in various brothels, and needed to keep that connection a secret.

Rosina Townsend was sacrificed because she knew far too much about her clients, and especially the owner of Number 41 Thomas Street.

Richard Robinson had not only murdered Helen Jewett; he had murdered other prostitutes in a war against women.

Hoffman knew his client was guilty, but defended him anyway because his fee was easy money, and he needed the support of Hoxie and other gentlemen of property and standing before declaring a run for mayor or perhaps governor.

Billy prepared to spend considerable time interviewing prostitutes, but before making arrangements, he needed some general information about the current conditions of prostitution in the city. Many things had happened since he had been away. He found a willing resource in the Female Moral Reform Society.

The Society had an acute sense of urgency, having unearthed a disturbing pattern of disappearances and deaths in the city. In one city block housing twenty brothels, the Society discovered the deaths of twenty-five women within three months that year. Several had died violently. The ladies of the Society were convinced that a man was in the community systematically murdering prostitutes.

Billy *had* to find proof of the fate of the girl named Emma Chancellor. Hadn't Robinson's own attorney, the reticent Mr. Price, acknowledged at the trial that his client had been heard saying he would kill Helen if exposed . . . "or any other woman?" That phrase, once said by Robinson to Billy, resounded in his ears. Then he looked up and saw Jamie Bennett enter the room.

The room fell completely silent.

Here was the one editor who still insisted on Robinson's innocence and rejoiced in the verdict in the face of almost universal condemnation. Earlier that morning Billy had been disgusted by Bennett's tender description of the aftermath of the verdict. But he was too angry to retch when he read in the *Herald*: "Mr. Hoxie was in tears; the kind, the noble, the eloquent Mr. Hoffman could restrain his tears; Price the hard-featured, the imperturbable Price, did not attempt to stop his. Robinson went with his father and uncle to Hoxie's, where he might pour into their ears, and theirs alone, the feelings of his heart, and his deep and lasting gratitude to that jury who had not sacrificed an innocent victim on the altar of an abandoned woman."

Billy felt the urge to accost Bennett that very minute, challenge his version of the truth, and insist that what Bennett had written was a fantasy, a cheap fantasy that was an obnoxious bid for favors from the rich and powerful.

But he hesitated when he noticed that everyone in the room had turned their heads to the back of the tavern, where James Watson Webb sat alone drinking ale. It had been less than a month since Webb had attacked Bennett *again* on Broadway. And once again, Bennett had responded with ridicule, advising Webb in the *Herald* to "stick to his paper—don't run about through the country, buying up whole countries of rocks at a couple of cents an acre—or lots in this town—or saltpeter."

Webb rarely came to the Windust. He was a well-known snob, preferring to drink and dine at more fashionable establishments, like Delmonico's. But he came today, no doubt anticipating the arrival of Bennett, who could never resist the opportunity to crow as the single voice of reason and justice in a city of fools. Webb had mostly ignored the entire Jewett/Robinson murder and trial, giving them only scant mention in the *Courier*. But he knew his enemy, and he sat at the back of the one place he knew Jamie Bennett could not avoid on the day after vindication.

No one heard clattering knives and forks, no slurping of beverages, no chewing of roasted meat, no whispered asides, no spitting. Everyone waited for Webb to do or say something.

He lifted his pewter cup as if toasting Jamie Bennett. This was a curious gesture. Whatever it meant, it could not possibly symbolize approbation. Billy decided that, without saying a single word, Webb was thanking Bennett for giving him the reason and opportunity to degrade him before everyone in town, not once but twice, and reminded the men assembled there that Bennett would never have the last word. A silent "Damn you" was more powerful than pages of editorial spleen.

And as usual, Jamie Bennett misread the sign, reacting as if given permission to reaffirm his preeminence before every journalist in New York. He nodded his head toward Webb and then said, turning to the men before him, "Well, gentlemen, my appearance tonight marks a grand opportunity to gloat.

I was right and *you* were wrong. Standing alone, triumphantly alone, has *distinct* pleasures."

Day propelled himself from his chair, and rushed like a battering ram toward Bennett, who didn't flinch even as a much younger man with tight fists came at him.

"You pompous bastard," snarled Day, trying to pull away from the hands and arms that held him back. "You damnable, pompous bastard!"

"No!" three of his colleagues urged him at once.

"Don't do this," said another. "Can't you see? This is just what he wants."

Billy jumped away, knocking over his chair and making room to watch the spectacle unencumbered by arms, legs, and fists. Somebody had to keep a clear head for describing the incident in graphic detail.

Day relaxed his arms and pulled against the arms of the men standing around him as his chest heaved with unspent rage. He shouted, "I will knock that other eye into the center of your face one day, and soon!"

"Sir, you are impudent and low bred," Bennett sneered. "Will you spit on me like Mr. Leggett did a few years ago?"

Then William Leggett of the *Evening Post*, who had remained seated during the assault, now rose from the adjacent table, as if provoked. But he was grinning and said sarcastically, "He will not waste *good* spit on you, sir, as I did in the days of my youth."

"You have *all* proven my unique standing in this community, and I will continue to supersede you all," Bennett countered.

Was the man trying to create a mob of angry reporters and editors? Was he mad?

A few cups were now hurled across the room, barely missing Bennett's head, and the chorus of curses intensified.

"Blackguard!"

"Bastard!"

"Damn you!"

"Fuck you!"

Billy heard himself saying, "You'd better get out of here, and I mean *now*, or you'll be a dead man."

For the first time, Bennett's resolve weakened, and Billy saw fear cloud the brightness of his self-righteous, squinting eyes.

"Go now," Billy insisted, needing James Gordon Bennett for another day, when he could expose Bennett's nefarious involvement in the acquittal of Richard P. Robinson.

Bennett pulled at his coat and hurried out.

The next afternoon Billy met Richard Locke, who agreed to loan his transcript of the Robinson trial. At the end of each session, no matter how late that session had ended, Locke translated his scrawl into words Ben Day could read the next morning. Locke had a good ruse, explaining, "He won't need these for at least a week, if then. I summarized the major points for the planned series of articles because he hates research. But you can only have them for a day; so if he asks for them, I will say I took them home and will bring back them tomorrow."

"What if he demands them immediately?" Billy asked, worried that his friend was near emotional collapse.

"He won't. He's lazy. The investigative reporter in him is dead, so he will wait."

"Thanks," Billy said. "I'm grateful."

"He never is, and I will be leaving him soon, very soon."

That evening Billy pored over the pages of note, looking for clues and leads. He made a list of promising possibilities and left his rooms the next morning with a sheet of paper jammed into his coat pocket filled with names, addresses, and questions. There was a prostitute he wanted to see. Her name had been mentioned in the press, and Billy thought it curious that of all the prostitutes considered persons of interest in the case, Lucy Preston, who came before the Grand Jury in April to attest to Robinson's promiscuity, was never mentioned during the trial. This omission then seemed trivial, but the trivial could have significant consequences.

Chapter Thirty-Six

After finding Lucy Preston at Ann Weldon's brothel, he came directly to the point.

"What do you know about Richard Robinson?" Billy asked.

Lucy's jaw was too big, her forehead too high, her breasts impressive. Her green eyes danced, as if everything they could behold fascinated and excited her, and they made him want to be her customer.

"It's about time someone important asked *me*," she said. "How did you find me?"

"That's not important. About Robinson, what do you know?"

"Helen was my friend, and she was very kind and generous, never difficult with us even though she was smarter than all of us together. But her judgment slipped when it came to him. She loved him desperately, as did Maria, and she is gone too. See what that man has done?"

"What are you suggesting?" He almost started to repeat the reports about the causes of Maria's death, but he waited to see to what Lucy had to say.

"It would flatter him to know that Maria died from a broken heart as well as from that terrible cold," Lucy replied. "She loved him too, even though she knew he was seeing Helen and other women."

"Then she was *not* jealous of Helen."

"She envied her, but Maria was too kind to hurt her, even though it tormented her to be in the room next to Helen's and hear what she heard. They were loud lovers."

"Then how could she *not* hear what happened that night?"

"I don't know, sir. She could only talk about the fire and the discovery of Helen's body. But I think she heard. She *must* have!"

"But she's gone, and we'll never know what she knew," Billy observed.

"She knew as much as I did," she countered.

"And what do you know?"

She straightened her shoulders as if to make an important announcement, and said gravely, "I know what they knew, but I'm not afraid of Richard Robinson.

And I certainly would never put myself in a position to be alone with him now."

"So you think he killed Helen?" asked Billy.

"Of course he did, because of what she knew about him."

"What did she know?"

"He embezzled money from Mr. Hoxie. He laughed about it, and I'm sure he was laughing about it still when Mr. Hoxie paid for all those fancy lawyers. Robinson spent a lot of money, but he didn't have much, certainly not enough from his job to pay for his expensive tastes. And his father didn't give much. He was always complaining about his 'cheap father.' Robinson threatened Helen, and she threatened him."

"I can see why he threatened her, but why did she threaten him?"

"She *needed* him, despite everything she knew about him . . . even when she knew about Emma Chancellor."

"What do you mean?" Billy asked carefully, suppressing his growing excitement.

"Helen told me she knew about the embezzlement, but she also knew that he killed Emma because of what Emma had threatened to tell."

"So Helen confided in you about this?"

"Yes, she told me. And she admitted that sometimes—and I mean *sometimes*—she was afraid of him. But at other times she wasn't."

"And she wanted to have him even though he *admitted* to murder?" Billy asked. "She was willing to see him even after she knew and *told* him she knew?"

This strained credulity, but he waited for an explanation. Helen had been almost irrational before he left town.

"He could charm her, I must say, as he could charm so many. He was so good with words, and those letters could make Helen just forget her fears and put aside her better judgment. She was a fool for this kind of love. I told her long ago, *never* fall for a client. And this one had no loyalty to her at all. He went about town openly seducing eager women, in and out of houses."

"Did he seduce *you?*"

Billy was now skeptical of her motives. Why hadn't she said something at the Grand Jury Proceedings in April? She'd talked about Robinson's multiple seductions, but nothing else.

"No, he did not *seduce* me!" she said hotly.

"Then was he ever your customer?"

She paused, clearly considering how she was going to answer the question. She closed her eyes and then opened them quickly. "Yes, he was, for a time."

"I see," Billy observed, deliberate and enigmatic, hoping to incense her and get even more information.

"But this was all *before* Helen told me about Emma," Lucy protested.

"But as her friend, you knew she favored him."

"But she didn't mind that he paid for other women. She only wanted him to see her as his favorite, his true love."

"Did you tell her that he was seeing you?"

"I was afraid to tell her, and we did not live together when she was so caught up with him."

"But she told *you* about Emma Chancellor? I can see her telling Maria Stevensm since they lived together, right next door, but why *you*?"

"I don't know," Lucy admitted. "I thought she was telling everybody. She was becoming so desperate."

"So that is why you didn't come forward? You assumed someone else would tell?"

"And looked what happened! Nothing they said mattered. No one seemed to care about Robinson's reasons for killing Helen."

"So you let him get away with it?"

Lucy didn't flinch. "He got away with it without *me*; and nothing I could have said mattered anyway. Look what they did to Rosina Townsend."

He was still not convinced; there were discrepancies and omissions. But he decided to go forward nevertheless.

"Do you think the lawyers knew?" he asked.

"I don't know anything about that, sir, but that would make things far worse, don't you think? All those judges and lawyers working together to keep secret a man killing two of us? And maybe, just maybe, he was killing the others, too."

"You don't know that," said Billy, surprised by his feeble genuflection to objectivity.

"He hated us all, you know," said Lucy, her eyes declaring a final, irreversible judgment.

"How do you know? And why would he hate you all?"

"He always thought we were laughing at him behind his back."

"What was there to laugh at?" he asked. "By everything we can see, he is a very handsome man. And the loss of hair was a late development."

She looked down and smiled mischievously.

"It was what *you* couldn't see," she observed. "That large, no, huge . . ."

"I see," he stammered, surprised that his own knowledge did not prevent his current discomfort.

She smiled delicately, as if enjoying his reaction, adding, "But you will discover more about her, and him, when you see her letters."

"I have seen a few," he replied, referencing his access to letters Robinson had shared with him. It pained Billy still that for all of her letter writing Helen rarely wrote to him. Yes, she jotted occasional brief notes, telling him where to meet and when, but the effusive rhapsodies she wrote to every other man were never his to receive or enjoy. Even when he was out west and reported his coach accidents, she only assured him about buying a requested item and mentioned the interests of another man.

"She made copies, especially of her favorites," Lucy continued. "She liked her own words and didn't want to lose some of them forever."

"Do you have them?"

"No."

"Then who does?"

"Her maid, the colored girl."

"The colored girl? How do you know that?"

"Helen told me. She said she trusted Sarah more than anyone else. At first I was offended, her trusting a *colored* girl over me. But she said she had her reasons."

"Did she ever write to you?"

"No. Never. I think she only wrote to men."

"Where does the colored girl live? Do you know?"

"No, but you can find out, can't you? You reporters find out all kinds of things. You found me."

Billy found out where Sarah Dunscombe lived and knocked on the door of her mother's rooms on the second floor of a flat in the Fifth Ward, not far from Rosina's Townsend's former establishment. It was after working hours, but not too late in the evening.

When he rapped on the door, a mature female voice answered, "Who's there?"

Summoning his kindest, most unthreatening voice, Billy replied, "It's Billy Attree of the *New York Transcript*, the newspaper."

"Go away," said the voice, now tinged with apprehension. "We don't need no newspapers."

"I'm here to see Miss Dunscombe, Miss Sarah Dunscombe."

"She did enough talking in that courtroom. She don't need to talk no more. She don't need to answer any more questions."

"I'm here to help, to help Miss Helen."

"She's dead," asserted Mrs. Dunscombe. "Bless her soul, she's dead."

"Yes, but Sarah can help her memory."

Billy could hear the unlatching of the door, and candlelight brightened the darkened hallway when Mrs. Dunscombe opened it. Behind her stood Sarah, a short, thin girl with prominent cheekbones, dark brown skin, and luminous black eyes, the image of the frightened witness in the courtroom denied by those unflinching eyes and her straight back. "I'm only letting you in 'cause she said it's all right," Mrs. Dunscombe explained.

"Thank you," answered Billy. "I won't take much of your time."

"Why do you want to speak with my daughter, sir?" Mrs. Dunscombe asked, stepping aside to allow him to enter. "I'm not going to let you hurt my girl like those men in the courtroom. They scared her, she said."

"I would never bring harm to her," Billy countered.

"That's what you *all* say," Mrs. Dunscombe said.

"Mama, please," said Sarah. "This isn't about me. It's about Miss Helen."

"Thank you, Miss Dunscombe." Billy had to move quickly to gain Sarah's cooperation. Careful courtesy could become cold refusal in seconds. "I need your help."

She looked to a chair, and gestured him toward it. "How?" she asked.

"You have some of her letters," Billy said evenly.

She waited, never looking away, never showing surprise or dismay.

"Someone told me," he explained, "and I would like to read them, get them published, so people will know her as she truly was. They didn't want to hear those letters at the trial. The man who killed her got away with it, and he can't be tried again. But I can show the truth about him through her words."

"Sarah, you don't have to say nothing," her mother interjected. "You don't even have to say you have them. This could bring us trouble, and we don't need no more trouble."

"No one has to know where they came from," Billy said. "I certainly won't say. The trial is over, and there can't be another."

"She can get into trouble for not telling about them letters," asserted Mrs. Dunscombe, her tone hardening as she tried to protect her daughter

"I didn't lie, mama," insisted Sarah. "They never asked about them letters, and so I didn't have to lie, and I didn't. I haven't read 'em. There are so many, but maybe some good will come."

"Do you know why she gave them to you?"

"She trusted me."

"But why?" Billy insisted.

"I don't have to say nothin'," Sarah said, refusing to look away. "I'm not in that courtroom now."

"I'm so sorry," said Billy, for fear of losing vital ground. But he could not help wondering, was the frightened girl on the witness stand just a role played by a far more mature young woman? Who was her teacher? Was it her mother, or was it Helen Jewett?

Sarah stood now and said with great dignity, "I'm getting them now, and you keep 'em as long as you want to."

Flabbergasted, Billy said, "But they are original, in her own hand. I can have them copied and bring them back."

"I was afraid to keep them, but I had to because she wanted me to. But now that she's gone, I don't have to."

She hesitated for a moment and then confessed, "I can barely read, sir, just my name and a few words. Maybe that's why she gave them to me."

"Are you sure about giving them?"

"Yes, I'm sure. Don't you agree, Mama? If I give them to Mr. Attree, we won't have to worry no more about people botherin' us. I loved Miss Helen, but she sure made love hard."

"What do you mean?" Billy asked.

"She told me what she wrote about in them letters, but you can read for yourself."

She handed him bundles of letters tied by long pieces of cotton cloth.

"Do you think she knew something was going to happen to her?" asked Billy.

Sarah sighed deeply and said, shaking her head, "She was just so happy he was coming back. She never talked about him hurting her. She never worried about that. She was unhappy sometimes, but she loved him."

"And she was good to Sarah," added Mrs. Dunscombe. "I'm sorry now for not letting her in when she came with things she sewed for Sarah when she was sick. I couldn't let her in, you know, 'cause she was what she was."

Mrs. Dunscombe shook her head, emphasizing her regret. "She was *good* in her own way," she added.

"These letters can help," said Billy.

Back in his room he finally read scores of Helen's letters, written in her delicate but clear penmanship. As expected, they revealed a highly intelligent and eloquent writer who had fallen deeply in love with the wrong man. She was young and she was foolish. Near the end, she was also desperate, controlling, and eager to lie. But Billy could not help himself; despite everything, especially her refusal to bestow on him the special favors she bestowed on Robinson, he could not stop admiring and loving Helen. He loved her then, he loved her still.

She was so different, with a mind of her own, and never dull. He wondered again about the dynamic energy of Helen's interest and experiences. She seemed fully engaged with the world, as if every moment demanded her attention, from the taste of a biscuit to a whispered line of poetry, from the rising of the sun to the promptings of her own bewildered and demanding heart. In these letters, some to Robinson and many to prominent members of New York society, she revealed herself as even more than he had known.

When he told Locke about his discoveries, Locke calmly observed. "There's nothing to prove Robinson's guilt. We already printed the November fifteenth letter. You will open the *Sun* to claims of forgery. The police have other originals, and the city has shown no interest in them."

"The police don't want the names of her clients in the paper," Billy said.

"And neither do the clients," replied Locke. "We can't open ourselves to libel suits. The *Sun* won't survive if every rich customer goes after us."

"They will come after us, one by one. And the money we'll need to defend ourselves will dry up. Our opponents can pay advertisers and subscribers to stop supporting any paper. You can denounce moral corruption, but name names about sleeping with prostitutes? *Never.*"

Pausing for a moment, considering the irony of Locke's concerns about libel and forgeries, Billy finally conceded, "You're right."

"Don't be surprised by the silence in the press," Locke added. "She's dead. He's free. It's already old news."

"Let's have a drink," Billy replied.

"Yes," Locke replied without hesitation.

"Let's get drunk, stinking drunk," said Billy.

"Agreed, but not at the Windust," Locke said. "How about your rooms?"

"What about your wife and family? Won't they worry?"

"They're used to my absences. Mr. Day is a convenient excuse when I need a drink."

"We'll toast Mr. Day then," said Billy.

"For being right, for hiring us, for finally seeing Helen Jewett for who she was."

"You still hate him," said Billy.

"Don't you?"

Billy hesitated, and then said, "He has his uses."

"I will resign soon," Locke replied. "I need to start my own newspaper, and it won't be another *Sun* or *Herald*. It will be different, very different."

"Then you won't be hiring me," Billy said. "You like science and philosophy. I like crime."

"There's room for more than one kind of newspaper. And competition will be less if Mr. Day leaves the *Sun*, like he's threatening. He says he is sick of it all now."

"Then I will be out of a job."

"You can always work for Jamie Bennett," said Locke, smiling.

"If the price is right," replied Billy. "I'm a whore too."

———•———

Benjamin Day meant to answer the questions about guilt, collusion, and conspiracy in his series of detailed articles published under the title, " A Solemn Farce," a title he said was "at once accurately descriptive of its object, and expressive of public opinion concerning it. It is one to which nine tenths of intelligent population have stood sponsors."

Starting on June fourteenth, Day reviewed over a two-week period every witness and piece of evidence introduced at the trial. He commented on the trial's circus atmosphere, created by a court that allowed rowdy men to cheer favorites and boo anything critical to the prisoner. He established the connections between Hoxie and the jury; several of them were personal friends. Hoxie, Judge Edwards, and Hugh Maxwell, one of the defense lawyers, all worked together at the New York City Temperance Society. And friends of Hoxie on the jury had heard Hoxie admit to having bribed Jamie Bennett to support Robinson in the *New York Herald*.

The juryman who had asked Furlong a question directly during the trial admitted to Day that he'd asked it, "merely to satisfy some of the jurors who did not know Mr. Furlong as well as some of the others." And Furlong himself, the man so crucial for establishing Robinson's alibi, was heard boasting a few days after the trial, "It was neck and neck with me and Rosina Townsend. But I was determined *not* be outworn by a whore."

After pointing out the unequal treatment of the witnesses, the incompetence of a district attorney who failed to call into court the six men at Rosina Townsend's on the night of Helen's murder, and the inappropriate behavior of Judge Edwards, Day claimed that a conspiracy of money and privilege had insured the trial's outcome. Robinson was guilty of the murders of Helen Jewett *and* Emma Chancellor, and those who defended him, including the judge, were all members of the same class, insisting on the right to murder lowly prostitutes with "perfect impunity."

One matter continued to bother Day and Billy. Why did Hoxie show such open favoritism for Robinson?

Of course, Billy could not interview Robinson. He had returned to his family home in Connecticut. And Hoxie refused to see Day or Billy.

But Billy found in a saloon the clerk who had mentioned almost casually the clock by which Robinson could tell his departure on the night of the murder. The time no longer mattered, but he wanted to know how Robinson's fellow clerk felt about that watch.

After accepting Billy's offer of another drink, the clerk said warily, "I know your kind, always trying to trick us honest men into saying something so you can have a story. Well, I told the truth."

"Did you like Robinson?" asked Billy.

The young man started, obviously surprised by the question. He paused for a moment and then whispered, looking around the room as if he feared being overheard, "Well, no, I didn't. All he did was boast about his way with women. He was a looker, but damn, I got tired of hearing about it. He even dared to tell me he was 'blessed' down there. But what made me really mad was that promotion he got from Mr. Hoxie."

"Why?"

"He wasn't that good. He made too many mistakes with the books, and he had no good reason for the missing money. Mr. Hoxie cared that the money was missing, but he never cared about the bookkeeping Robinson did. And he *promoted* that lazy, stupid fool over me!"

Billy offered a sympathetic lie. "That happened to me once. I know how that feels."

"And Mr. Hoxie *gave* him that watch. Robinson waved it into my face like some kind of proof."

"Of what?"

"I don't know for sure," the clerk replied, lowering his voice as he looked around the room again. "But Mr. Hoxie came into the clerk office many times and stood next to Robinson, put his hand on his shoulders, whispered into his ears, even touched his hand once. After that, I wasn't surprised that Mr. Hoxie was with him at the trial every day."

"Do you know what you are saying?" asked Billy, still careful even as the obvious became apparent. Billy had arranged clandestine meetings for a few wealthy gentlemen with Robinson, but he had never heard anything about any *relationships.*

"I don't know what I'm saying," the clerk said, leaning back in his chair and looking down at his drink. "All I know is he treated Robinson like a son. No, like *more* than a son."

"*More?*"

The clerk stood. "I have nothing more to say. I said too much already, and I need my job. If you say anything, I will deny it. Everyone knows you're against Robinson. I should have known that you would buy some drinks to get me to say something *stupid*. You people are all shits."

Billy sat still, taking in the implications of what he'd heard. Maybe Joseph Hoxie loved Robinson, and did what he needed to do to keep the full extent of his relationship private, even if Robinson was embezzling from him. No influential, wealthy man could face a scandal of that magnitude.

And if Helen Jewett knew about it, then Robinson *had* to kill her.

Darkly, he thought of another possibility—that Hoxie asked Robinson to kill her and *paid* him to do it.

Excited as he was about these speculations, Billy knew the absolute impossibility of printing the allegations; they were too volatile. The entire city would rise up against him and he would lose everything. He needed to work.

Ben Day had similar misgivings.

His cowardice disappointed, but if nothing else, it clarified his future course. Day was done with the newspaper business. If he could not tell the truth, then why publish?

Amused by the irony, he laughed. For a year he had gladly published complete fabrications and made piles of money from the Maria Monk and the Moon Series. Now he cared about truth and justice?

Yes, he concluded proudly, even though he recognized that truth and justice were not absolutes. He had abandoned an earlier commitment to them in the pursuit of success and wealth. But now he was a different man, thanks to Helen Jewett and the trial. And he would live a different life. He would sell the *Sun* to his brother-in-law.

In the meantime his "Solemn Farce" received congratulations from most of his penny press colleagues. But the series did not sell out.

About "Solemn Farce," Hoffman, Maxwell, Hoxie, and Edwards had absolutely nothing to say.

Jamie Bennett responded to the series using a familiar tactic: denounce and mock the whore. He claimed that Emma Chancellor was not dead, and he described Robinson's first meeting with her: "He danced, he talked, —he took her in his arms—he kissed her—he fondled her ripe, rich, ruby lips."

After branding Day a consorter with prostitutes, he recalled the day when the prostitutes appeared in court, his judgmental sarcasm unmistakable.

"Who can forget the spirit displayed in the testimony of the lovely but bitter Emma French, the cool but enchanting Eliza Salters, the calm but persuasive Elizabeth Stewart, the affectionate Mary Gallagher, and the vindictive bright eyed Rosina Townsend?"

Then he offered his final judgment with another question: "When will the lightning of High Heaven purify the immoral atmosphere of this Sodom and Gomorrah?"

To charges of bribery, Bennett had a simple explanation: Yes, he had accepted money from Hoxie to print his support of Robinson's innocence. But this was paid advertising, not bribery. After all, a bribe applies when you accept money to print something that you know is not true. When Barnum came to him and asked him to print advertisements for Joice Heth, he had refused, knowing she could not have been George Washington's nurse. Accepting money to print articles about Robinson was simply payment for what he would have said anyway. This was no different than accepting advertising money for soap, perfume, cigars, buttons, and abortion medicines.

Then Robinson broke his silence.

Chapter Thirty-Seven

By mid-July, Robinson had returned to his parents' house in Durham, Connecticut. Having seen the great city, he now hated the country even more and impatiently waited for his escape. He missed New York and wanted to go back there, but he had to bide his time. His acquittal was popular with young men who admired his success with the "ladies," but the city press, except for Bennett's *Herald*, had universally condemned him and seemed ready to hound him if he ever returned. Ben Day of the *Sun* clearly hated him, and was now suggesting all kinds of nonsense to explain what had happened. When Winthrop Beale collared him about an interview for future publication, Robinson seized the opportunity to set the record straight.

He needed to pay off a debt to Winthrop, and he expected the earned profits from the publication to cancel that debt. After all, Robinson was famous and readers would eagerly pay money to read what he had to say about the murder of Helen Jewett and his trial.

Preparing for the interview, Robinson carefully reviewed the past April.

The decision in that cold spring was simple and came easily.

Helen's demands were endless, and his responses were never enough. She needed more and more and could never be satisfied. He'd begun to dread her letters, sent to him two and three times a day, a relentless torrent of whining, complaint, pleading, threats, pestering, and declarations of love and hate.

He knew they would never end. Helen was jealous and unforgiving, despite her claims to the contrary. And he had realized, sitting beside her at the theater during that performance of "Norman Leslie," that Helen had to die.

He felt no remorse. He had a job to do, and it had to be done quickly, without hesitation or moral equivocation. After all, Helen Jewett was just a prostitute—a beautiful, intelligent, and skilled prostitute, but still only a prostitute. No one would seriously mourn or notice her passing. Prostitutes disappeared or died violently all the time. How could one more dead whore matter in the end?

He had asked to see her that night, and she'd agreed.

Working that day, he was cheerful and resigned. It was his birthday, and he knew that a sudden blow to Helen's head with a small hatchet from Mr. Hoxie's store would make his birthday complete.

He finished work at Mr. Hoxie's at five thirty and celebrated at a saloon. To keep his mind clear he only sipped his liquor. He told his friends he needed to have complete control of his faculties for what "he had to do." They had laughed, winked, and leered, assuming what he meant. They separated on Beekman Street between eight and nine, and after saying he was going to the Clinton Hotel, Robinson walked back south to Maiden Lane, retrieved the hatchet, tied it in place under his cloak, and hurried north to Thomas Street, a half mile away. He arrived around nine-thirty.

When Rosina answered the door, he partially covered his face with his cloak, even though he knew she knew him as Frank Rivers. He was expected. Nevertheless, discretion was a habit when visiting famous brothels at night. You never knew who you might encounter, especially when a brothel had prominent and wealthy customers.

Rosina led him to the parlor where Helen waited. They walked to the top of the landing, where Helen said sweetly, "My dear Frank is here."

He was not moved. She'd said this for Rosina's benefit. It was just another trick, a cheap endearment to be followed by the inevitable kick in the balls.

Her room had a fire and was immaculate. Helen's colored maid had been there earlier in the day, and as usual had done an excellent job preparing the room for whatever Helen had planned for that night. He didn't care that she had seen another man earlier that evening.

Helen thanked him for coming, and asked if they could read Byron together. She mentioned nothing about the request for returned letters and his miniature.

As usual, she had selected passages. But this time, to his great surprise, she asked if he had any favorites that he wanted read. He said, "Yes," and identified four favorites. They read Byron lyrics and selections from his dramas for about an hour, until Helen decided to go down and ask for more champagne.

While she was gone, he looked for his miniature. He found it almost immediately under some delicate undergarments in the top drawer of the dresser. He decided to retrieve it later rather than take it right then. He didn't want Helen to discover he had gone through her things without permission. He didn't want another argument, not tonight.

Within minutes Helen returned and stood at the door talking to Rosina. Rosina could see into the room, but Richard had made sure to sit on the bed with his back turned, so that Rosina could not see his face.

After Helen closed the door, she said, "We have two causes for celebration, your birthday and our reconciliation. It's not yet truly spring, but the winter of our discontent is over."

He could tell she was quoting something, even though she made no reference to a writer or his work. Her face always brightened when she quoted, as if the recollection of the words fired an inner lamp. And her tone of voice, usually light, darkened with the coming of a profundity from which he had to learn.

I am your teacher that voice said, and you need *to listen,* her voice implied.

He hated that change of voice. No matter her protestations to the contrary, she could not resist her need to demonstrate her absolute intellectual superiority over him. At first he was impressed and charmed by her knowledge. But all too quickly, admiration became envy, resentment, and then pure hatred. She was a whore, and she had the nerve to remind him repeatedly that he was ignorant, unschooled, and shallow? He couldn't count the times he'd had to resist the impulse to punch in her in the face, and say, "Shut the fuck up, you cunt, or I'll knock you off that high horse. Just shut the fuck up!"

Looking at the bubbles rise in their glasses of champagne, he felt rage rising up from the pit of his stomach. It soured his gut and filled his chest. He had to act quickly, or his plan would unravel.

He took a deep breath, sighed, smiled, and raised his glass.

"To spring."

"To spring," Helen repeated, smiling. She took only a sip, placed the glass on the tray, and gave him her hand.

"Let's go to bed and celebrate there," she said. "Then sleep, oh, gentle sleep."

They undressed slowly, savoring the gradual exposure of flesh, the rising heat of their skin, the moisture at their fingertips. He was surprised by the speed of his erection. He had anticipated that murderous intent would hinder his response.

Robinson kissed her deeply, his tongue tasting the contours of her mouth. He hoped it muted the guttural groan at the back of his throat, for he feared she would know that she had reduced him, once again, to an animal.

He stopped suddenly, pulling away from her. Why should he care what she thought or felt? Why should he worry on this night of all nights? Within a few hours she would be dead, and what she thought would matter not at all. Noticing her confusion at this sudden interruption, he almost laughed at the absurdity of his concern. But he had to remain focused, and not arouse suspicion.

"I want you now."

"I love you," she said as he mounted her.

He wished she had not said it. This particular endearment was another trap, her way of forcing him to repeat her favorite line. He resisted, but then complied. He had nothing to lose, and she would die happy.

"I love you," he whispered.

Quickly, they were done.

As she touched him on the cheek, she whispered, "We can do it again, just before you go in the morning."

"Yes," was all he said.

She stepped out of bed to retrieve her nightgown.

"Do you want any night clothes? It's cold still."

She kept a supply for her clients, but Robinson said, "No." He did not want to have to burn clothes spattered by her blood. If he got blood his skin, he could wipe it off with a cloth and toss that into the consuming flames.

As she was about to rest her head on her pillow, he noticed a delicately embroidered handkerchief on it. He had never seen it before, and said casually, "That's beautiful. Where did you get it?"

His next conquest would appreciate such a gift.

"Oh, it's nothing," she replied before falling asleep.

He waited until two o'clock in the morning. It was cold and dark. The gas lamp on the nightstand was still burning, producing enough light for Robinson to watch Helen sleeping on her side.

He climbed out of bed, retrieved his cloak, and untied the hatchet. He walked to the bed and looked down at Helen to make sure she was asleep. Her eyes were closed, her breathing gentle and steady.

There was no time for reflection, no time for recollection, no time for anticipation. The past was past, what was done was done, and a future unencumbered by a controlling, jealous woman lay ahead. He had a job to do.

He raised the hatchet, selecting the exact point in her skull for the blow. Then he tightened his grip, tensed the muscles in his arms and shoulders, and pounded Helen's forehead once.

The impact surprised him. The skin split, and small but thick streams of blood flowed out. But the blade did not go deeply into the skull. It was harder and thicker than he had thought. So he pulled the hatchet out quickly and pounded again, making a deeper cut and causing more blood to flow.

Helen's body convulsed, and Robinson panicked, thinking she might wake up, see him, and fight for her life. He straddled her chest and pinned her arms with his knees. Then, with all the force his fear and rage could muster, he struck her for a third time, this time embedding a piece of her skull into her brain.

Blood covered her face and his midsection; even his groin was splattered with thick red drops. He lifted himself away from the body and then stepped off the bed to get to the water and bowl provided each night by the maid. A folded cloth lay on the stand, and he dipped it into the water before applying it to his skin. He shuddered at the cold, but he needed to wash away every last drop of blood before he donned his clothes. He tossed the dark cloth onto the bed; it would burn with the bedclothes.

He dressed quickly, putting on his cloak, and retrieved the miniature from Helen's bureau drawer. He reached for the lamp and looked down at the end of the bed. He considered for an instant the possible consequences of igniting a fire in a room of a brothel filled with people. The previous December, a fire in a warehouse eventually consumed entire city blocks. Thomas Street was narrow, all the houses attached in rows. A fire could spread with deadly efficiency.

He didn't care. Maybe Rosina Townsend or one of the other whores would smell smoke and call for the fire brigades; maybe all of them would die in their sleep from the smoke.

He couldn't worry about that. He found some paper, put the paper to the lamp, and set a fire in the blankets and pillows near Helen's head and back. Soon, her body would burn beyond inspection or even recognition.

Robinson took the hatchet with him, in case he encountered someone in the house on his way out.

Fortunately, the upper landing was dark. Heart pounding, he crept down the stairs, taking one step at a time and cringing at each groan of the wood under his feet.

Finally, he reached the bottom. He crept down the hallway to the rear parlor, placed the lamp on the marble topped table, found the bar to the keyless double doors, lay it aside, slowly opened the door, and went into the backyard.

He tossed the hatchet to the ground. He had wiped the blood off of it before leaving Helen's room. He didn't need it anymore. He just needed to find a way to get out of a yard with an eight-foot fence.

Robinson scanned yard, taking a quick look at the garden, the tables, a cistern, and the privy. He figured out what he would have to do; he would climb the fence behind the privy into the yard of a house fronting Hudson Street.

Using the privy as a ladder, he climbed up and over the fence easily enough. But he made two mistakes. He managed to smudge one leg of his blue pantaloons with the fresh whitewash on the fence and, frustrated by the encumbering cloth of the long cloak, he tossed it aside.

That was stupid, incredibly stupid, he immediately realized when he reached the street and hurried south to his boardinghouse. The cloak's velvet collar and facings, the frog closures down the front, and the black silk tassels made it distinctive. It could be linked to him. Robinson had worn it proudly, showing off its workmanship to Eliza Salters and other prostitutes.

If it could be proven that he had been at 41 Thomas that night, was the last to see Helen alive, and had worn that cloak found in the backyard, he could be arrested for murder. Then he dismissed the concern, running through the narrow streets of Manhattan. The shadows of the walls seemed to shelter him, silently promising that no harm could come to him. He had friends in high places; they would protect him, the adopted son whom no one could resist in his city of desire.

———•———

Winthrop was only two years older than Robinson, but he seemed much older, his brown eyes hardened by sleepless nights and perpetual skepticism. He had come prepared to take down every word Robinson had to say, and would write as Robinson answered the questions.

Sitting in the Robinson parlor, Winthrop dispensed with pleasantries and asked his first question, "Have you as much pride as ever, Robinson?"

Robinson hadn't expect the question, but he was prepared to use any question as the opportunity to declare the lessons he had learned about life in general, and to teach the world *his* truth.

"No, I have run my career," he replied. "I have nothing more to hope from the patronage of this hypocritical world. I have no desire to flatter it. Mankind, I love you not. I will no longer pretend to see you as you would seem to others. I know your disguise; I have worn it. I know your arts; I have practiced them. I know the trickery of the stage; I have myself been behind the curtains, examined the scenes, scrutinized the tinseled wardrobes, sneered at the elements of a thunderstorm. I can unmask one half of New York and uncloak the other. I know that city, web and woof, male and female, from the East River to the North, and from Castle Garden to Washington Place. I have not only surveyed its length and breadth but sounded, also, its depths, even from La Fayette Place down to Corlear's Hook."

Robinson smiled, satisfied with his declaration as the preeminent guide to New York's darkest and deepest dens. He smiled even more when Winthrop ignored his eloquence and asked the next question: "Does your conscience *trouble* you?"

"Not a bit," Robinson replied. "Did it appear in the court when I was charged with murdering Helen Jewett? Do you think I would have ruined my brilliant prospects?"

Winthrop frowned.

"Robinson, I am asking the questions. Because of that trial, you are a celebrity. Do you *deserve* it?"

"What entitles me to be gazed at as the young lion of the day?" Robinson replied. "I fear I am unworthy of such universal admiration. What great action have I performed, that the eyes of all mankind should be thus turned upon me? Indeed I am honored over-much. My modesty is burdened."

Winthrop replied, "Admiration? The public views you as worse than a savage."

Robinson snapped, "The public is a damned, long-eared ass."

Without warning, Winthrop shifted to accusation. "Did you do it, murder that girl?"

"Only a bungler would use a dull hatchet to cut up a girl," said Robinson evenly. "I would sooner use a jack knife."

"All the lithographs sold in the stalls on Broadway have you doing it. Have you seen any of them?"

Robinson smiled wanly and said, "How damned *innocent* they made me look! I should take myself for one of the babes in the woods. I look as harmless as an infant Jesus. If that were a correct copy of my countenance, Ogden Hoffman ought to be thrown over the Bar for not setting up idiocy in my defense. My face would have furnished an irresistible argument to any jury. As for Helen, poor thing, she looks so brazen in the print, as Mary Magdalene; in truth, she was a fine intellectual-looking woman. They say these caricatures are put up at the windows of the print shops and hawked about the country by vagabond boys. Never mine. The romancers may yet make us the Eloise and Abelard of the Age."

Winthrop raised his eyebrow, but did not comment, asking instead about Furlong, whose testimony had been so crucial to Robinson's acquittal.

"Were you surprised that Mr. Furlong remembered so many details about a night, before the murder, that seemed so ordinary?"

"Mr. Furlong has an excellent memory, much better than mine," Robinson replied. "And thank goodness Mr. Furlong was in the business of selling cigars. Smoking may kill other folks, but it keeps me alive."

Robinson enjoyed his little joke.

"There is a correct way, you know, for opening a cigar box and lighting a cigar. I like to see things done exactly right—for example, the tying of a cravat or the folding of a letter." He turned to the small wooden box on the adjacent table, and said, "Let me show you."

"Another time," said Winthrop, annoyance rising in his voice. "Did Helen love you?"

Robinson had another well-prepared answer: "How could she help it? Half the women in New York were in love with me. Someone how I pass for 'a marvelous proper man.' I can go back to Gotham and marry an heiress. But out upon matrimony, say I. I am not fond of *cold ham*."

"Will you return there, to New York?"

"I wish I were back there. Connecticut is a very stupid little state," Robinson scoffed.

"How could you afford what is required to attract an heiress?" Winthrop asked.

"When you need five dollars, you beg it, or borrow it, or get it in any of forty ways," Robinson replied, deliberately vague. He didn't want to answer any follow-up questions about embezzled funds, and was thankful Winthrop did not pursue that line of questions.

"Were the prostitutes in New York attractive?" Winthrop asked, his random questions obviously intended to disorient Robinson. Robinson was not fooled and remained calm. "Did they have qualities that would have merited your hand, if they were not fallen?"

"Some of them surpass all women I have ever known, in beauty, but above all, in eloquence, " Robinson replied. "They can tell piteous tales of their wrongs and sufferings, tricks of the trade, though, tricks of the trade, I *do* assure you."

"Eloquence?"

"It has its uses," Robinson, "especially if you tell tales of seduction and fall."

"Then she *used* you?" Winthrop asked.

"She had her *tricks*, as they all did, but she was especially good with her tricks."

"Did you love her?"

"Sort of."

Winthrop suddenly changed the subject again, returning to the trial. But this time he was commanding, almost hostile.

"Look at me in the eye, if you can," he pressed, "and deny that you dropped the cloak there, yourself."

"Deny!" exclaimed Robinson. "Why should I deny . . . or confess?"

"Why then did you deny that you owned the cloak when you were arrested?"

"It was none of Brink's business to inquire into the state of my wardrobe. I told him a lie because it was natural. Clerks and merchants in New York lie. Lying is their vocation; 'tis too common to be considered even an accomplishment. Would you hang up a poor counter-jumper for lying? If all the liars in New York were killed, there would be few people left for mourners."

"So you admit to being a liar?"

"I was surrounded by corrupters, and I sank deeper into a cesspool of roguery until I was doing things that I could no longer recognize as the work of Richard Robinson of Durham Connecticut," he answered. "It came as a relief when I was finally jailed. My jail kept me away from the rascally world. In there I was safe."

"Then you *are* a liar?" insisted Winthrop.

"I have nothing more to say about it," said Robinson.

He had tried to maintain a light, even bantering tone in his comments. But finally he had lost his patience, and spoke with severe composure:

"My conscience does not hurt me. Don't report, now, that I confess myself guilty, look like a criminal, etc. I didn't confess *anything* at all. They can't prove that I ever saw Helen. It might have been somebody else. There was a dark passage. I deny the whole affair—handkerchief, miniature, letters, cloak, and all."

Then he pulled out a letter from his inner coat pocket, saying, "I have a letter from New York, from one of my married admirers. Oh, I would give worlds to be with her again for a single hour."

"You can still accomplish it when you return to New York."

"No, I will not be returning. I intend to go to Texas and join that devoted band of desperadoes defending Texas from the Mexicans. I am now getting the needed shirts, blankets, boots, a gun, compass, a tinderbox, and matches."

Winthrop remarked, "You're making plans, and getting prepared? A person of forecast, indeed."

Robinson smiled, despite the cutting compliment. He knew he was impulsive. But a move to Texas and the joining of the Army there required planning and supplies . . . and a new name.

"I will have an new name too," he replied. "I have been Richard the Fourth long enough for my interest and safety. The world has somehow got a grudge against me."

"Somehow?" asked Winthrop.

"I am sick of popularity," sighed Robinson. "Like Byron, I have drained the bowl of dissipation to its dregs. I have felt the intoxication of fame, and am now about to become a martyr to the cause of liberty in Texas, where the brand of Cain is honorable."

As soon as he mentioned Cain, he knew he had gone too far. He was not making a confession; he was only admitting to being branded as one. But he feared that Winthrop would not see or make the distinction and quickly added, with all the obfuscating pomposity he could muster, "The past is sealed. It is even to me, as a dead letter. But the future is open, and I go into exile with all the firmness of a martyr."

"When are you leaving?" asked Winthrop.

"At the end of the month. I'll travel on Clinton's Ditch to a lake steamer, go on canal boats through the Scioto Valley to the Ohio River, and board a steamboat to New Orleans; then on to Galveston."

"Are you afraid to die?"

"No," replied Robinson, standing up. "I'm done with today's interview, but we can fish together, and you can watch me and ask more questions for your readers."

Robinson grinned and extended his hand, feeling triumphant. He had managed to remain in control and protect the essential core of his narrative. There was no great risk in being gracious and sociable on the Quinipiac River in July, when nothing could be finer than fishing in the summer morning before the sun burned the skin and the humid air became thick with flies. Winthrop would just see more of the same—a man of untroubled mind, in excellent health, and with great prospects.

He could maintain the lie until the end.

The primary fact was irreversible: He could not be tried again for the murder of Helen Jewett. And as much as he didn't like to admit it, he had been lucky. That tossed away cloak could have unraveled everything. But he had been shrewd, too, accepting the advice of his lawyers to keep his mouth shut.

His triumph now consolidated by *another* willing member of the press, Robinson grinned, gave his hand to Winthrop, and asked, "What shall you call this interview? Do you have a title yet?"

"Of course," Winthrop, all smug satisfaction in just two words. "I will call it 'Robinson Downstream: Containing conversations with the Great Unhung."

Robinson hesitated for only a moment and then said, nodding his head, "Splendid, just splendid. Come. Let's get to the river. Even with the fish I have great prospects."

Historical and Source Notes

This is a novel; a work of historical fiction based on actual events and real people whose lives inspired an imagined tale. However, the public history of New York City was not changed in this book; and sources for this history can be found in newspaper editorials and articles, court records, diaries and letters, and histories written by journalists and scholars. The characters lived in early nineteenth-century America, but their emotional and psychological lives were usually hidden behind codes of decorum, discretion, and obvious silences, a wall that scholars can sometimes penetrate with skillful, relentless, painstaking research. Their work is essential for historical fiction, but novelists don't have the historians' constraints and can imagine thoughts and create dialogue without documented evidence. This is liberating. Nonetheless, I must honor the research of others, and admit that without their work, *City of Desire* could not have been written.

I consulted several works, all of which I am not going to identify here. But there are some books I depended on heavily, and they deserve my acknowledgement and gratitude: Patricia Cline Cohen, *The Murder of Helen Jewett: The Life and Death of a Prostitute in Nineteenth Century New York* (Alfred Knopf, 1998); Matthew Goodman, *The Sun and the Moon: The Remarkable True Account of Hoaxers, Showmen, Dueling Journalists and Lunar-Man Bats in Nineteenth Century New York* (Basic Books, 2008); Andie Tucher, *Froth and Scum: Truth, Beauty, Goodness and the Ax Murder in America's First Mass Medium* (University of North Carolina Press, 1994); Christine Stansell, *City of Women: Sex and Class in New York, 1789-1860* (University of Illinois Press, 1982); Timothy J. Gilfoyle, *City of Eros: New York City, Prostitution, and the Commercialization of Sex, 1790-1820* (W. W. Norton and Company, 1992); Marilyn Wood Hill, *Their Sisters' Keepers: Prostitution in New York City, 1830-1870* (University of California Press, 1993); Eric Homberger: *Scenes from the Life of a City: Corruption and Conscience in Old New York* (Yale University Press, 1994); and Edwin G. Burrows and Mike Wallace, *Gotham: A History of New York to 1898* (Oxford University Press, 1999).

From these works I found innumerable details that were used for narrative purposes. The exhaustive research of Patricia Cline Cohen was indispensable, and her more than fifty pages of notes at the end of her book, led to more detective work. Finally, I want to honor an earlier novel about Helen Jewett's murder by the late Raymond Paul, *The Thomas Street Horror: An Historical of Novel of Murder* (Viking Press, 1982). Paul's novel exonerates Robinson and charges Maria Stevens with the crime. I came to a different conclusion, unwilling to ignore the fact the Maria Stevens, another prostitute, died before the trial and could not have confessed to murder on the witness stand after cross examination by the novel's fictional hero, the rogue attorney, Lon Quinncannon. Nevertheless, I appreciate Professor Paul's detailed description of 55 Thomas Street, including a map of the house and surrounding yards, and his extensive quotations from the press of that day. He was thorough and accurate about New York and its newspapers, a model user of primary source material for fictional purposes. He inspired me to match his standard. I hope I succeeded.